### *Murder with All the Trimmings*

"Viets milks much holiday humor in her novel, pulling out all the wonderfully garish stops." —*Pittsburgh Tribune-Review*

"Elaine Viets writes exciting amateur sleuth mysteries filled with believable characters; the recurring cast starting with Josie adds a sense of friendship that in turn embellishes the feeling of realism." —*Midwest Book Review*

"This series gets better with every book. . . . A wonderful holiday read . . . a book to be savored by a cozy fire with a good cup of hot chocolate." —*Gumshoe*

"Viets brings a sense of humor to a variety of difficult family situations in this fun novel." —*Romantic Times*

### *Accessory to Murder*

"Elaine Viets knows how to orchestrate a flawless mystery with just the right blend of humor, intrigue, and hot romance. If you are looking to complete your wardrobe for the fall, you just found the most essential piece." —*Fresh Fiction*

"The writing and plot are superb . . . no wasted words, scenes, or characters. Everything advances the plot, builds the characters, or keeps things moving. It's what her many fans have learned to expect." —*Cozy Library*

"A funny, laugh-out-loud whodunit. Elaine Viets has created characters that you can identify with. . . . This is one book you don't want to miss." —*The Romance Readers Connection*

"A well-thought-out whodunit starring a sleuth who is totally believable and a bit quirky." —*Midwest Book Review*

"A very interesting series. . . . I'm looking forward to the next book." —*Deadly Pleasures*

*continued . . .*

"An intelligent heroine."
—Charlaine Harris, author of *A Secret Rage*

"An entertaining new series with just the right touch of humor."
—*The Miami Herald*

"It's Janet Evanovich meets *The Fugitive*."
—Tim Dorsey, author of *Big Bamboo*

### Dying to Call You

"Viets writes a laugh-out-loud comedy with enough twists and turns to make it to the top. . . . In fact, she's been nominated for a truckload of awards this year. . . . There is a good reason why Viets is taking the mystery genre by storm these days. . . . She can keep you wondering 'Who done it?' while laughing all the way to the last page."
—*Florida Today*

### Murder Between the Covers

"Wry sense of humor, appealing, realistic characters, and a briskly moving plot."
—*South Florida Sun-Sentinel*

"A great writer . . . simply superb."
—*Midwest Book Review*

### Shop Till You Drop

"Fans of Janet Evanovich and Parnell Hall will appreciate Viets's humor."
—*South Florida Sun-Sentinel*

"Elaine Viets's debut is a live wire. . . . Helen Hawthorne takes Florida by storm. Shop no further—this is the one." —Tim Dorsey

"I loved this book. With a stubborn . . . heroine, a wonderful South Florida setting, and a cast of more-or-less lethal bimbos, *Shop Till You Drop* provides tons of fun. Six-toed cats, expensive clothes, sexy guys on motorcycles—this book has it all."
—Charlaine Harris

"Fresh, funny, and fiendishly constructed . . . a bright start to an exciting new series. This one is hard to beat."
—Parnell Hall, author of the Puzzle Lady crossword puzzle mysteries

**Also by Elaine Viets**

Josie Marcus, Mystery Shopper Series

Dead-End Job Mystery Series

# THE FASHION HOUND MURDERS

JOSIE MARCUS, MYSTERY SHOPPER

*Elaine Viets*

AN OBSIDIAN MYSTERY

OBSIDIAN
Published by New American Library, a division of
Penguin Group (USA) Inc., 375 Hudson Street,
New York, New York 10014, USA
Penguin Group (Canada), 90 Eglinton Avenue East, Suite 700, Toronto,
Ontario M4P 2Y3, Canada (a division of Pearson Penguin Canada Inc.)
Penguin Books Ltd., 80 Strand, London WC2R 0RL, England
Penguin Ireland, 25 St. Stephen's Green, Dublin 2,
Ireland (a division of Penguin Books Ltd.)
Penguin Group (Australia), 250 Camberwell Road, Camberwell, Victoria 3124,
Australia (a division of Pearson Australia Group Pty. Ltd.)
Penguin Books India Pvt. Ltd., 11 Community Centre, Panchsheel Park,
New Delhi - 110 017, India
Penguin Group (NZ), 67 Apollo Drive, Rosedale, North Shore 0632,
New Zealand (a division of Pearson New Zealand Ltd.)
Penguin Books (South Africa) (Pty.) Ltd., 24 Sturdee Avenue,
Rosebank, Johannesburg 2196, South Africa

Penguin Books Ltd., Registered Offices:
80 Strand, London WC2R 0RL, England

First published by Obsidian, an imprint of New American Library,
a division of Penguin Group (USA) Inc.

First Printing, November 2009
10 9 8 7 6 5 4 3 2 1

Copyright © Elaine Viets, 2009
All rights reserved

OBSIDIAN and logo are trademarks of Penguin Group (USA) Inc.

Printed in the United States of America

*For those who speak for the ones who cannot—
the animal rescue organizations*

# Acknowledgments

Thanks to the staff of the Humane Society of Missouri, who save animals every day. Debbie Hill, vice president of operations, and Jeane Jae, director of communications, were especially helpful.

Rachelle L'Ecuyer worked long hours to answer my questions about her city, Maplewood. She even e-mailed me at ten at night, long after she should have been at home.

Karen and David Reibman did adopt two Missouri puppy mill dogs, Joey and Magic. Karen believes the little dogs give her more than she gives them.

St. Louis is my hometown, and I depend on my local experts, Jinny Gender, Karen Grace, and Janet Smith.

Thanks also to Valerie Cannata, Anne Watts, and Kay Gordy. I consult Kay, proud grandmother of Sage, for early childhood behavior. Kay is an even better cook than Alyce.

Thanks to Emma, my expert on nine-year-olds. Emma gave me deep background on what it's like to be nine years old. I wish I could use her real name, but the world is a dangerous place these days for young women.

As always, thanks and love to my husband, Don Crinklaw, for his extraordinary help and patience.

My agent, David Hendin, is still the best.

To my editor, Kara Cesare, and her assistant, Lindsay Nouis, thank you. Their critique made this a better book. Thanks to the Obsidian copy editor and production staff and to hardworking publicist Megan Swartz. I am one of the lucky writers who likes her publisher.

Many booksellers help keep this series alive. I wish I had room to thank them all.

Special thanks to the law enforcement men and women who answered my questions on police procedure. Some police and medical sources have to remain nameless, but I want to thank them all the same. Particular thanks to Detective R. C. White, Fort Lauderdale Police Department (retired), and Synae White. Any mistakes are mine, not theirs.

Thanks to the librarians at the Broward County Library and the St. Louis Public Library who researched my questions. Their knowledge and patience are appreciated.

# Chapter 1

Josie's boss was coated in pork grease from his lips to his chin. Harry the Horrible sat at his desk in Suttin Services, munching happily on pork crackling.

*Crack!* Every time he took a bite, the crackling sounded like ice breaking in a pond. Particles of pork grease seemed to hang in the air.

It was seven thirty in the morning. Josie's stomach turned at the thought of pork skin for breakfast. But the way Harry ate, he could be starting lunch. She'd been summoned to appear at Suttin's rat trap of an office for a surprise mystery-shopping assignment. Harry's surprises were always unpleasant.

Even in the sad, gray winter light, Josie could see the Suttin office needed a good cleaning. Battered file cabinets huddled together like refugees. Dented desks held tottering piles of yellowing reports. Harry was the head troll in this dank cave.

Josie was glad she wasn't imprisoned at a dusty desk. She was a mall moll, and blended in with the splashing fountains, shiny marble, and cheerful plants of St. Louis's shopping centers. Small, brown-haired, and cute, Josie was the invisible shopper, on a mission to save Mrs. Minivan from retail indignities.

"You're always whining that I give you dog assignments," Harry said. "Well, this one is a real dog. Except now you're gonna thank me."

"I am?" Josie said.

"Trust me," Harry said.

She didn't. Josie couldn't imagine calling a helpless newborn Harry, but her boss had grown into his name. Harry was hairy. Little dark hairs, like clumps of weeds, grew in his ears, in his nose, and on his knuckles. More hair peeked between the tightly stretched fabric of his white shirt and was tangled in the links of his stainless steel watchband. In fanciful moments, Josie wondered whether Harry was a were-wolf. She watched carefully, but his hairiness never waxed or waned with the moon.

This morning his hands were slippery with pork grease. Harry waved the slab of crackling at her. "That's all you have to do. Look at little puppies."

"Where?" Josie asked.

"You're supposed to mystery-shop Pets 4 Luv. Cute name. Cute stores."

*Crack!* Harry took another crackling crunch and gave a crocodile smile. He looked even slipperier, thanks to his glistening coat of pork fat.

"First, ask the pet store clerk a few simple questions." He counted on one greasy finger. "Then take some video of the doggies." Another finger. "Then turn in your report. Easy as one, two, three. You get to use this cool purse cam. The video camera is in the purse strap. It has audio, too. This purse is a complete covert surveillance system. Real James Bond stuff."

He held up a lumpy black purse and grinned. Josie could see his greasy prints on the fake leather.

"Harry," Josie said, "the purse looks like something my grandmother carried. It's huge."

"Big purses are in style," Harry said.

"That looks like a suitcase with a strap," Josie said. "It's ugly. I might as well have a neon Shoplifter at Work sign. A mystery shopper is supposed to blend in, remember? Anyway, how do I get people to talk into the purse strap?"

"The strap is adjustable," Harry said.

"So I say, 'Wait a minute, let me fix my purse so I can hear you'? Why do I need a hidden video camera for this assignment? I've always turned in written reports."

"Time to keep up with the new technology, Josie." Harry grinned again. The grin slid off his face when he saw Josie's eyes narrow.

"What aren't you telling me?" she asked.

"Nothing." Harry sounded like her ten-year-old daughter, Amelia, when she was lying.

"Is that purse cam legal?" Josie asked.

"Sure," Harry said. "There's nothing wrong with taping your own conversation."

"What about taping someone who doesn't know I'm packing a purse cam?"

"Josie, if the salesclerk is doing her job, she has nothing to fear. All you have to do is ask some simple questions. Let me worry about the legal stuff."

"What are those simple questions?"

"Uh, I don't have them yet," Harry said. "I'll fax the questionnaire to you as soon as I get it. Pets 4 Luv is a big national chain, Josie. Those little pups are adorable. You'll get paid to look at cute puppies."

"Right," Josie said. "Like I get paid to shop. Fax me the questions, Harry, and then I'll let you know if I want this assignment."

Now Harry looked like a hurt puppy. "You're turning me down?"

Josie swore the man whimpered. "No, but I need more information before I agree," she said.

"Okay, Josie. But don't forget Christmas is coming and

you've got a kid." Now his smile turned into a sneer and his small eyes glittered amid the pork fat.

"Are you threatening me?" Josie asked.

"No, no." Harry held up his greasy hands in protest. "It's just that Pets 4 Luv heard you're good, and they want you."

"I need to know more before I want them," Josie said. "When will you have the questions?"

"In about an hour or so." Harry tore off a chunk of pork rind with fat still clinging to it and said, "Would you like some crackling? It's from my mom's pork roast. She's a fantastic cook."

"Uh, no, thanks," Josie said. "Gotta run. I'll wait for your fax."

She fled, afraid he might shake her hand good-bye.

Outside in the parking lot, the cold air felt refreshing after Harry's pork-perfumed office. As she threaded her gray Honda through the heavy morning traffic, Josie tried to figure out what was wrong. Harry never gave her good mystery-shopping assignments.

Pets 4 Luv. Why did that name seem familiar? Josie didn't buy pet food. She knew it was a national pet chain with several locations in St. Louis. She'd seen the ads, but had never been inside a store. Harry wanted her to visit two, and one was in—

The shiny black Cadillac in front of Josie slammed on its brakes. Josie skidded to a stop millimeters from its rear bumper. The car's owner flipped her off. Horns honked.

Josie's hands shook. She took a deep breath. That was way too close. She needed to get home, fortify herself with coffee, and research this assignment. Josie was glad her mother was driving Amelia to school this morning. She was too distracted to be behind the wheel with her daughter.

Josie parked in front of her two-family flat. Her mother lived upstairs. She was Josie's landlord and live-in baby-sitter. The only way Josie could survive on her mystery-shopping money was with Jane's help. She crunched across the frozen grass to the sidewalk. There were salt stains on the concrete and dirty patches of ice in the corners of the wide porch. St. Louis had had six inches of snow three days before, but it was mostly gone.

She opened her front door and called, "Hello?"

Silence. Amelia's coat and backpack were gone. Their home seemed empty without her daughter. Amelia had been too quiet since her father, Nate, had been murdered. She'd even cut down on visits to her best friend, Emma. Josie wished there were a way to restore the spark in her daughter.

She fired up the computer in her bedroom office—a grand name for a garage-sale table and a fax machine—and Googled "Pets 4 Luv." After one headline, she knew why the chain was familiar:

PUPPY LUV 4 SALE: NATIONAL CHAIN CAUGHT BUYING ABUSED PEDIGREED PUPS.

Josie's stomach turned as she read the details. Two years ago in August, law enforcement and animal rescue workers had raided a puppy mill in southwest Missouri. More than two hundred pedigreed pups were carried out. Later, forty died of disease, illness, and dehydration. The conditions at the puppy mill were horrific. The animals had no water, no medical care, and they lived in dirty cages. Breeding females were forced to have one pedigreed litter after another until they died from exhaustion. The southwest Missouri mill had been operating for years. A tractor-trailer load of Chihuahuas, pugs, and Pomeranians shipped from the puppy mill had been traced to Pets 4 Luv. Records showed the chain had bought more than fifteen thousand puppy mill dogs at cut-rate prices and sold them for four or five hundred dollars each. That was six million dollars' worth of misery— minimum.

Puppy mills fed the demand for celebrity dogs, Josie thought. Pop princesses were photographed with their pampered pups. Young women wanted tiny dogs they could carry in cute pink purses. Puppy mill dogs were cheap pedigreed pups sold for high prices. Their new owners didn't understand the cruelty behind their four-legged accessories.

Josie clicked through photos of Hilary Duff and Paris Hilton with tiny Chihuahuas. Jessica Alba had a pair of pugs named Sid and Nancy. Christina Aguilera walked her fluffy papillons. Why did Christina's pretty dogs have those revolting names, Stinky and Scratchy?

The celebrities and their dogs were well fed and well groomed. The puppy mill dogs were not so lucky. Josie winced at the videos of rescuers carrying out tiny dogs with matted fur, runny eyes, and open sores. The dogs shivered and whimpered. Their rescuers looked ready to burst into tears.

Pets 4 Luv claimed it didn't know its dogs were from puppy mills. "All our purebred pups are raised at USDA-inspected facilities and have American Kennel Club papers," a company spokesperson said.

That was true. But animal rescue agencies said AKC papers were no guarantee of humane care, and the USDA didn't have enough staff to inspect all the facilities. The pet chain escaped legal action, but the scandal damaged its reputation. It was boycotted by animal lovers. They campaigned for people to get animals from breed rescue organizations, shelters, or humane breeders and avoid buying dogs from chain stores.

Good, Josie thought.

But why did Harry want her mystery-shopping these stores now? My boss isn't just slick with pork fat this morning, Josie thought. He's trying to slide something by me.

Her fax machine rang, then churned out the list of mystery-shopping questions.

Josie was supposed to visit two stores. She had to buy a twenty-pound bag of puppy chow at each one and ask the following questions:

1. Where are your pedigreed puppies?
2. May I see their breeder paperwork?
3. Do you have their AKC registry papers?
4. What are the name and address of the breeding facility?
5. Do you have the veterinary records for the puppies and their parents?

These questions, Josie had learned from the animal rescue Web sites, were designed to help spot puppy mill animals. What was Harry getting her into? Josie dialed his office number.

"So, Josie," Harry said in a too-cheerful voice, "did you get the questions?" *Crack!* He was still eating pork cracklings. Josie wondered whether he'd slide right out of the chair.

"Yes," Josie said. "What I don't get is why I'm mystery-shopping puppy abusers."

"Aw, Josie, don't be that way." *Crack!* "Are you going to do the job or not?"

"Not. Not unless you tell me what's going on, Harry. I saw the news stories about Pets 4 Luv. They're a terrible company."

Harry fell into a friendly, wheedling tone. "Look, Josie, it's not a big deal. A couple of years ago the chain took a shipment of dogs from a Missouri puppy mill. The home office didn't know anything about it. Some young district manager was trying to cut costs."

"He cost them a lot of business," Josie said.

"That's why they fired him," Harry said. "They also stopped buying dogs from puppy mills. It's company policy. They put it in writing. And really, what damage did they do? All those pups went to good homes."

"How do you know?" Josie asked. "Anybody who plunked down the money could buy a pup. I bet the stores never interviewed the new owners."

"Hey, what are you?" Harry said, turning suspicious. "One of those animal rights loonies? Since when did you care about puppies?"

"Since I saw the Humane Society videos about puppy mills. Consider me a convert."

"Well, since you're such an animal lover," Harry said, his voice dripping sarcasm, "you'll really want this assignment. Pets 4 Luv says it's reformed. The head office in Milwaukee is suspicious of two St. Louis outlets. The stores are selling a really low number of pedigreed dogs—a lot fewer than the chain's other stores in similar neighborhoods. The managers say it's because of the bad publicity. But the Milwaukee headquarters isn't sure. It would be easy for the store managers to buy a load of Missouri puppy mill dogs and pass them off as okay animals, then pocket the profits. Everyone wants pedigreed dogs since that Paris girl—I can't think of her last name, some hotel—Marriott, Westin—"

"Paris Hilton," Josie finished.

"Right, one of those slutty blondes. Anyway, the girls all want them after Paris pranced around with that skinny thing that looked like a shaved rat."

"Paris's dog is a Chihuahua," Josie said.

"Yeah, well, Pets 4 Luv got you a purse cam to mystery-shop their suspect stores."

"I'm a mystery shopper," Josie said. "I have a ten-year-old daughter. I can't get involved in something dangerous. Who's going to raise Amelia if anything happens to me?"

"It's not dangerous, Josie. Anyway, you've got your mother," Harry said. "She can bring up your daughter."

"My mother! She doesn't need to raise a child at age sixty-eight. I am not a private eye. Tell the chain to hire one. They have the money. Don't the animal protection agencies investigate these matters?"

"That's what they're trying to avoid, Josie. Pets 4 Luv can't risk more bad publicity. Private eyes can be bought. Reporters can cause more damage to the chain's reputation if this story gets out. And it will get out. There's nothing TV news likes better than pictures of dying doggies."

"Harry," Josie said, "I am not a private eye. I am not a reporter. The answer is no."

"Think about it," Harry said. "I'll call you back."

There was a pork-splitting *crack!* and Harry was gone.

# Chapter 2

"I can give you another fifty bucks if you'll do the pet store job," Harry the Horrible said. Josie's boss had waited until eight thirty that morning to call her back with the news.

More money? Josie thought. Harry never offers me more money. The man is desperate. He's not even eating anything as he talks to me. Something is really wrong with this assignment.

"Fifty dollars per store, or fifty bucks total?" Josie asked.

"Total, of course. What do you think I am?" Harry sounded shocked.

"I'm supposed to risk my life for fifty bucks?" Josie asked. "That will barely cover the gas to the two stores."

"Don't be melodramatic," Harry said. "What's dangerous about stores that sell little puppies?"

"They aren't selling little puppies. They're peddling abused animals."

"You don't know that," Harry said. "That's why the company needs someone to investigate."

"So hire an investigator. This isn't my job. I'm a mystery shopper. I evaluate the sales personnel and the store's appearance."

"A couple of these stores may—and I mean *may*—be selling puppy mill dogs. Big deal."

"It is a big deal, Harry. A pedigreed Chihuahua sells for

around four hundred dollars. The news reports said this chain bought fifteen thousand puppy mill dogs cheap and sold them at inflated prices. We're looking at some six million dollars in sales. That can attract a murderer."

"Don't be a drama queen," Harry said. "You're going to a pet store. It's perfectly safe."

"Then you go," Josie said.

"I can't," Harry said, a little too quickly. "I have to manage the office."

"The faxes will come in by themselves," Josie said. "The answering machine will take your calls."

"Pets 4 Luv wants you, Josie." It must have hurt Harry to make that admission. "They asked for you by name."

"Let them pay for the privilege."

"Josie," he said, his voice hardening, "jobs are getting harder to find. Ever notice how many stores that we used to mystery-shop are now out of business? Others are laying off people. They can't afford mystery shoppers. You're lucky to have a job."

"I'm not lucky if I get killed," Josie said.

"Who says you'll get killed?" Harry asked. "All you have to do is look at puppies."

Josie hung up while Harry was still protesting. Fifty lousy bucks! She was supposed to risk her life for that? That was barely a bag of groceries.

She flopped down on her sagging couch and surveyed her living room. The rug had spots that wouldn't come out. The end table was decorated with dust and drink rings. There were cobwebs in the corners of the room.

My house looks like a secondhand furniture showroom, Josie thought. She swiped at the dust on the end table. Ugh. Her hand came away gray. She remembered her grandmother saying, "We were never so poor we couldn't afford soap."

Maybe cleaning the room would make it look better. Josie pulled out the furniture polish, dust rags, and vacuum and set to work, cleaning, polishing, and hating Harry. An hour later, the shabby living room shone. That made it look worse. Now the stains stood out in the freshly vacuumed rug. The drink rings were more visible. Maybe she should buy slipcovers for the ratty couch. But nothing could disguise that sagging middle.

Sagging middle. That reminded her of Stan, her muscle-bound boyfriend. Nothing sagged on that man, except maybe his interest in Josie. Last winter, her formerly nerdy neighbor had buffed up and bought new clothes. Now Stan was definitely eye candy, and they'd started dating. But things weren't clicking between them. Under that hot exterior lurked a lukewarm little old man.

Stan lived next door, but the gym was his new second home. He used to manage a hardware store. Stan had enjoyed recommending the right showerhead and the proper paintbrush. He'd happily searched for shovels and garden sprinklers. He was endlessly patient with puzzled home remodelers.

But the hardware store went out of business about the time Stan became seriously interested in bodybuilding. Now he had a job at 2 Ripped. When he wasn't working, he was working out. The man was obsessed.

The receptionist answered the phone with a sultry, "Welcome to 2 Ripped, where we have our December two-for-one Get Ripped for the Holidays sale."

"May I speak to Stan?" Josie could hear the workout music thumping in the background.

"Oh, it's you," the receptionist said, turning off the charm.

"Hey, Muscle Dude! It's your old lady," she yelled. "Pick up the extension."

More thumping music. Then Stan said, "Hi, honey. Howie and I are going for a run tonight at five. Want to join us?"

"It's too cold," Josie said.

"Not once you start moving," Stan said.

"There are other ways to warm up," Josie said. "I could fix you dinner. I could make us two nice, lean steaks. Mom will watch Amelia. Then we could go to your place."

"Thanks, sweetie, but I'm in the carbohydrate phase of my diet. I have to eat thirty-three grams of carbs every three hours. I'm limited to sweet potatoes, oatmeal, and whole wheat pasta. Besides, I have to get up for a six-o'clock run tomorrow. I burn more fat if I exercise before breakfast."

Josie was almost lonesome for the old Stan, who compared bargain prices on paper towels. "But you liked the steak I fixed two Fridays ago," Josie said.

"That was during my high-protein phase," Stan said. "I have to alternate. Now I'm in carb mode. I control my protein cravings with a tablespoon of low-sodium peanut butter."

What about my cravings? Josie wondered. Peanut butter won't help me. I'll be thirty-two soon. A woman has needs, and peanut butter isn't one of mine.

"I can't look cut if I'm not lean," Stan said.

"If you were any more cut, you'd have a Waterford label," Josie said.

More thumping music. Stan had missed the joke. Maybe he'd overdeveloped the muscles in his head.

"Waterford is cut crystal," Josie tried to explain. "It's something else to admire."

He still didn't get it. The man looks like a Greek god, Josie thought, but I'd get more action from a marble statue.

Stan skittered away from the dicey topic of sex. "Is your dishwasher okay? Anything you want me to work on around the house?"

Yes! Josie wanted to scream. Me!

"No?" Stan said, before she could answer. "Gotta run. My first client is here. See you."

See you. That's exactly what she'd do. Stare at her smoking-hot boyfriend. Stan looked like he could stop a cattle stampede with one hand while he carried a swooning heroine in the other. But he didn't make Josie swoon. She'd spent more exciting nights in the ceiling fan section at Home Depot.

Josie felt almost grateful when her doorbell rang, interrupting her anti-Stan list. She peeked out and saw her mother bundled in a dark coat, scarf, and boots. A black wool hat was mashed down on Jane's iron gray hair. It must be beauty shop day.

"Come in, Mom," Josie said.

"I found a nice beige couch at a moving sale this morning," Jane said. "It looks brand-new. It's perfect for your living room and it's only two hundred dollars."

"That's lovely, Mom, but by the time I get there, a bargain like that will be gone."

"No, it won't. I bought it for you. It's your birthday present. Early."

"Thanks, Mom. You didn't have to—"

"No, I didn't. But I wanted to. I've just talked to Stan. He's going to borrow his friend Howie's truck and deliver it tonight."

Aha. This was a gift with strings. Josie's mother was crazy about Stan. Jane had been trying to snag him as a son-in-law for years. "Call him and find out what time."

"But Mom—"

"Enjoy your new couch," Jane said. "Don't forget that Amelia is coming upstairs to my kitchen for a cooking lesson after school. If you want, I can keep Amelia late so you and Stan can have some private time."

Josie wondered whether her mother's clumsy matchmaking efforts had helped cool Stan's spark. It was difficult to have hot thoughts about a woman with her mother hovering in the background.

"He's busy tonight."

"I know he can deliver the couch, Josie. I just called him.

Maybe if your cooking were better, he'd see you more often. Amelia and I are making chili tonight. There's enough for you and Stan both. No man can resist a good bowl of chili on a cold winter night."

"This one can. I wish he'd get off this health kick."

"Just be glad he doesn't go drinking with the boys," Jane said.

"It would be better if he did, Mom," Josie said. "That's normal. Eating thirty-three grams of sweet potato is not."

"Josie, you're not getting any younger. Your daughter needs a father. You shouldn't let him get away."

"If I were a barbell, Mom, he wouldn't be able to keep his hands off me."

Jane thrust out her jaw in that stubborn bulldog stance. "I can't talk to you when you're being silly. I'll be at the beauty shop." She stomped off toward the garage, her back rigid with anger.

How could she explain to straitlaced Jane that Stan was more interested in working out than making out? Josie tried hard not to giggle. She needed her mother, but she put up with a lot for that help.

What if a grown-up Amelia came to me with that problem? Josie wondered. I hope I'd be wise and witty, but I'd probably flub it. I did a lousy job of telling my daughter why I didn't marry her father. Amelia was nine when Nate reappeared on my doorstep, and I still hadn't found the right time for that talk.

Josie tried to count her blessings. At least the ratty couch would be out of there. She'd call Stan again and find out what time he could bring the new couch.

"Muscle Dude, it's your old lady. Again," sang out the receptionist.

"Josie, I can't talk. I have a client." Stan dropped the phone and apologized. "Sorry, my hands are slippery with sweat. I've been working out."

"Mom said you were going to deliver my couch tonight, but it can wait. You're busy."

"No, Howie and I will bring it after our run, about seven thirty. He'll help carry it in. Will that work?"

"Do you need Howie?" Josie said. "With your muscles, you could carry it in single-handed."

"Thanks," Stan said. "But this is my 'cutting' week. I've been working my chest, shoulders, arms, and abs. I don't want to overdo it."

Overdo it? The man measured his food on a scale and kept a workout diary.

"What if I make you and Howie dinner after you deliver the couch, as a thank-you? I can bake a potato."

"Thanks, sweetie, but Howie is into raw food."

"I can make that," Josie said.

"He only eats organic. He needs his meals specially measured. Gotta run. See you tonight."

Josie wondered what else she could do to spice up their romantic life. She'd tried lacy underwear, candles, special dinners, and scented oils. She'd read books about how to turn cool men into red-hot lovers. She'd tried tactful ways to tell Stan what she liked. Despite his hunky body, Stan was as sexy as baggy sweatpants.

Maybe I should admit it, Josie thought. Stan was like a sweet older brother. He enjoyed puttering around fixing things at her flat. His wardrobe used to look like it had been stolen from a nursing home. Stan had favored baggy brown *Father Knows Best* cardigans and nerdy shirts. For years, he'd been content to admire Josie from afar.

Then, last Christmas, when her romance with Mike the plumber had fallen apart, she'd suddenly noticed Stan was a hottie. Actually, Amelia had noticed first. Josie had started dating Stan on the rebound. She couldn't marry Mike: He had serious problems with his daughter. Heather needed a psychiatrist, not a stepmother. Worse, Heather hated Amelia, and Josie couldn't sacrifice her daughter for her personal happiness.

Nate, her first hot lover, had been a romantic figure: handsome, passionate, impulsive, and generous. Josie assumed Nate had family money. After she was pregnant, Josie discovered he was a drug dealer with dangerous friends. She refused to marry him. Nate spent nine years in a Canadian prison, then came back for her and Amelia. He was murdered and died on Josie's doorstep. Josie turned gratefully to sweet, safe Stan.

He was still sweet and safe. Stan didn't care that Josie wasn't as ripped as he was. Stan never looked at other women. At the gym, the women (and a few men) ran after Stan like greyhounds after a mechanical rabbit. One woman with abs like cobblestones even bought him a T-shirt that said MUSCLE DUDE.

Stan kept the shirt, but ignored the flirt. "I like women to be a little shy, you know?" he told Josie. They were watching TV at the time. They were always watching TV, unless Stan was mowing Josie's lawn, shoveling her sidewalk, or raking her leaves. Her all-around handyman did everything but heat up the bedroom.

Josie's phone rang.

"Is this Ms. Marcus?" a clipped, nasal voice asked. Josie recognized the superior tone, if not the person. It was the Barrington School for Boys and Girls. She was the single mother of a full-scholarship student. Major donors were treated with hushed respect.

"Ms. Marcus, my name is Wendell Worthington, with the Barrington School for Boys and Girls. I'm afraid I must give you some bad news."

"Is my daughter okay?" Josie asked.

"She's fine," Worthington said, with a false chuckle. "An excellent student. Top notch. A credit to Barrington. And to herself, of course. I'm the school's financial officer. It is my unfortunate duty to tell you that we can no longer give your daughter a full scholarship."

"What!" Josie said.

"As you know," Worthington continued smoothly, "these are troubled financial times. Our school trust was heavily invested in Edgar Smathson's fund."

St. Louis's answer to Bernie Madoff had stripped his country club pals down to their monogrammed boxer shorts.

"Mr. Smathson was such a generous donor and a good man. We had no idea he was running a Ponzi scheme until the indictments. Our trust lost only twenty percent, which is quite good in this market."

Worthington took time to pat himself on his back before he stabbed Josie's.

"We are forced to ask every parent to contribute a little something."

"But I'm a mystery shopper," Josie said. "And so many stores are closing that I'm losing work. I'm making less money. I can't afford—"

Worthington interrupted her. "I understand, Ms. Marcus. We're not asking for the full twenty-thousand-dollar tuition. The amount we need is based on your ability to pay. We don't want to make it impossible. Our accrediting agency requires twenty-five percent 'diversity' for Barrington students."

That was the school's word for poor. Amelia didn't qualify as "ethnically" diverse, but Maplewood was "urban" by Barrington standards, and that put Amelia in the diversity category.

"We've been able to recruit 'full boat' payers from the Asian and Indian communities. Many are the children of physicians and researchers attracted here by St. Louis's fine medical facilities and universities. They are excellent students and their parents can afford full tuition. But they tend not to be donors. That's not a criticism. They have different cultural values. We are forced to go back to our regular donors, and they have suffered severe financial distress. We're asking all our scholarship students to pay a little something. Even a student who has a mother on welfare will contribute one hundred dollars. We're asking you for only one thousand dollars."

"Only!" Josie said. She felt dazed. "But—"

"We don't need it tomorrow, Ms. Marcus. But we do need it."

"I'll—I'll get it, Mr. Worthington. Just give me a little time."

Josie hung up the phone. She felt like both couches—her old and her new one—had been dropped on her. One thousand dollars. At Christmastime.

Amelia was thriving at Barrington. She needed stability. But where would Josie get that kind of money? Her mother didn't like Barrington. Jane wanted to send Amelia to St. Philomena's Catholic School. She had even suggested that the combination of public school and the church Sunday school would do, until Josie showed her the statistics on guns in public schools.

Her phone rang again. It was Harry. "Pets 4 Luv will double your fee," he announced, without bothering to say hello. "*Double your fee*. But that's their last offer. Take it or leave it."

Josie felt a flood of relief. That fee would pay a nice chunk of her daughter's tuition. The job was still dangerous, but the money made it worth the risk.

"I need an answer now. You have to start this morning," Harry said. "You have to return the purse cam to Suttin by three this afternoon, then e-mail me the report."

Josie heard his desperation. "I can return the camera by three o'clock," she said. "But I have to pick up my daughter at school. I can e-mail the report later this afternoon."

"The office will be closed then," Harry said. "Uh, it's a one-time thing."

Josie translated that as Harry was taking some unauthorized hours off work.

"Couldn't your mother pick up the kid?" Harry asked.

Josie knew she had the upper hand. "Harry, I have to take my daughter to school and pick her up. I depend on my mother too much as it is."

"Okay, okay. Get it in early tomorrow. Just take the freaking job. Please," Harry said.

"I love it when men beg me," Josie said.

# Chapter 3

"Are you sure you want to do this?" Josie asked. "You can still go home."

"Why?" Alyce said. "We mystery-shop together all the time. I'm your cover, your generic housewife. I'm the invisible woman."

"Not that invisible," Josie said. "You showed up on short notice when I needed you this morning."

"Thank my nanny," Alyce said. "She's watching Justin."

They were sitting in Alyce's plush SUV on the parking lot of Pets 4 Luv. Josie's car was parked next to it, but Alyce's SUV had the better heater, so they sat inside it and waited. The store was supposed to open in five minutes. A woman in a blue winter coat paced outside the doors.

"You seem uneasy. What can go wrong at a pet store?" Alyce asked. "We're in Kirkwood, one of the safer suburbs in St. Louis County."

"There's something flaky about this store," Josie said.

The blue-coated woman rattled the doors impatiently, but they stayed locked.

"Looks like a normal store to me," Alyce said. "The employees don't want to open until they absolutely have to."

"I'm getting paid too much money for this job," Josie said.

"Nice problem," Alyce said.

"Harry the Horrible isn't telling me something."

"Harry never tells you anything," Alyce said.

"True," Josie said. "But I have to use this stupid purse video camera." Josie held it up.

Alyce studied the purse. "I wondered why you carried that. It's seriously ugly. But I didn't want to say anything."

"You're a true friend," Josie said.

Alyce was Josie's best friend and complete opposite. Josie was small and dark haired. Alyce's skin was so white, it was almost translucent. She had pale blond hair and a generous figure.

Alyce was fairly rich. Josie was strapped for cash. Alyce lived in a new, upper-crust suburb. Josie preferred older, more urban Maplewood, on the edge of St. Louis. Alyce enjoyed being a stay-at-home mom. Josie liked mystery shopping. She cooked with battered pots and old knives. Alyce adored kitchen gadgets and lusted after a hundred-dollar panini press. That was a love Josie could never understand, but their odd friendship worked. Their personalities blended perfectly, like the offbeat ingredients in Alyce's recipes.

Alyce surveyed the beige brick building and almost-empty parking lot. "Looks like your basic big box store. Tell me why Pets 4 Luv is dangerous."

"The chain's headquarters suspect some of their stores are selling puppy mill dogs."

"That's cruel to the little dogs," Alyce said, "but I'm not sure how it's dangerous to people."

"Millions of dollars are at stake," Josie said. "There's major money in selling puppy mill pets."

"Has anyone been threatened?"

"Not that I know of." Josie watched the blue-coated woman push through the doors. "Finally. The store is open. I'm turning on the purse cam. We're going in."

Alyce giggled. "You sound like a SWAT team leader," she said.

Pets 4 Luv was bigger than Josie's supermarket. End-less aisles were crammed with toys, treats, pet clothes, and food.

Josie didn't have to ask the first question, Where are your pedigreed pets? The animals were displayed near the doors. Cats were in common wire cages with carpet-scrap floors. Long-haired Persians looked down their short, flat noses at ordinary striped kittens. Mice, rats, hamsters, and other pet rodents were in plastic corrals. Bright parrots, parakeets, and canaries were protected from drafts in Plexiglas cages.

The pedigreed pups were showcased like fine jewelry behind heart-shaped windows. Portugese water dog pups, the First Dog choice, had pride of place.

"The water dogs' popularity went up since they became the White House pet," Josie said.

"I see plenty of pop princess favorites," Alyce said. "Those Chihuahuas, Pomeranians, and papillons are real fashion hounds."

"I may overdose on cuteness," Josie said.

Piles of pups slept, yipped, or wrestled with one another. A tiny pug chased his own curly tail. A few pups pawed the glass and whimpered for attention.

"May I help you?" The store clerk had a face like a gray-ing basset hound. He seemed too dignified for the bright yellow Pets 4 Luv shirt. His name tag featured a plastic puppy saying, I'M JIM, PANTING TO HELP YOU. Josie almost felt sorry for the man.

"I was admiring your pedigreed puppies," Josie said.

"Cute, aren't they? All our puppies are purebred," Jim said. "They're USDA inspected and have American Kennel Club papers."

Jim reached into a cage and handed Josie a pug so tiny she could hold the warm little creature in the palm of her hand.

"There," he said. "It doesn't cost anything to hold one. Isn't he sweet?"

The puppy squirmed. Josie was afraid she'd drop the little fellow.

"He is cute," Josie said. "May I see his breeder paperwork?"

"Sure, sure," Jim said. "I don't have it right this moment."

"What about the vet records?"

"I can't get those right now, but all our pups are veterinarian inspected and perfectly healthy."

"Terrific," Josie said. "Would you put that in writing for me?"

"What?" Jim looked like a cornered animal.

"Would you put it in writing that your pups are vet inspected and perfectly healthy?"

"Uh, I'm not authorized to do that," Jim said.

"May I speak to the manager?" Josie asked.

Jim looked wildly around the store, then said, "She's not here. I have to unload a shipment of cat litter." He disappeared down a dog food aisle like a gopher down its hole.

"Wait!" Josie called. The pup in her hand tried to wiggle free. She struggled to hang on to the slippery little fur ball, but he made a leap and landed on a stack of dog food bags. The pup looked outrageously happy on the dog food mountain. He tore at the paper bag with tiny, needle-sharp teeth.

Josie grabbed the pup and shoved him back into his cage. He gave a heartbroken howl.

"Is he crying for you or the food?" Alyce asked. Then she started laughing so hard she sat down on the stack of dog food bags. "You've broken his heart. And he's only eight weeks old."

"You can console him. I have to buy a twenty-pound bag of puppy chow." Josie ran down the dog food aisle. She found the puppy chow, but saw no sign of Jim.

Alyce joined Josie at the cash register. Shirley wasn't exactly panting to help, despite her name tag, but she did ring up the dog food.

"Is Jim around?" Josie asked. "He was helping me pick out a puppy."

"Jim had to go to lunch," Shirley said.

"At ten fifteen?" Josie asked.

"We get really busy during the noon hour," Shirley said. "Is there something I can help you with?"

"Yes," Josie said. "I'd like to see the names and addresses of the breeders for your pedigreed pups."

"Our manager has those and she's on vacation," Shirley said. "But if you want to buy a pup, we can mail you the paperwork later."

"No, thank you," Josie said.

When they were back outside, Alyce said, "They're lying. Both of them. I hope you got that on tape."

"Me, too. Let's get some coffee and check the tape, or chip, or whatever it is," Josie said. "The other store is in Rock Road Village, by my place. There's a coffeehouse, Foundation Grounds, nearby on Manchester Road. Their baked goods are organic and their coffee is free trade."

"I'm not sure I can stand too much virtue," Alyce said. "But I could use a cappuccino."

"The baked goods are wicked," Josie said.

"Sold," Alyce said.

They formed a two-car caravan for the six miles to Foundation Grounds in Maplewood. On the short drive, Josie remembered the wiggly little pug. Maybe she could make sure other pups got a better start. Josie Marcus, defender of baby animals, she thought. She didn't feel noble, but at least she was doing useful work—and helping pay her daughter's tuition.

Foundation Grounds' coffee-scented interior was welcoming on a gray day. Josie and Alyce found a quiet corner and settled in with their scones and cinnamon-sprinkled cappuccinos.

"I like the funky decor," Alyce said. "Wish there was a way to just get a cup of foam." She ate hers with a spoon. "Did your purse record everything?"

Josie put in the earpiece, then did a quick check of the sound and video. "Every weaselly word. And I mean no disrespect to weasels. I'll bet anything that store is selling puppy mill pets."

Alyce finished her cappuccino and Josie polished off her scone. "Want more coffee?"

"Let's finish this assignment," Alyce said. "I can hardly stand to look at those poor animals. It's like they're begging me to save them and I can't."

"This isn't your job," Josie said. "It's mine. I understand if you want to go home."

"I'm not a quitter," Alyce said.

The second Pets 4 Luv store in Rock Road Village was nearly a copy of the first, down to the pedigreed dogs behind the plastic hearts. This time, Edna was supposed to be panting to help Josie. Edna was a sturdy, sensible woman with tightly permed dark hair. She offered Josie a carob chip cookie. "What do you think?"

Josie took a bite. "Not bad," she said. A little bland, but okay, she thought.

Edna had a wicked gleam in her eye. "It's a dog treat from the bulk food bin, but a lot of humans eat them."

Josie nearly spit out the rest of the cookie.

"It won't hurt you," Edna said. "They're the same carob cookies you see in the bulk food bin at supermarkets."

A Chihuahua that was, all eyes, ears, and twig legs, pawed a heart-shaped window. Josie was tempted to feed it the rest of her cookie.

"I'll take half a pound," Josie said. "I want to get a puppy for my ten-year-old daughter. It's a present."

She asked the required questions. Edna gave evasive answers, but Josie could see the panic in her eyes.

"Bichons require a lot of grooming," Edna said. "Would your daughter do that chore? Let me show you the grooming supplies you'll need."

Alyce pretended to look at leashes while Josie followed the woman to an aisle lined with brushes and other grooming tools.

"There's no security camera here," Edna said, dropping her voice. Josie hoped the purse cam could still pick it up. "Turn off that thing."

"What thing?" Josie said.

"I don't have time for games. Any idiot can see you have a recording device in that purse. You're too young and stylish to carry an old woman's purse."

Josie put her hand inside the purse and pretended to fiddle with a switch. "It's off," she said.

"You're one of them," Edna said. "You're an animal rescue investigator. They've been sneaking into this store, driving my manager crazy. Dave is up to something. He watches the security cameras like it's the bottom of the ninth in the World Series."

"I could be with the other side," Josie said.

"No, I'm a good judge of people," Edna said. "I've been in retail more than thirty years. I get off work at six thirty tonight. Come back and I'll 'accidentally' run into you outside by the door. You'll be a friend I haven't seen in ages. Gotta go, or Dave will come looking for me."

"Are these puppy mill dogs?" Josie asked. "Are they—"

An announcement on the store speaker system interrupted her. "Edna to register two. Edna to register two."

Edna went white with panic. "That's Dave!" She pushed Josie toward another aisle. "I'll see you tonight at six thirty. And leave that big purse at home."

Josie bought the sack of dog food and the carob cookies, but not at register two. Jennifer was not panting to help her, but she did take Josie's money.

"What was that all about?" Alyce asked as Josie loaded the purchases into her car.

"Edna figured out I was recording her conversation,"

Josie said. "I told Harry that purse was too obvious. She thinks I'm an animal activist and wants to meet me tonight at six thirty. She'll tell me what's going on."

"You are not doing that," Alyce said. Her pale face was pink with anger.

"I have to. I'm pretty sure these two stores are selling puppy mill dogs. If I can get a name, I can file an anonymous complaint with the Humane Society and stop them."

"Pets 4 Luv will do that when your report is filed," Alyce said.

"Maybe. I can't count on them," Josie said. "Harry will cover up any crime for a customer. I have to turn in the purse cam by three, but I don't have to turn in my report until tomorrow morning. My name's not going on it until I know it's accurate. Then I'll file my complaint and stop this."

"Josie, this is too dangerous. It will be dark at six thirty."

"Not with all those parking lot lights."

Josie thought of the warm pug puppy on his dog food mountain. "I'll be fine. This is a safe neighborhood."

"You need backup and I can't help you. I'll be home with Justin and Jake."

"I'll call you when I get to the store and again when I leave. You'll be my backup."

"You promise?" Alyce said.

"Pinkie swear," Josie said.

They locked little fingers. "If you don't call me at six thirty, Josie Marcus, I'll use the ultimate threat," Alyce said.

"I don't think you can call a cop for this."

"I'm calling someone much scarier—your mother."

# Chapter 4

"Mom, can I get a cat?" Amelia Marcus asked.

Josie choked on her brownie. Her ten-year-old daughter had a real talent for asking difficult questions at inopportune moments. Usually Amelia chose the car while Josie was trying to maneuver her way through after-school traffic. It was Amelia's preferred place to discuss volatile issues. Maybe, Josie thought, because we're both belted into our seats.

But there were no seat belts at the kitchen table.

Amelia had made one of Josie's favorite winter meals: chili and a salad with ranch dressing, plus brownies for dessert.

Josie realized this wasn't a dinner with her daughter. It was a seduction. Amelia had waited for dessert to pop the question.

"Why do you want a cat?" Josie asked, stalling for time.

"Zoe got a registered, pedigreed Himalayan show cat," Amelia said.

Zoe. Josie should have known. The class troublemaker was the first to have every designer fashion. Now she had a pedigreed cat.

"It was twelve hundred dollars," Amelia said.

Josie swallowed the rest of her brownie in one gulp and said, "I can get you twelve hundred cats for that price. Well, maybe a thousand. It would cost something to neuter them."

"I don't want a thousand cats. I just want one," Amelia said.

Josie saw the tears puddling in her daughter's eyes and trickling down her nose. Amelia hated her freckled nose and thought it was too big. Josie thought in a few years it would give her daughter's face a distinction that her own lacked.

"We don't have a thousand dollars," Josie said. She didn't mention Barrington's demand for a thousand dollars. Her daughter had enough troubles.

Amelia was shrewd enough to see that argument wasn't working. She tried another. "Zoe's mom let her have the cat because it's a good way for Zoe to learn responsibility."

"How often does Zoe clean the cat box?" Josie asked.

"The maid does that, every morning."

"Good," Josie said. "Our maid can clean your cat's box."

"Really?" Amelia asked. "We're getting a maid?"

"Sure, as soon as I grow two freaking heads," Josie said.

"Oh. You were being sarcastic," Amelia said.

"Of course, I was," Josie said. "We live in the flat downstairs from your grandmother. You go to a rich kids' school on a scholarship. I make my living as a mystery shopper, and most of those designer clothes you love so much were bought at garage sales or consignment shops. So how am I going to afford a designer cat?"

"I'll clean the litter box, I promise. I've never had a cat. Please, Mom." Amelia dragged the "please" out to at least four syllables.

Josie sighed. But she was secretly delighted that her daughter was asking for something. Amelia had been remote and listless since her father's death. They were approaching the first anniversary and Josie was worried. Fighting for a cat was a sign of life after Nate's murder.

"Let me look into it, honey," Josie said.

"That means no," Amelia said.

"It means I want to look into the situation," Josie said. "It's time to clean up."

Amelia rinsed the plates and put them in the dishwasher, wrapped the brownies in plastic, and cleaned off the table like a model child. She even swept the floor. Josie knew this was her daughter's way of demonstrating she could take care of a cat.

"The kitchen looks terrific," Josie said. "Now you need to finish your homework."

"Are those cookies?" Amelia asked, spotting the bag of carob chips Josie brought home.

"Sure, have one," Josie said.

"Did you make them?" Amelia asked.

"No, I bought them at the store," Josie said.

"Good, then they'll probably taste okay."

Josie was used to digs about her cooking. This would be a sweet payback. Amelia crunched the cookie and said, "Not bad. A little flat. The chocolate chips suck."

"They're carob chips," Josie said. "They're healthier than chocolate."

"Oh, healthy," Amelia said, as if that were an explanation. She had her mother's distrust of health food.

"Chocolate's not good for dogs," Josie said.

"Dogs?"

"Those cookies are from Pets 4 Luv," Josie said. "Look at the bag."

Amelia made gagging sounds. "You gave me dog food? I'm calling the child abuse hotline."

"It's not dog food," Josie said. "People eat them, too. It's an interspecies snack. Those cookies aren't dangerous. I ate one."

"So? You drink beer and I can't," Amelia said. "What if I made you a cat-food burger?" She had the same stubborn look as her grandmother.

How did that gene get passed on? Josie wondered. "I might be too sick to consider that cat," she said.

The phone rang. "I'll get it," Amelia said.

Josie let her answer the phone. The caller was probably for Amelia, anyway.

"It's Grandpa Jack," Amelia said. "He says to tell you hello."

"Give him my love," Josie said.

Amelia retired to her room to talk with her grandfather. Jack Weekler was one of the few good things to come out of Nate's death. He'd rushed to St. Louis when he'd discovered his only son was dying, and met Amelia and Josie for the first time. Grandpa Jack lived in Toronto, but he e-mailed often and called several times a month. Amelia asked him questions about her late father, and Jack told her stories about Nate. Nice, normal stories that gave no clue as to how his son had ended up a drunk and a drug dealer.

Amelia came running out of her bedroom and said, "Grandpa said Daddy had a cat when he was a little boy. He used to feed it buttered carrots and anything else he didn't like on his plate. Daddy's cat was brown with black stripes and had a little white vest. Grandpa calls stripy cats 'tabbies.' He said it was a stray."

"Not a registered, pedigreed show cat?" Josie said. She couldn't resist.

Amelia ignored her. "The cat followed Daddy home from school when he was six. He called it Cookie. When Grandpa asked him what color Cookie was, Daddy said, 'Dirty.' "

Josie laughed. "That sounds like your father."

"Grandpa's going to e-mail me a picture of Daddy and his cat."

"Good," Josie said. "I'm sure your grandfather also wanted you to do your homework."

"He did ask if I was getting good grades."

"Then don't disappoint him."

Bringing up Amelia was easier with a benevolent grandfather, Josie thought. It cut her nagging in half. Maybe Grandpa Jack's story about Nate's cat would tip the scales toward a mixed breed. Josie got on her computer to check out feline adoptions.

She found pedigreed cat rescue groups, where people could adopt a cat for little or no money. Josie learned that Himalayans were a cross of the Persian and Siamese breeds. She also saw that Himalayans and Persians were prone to health problems. These included a progressive brain disease, breathing difficulties, and hip joint problems. Josie wondered if Zoe's cat cost so much because the breeder had to be aware of these conditions. For Josie, they meant massive vet bills. She knew no cat's health could be guaranteed, but why go for a breed with built-in trouble?

Also, a Himalayan's long coat required constant brushing. Josie figured Amelia would get tired of that chore after a few weeks.

The Humane Society of Missouri did have a "breed interest e-mail notification" program for people who wanted a pedigreed cat or dog. Josie could register, if Amelia really wanted one.

Josie looked at the society's list of mixed-breed cats. These looked more affordable. The adoption price of one hundred twenty-five dollars included shots, a feline leukemia test, worming, flea treatment, spaying, tracking microchip, collar, a tag, and more. There was an extra charge for declawing.

Josie thought Amelia could find a cat here. She was about to examine the online photos of cats available for adoption when her phone rang. It was her mother, Jane.

"Hi, Mom," Josie said. "Thanks for another cooking class. Amelia made a terrific dinner."

"You could come, too, and learn how to cook," Jane said.

"I don't have the knack. The kid's a natural."

Jane sniffed her disapproval. "You don't even try."

"I did try. Your granddaughter doesn't like my cooking. That's what drove her upstairs to your kitchen. I've done her a good turn."

"Must you make everything into a joke?" Jane said. "I

wanted to talk to her about our next cooking lesson. Can she come tomorrow?"

"I don't think so. We're probably going to the Humane Society to adopt a cat."

"A cat! You know I hate cats," Jane said. "Sneaky, slithery things. I can't stand how they rub up against my ankles."

"The cat will stay downstairs, Mom. Your ankles are safe."

"This house will stink like cat pee," Jane said.

"Not if your granddaughter cleans out the litter box every day."

"What if that cat uses Mrs. Mueller's flower bed for a litter box?" Jane said. "You know how particular she is about her yard."

"A little fertilizer is good for flowers." Josie could almost hear her mother levitating. Mrs. Mueller was their troublesome next-door neighbor. Any cat of Josie's would immediately head out the front door and water Mrs. M's shrubbery.

"Mom, calm down," Josie said. "If we get a cat, it will be an indoor cat. They're healthier and they live longer. Besides, your granddaughter wants this cat, and it's the first thing she's cared about since her father died."

"Well—," Jane said. For once, she was at a loss for words. Jane loved Amelia.

"I'll go get Amelia," Josie said. "Could you watch her for an hour or so? I have to go back to work at six thirty."

"Why are you working at that hour?"

"I'm being paid double and Christmas is coming," Josie said.

"Isn't Stan delivering the couch tonight?"

"He and Howie are coming at seven thirty. I should be back by then. Here's Amelia." Amelia appeared in the doorway like a rescuing angel. Josie gratefully handed her daughter the phone, eager to escape more meddlesome matchmaking.

While Amelia talked to her grandmother, Josie looked at

pictures of cats on the Humane Society of Missouri's Web site. Several were brown tigers like Nate's cat, Cookie.

"I'll be right up, Grandma," Amelia said, and hung up the phone.

"Honey, look at my computer," Josie said. "The Humane Society has more than a hundred cats for adoption, and some of them look like your daddy's cat."

"Tigers!" Amelia said. "That one has a white vest. When can we go look at them?"

"After school tomorrow night," Josie said. "If you find one you like, we'll talk about adopting it."

"Thanks, Mom!" Amelia said.

"They also have a service where they'll e-mail you if they have a Himalayan or a Persian for adoption," Josie said.

"I want a tiger cat like Daddy's," Amelia said. "Are we going to get it declawed?"

Josie thought of her new couch. "Yes," she said.

"Isn't that cruel?" Amelia said.

"If we leave the back claws, the cat can still defend itself," Josie said. "Ruining my new couch would be cruelty toward Mom."

Amelia laughed and went upstairs.

Josie arrived at the Pets 4 Luv in Rock Road Village at 6:28 p.m. and called Alyce.

"I'm here. I'm going to talk to Edna now."

"Don't forget to call afterward," Alyce said.

Edna was coming out the automatic doors when Josie reached the store's sidewalk. The saleswoman's shoulders had that weary, end-of-the-day slump. She wore a black coat, a thick red scarf, and a red wool hat. Even Edna's dark hair looked tired.

"Edna!" Josie cried, as if the salesclerk were a long-lost friend.

"Good to see you," Edna said, and gave Josie a hug. Josie realized Edna didn't know her last name. The saleswoman steered Josie away from the store.

"Amelia is adopting an animal from the Humane Society," Josie said.

"Good," Edna said. She glanced at Josie's small purse and whispered. "Is that thing on?"

Josie unzipped it and showed Edna the inside. "It's too small to hold a recorder. Just a plain black bag."

"I don't have much time." Edna was talking so fast Josie could hardly understand her. "Do you work with Nedra?"

"No," Josie said. She didn't explain that she was a mystery shopper.

"Nedra's one of the good guys. The store manager, Dave, is not. He'll do anything for money, even sell abused puppies. He flew to the head office this afternoon. If Milwaukee has an ounce of sense, they'll fire him for this scam."

"Who's the store's supplier?"

"I tried to get into Dave's office to check, but I don't have the key. I've heard him talking to the guy on the phone. The puppy mill is in the woods somewhere in St. Louis County. The miller—that's what we call them—delivers the pups in a dark, beat-up truck. He smears mud on the plates. He has a funny first name, like something in the Bible. I can't remember it. Don't be fooled by the Bible name. He's greedy as the devil."

"Do you know his last name or the name of the mill?" Josie asked.

"No. All I can tell you is he says the road to his kennel is so bad he nearly broke an axle coming here after that snow. And he complains about his help. He says the boys don't work hard enough. He's such a horrible man. I'm sure that's how he talks about black people. I'm quitting as soon as I get my paycheck in two weeks. I don't care if I don't find another job. I can't stand it here anymore."

The automatic doors whooshed open. Edna clutched Josie's arm and said, "That's Jennifer. She spies for Dave. I have to run."

"Wait!" Josie cried.

"Good luck with your new pet," Edna called, waving good-bye. "Nice to see you." She cut through two rows of cars, heading for section D.

Josie watched a dark pickup cruise past a row of parked cars. The truck moved slowly, as if the driver were looking for a parking spot. Edna, keys in hand, was heading for a red Saturn. The truck sped up, hurtling straight toward her. Edna didn't notice.

Josie screamed, "Edna! Look out!"

But Edna didn't see the truck until it was almost on top of her. Then she tried to run. The truck bore down and struck her in the back, knocking her sideways. Edna was dragged several feet by her long scarf. Her hat flew off and landed on a car hood.

Then the truck was gone. Josie saw the sparkle of broken glass near the body. Edna didn't move. Her head was at an impossible angle.

# Chapter 5

"No! Edna no! You can't be dead. Please," Josie wailed, as she wept beside the woman.

The shrieks of the sirens mocked her screams and the blazing lights were from some hellish disco.

Josie heard the slam of a car door, and a uniformed officer swaggered over to her.

"Please help Edna," Josie begged him. "A truck ran her down and drove away."

"Step away, please, ma'am," the officer said, "so the paramedics can take care of the lady."

Four paramedics expertly loaded Edna onto a gurney and roared off to Holy Redeemer Hospital. Josie had the horrible feeling there was no need for their haste.

While she waited to talk to the police, Josie called her mother. "Mom, I witnessed an accident. The police are talking to me."

Jane gave a startled cry. "Are you okay?"

"I'm fine, but I don't think the poor woman who got hit will be so lucky. Yes, I know Stan is delivering the couch in a few minutes. Tell him hi for me. I'll be home as soon as I can. Please call Alyce and tell her I'm fine."

"How do I know that unless I see you?" Jane asked.

"Mom, I'm talking to you, aren't I? That should be

proof. Call Alyce or she'll worry. I'll be home as soon as I can."

The uniformed officer was standing over Josie. "I'd like to ask you a few questions," he said. His name tag said RICHARDS.

Her teeth were chattering and she was shaking so badly she could hardly talk. Officer Richards led Josie inside the store to the employee break room, a bare, white-walled room with a long folding table, six chairs, a soda machine, a fridge, and a microwave. The only decorations were OSHA and minimum-wage posters. The air smelled of red sauce and cardboard from countless microwaved dinners.

Officer Richards handed her a cup of heavily sugared hot coffee. Josie took a sip, then wrapped her hands around the cup to warm them. She still couldn't stop shaking. She heard the break room door shut. Officer Richards had a round open face, short brown hair, bulging gym muscles—and a bad cold. He kept sneezing. Josie pulled her coffee away from him, and hoped it was out of range.

Between sneezes, Richards asked Josie the standard questions about her age, name, marital status, and what she did for a living.

After a few sips of coffee, she felt a little better, but so tired she had to struggle to keep her eyes open.

"How long have you known Edna Prilosen?" Richards asked.

"Is that her last name?" Josie said. "I didn't know it. I met her today when I was mystery-shopping this store. Edna advised me not to buy the puppies because they were from a mill."

"An employee told you not to buy a product her store was selling?"

Josie could hear the disbelief in his voice. He gave a mighty sneeze and pulled a white handkerchief from his pocket.

"Yes," Josie said. "Edna said the puppies were unhealthy, and her manager—Dave—bought them from a puppy mill."

"Miss Marcus, could you tell me what kind of truck hit the victim?" That question set off another attack of sneezing and wheezing.

Josie waited until he finished. It gave her time to think. "My ex-boyfriend had a Ford F-150 pickup. This pickup looked like his, only dark gray or black. The color was hard to tell under the mercury vapor lights. I think it was older, too. The truck had a lot of scrapes and dents. I guess it has a busted front light now. There was broken glass or plastic all over the blacktop."

"Did you get the truck's license plate?" Officer Richards asked. "Even a letter or a number would help."

"The plate was smeared with something dark, like mud," Josie said. Mud, she thought. What did Edna tell her about mud?

"Did you see the driver?" Richards asked.

"I think he was wearing a black ski mask."

"He?" Officer Richards sneezed again.

"I didn't see his face, but he seemed tall and his shoulders were broad like a man's."

"Tell me again from the beginning about your encounter with Edna Prilosen," Officer Richards said.

Josie tried to think back to the morning when she'd met Edna. It seemed another lifetime. It was. Edna was alive and healthy and trying to save abused animals this morning. Josie's eyes filled with tears. She talked fast to keep them from spilling down her cheeks.

"I was mystery-shopping the store. Edna was very helpful. She gave me a free cookie from the bulk bin. It was a carob cookie treat for dogs. I took a bite and she said people ate them, too. I got half a pound, as a joke. I don't have a dog.

"Then I asked her about the store's pedigreed dogs—their papers, parents, their veterinary care. She avoided a direct answer. When I said my ten-year-old daughter wanted a puppy, Edna became agitated. She dragged me to a 'dead zone' where she couldn't be seen on the store's security cameras."

"What did she tell you?" Officer Richards unleashed a mighty sneeze. Josie backed her chair away an inch. She thought she heard someone rattling the break room door.

"She said I shouldn't buy a puppy there because the dogs weren't healthy. She thought I was an animal activist. Edna told me to come back tonight when she got off work because the store manager was suspicious that she was on to him. She wanted me to meet her outside the store at six thirty. Then her manager called her to register two. Edna panicked and ran up there. I bought a bag of dog food and left. I feel like this is all my fault."

"It is all your fault, Miss Marcus," said a voice behind her. "When amateurs meddle in police work, innocent people get killed."

Josie turned and saw her Rock Road Village nemesis, homicide Detective Gray, leaning against the break room doorway. As usual, he was wearing a gray suit and dark tie. Josie had met him when Nate was murdered. He didn't like her then, and she could see the same distaste in his shrewd eyes.

Officer Richards looked up in surprise.

"Miss Marcus and I are old friends, officer," Detective Gray said. "And wouldn't you know it? She's connected with another murder."

"Murder?" Josie asked. "Edna's dead?" The news wasn't a surprise, but the reality was a punch in the gut. Josie clung to her coffee cup as if it could save her from slipping off the earth.

Detective Gray regarded Josie without warmth. "It's interesting," he said. "I haven't seen you for almost a year, when your ex was murdered. But I stop in here and the first words out of your mouth are lies."

"What lies?" Josie said.

"Don't bullshit me, Miss Marcus. I just saw the parking lot security video. If you met the victim today, why did you greet Edna Prilosen outside the store at six thirty-two tonight like she was your oldest friend? There's no sound on that video, but I saw you hug that woman. Do you always embrace strangers?"

"That's what we agreed to do when I met her this morning. It's all on my tape."

"Your tape?" Detective Gray raised one eyebrow.

"I had a purse camera for my mystery-shopping assignment. It recorded our conversation."

"You've got audio?"

"Not with me. Harry, my boss at Suttin Services, has the tape now. He said it was legal to record myself in Missouri. I hope there's not a problem."

"Officer Richards, call the PD Geek Squad and have them make a mirror copy of the store's security video system's hard drive," Detective Gray said.

"The Geek Squad, sir?"

"The police tech services unit. I need a copy of that store security video to see if it tallies with her account. When did you have this conversation with the victim, Miss Marcus?"

"A few minutes after the store opened at noon," Josie said.

Detective Gray turned to Officer Richards. "Tell them the hour between noon and one is most important. Secure the room where the machine is. These tapes have a habit of erasing themselves."

"Yes, sir. Do we need a warrant?"

"Let's seize the tape first and then get a judge's permission to view it. Where's the manager, Dave?"

"He was called to the store headquarters in Milwaukee this afternoon," Officer Richards said.

"Have someone get hold of them and track him down. Now."

"Yes, sir." Officer Richards dashed out of the room.

Detective Gray turned back to Josie. "What's your boss's last name?"

"I don't know. I've always called him Harry." She left out "the Horrible." Josie was pretty sure he wasn't listed that way in the phone book.

"Where's he live?"

"I don't know," she said.

"You must have an emergency number."

"I do, but it's at home."

"When we finish here, I'll have an officer accompany you to your home for that phone number. Did you have a tape running when you talked with Miss Prilosen in the parking lot?"

"No," Josie said. "She'd spotted the recording device in the store and asked me not to bring it. So I just had this. She checked it." She held up her black purse.

"What did she tell you before she was run over? And remember, Miss Marcus, if you hide anything, there will be serious consequences. A woman was murdered because of your meddling."

"Edna said she tried to get into Dave's office to check his records, but she didn't have a key. She did hear him talking to the puppy mill owner on the phone. Edna said the mill was somewhere in St. Louis County."

"That's real helpful," Detective Gray said. "We're only talking about some five hundred square miles. What else?"

"The puppies are delivered in a dark, beat-up pickup," Josie said. "The miller smears mud on the plates. He has a funny first name, like something in the Bible."

"More useless information," he said.

"Well, at least you know the killer isn't named Cliff or Bruce."

"Is that a joke?" Detective Gray asked.

"Not a very good one," Josie said in a small voice. "That's all I know."

"Well, it isn't a whole hell of a lot," he said.

"Edna started to tell me more, but then Jennifer came out of the store. She's another saleswoman. Edna said Jennifer was Dave's spy. She got scared and ran away and—" Josie couldn't say the rest. It was too horrible.

"Looks like we'd better have a talk with this Jennifer," Detective Gray said. "In the meantime, let's go over your statement again, from the top."

They went over the details twice more. Then Josie signed a statement. "I'm really tired," she said. "It's been a terrible night."

"It wasn't a whole lot of fun for Edna, either," Detective Gray said.

Josie fought back the tears.

"Officer Richards will follow you home," Detective Gray said. "You will give him your boss's after-hours phone number. If you don't cooperate, I'll throw you in jail as a material witness."

It was nearly two in the morning when Josie pulled in front of her flat. Officer Richards parked behind her. Josie saw the lights on in her flat. She parked the car and sleep-walked past the couch out by the curb. Officer Richards walked next to her. He stank of menthol and made crunching sounds. Josie guessed he was chewing cough drops.

Jane was waiting for her at the door.

"Mom, I have to get some information for this officer, and then he's going home."

"You look tired," Jane said to the officer. "May I get you some coffee or a brownie?"

"Thank you, ma'am, but if I don't get back, I'll be skinned alive."

Josie found Harry's emergency number in her bedroom office. As she passed Amelia's room, her daughter called softly, "Mom, are we still getting the cat tomorrow?"

"After school, sweetie. That's a promise."

"Good," Amelia said.

Josie handed the information to Officer Richards and

walked him to the door. She noticed Mrs. Mueller peering out the slats in her blinds. The old snoop was on duty even in the middle of the night.

Josie closed and locked the front door. She expected her mother to be angry. Instead, Jane was sympathetic. "You look tired," she said softly. "How are you, sweetheart?"

"I'm fine, Mom," Josie said. "But Edna's not. She's dead."

The tears that Josie had held back all night suddenly burst forth. Jane folded Josie into her arms and Josie cried on her mother's shoulder for the first time in years.

"It will be okay. It will be okay." Jane patted her daughter and held her like a child. "Sit down and I'll bring you some hot tea."

Josie didn't even realize she was sitting on her new couch.

# Chapter 6

Josie spent the night drifting in and out of an uneasy sleep. She remembered tiny, terrible details from Edna's murder: The broken glass glittering in her dark hair like stardust. The sad, inhuman angle of her neck. The dark pool of blood under her back.

And the deep suspicion in homicide Detective Gray's intelligent eyes.

After several restless hours, she staggered out to the kitchen for coffee. Then Josie sat on her new couch, reveling in its soft cushions and unstained upholstery.

Josie wrote her report and e-mailed it to Harry, along with a note explaining what happened last night. Maybe she should call and warn him. It was six thirty in the morning. She dialed the emergency number, but there was no answer. She didn't leave a message.

She assumed that was his home number and wondered when he would come into the Suttin office, read her report, and erupt.

Her phone practically jumped off the kitchen wall ten minutes later. Josie took a quick gulp of coffee before she answered.

"Josie Marcus, why did you tell the cops about that purse cam video?" Harry thundered. "Why didn't you call me?"

"Did I do something wrong?" Josie sounded overly innocent. "You told me the camera was legal. I tried to call you at the emergency number, but no one answered."

"I was spending the night somewhere," Harry said.

Josie wondered who the unlucky woman was.

"Mom fixed me dinner last night," he said, answering her unspoken question. "If you'd left a message, I could have called you sooner. That's how Pets 4 Luv found me. I'm at the office early trying to clean up your mess. And it is one hell of a mess.

"You shouldn't have told the cops. You know our client reports are confidential. I'm looking at a goddamn subpoena. They just served me." There were no cracking or crunching sounds. Harry was too upset to eat.

"But, Harry, if we didn't do anything wrong, we have nothing to fear—and neither do our clients." It was a sneaky echo of his own words. Eat those, Josie thought.

"The whole reason Pets 4 Luv hired us was to avoid publicity," Harry shouted. Josie held the phone away from her ear and waited until the screaming stopped. Josie didn't know a man's voice could go that high.

"Harry, an innocent woman is dead," Josie said. "I saw her get hit by a truck. It was horrible."

"What's that got to do with me?" he said.

"It was the Pets 4 Luv saleswoman, Edna. I talked with her. Our conversation is on the purse cam video. Her boss was suspicious about her activities. He thought she was helping the animal activists. If you ask me, Edna's death is the store's fault."

"I didn't ask you. And I don't care if she's dead."

"Well, I do. If Pets 4 Luv suspected something was wrong, they should have brought in private investigators instead of trying to cover it up. If the chain gets unfavorable publicity, they deserve it."

Josie heard Harry take a deep breath, as if he was trying to calm down. "They've already fired Dave, the Rock Road store manager," he said. "They called him to Milwaukee yesterday. I e-mailed them the video at three o'clock. I did what I was supposed to."

His word hung in the air like an accusation.

"Corporate saw the video, then met with Dave at four o'clock and told him they wanted the pedigreed-dog sales records. Dave said they were in his rental car. Four supposedly smart people—the CEO, the human resources woman, and two high-priced lawyers—were there for the firing, and they didn't have the brains to send a security guard with Dave when he went to the parking lot. Dave took off.

"The idiots sat on their asses for thirty minutes before they realized he wasn't coming back. The cops rousted the CEO early this morning and he called me. He was furious with me."

"It's not your fault," Josie said. "The store let Dave get away."

"The cops traced Dave as far as Chicago. He left the rental car at O'Hare about six thirty last night. From there, he could fly or drive anywhere, especially if he had fake ID."

"I wonder if they'll ever find him," Josie said. "I'm betting Dave has at least a million dollars stashed away from that puppy mill scam. I think he had fake documents and was ready to run. Well, if he was at O'Hare at six thirty yesterday, at least we know he didn't kill Edna."

"No, but he could have called someone to do the job," Harry said.

"Uh, Harry, about my money for this job—"

"You'll get it," he said. "But if you ask me, you don't deserve it. This was supposed to be an easy job. Now Pets 4 Luv is all over me and the cops can't find that crooked manager. But they sure as hell found me."

"I'm sorry," Josie said.

Even Harry could hear the insincerity in her voice. He slammed down the phone.

Extra money and a harassed Harry, Josie thought. There is some justice. He'll get even with me later, but right now he's in hot water and he deserves to be. She hummed a little tune as she poured another cup of coffee.

Fortified with caffeine, she went to wake up Amelia. They'd have to leave for school soon. Amelia was awake, but still in bed.

"Are we still going to get my cat this afternoon?" Amelia asked.

"Of course."

Amelia leapt out of bed without protest. She was ready for school in record time.

"Did you have nightmares and stuff last night after watching that poor lady die?" Amelia asked on the way to Barrington.

"How do you know about Edna?"

"I heard you talking to Grandma when you came home. You were crying. You never cry."

"I was just tired," Josie said.

"Yeah, right," Amelia said.

"Is Harry going to chew you out?" Amelia asked.

"He already did this morning," Josie said.

"I'm sorry," Amelia said.

Josie shrugged. "He's a jerk. He's not even sorry that poor woman died."

I'm having a real conversation with my daughter, Josie thought. Unlike her mother, she's going to be a thoughtful, sensitive person. She pulled into the circular drive of the Barrington School for Boys and Girls. The Georgian-style redbrick buildings with their crisp white trim and dignified fan lights told the parents they were special. It wasn't necessary. Most of them already believed that.

"There's Emma!" Amelia reached for her backpack, slammed the door, and ran out of the car to greet her friend.

Josie waved to Emma's mother, then inched down the Barrington drive. Students drifted in front of the moving cars with the confidence of the well protected. They had no fear of being hurt. The world always did what they wanted.

I wish my daughter had their self-assurance, she thought. I wish we had their charmed lives. But she knew there were no charmed lives. Even rich kids and their parents were short of money, and they worried in their way as much as Josie and Amelia.

Josie's phone rang as she was leaving the Barrington driveway. It was Alyce. Josie pulled into the parking lot alongside the school to talk to her friend.

"How are you?" Alyce asked. "And what happened last night?"

Josie told her, while Alyce made sympathetic sounds. "Do you want to come here for coffee?"

"No, thanks. I want to get some supplies for Amelia. We're going to pick out a cat at the Humane Society tonight."

"That will be a good distraction for both of you. Tell me you aren't going to Pets 4 Luv."

"I'm going to their competitor, the Puppy-Kitty Superstore."

"Good," Alyce said. "Call me if you need to talk. You had a very upsetting evening."

Josie stopped at the giant warehouse store and bought a cat box, litter, dry food, and cat toys, including toy mice and a bag of colorful yarn balls. She also bought a long-handled device with red feathers on the end. The saleswoman assured her cats went crazy over it.

Jane was waiting for Josie when she came home loaded with her packages. Her mother seemed tired and pricklier than usual this morning.

"How are you?" Jane asked.

"Fine, Mom. I bought some cat supplies. We're going to pick out a cat tonight."

"Are you really going through with that?" Jane didn't bother to hide her disapproval.

"Yes, Mom. It will be good for Amelia."

"A cat is not a vitamin pill, Josie. What if the animal has fleas?"

"The Humane Society checks the cats," Josie said. "The cat will be flea free. They'll clean out the ear mites and worm it, too."

Jane wrinkled her nose. "Thank you for that lovely image."

# Chapter 7

"And Amelia Marcus."

Five more students came running out of the Barrington School for Boys and Girls. Sleek SUVs, Mercedes, and BMWs awaited them, along with Josie's humble gray Honda. Her car was the alley cat in this well-bred automotive herd. Barrington teachers drove cars like Josie's—small, old, and anonymous.

Barrington students did not walk out of school. They had to wait for their rides to arrive and their names to be called. Most of their parents had six-figure incomes, trusts, and hedge funds. Their children were one more valuable asset.

At least my daughter's safe, Josie thought. I couldn't raise any ransom money. But Josie had turned worrying into a fine art. She went through the lists of what-ifs:

What if some lowlife thought Amelia was a rich kid?

What if the kidnapper hurt my daughter when he—or she—learned the truth?

What if—?

"Hi, Mom," Amelia said, opening the car door. She threw her backpack on the rear seat and flopped down on the front one.

Josie's worries were smothered by parental pride. My daughter has grown up in the last year, she thought. Amelia looks so much like her late father, it hurts my heart.

Josie smoothed her daughter's dark bangs and kissed her hello. In another year or so, Amelia wouldn't permit that liberty in public.

"How are you feeling?" Amelia asked, with one of those spooky flash-forwards to adulthood.

"I'm fine. Ready to pick out a new cat," Josie said. "Do you want to check the computer at home again for pictures of adoptable cats?"

"I printed them out last night." Amelia reached around and rummaged in her backpack for some folded papers. "Let's go to the shelter before someone gets my cat. I have my list down to two. I read their biographies on the Web site and looked at their videos. I want the playful one."

"Tell me about your picks," Josie asked.

Amelia read from the paper in her school essay voice. "'Teddy is two years old,'" she said. "'He's a brown tabby with a white vest. He has a great personality and is very playful. He's been declawed and has a loving nature.'"

"Declawed?" Josie asked. "He's got my vote."

"Don't I get one?" Amelia asked.

"Of course you do, honey. Let's hear about the other cat."

"'Harry is eight months old,'" Amelia read. "'Harry is a domestic shorthair with green eyes and a white vest. His family had to relocate and they brought him back. He's been neutered. He is very clean and likes people.'"

"Doesn't sound like the Harry I know," Josie said.

"It's not the cat's fault he has the same name as your boss," Amelia said.

"I'm sure Harry the cat has better manners," Josie said. "If you get the cat Harry, are you going to change his name?"

"Maybe. I don't think I'd like to have my name changed once I got used to it. What if you decided to call me Sarah? Besides, if I pick Harry, he'll be getting a new home. That's a lot of change for a little animal."

"Very thoughtful." Josie swallowed a lump in her throat. Her daughter was learning to consider others' feelings, even cats'.

"We're here!" Amelia said. The Macklind Avenue shelter was a restored warehouse. Josie thought the inside was surprisingly clean and bright. She could hear a few meows and barks. The adoptable adult cats lounged in a glass-fronted cattery.

"Look at that big orange cat," Amelia said.

"Your great-grandmother called those marmalade cats," Josie said, "because they look like orange marmalade."

"I like that big fluffy brown one," Amelia said.

"I think that's a Maine coon," Josie said. "They're supposed to be gentle."

Some cats slept, some curled into balls, and some paced like tiny tigers in a zoo. Others wrestled and chased one another. Josie was relieved to see at least one brown striped tabby rolling around with a toy mouse. She hoped the cat stayed in a playful mood.

"You can still get a Persian or a Himalayan like Zoe's," Josie said.

"I want a cat like Daddy's," Amelia said.

An adoption counselor asked them questions about cat food, litter boxes, health care, and other pet issues. She looked like the kind of woman you could go to if you were in trouble.

"Will your cat be indoor, outdoor, or both?" the counselor asked.

"He's staying indoors," Josie said.

"Good," the counselor said. "Indoor cats live longer."

They filled out a one-page application. Amelia asked for either Harry or Teddy. Teddy had been adopted earlier that day, the adoption counselor said, but Harry was still available. Amelia could meet him in the "get acquainted" room.

Josie and Amelia sat with a nervous Harry in the cell-like room. Harry was an optical illusion. He looked skinny, but he was a solid fellow with long legs and a whiplike tail. His short brown fur had thick, squiggly black stripes. The colors were muted brown and black, but the effect was oddly loud.

Shining out of these winter forest colors were enormous green eyes. Harry's huge ears moved like satellite dishes, following the conversation.

"He looks scared, Mom," Amelia said.

"He should be. What happens today will determine the rest of his life." Josie wished she hadn't sounded so solemn. "Don't worry, honey, he's not the only cat in the world. If he doesn't work out, we'll keep coming back until we find the perfect one for you."

Amelia unfolded the photo her grandfather had e-mailed to her. Young Nate had Cookie the striped cat hoisted on his shoulder. Both had carefree grins.

"Daddy's cat looks just like Harry," Amelia said. "See how Harry's stripes turn into sort of circles on his sides? He has a white chest and white fur around his mouth. He's the reincarnation of Cookie."

"He's very pretty," Josie said. She didn't have the heart to say that nearly every brown tabby looked like Nate's cat. I'm sort of a human tabby, Josie thought. I'm cute, brown-haired, but nothing special.

Harry approached them, sniffing loudly. Amelia sat perfectly still and didn't try to touch the cat. Harry sniffed her shoes, then checked out Josie's shoes. He tentatively batted Josie's key chain with one brown paw, then stalked and attacked her purse, tangling himself in the long strap. Josie carefully unwound the cat from her purse.

Amelia giggled.

Harry pounced on Amelia's shoestring.

"He's so cute," Amelia said. "Can we get him, Mom?"

"As long as he's declawed," Josie said. "Let's ask the counselor about that."

"Only the front claws are removed," the adoption counselor said. "Cats need their back claws to defend themselves. You could get a good scratching post rather than declaw him. Many people think declawing is cruel."

"So is attacking my couch," Josie said. "I won't be home all day to guard it. Declawing is better than no adoption."

"Let me call our veterinarian staff." The counselor punched in a number, then reported back. "Your cat can be scheduled for the procedure at seven tomorrow morning. Harry can stay here tonight."

"But what if someone adopts him?" Amelia said.

"They won't. We'll put your name on his temporary collar. You can pick him up tomorrow after his surgery. We'll give you a call when he's ready."

"Can't we take him home now?" Amelia asked.

"You could, but you'd introduce him to a strange house for one night, then bring him back here again early in the morning. That's very stressful. We'll prepare him for surgery and make sure he has no food or water after midnight. These are familiar surroundings for Harry right now."

Josie paid the adoption fee and collected her paperwork and discounts for cat food and medical care. "That was quick," she said. "We were out in an hour."

"What if Harry dies during surgery?" Amelia asked as they hurried down the broad sidewalk to their car. It was growing darker and colder.

"The Humane Society has good vets. Harry is young and healthy. He won't die."

"But Daddy died in the hospital," Amelia said.

"Your daddy was very sick," Josie said.

Your daddy was a drunk and he was murdered, she thought. But Josie was still worried. My daughter has had too many losses. What will I do if that cat dies? People die during minor surgery all the time. They die from simple tonsillectomies. You never know—

A yellow fur ball came hurtling across the brown winter grass and collided with Amelia, knocking her to the ground.

A golden-haired puppy trailing a red leash sat on Amelia, licking her face. A small dog wearing a blue sweater bounced up and yapped by her foot.

"Chloe!" a despairing male voice said.

"Bruiser!" an angry woman cried.

Bruiser? My child was attacked by Bruiser? Josie thought. Let me at him.

It took a few minutes to sort out the fur and people. Bruiser turned out to be a scrawny brown Chihuahua. Chloe was the fat yellow lab mix who'd knocked Amelia to the ground. Her owner grabbed the red leash, then said to Amelia, "Are you okay, honey? Are you hurt?" He looked worried.

"I'm fine," Amelia said, brushing off her jacket. She scratched the pup's ears. Chloe did a full-body wag and gave Amelia another slurp.

"That's a relief," the man said. "I'm sorry. Chloe is still learning her manners. My name is Jerry."

Jerry looked rather like a puppy himself, with soft brown eyes, unruly blond hair, and big feet. He offered a huge paw and pulled Amelia up off the ground.

Behind Jerry, a pale young woman in a long dark dress and navy wool coat clutched Bruiser. Her drab brown hair was tied back and her face was grim. Josie thought she looked like a member of a religious cult. "I'm terribly sorry," she said in a soft voice. "Bruiser is small, but strong. Are you okay, little girl?"

Amelia's mouth tightened. She thought she was too old to be a "little girl."

"My name is Nedra." Bruiser's owner stuck out her hand.

"I'm fine, really," Amelia said, ignoring the handshake.

"Are you here with Jerry?" Josie asked Nedra.

"No, I live nearby. I was walking Bruiser when he saw the yellow pup and went running up to play. Bruiser is adopted from this shelter. I like Chihuahuas, but I was afraid I'd get a puppy mill pet if I bought one at a pet store. A pound puppy is the only way to end the cruelty." Nedra kissed her little dog on its round dome.

"People who run puppy mills should get the death penalty for what they do to innocent doggies, shouldn't they, Bruiser?" Nedra smooched the dog again. "I'm trying to leash train Bruiser, but he still makes some mistakes."

Amelia gave Bruiser an ear scratch while Chloe begged for more attention. She tried to pet both dogs at once, but her arms weren't long enough.

Nedra? Where had Josie heard that name before? "Did you know Edna, a saleswoman at Pets 4 Luv?" Josie asked.

"She's the woman who was murdered last night," Nedra said. "I saw that terrible video on the news this morning."

"I talked with her yesterday," Josie said. "Edna thought you were one of the good guys. She said you were investigating her store for puppy mill dogs."

"I belong to People Are Animals, Too," Nedra said.

"I've never heard of that organization," Josie said.

"They're headquartered in New Mexico," Nedra said. "Near Santa Fe. If you ever vacation in that area, you should stop in at PAT. They do good work. PAT is more forceful than most pro-animal agencies. They haven't compromised their ideals."

Josie wondered if those ideals—and some clumsy investigation on Nedra's part—had made Dave suspicious and led to Edna's death.

"We just got a cat," Amelia said. "He's at the vet's here, getting fixed."

Josie was relieved that Amelia didn't go into details. She suspected Nedra would disapprove of declawing.

Nedra handed Josie a couple of business cards and said, "If you need a veterinarian again, let me recommend this one. He loves animals. His office is near Maplewood. He works weekends and he'll even come to your house. I'd better get Bruiser home. He's shivering from the cold, aren't you, sweetie?"

She left, kissing and cuddling Bruiser.

"May I buy you a hot chocolate or a cupcake?" Jerry asked.

"No, thanks," Amelia said. "But I make a good brownie, if you want to come to our house."

"Amelia!" Josie said, her cheeks flame red. "Sorry. My daughter, like your puppy, can be a little overly friendly." She shot Amelia a glare.

"I understand. You shouldn't invite strange men to your house, even if they do have cute dogs," Jerry said. "How about if you have coffee with me someplace away from your home?"

Josie studied Jerry. He wasn't ripped or cut like Stan. Josie couldn't bounce quarters off his abs. The man was no hunk. But he was cute. A tabby like me, Josie thought. Maybe it's time to see someone who isn't obsessed with carbs.

"Thanks, but I've had too much coffee today," Josie said. "I'm wired. Do you live near Maplewood?"

"Better. I live in Maplewood," he said. "It's a cool place."

"I do, too," Josie said. "Maybe we could walk your pup to Airedale Antics and get her a treat. Do you know that shop?"

"Sure do. It's on Manchester between Sutton and Marshall. They have two Airedales—Sassybear and Harrybear. The dogs greet everyone with wagging tails. Chloe thinks they're her buddies. We'll meet you there tomorrow night about six o'clock. Bring Amelia."

"I will," Josie said. "On a leash."

# Chapter 8

"I can't believe you asked that man to our house, Amelia Marcus." Josie's voice was rapidly rising to a shout. "You are grounded. Grounded! Give me your cell phone."

"But Mom," Amelia said, "what if something goes wrong and I need it?"

"There wouldn't be any emergencies if you didn't do stupid things, Amelia."

"I was only thinking of you," Amelia said.

"Me!"

"Well, I thought Stan was a hottie and you started dating him. That made Grandma happy, but he turned out to be really boring. I tried to give Stan a brownie last night and he said he didn't eat bad carbs."

"Now you know how it feels to have your cooking insulted," Josie said.

"But I'm a good cook!" Amelia said.

"And I'm not?" Josie knew the answer. She took deep breaths to calm herself. Amelia said nothing.

"Look, Amelia, Stan turned into a fitness fanatic. And he is dull. But he does help us and he's still a nice man." A nice dull man, she thought.

"Jerry seems to be nice, too," Amelia said. "He's not ripped or anything, but I thought he'd be more fun. Stan is nutso-crazy about exercise."

"I can take care of my own love life, thank you," Josie said, her voice crisp as new lettuce. "I don't need a man. Millions of women survive without them. Jerry seems nice, but we don't know anything about him. He could be a serial killer using a puppy to lure his victims. We could all wake up dead one morning."

Josie realized she was sounding a bit crazy herself.

"Well, you're the one who agreed to meet him at Airedale Antics, Mom," Amelia said.

"In a public place on a busy street," Josie said. "With people around. I didn't invite him to our house. He doesn't know where we live. Do you see the difference?"

"Mrs. Mueller, dead ahead," Amelia said, sounding relieved. "She's in our front yard and she looks like trouble."

Mrs. Mueller always looked like trouble. Her arms were crossed and her face was grim. Her iron gray hair was sprayed into place and didn't dare move, even in the brisk winter wind. Mrs. Mueller's gray coat could have been swiped from a Soviet prison matron. She was frowning at Josie's old couch sagging by the curb. It looked depressingly frayed, even in the dim streetlight.

"Go on inside," Josie said. "I'll handle her."

She parked the car in front of her flat. Amelia ran for the front door. Josie wanted to join her daughter, but she climbed out of the car and locked it. "Hi, Mrs. Mueller." Josie forced herself to sound casual.

"What is this couch doing in your front yard?" Mrs. Mueller asked in a voice like thunder.

Several wrong answers popped into Josie's head including, "The backstroke" and "Whatever it wants."

"It's waiting for the city's bulk-item pickup," Josie said.

"Couldn't you give it to Goodwill?" Mrs. Mueller said.

"I wouldn't inflict that on the poor," Josie said. "Maplewood has free bulk-item pickup. It will be disposed of properly."

"Not for a week! Remove that object immediately," Mrs. Mueller said, pointing at the couch.

"I can get Stan and Howie to carry the couch onto my front porch," Josie said. "But I can't guarantee they'll move it after that. It could just stay there permanently. It would be cheaper than porch furniture and more comfortable. Now, if you'll excuse me, I have to get our house ready for the new cat." Josie sidled past Mrs. Mueller.

"Cat!" shrieked Mrs. M.

She knew it was wrong, but Josie couldn't resist. Mrs. Mueller made Josie feel fifteen years younger, which turned her age back to sixteen, when Josie seemed to spend most of her young life in trouble. Her nosy neighbor spied on Josie and reported any infractions to her mother, Jane. Josie was kissing a boy at ten o'clock at night in his car. Josie was smoking cigarettes by the Dumpster. Josie was riding on a motorcycle with Joe, who dropped her off a block away from her home.

Josie's mother revered the old bat. Mrs. Mueller was the church power broker, controlling the choice committees.

Amelia held open the front door for her mother. "She went ballistic when you mentioned the cat."

"That means you'll have to be doubly careful," Josie said. "If that cat ever gets out, Mrs. Mueller will have animal control here before his paws hit the yard."

"Can we get our home ready for Harry?" Amelia said.

"We're supposed to keep the new cat in a small room until he feels secure."

"How about my bathroom?" Amelia said. "I'll shut the door when I go to school."

"Good," Josie said. "That way, if Harry has an accident, it will be easy for you to clean up."

Amelia wrinkled her nose.

Josie brought a soft, fluffy throw rug for the new cat to sleep on next to the bathroom radiator. She added the litter box but no litter. "We're supposed to use shredded newspaper until his paws heal."

"Who's going to chop up the newspaper?" Amelia asked.

"Guess," Josie said, and handed her the scissors.

"I can't wait until tomorrow when I see Harry." Amelia dutifully cut up copies of the *St. Louis City Gazette*.

When she finished, Josie handed her a bag. Amelia pulled out something that looked like a long-handled feather duster. "Am I supposed to dust the cat?" Amelia asked.

"That's a cat toy," Josie said. "The saleswoman swears cats love it. The little mice are fake fur, not real. That's a bag of yarn balls. Cats supposedly go crazy batting them around."

"Will the cat play with me when he has all these toys?" Amelia asked.

"He'll have to do something while you're at school," Josie said.

"You didn't buy them from that place, did you?"

"They're from a competitor."

"Good," Amelia said. "I don't think we should support them."

"Me, either," Josie said.

"I'd like to go to bed early," Amelia said.

"You would? Are you sick?"

"No, it will make tomorrow come faster."

The next morning, she was up without Josie having to wake her. She fixed herself breakfast and was ready to leave for school on time. All the way to Barrington, Amelia talked about Harry. Josie waved good-bye to Amelia and went back home feeling happier than she had since Nate's death. One small cat was making a big difference—if he survived the surgery.

When the phone rang at ten a.m., Josie nearly tripped over a kitchen chair running to answer it. The call came from the wrong Harry. Her boss wanted her to mystery-shop three small pet boutiques.

"Any puppy mill pets at these stores?" Josie asked.

"They don't sell pets at all," Harry said. "And you won't need a purse camera."

"Good," Josie said.

Josie paced the floors for another hour, waiting for news about Harry the cat. The Humane Society veterinarian's office called. Harry's operation was a success. She could pick up the cat after three o'clock.

She was nearly weak with relief. Josie filled the cat's bowls with food and water and put a soft toy mouse and a yarn ball on the cat's rug. There. The room was ready. Now she needed to get Amelia at school.

Amelia fairly skimmed over the ground as she ran to her mother's car that afternoon.

"Is Harry okay?" she asked.

"Good afternoon to you, too," Josie said. "Harry is fine and we're going to pick him up, unless you have something else you'd rather do."

"No," Amelia said, as if her mother had asked a serious question.

"Don't be too disappointed if he doesn't want to play," Josie said. "He's had surgery. His paws are hurting and he'll be groggy. He'll probably want to go to sleep."

"I understand," Amelia said.

All the way to the Macklind Avenue shelter, Amelia texted Emma about her plans for the cat in that strange shorthand kids used. Josie was grateful for the quiet.

Amelia insisted on carrying in the pet caddy herself.

Josie was impressed with how the vet tech handled the cat. She'd carefully wrapped Harry in a scrap of old blanket, then packed him into the new caddy. Harry looked sleepy and flopped down inside like a rag doll. Josie felt a pang of guilt when she saw his stitched front paws.

Amelia held the cat carrier on her lap on the way home and peppered Josie with questions. "When do you think he'll come out and play, Mom?" "How long will he sleep, Mom?"

"Will he get any bigger, Mom?" "When's he going to be well, Mom?"

Josie answered, "I don't know" until Amelia gave up. She refused Josie's help carrying the cat inside. "He's not heavy, Mom."

Harry was carried into the purple bathroom with great ceremony. He didn't make a sound. When Amelia opened the door to his carrier, Harry poked out his head and looked around cautiously.

"He's coming out!" Amelia said, as if she'd spotted a rock star.

Harry crawled under the claw-foot bathtub and refused to budge.

"Harry, come out and play," Amelia called.

"Let him alone, honey," Josie said. "He's had a hard day."

"Can I ask Grandma to come see him?"

"You can, but she doesn't like cats."

Josie called her mother.

"Are you seeing someone besides Stan?" Jane asked when she picked up the phone.

"Not yet."

"Josie, you won't find a better man," Jane said.

"That's the problem, Mom," Josie said. "I'm looking for someone who's not quite so perfect."

"Humph!" Jane said. "There are plenty of drug dealers. And that last one you dated, that plumber—well, I won't mention his family."

"Me, either, Mom," Josie said, interrupting Jane. "Your granddaughter wants to know if you'll come downstairs to see her cat."

"I am not entering your home with that wild animal running loose," Jane said.

# Chapter 9

"So that's all I can tell you about me," Jerry said, scratching Sassybear's ears. The friendly black and tan dog was one of the official greeters at Airedale Antics. Amelia was petting Chloe and checking out the cat treats.

After some coaxing, Jerry began to talk about himself. "I work at the post office. I rent a house in Maplewood. I'm single and I have a dog named Chloe. Not real exciting." He dismissed himself with a shy little shrug. Josie wanted to scratch his ears and pat his blond head.

Down girl, she told herself.

"Uh, how do you feel about exercise?" she asked.

He patted a nearly nonexistent paunch. "I should do more," he said. "But I don't. Too busy."

"That's good," Josie said.

"It is?" Jerry tilted his head like a puzzled pup. "My doctor says I need to work out more. So does my mom. I wouldn't have a weight problem if Mom weren't such a good cook. I don't get much exercise standing behind a post office counter. That's why I got Chloe. I thought walking her would help me lose weight. Could I buy you some wine? I mean, your cat?"

"Harry might like the Meowlot," Josie said. "You could buy him a drink."

"Can cats have wine?" Amelia asked. "Isn't it bad for them?"

"It's not real wine, honey. It's all-natural gravy with vitamins and minerals," Josie said.

"I'm getting Chloe a bottle of Barkundy," Jerry said.

"Is Jerry short for Gerald?" Amelia asked. "We have a Gerald in my class."

"No, it's for Jeremiah," he said. "My dad was a born-again Christian."

"Oh, the prophet," Josie said.

"The brokenhearted prophet," Jerry said. "No one listened to his prophecies. I use Jerry. My father died two years ago. Cancer."

"My father died, too, last year," Amelia said. "I miss him."

"I miss Dad, too," Jerry said. "So does Mom."

There was a long silence.

Then Jerry said, "But enough about me. Tell me what a mystery shopper does, Josie. Do you really get paid to shop, like the ads say?"

"Those ads are usually scams," Josie said. She spent a half hour talking about her work. Jerry listened and asked questions. Jerry really did seem ordinary, in the best sense of the word. Josie knew she wasn't always a good judge of men, but in the last hour, Jerry hadn't hit on her, talked about his ex, or done anything that set off alarms.

"Are you seeing anyone seriously?" he asked. Jerry noticed her slight hesitation.

"Sorry," he said. "I shouldn't have said anything. I don't mean to go too fast. But I was so happy you didn't start singing 'Jeremiah was a bullfrog' when I told you my name. I'm really tired of that song."

"Can't blame you," Josie said.

"Could Chloe and I walk you two home?" Jerry asked.

"It's not too cold tonight," Josie said. "I definitely need a walk. I'm embarrassed to say our home has an old couch out in front, but that will be picked up next week."

On their walk, Chloe stopped to sniff every bush, tree, and light pole on the street. Amelia solemnly held the red leash while Jerry and Josie talked. Chloe stopped for frequent pats and ear scratches, and even rolled over and presented her belly for scratching. "Her fur is so soft, Mom. Almost as soft as Harry's," Amelia said. No animal could compare with Harry.

When they reached Josie's home, Jerry said, "We're practically neighbors. You live only two blocks away."

Chloe streaked across the sidewalk, with Amelia hanging on to the leash. The pup stopped to anoint the couch by the curb. "Chloe! No!" Jerry shouted. He ran up and yanked her leash.

"Once it's outside, the couch is fair game," Josie said.

"I'm not sure Chloe knows the difference between outside and inside couches. She has enough bad habits."

Josie could see Mrs. Mueller peering through her blinds. Josie waved at the old sourpuss, and the blinds snapped shut.

They stood outside Josie's flat while Amelia talked nonstop about her new cat. "I wish he'd come out and play," she said. "All I saw of him since he came home was the tip of his tail under the bathtub."

"Well, that's progress," Jerry said. "He's eating, right?"

"And he uses the litter box," Amelia said. "He's really good about that. It's my least favorite chore. I just wish I could see him."

"It takes time," Jerry said. "Cats don't like change. I should know. My mom has thirty-seven. If you want to see cats, you should come to our house for dinner tomorrow night. Mom would let you play with her cats. How about it, Josie?"

"Uh, it's a little soon," Josie said. And it could become an endless evening if Josie and Jerry's mother didn't hit it off.

"Mom loves company," Jerry said. "Amelia can play with the cats and with Chloe."

"Yeah, Mom," Amelia said.

"But we have a lot to do on Saturday," Josie said, stalling for an excuse.

"We can sleep late Sunday. I don't have school," Amelia said.

"Good," Jerry said. "It's all settled. I'll pick you up at five. It will be just a few hours. I'll make sure you're home early. What can go wrong?"

A million things, Josie thought. But I'll have my cell phone. I can call for help if there's a problem.

She said yes. She knew she would regret that decision. She didn't realize how much.

# Chapter 10

Josie and Amelia were squeezed shoulder to shoulder in the front seat of Jerry's dented black Ford pickup. Chloe the pup squirmed on Amelia's lap, her tail wagging happily. *Thump! Thump!* The pup's tail kept whipping Josie's arm while Amelia scratched the dog's ears.

Amelia was in a good mood. Harry had poked his head out from under the bathtub this morning and allowed her to pet one paw before he scurried back to shelter. Amelia had texted this triumph to her friend Emma.

Now she told Jerry about her encounter with Harry. He listened carefully and asked the right questions. Josie marveled at his patience.

The old truck bounced along a gravel road in Wildfern. Tiny rocks pinged off its chipped dark paint. Wildfern was a remote suburb in West St. Louis County that lived up to its name—it was mostly wildwoods. In the summer, dark leathery ferns grew in their shady depths. Wildfern had more unpaved roads than any other part of the county. Bare trees almost grew across the narrow road, and their branches left more scratches on the truck's sides.

Josie was uneasy. They were in the middle of nowhere with a man she barely knew. It was dark. She wondered if she could even get cell phone service out here and quickly checked her phone. Oops. One thin bar.

"Something wrong?" Jerry asked.

"Thought I might have a message from my boss," Josie said. "But he's decided to leave me alone today."

It was growing dark, but not cold. It was supposed to be unseasonably warm for the next few days, so she and Amelia wouldn't freeze to death in the deep woods.

"We'll be bouncing in these ruts a little while longer," Jerry said. "You'll see Mom's house after the next rise. It will be on the right."

*Whump!* The front wheels dropped a foot or two, and the truck lurched. So did Josie's stomach. Jerry steered the battered pickup back into the ruts, while putting out a hand to protect Amelia. The pup nearly slid out of Amelia's lap. She caught it and Chloe squealed.

"Easy, girl," Jerry said.

Josie wasn't sure if he was talking to the truck or the dog. "Sorry. That was a deep rut. It's about time for the neighbors to pitch in and get another load of gravel for this road or I'm going to break an axle. Are you okay, Amelia?"

"I'm fine," she said, and smiled at Jerry. Break an axle, she thought. Why did that sound familiar?

"Those sure were good brownies, Amelia. Mom will love them."

My daughter is lonesome for her father, Josie thought. She'd insisted on baking Jerry a batch of brownies. Jerry had happily eaten three before they left for dinner at his mother's house. The rest were wrapped in aluminum foil for his mother. Josie held those and hoped they weren't covered with dog hair.

"Uh, before we get there, I should tell you my mom is a little unusual," Jerry said.

"So is mine," Josie said.

"That's her duplex there," Jerry said.

Josie saw a one-story, pale green rambler surrounded by an acre of brown winter lawn. She was glad she didn't have to mow it. The long concrete slab porch was sheltered by a brown vine and a green striped awning. "That's Mom's moon vine on the porch. In the summer, it has the prettiest flowers. She has honeysuckle growing up the side trellis. Mom loves flowers."

Bernice "Call Me Bernie" met them at the door. She had a comfortable figure and an old-fashioned apron protecting a flowered housedress. She gravely thanked Amelia for the brownies and asked her recipe.

"I've made apple pie for our dessert," Bernie said. "But your brownies will make a good bedtime snack."

Three cats crowded around Bernie's feet. Two more slept curled on top of the television. Brown, white, black, and gray cats perched on couches and chairs. An old hound slept near the furnace grate, a kitten nestled in his paws. Jerry had to restrain Chloe from bounding over to join them.

"Let me see my grand dog," Bernie said, after the people were introduced. Chloe pranced and twirled, got tangled in her leash, and had her ears scratched.

"Come into the kitchen," Bernie said. "I'm making pork chops."

A fluffy black cat boldly strutted across the table and sat in the bread basket. Josie's stomach turned. Bernie swatted the cat with a dish towel. "Blackie, get off the table. You know better."

Blackie stared defiantly at Bernie. Bernie picked up the cat by the scruff and dropped it on the floor. Chloe sniffed the cat and Blackie planted his claws in Chloe's tender nose. The pup howled in pain.

"Is she hurt?" Amelia asked.

Jerry checked the pup's nose. "No blood. She's learned her lesson."

"Put Chloe in the backyard," Bernice said. "Otherwise, she'll wake up poor old Hound Dog. He's getting a bit creaky. Fix her a bowl of water and some kibble. Would you like a beer or diet soda, Josie?"

"Diet soda. In the can, please," Josie said as she watched cat hair float across the room.

"Have a seat at the table there," Bernie said. "Dinner will be ready in a sec."

Bernie shooed a yellow cat off a chair and pointed with the meat fork for Josie to sit down. Amelia took the chair next to her mother.

More cats came shyly out of corners to study the newcomers. Many didn't look healthy. One tabby had a weepy eye. A calico had bald patches in its coat. Josie hoped she didn't take a skin disease home to Amelia's cat. The thought made her itch.

"Where is your bathroom?" Josie asked.

"That door there," Bernie said, waving toward the back of the kitchen.

In the mirror on the bathroom door, Josie saw that she was covered with cat hair. She looked like she was wearing fur pants. Well, she could clean that off.

Quit judging Bernie, she told herself. She's a nice lady even if she is a bit lax with her housekeeping. You're not exactly Martha Stewart. Josie washed her hands and went back to the kitchen.

Bernie had piled a platter with pork chops. There was a big bowl of creamed corn, another of fried potatoes and onions. In the center of the table were jars of homemade relishes, a bottle of ketchup, and a stick of butter on a small plate.

"Sit! Eat!" Bernie said.

"Looks good, Mom," Jerry said, forking two chops onto his plate. "Mind if I have a sandwich?"

"Eat them any way you want, son," Bernie said.

"Josie?" he asked. "Bread?"

"Uh, no thanks," Josie said. She could see cat hair on the bread. She took a chop and a spoonful of corn. They looked hairless.

"You sure have a lot of animals," Josie said.

"Thirty-seven cats and three dogs," Bernie said with pride. "All of them abandoned out here by stupid people who think pets can fend for themselves in the wild. One was a toy French poodle. She was white and would have stood out like a ghost in those woods. A hawk would have carried off FiFi in two minutes if I hadn't taken her in."

"Do you call the Humane Society when you rescue an animal?" Josie said.

"Don't need to," Bernie said. "I can take care of them better than any society."

"We just adopted a cat," Amelia said.

"Good for you," Bernie said. "If you like animals, you should meet Paul. He's my renter. Lives in the other half of this duplex. Paul's very big in animal rights. He loves all creatures—more than people, if you ask me. Paul collects exotic snakes. You can watch him feed the snakes live rats if you want."

"Uh, no thanks," Josie said.

"It's only natural," Bernie said.

"It's a little too natural," Josie said. She was relieved Amelia wasn't interested in the snake feeding.

"Good pork chop," Josie said. She was creeped out by the snake talk and hoped her compliment would change the subject.

"Thank you," Bernie said, and returned to her favorite subject. "Snakes are useful creatures. I know girlie girls don't like them, but they eat mice, rats, and other vermin. You need snakes in the country, but you need the right kind. Someone dumped a big old boa constrictor on my front lawn. An albino snake. All white, head to tail. I came home from church and found it in the sun by the porch. I thought it was a piece of PVC pipe until it moved its head. I liked to died when I saw it. Paul wanted that albino snake so bad. He said he'd keep it at his brother's condo in Florida—he spends several months down there—but I said no way.

"I like animals, but I know where to draw the line. That's the one time I did call the Humane Society. I couldn't kill it. The society got in touch with some exotic snake club and they took the boa constrictor. They said it would have died in the woods come winter when the weather got cold. It was someone's pet and they abandoned the animal. That's no way to treat a pet, even a snake."

Josie was glad when Bernie served the pie with vanilla ice cream. She was itching to leave, in more ways than one. She wanted away from the cat hair. After dinner, she jumped up from the table to help Bernie wash the dishes. Amelia helped, too. When the dishes were loaded in the washer and the pots were scrubbed, Josie said, "We'd better get back home, Jerry. Amelia and I have a big day tomorrow. It was a pleasure meeting you, Bernie."

"It was nice of you to bring me homemade brownies, Amelia," Bernie said. "You two ladies come back anytime, with Jerry or without him. He almost never brings home any of his girls, and the ones I've met looked like real tramps."

"Mom!" Jerry said. His face was an endearing red.

"I'm glad my boy has found a nice girl, that's all. One with no tattoos."

Oops, thought Josie. Let's not go there. She practically pushed Amelia out the front door while Jerry collected Chloe from the backyard. When a fat gray cat crossed the pup's path, Chloe yelped and hid behind Jerry.

"She really did learn her lesson," Amelia said.

"The hard way, like most of us," Josie said.

A dented, dark pickup was parked behind Jerry's truck.

"Rats. I've got to get Paul to move his truck," Jerry said. "He's blocked me in."

He knocked on the door and said, "Paul! Leave your slithery friends alone and move your truck."

Paul was a tall, rangy man whose wifebeater shirt showed off his big shoulders. He came out, drying his hands on a dish towel. "Sorry, son," he said. "I wasn't thinking."

"Is that another dent in front on your truck?" Jerry asked.

"Slid into the mailbox. You've got a few dents yourself, you know."

Paul flipped the dish towel on his shoulder, moved his truck, and honked good-bye.

Chloe barked her own farewell.

"Paul's a nice guy," Jerry said as he backed out of the driveway. "I'm glad he's there to keep an eye on Mom. It's lonely out here after dark."

Shortly after the pickup turned out of Bernie's driveway, they passed a white-painted sign: DEERFORD KENNELS—ONE FOURTH MILE.

As they approached the kennels, Josie saw a wide lawn edged with ornamental cabbages and a white picket fence.

"Do you know the man who runs Deerford Kennels?" Josie asked.

"Old Jonah," Jerry said. "He's a great guy. Friend of my mom's. He breeds puppies. I hear he makes a mint off those dogs, but you could never tell by looking at him. He drives a beat-up old pickup. I should talk, but his truck is even more dented than mine.

"Jonah says dogs are the best cash crop of all. They saved his family farm. The land around here isn't much good. It doesn't have the rich topsoil you'd find in Iowa or Kansas. Jonah was about to lose everything, when he figured out dogs were one crop that never failed. He says you can make more money with puppies than with corn and soybeans. He always has puppies you can pet—dachshunds, bichons, Chihuahuas, even teacup poodles. I can take you there now if you want to see them."

"Puppies!" Amelia said. "I love puppies. Please, Mom."

"You have your cat, Amelia," Josie said. "And you have Chloe on your lap. Isn't that enough for one day?"

"Aww, Mom," Amelia said, dragging it out for several syllables. "Please let me pet them. They'll like it, too."

"It's only seven," Jerry said. "We'll be home by ten at the latest. I promise."

Josie was wavering. Jerry steered the truck around a rut and gave Josie his own sad-puppy-dog look. "Just a few minutes," he said. "We'll stop in, say hello, and go."

The blacktop road leading to Deerford Kennels was beautifully kept.

"Okay," Josie said. "You can look, Amelia, but you can't take a pup home."

"I'm happy with Harry," Amelia said. "I wouldn't want to upset him."

Jerry's truck turned up the wide, smooth blacktop road. Winter mums bloomed around a spotlighted DEERFORD KENNELS sign. Josie remembered Jerry's remark about breaking an axle on the road. She was out in the country. In a dark, beat-up truck. With a man who had a funny first name, "like something in the Bible," Edna had said. The late Edna Prilosen. Who named all four of those facts as clues to the puppy miller.

Jeremiah. Was Jerry part of the puppy mill ring? Was he helping Paul? Paul was a name from the Bible, too.

Josie's heart was pounding. If anything went wrong, she could appeal for help to the man who had pretty mums and white-painted fences. He'd help her. He was the only civilization for miles around.

"Maybe we can stop for a minute or two," Josie said.

# Chapter 11

The smooth blacktop ended abruptly once the Deerford Kennels entrance was out of view. Jerry's pickup lurched into more muddy ruts. Gravel ricocheted off the undercarriage. The truck rattled until Josie feared it would break apart.

Finally, the truck slowed and growled to a halt. Harsh security lights glared down on a rusting turquoise mobile home plunked in front of a two-story farmhouse with a rotted porch and boarded windows. The house's gray wood was scabbed with yellow paint.

"Spook house!" Amelia said.

"Doghouse," Jerry said. "You are looking at the world's largest doghouse. Jonah keeps his dogs in the farmhouse. He lives in the trailer with his two boys, Bart and Billy. Billy's the baby."

Dogs barked and whined.

"Ew, it smells bad," Amelia said, wrinkling her freckled nose.

"The boys get behind on their chores sometimes, but the animals are well fed and cared for," Jerry said.

"Is there a Mrs. Deerford?" Josie asked.

"Allegra took off years ago," Jerry said. "She left no forwarding address. Abandoned those little boys. Poor Jonah has done his best to raise them."

Josie could see why the woman left. The place was dismal. The muddy yard was crisscrossed with dozens of foot-prints. Abandoned truck parts, broken lawn mowers, bald tires, and other junk edged the property.

Chloe, excited by the sounds of other dogs, gave a few sharp yaps and lunged for the truck's door.

"Hold on to her, Amelia," Jerry said.

Amelia held the squirming pup and scratched her neck fur. "Easy, girl," she whispered.

"We're going to have to leave Chloe in the truck," Jerry said. "I don't trust her around all those dogs. There's Jonah coming out of the shed. Don't be put off by his looks. He's a diamond in the rough."

Jonah could have stepped out of an 1890s photo. His thick black hair was long and handsomely streaked with gray. His bushy, untrimmed beard hid his neck and his shirt collar.

Jonah wore overalls, a brown fleece-lined barn coat, a flannel shirt, and leather work gloves. He was followed by two boys who looked younger than Amelia. Their jeans were dirty. Their jackets were too light for the night chill. Josie wanted to clean them up, wrap them in heavy sweaters and winter coats, and buy them gloves and hats.

Their poor round heads were shaved to the scalp, which made the boys look like space aliens. Josie wondered whether Jonah was doing his own barbering or if the boys had had head lice. Shaving off the hair was the quick, cheap treat-ment. Well, lice happened at even the best schools, and the critters spread quickly.

But there was no excuse for those small, red hands pro-truding from the boys' worn jackets. What kind of mother would abandon her boys?

"Jerry!" Jonah took off his work gloves and stuffed them in a pocket. "Why didn't you warn me you were coming?" His smile showed crooked teeth, but there was no warmth in it. Josie saw his eyes were steely with suspicion. Jonah was not pleased by his uninvited visitors.

"We came to pet the pups," Jerry said. "But we can leave if you want."

"No, no, might as well stay now that you're here," Jonah said ungraciously. "Is that a new puppy I see in your truck?"

"That's Chloe," Jerry said. "She's a yellow Lab mix. Got her at the Humane Society."

"Now, Jerry, why did you go and do that, paying their fancy prices? I could have gotten you a good deal on an AKC-registered pup and you wouldn't have had to have it spayed, either. Could have had yourself a good little moneymaker, once you bred her."

"Thanks," Jerry said. "But you've got all those froufrou dogs."

"The ladies like the little dogs," Jonah said. "I've got Pekes, Chihuahuas, bichons, toy poodles, miniature dachshunds, all good sellers. You can put any of my dogs in a purse."

"I don't carry a purse," Jerry said. "I needed a guy dog, Jonah. Let me introduce my two friends, Josie and Amelia. Amelia likes pups."

"She can't buy one," Josie said quickly, hoping Jonah would ask them to leave. She hated this place. The air seemed thick with neglect and cruelty, as well as evil odors.

"Uh, Jerry, could I talk to you for a minute. Alone?" He pointedly escorted Jerry back by a shed. Five minutes later, the two were back.

"Well, come on in, little lady," Jonah said, with another insincere smile and a too-cheerful, "It doesn't cost anything to look." Josie thought that should be the puppy mill's motto.

Jonah's mud-spattered work boots thunked across the wooden porch. Josie stepped carefully, avoiding the loose boards. Amelia followed. The two blond boys trailed behind her.

Their skin was so white, Josie could see the blue veins under the nearly transparent skin. They were too skinny.

"Hey!" Jonah said to the boys. "You two boys have work to do. Go clean out the shed."

The boys shuffled off without a word, like tired old men. There were none of the ritual protests kids gave when confronted with a job they didn't want to do. Billy had a dark bruise on his right wrist.

Jerry was still teasing Jonah about his pedigreed purse dogs. "God gave dogs legs so they can walk," he said.

The house's old front door had pretty carving around an oval opening that had once held beveled glass. Now it was covered with unpainted plywood. Jonah opened it and the three followed Jonah into what used to be a large living room. It still had faded rose-covered wallpaper with lighter places where pictures once hung. He flipped on an old brass chandelier with three bare bulbs hanging from a cracked plaster ceiling. Worn yellow linoleum covered the floor.

The room was jammed with wire cages set over a series of troughs to catch the waste. The troughs were badly in need of cleaning. To the right was a former kitchen, now filled with enormous sacks of dog chow, dog dishes, and plastic garbage cans desperately in need of emptying. Three long-handled spades stood in the corner.

Josie heard a chorus of whines and whimpers. Four mouse-sized Pekingese huddled together in one cage near an overturned water dish. Their food bowl was empty. In other cages, tiny pups yipped and scratched at the wires. Four or five pups slept on top of one another. Others stared straight ahead with empty eyes. A few scratched their fur. Watching the scratching pups, Josie felt her own skin itch.

With one finger Amelia was petting a dirty white bichon. Josie wished her daughter wouldn't touch the animal. Its red weepy eyes didn't look healthy.

"It's cold in here," Josie said. "How do the dogs stay warm?"

"They're wearing fur coats, honey. And they've got each

other," Jonah said, indicating a roiling, wriggling pile of puppies in a wire cage.

"Is that enough?" Josie asked.

"They're animals," Jonah said. "Nature meant for them to live outside. I keep them in a nice house. Do you worry about cows in a barn? Do farmers tuck them into beds? This is my farm and these are my animals."

But cows get straw, Josie thought, and food and water and medical care.

"That wiener dog isn't moving," Amelia said, pointing to a brown dachshund lying on its side on the floor near the door.

"That's Daisy," Jonah said. "She died, poor thing. We need to bury her, but we haven't had time with all the chores."

What chores? Josie wanted to say. This place is filthy, and the dogs need food and water.

"What did she die of?" Amelia asked.

"Old age. She's six."

"That's not very old," Amelia said.

"It is in dog years," Jonah said.

The scene was so grim, Josie wanted to run. She couldn't stand it a minute longer.

"I want to leave," Josie said. "I'm not feeling so good. I think I'm coming down with something." She pasted on a smile and said, "Thanks for your time, Mr. Deerford. Sorry we interrupted you."

"Come back anytime you want a dog," Jonah said, which she translated as, "Don't bother me again unless you're buying something."

Josie, Amelia, and Jerry walked back to his truck in silence. Josie didn't try to hide her relief as she climbed into the cab. She hoped she didn't have fleas from Jonah's animals.

As he started the truck, Jerry tried to defend Jonah. "He used to be a farmer. He doesn't have the sentimental attitude toward animals that city people do."

"I don't think clean cages are sentimental," Josie said. "Neither is feeding his kids. Those boys looked like they could use a good meal and a bath. They didn't even have gloves and it's chilly tonight."

"Boys lose gloves," Jerry said. "They aren't careful like girls."

"Hah!" Josie said. "Do you know how many pairs of gloves I've bought Amelia so far this winter? Three. I told her if she loses one more pair, I'm getting her a set of mitten clips for her coat, like a first grader."

"Mom!" Amelia was indignant that her mother revealed this personal information.

"What did Jonah want to talk to you about in private?" Josie asked.

"Jonah was worried you were some kind of animal rights spy. He thinks some radical vigilante types are trying to close down his kennels. He started taking down license plates and names of people who 'drop by' for a visit. I told him you were a harmless mystery shopper, checking out ladies' clothing stores and stuff."

"Right," Josie said. "I do cute clothes."

"You can see why he'd be upset about spies. His family farm means everything to him."

"Absolutely," Josie said. "But I wish Jonah wouldn't let those boys outside dressed like that. They're working at night. They could use a good meal. And why does the younger one have a bruise on his wrist?"

"Boys will be boys," Jerry said. "They're active kids, always getting into trouble. Jonah says the boys are clumsy. They take after their mother, I guess."

I don't think so, Josie thought. What I saw tonight was horrible. I'm not making excuses for Jonah. I'm calling the child protection agency and the Humane Society of Missouri. I'm reporting Jonah for cruelty to children and animals.

She felt better now that her mind was made up. She had

the power to stop this horror. She wondered if she could make Jerry open his eyes and really see Jonah Deerford.

"Why didn't you buy your pup from Jonah?" she asked.

"Like I said, he raises girlie dogs. And he charges too much. His teacup poodles drive you crazy with their yapping. Their bones are so brittle, one dog broke her leg jumping off a chair.

"The only dog I'd consider buying from him was a dachshund, but they like to dig. If one dug up my yard, my landlady would shoot me. Besides, I had a dachshund as a kid. It had back problems. Goes with the breed. Poor dog needed surgery. I'd rather have a good, healthy mutt like Chloe."

He gave his nonpedigreed pup a pat. Chloe seemed fat and happy compared to the sad, well-bred prisoners in the farmhouse.

As they pulled out of Jonah's yard, they heard a long, lonely howl rise from the house. The hair rose on Josie's neck.

Chloe threw back her own head and answered. The howl died in the dark winter woods.

# Chapter 12

Jerry's truck landed on the paved road with a bolt-rattling thud. Amelia clung to Chloe to keep the puppy from falling on the floor, and Josie put an arm out to protect her daughter.

They were on a winding, two-lane road at the bottom of a wooded hill—a paved road, finally. A streetlight outlined a silver septic tank next to a split-level home.

Civilization, Josie thought.

Jonah's rutted road went back into another world, one she hoped she'd never visit again. Josie shuddered when she thought of those poor, cowed boys with their dirty clothes and cold-reddened hands. Jonah's sons had no boyish mischief, no playful banter with their father. Bart and Billy also had no childhood. They were condemned to work at their father's kennels. The man wouldn't even buy them warm coats.

Boys. Josie remembered Edna's words the day she died: *He complains about his help. He says the boys don't work hard enough. He's such a horrible man. I'm sure that's how he talks about black people.*

Jonah Deerford was a horrible man. But he wasn't talking about black people. He was complaining about his own sons. Their sad faces stuck in her mind. The boys seemed to be begging for help. Where was their family?

"Do Bart and Billy have any grandparents?" Josie asked when they were cruising along the road.

"Jonah's parents are both dead," Jerry said. "He inherited their farm and saved it from the IRS. His wife's parents are old hippies who live somewhere out west. When Allegra ran away, Lance and Linda wanted to take the boys and raise them, but Jonah refused. He said they'd turn the kids into wusses."

And Jonah would lose his cheap help, Josie thought.

"There's some bad blood there," Jerry said. "Lance and Linda said their daughter would never leave her children and they reported her missing. They filed for custody of the boys, but they live on some kind of New Agey commune and that didn't sit well with the Missouri judge. Jonah said those kinds of people used drugs. He told the court that the boys were homeschooled in a Christian manner and did their chores. Jonah's minister testified that those boys were in church every Sunday. Jonah got custody of the boys. The grandparents said they'd fight him in court, but they ran out of money. They didn't even have steady jobs. They weren't a good influence. Boys need discipline and the judge agreed with Jonah."

"He did seem a little hard on the boys," Josie said, proud of her tact.

"Jonah's trying to teach Bart and Billy responsibility. It's not easy to do."

"I don't think keeping your kids cold and hungry teaches them anything useful," Josie said, the last of her tact evaporating.

"Life on the farm is tough, but it builds character," Jerry said.

"They could use less character and more food," Josie said. "They're too thin."

"Josie, you can't mollycoddle boys. They're different from girls. My cousin Allison was going to raise her son without all that old-fashioned gender bias. But no matter what she gave him, from a doll to a box, he turned it into a soldier."

Josie was beginning to think that the more time she spent with Jerry, the less she liked him. Maybe they'd just been together for too long too soon. Maybe he didn't understand, since he had no children of his own. But then another, scarier thought crossed her mind. Maybe Jerry was in league with Jonah. So were his mother and Paul. They lived in the country. Jerry and Paul drove beat-up old trucks—and had names from the Bible. They lived right down the road from the kennels. And Jerry thought there was nothing wrong with Jonah's cruelty to his children and animals.

She stared out the window at the passing houses and fields, until a safe subject hopped into view. "Look, Amelia, there's a bunny running across the road," Josie said.

Jerry slowed the truck to make sure the cottontail was safe, then said, "I know we just had a big dinner, but would you like to stop somewhere for ice cream?"

"Your mom fed me too well," Josie said. "Thanks."

"What about you, Amelia?" Jerry asked. "Your mom says you like MaggieMoo's. How about some ice cream?"

This was Amelia's great temptation. Please say no, Josie pleaded mentally. She visualized the words in huge black letters and tried to mentally send them to her daughter's mind: No, no, no.

Either the trick worked or Amelia didn't want any ice cream—and that was almost unprecedented, even in winter.

"I'd better go home and check on Harry," Amelia said. "What if he quit being scared and came out from under the bathtub and I missed him?" She struggled to hold the pup. "Chloe is getting squirmy."

"I think she needs a walk," Jerry said. "I should get her home. I don't want Chloe to use your yard. Your crazy neighbor will have a fit."

For once, Josie was grateful for Mrs. Mueller.

Jerry drove home to Maplewood at the fastest legal speed. The old truck was in front of Josie's home in forty minutes. Darkness had slipcovered the couch by the curb into a shape that could have been a well-trimmed hedge, if she didn't look too closely. At least it didn't seem so embarrassing at night.

The lights were off in Stan's house. Josie figured he was at the gym, as usual.

Jane was home. Josie could hear her mother's TV as she unlocked the front door. Jane was getting a little deaf and tended to fall asleep in front of the set. Josie hoped her mother was asleep. She didn't want another lecture on why she should date a man who drove an elegant Lexus or BMW instead of a pickup.

The life Jane dreamed of for her daughter was a version of her own before her unwanted divorce: a husband who had a well-paid professional job, while Josie was occupied with worthy causes and charity lunches. Jane never seemed to understand that her daughter would be bored silly with that life.

Amelia gave the pup one last hug. Chloe licked her nose as Amelia passed the little dog to her owner. Jerry held firmly on to the dog while Josie and Amelia climbed out of the truck.

"Thank you so much," Josie said, hoping her relief didn't show.

Once the truck's passenger door was safely shut, Chloe stood on her fat hind legs, pawing the window glass and barking good-bye.

Amelia waved. Then she and Josie ran for the house as if they were being chased by hungry Dobermans.

Once inside, Josie said, "You have dog hair all over you. Please wash your hands after handling those dogs at Deerford Kennels."

"That place was so gross. I want a shower," Amelia said.

"Good idea. Just save me some hot water," Josie said.

"Those poor dogs were really sick, weren't they, Mom?"

"Yes," Josie said. "I hope we didn't bring something home to Harry. Go downstairs and drop your clothes and shoes into the washer—even that parka. I'll wash mine, too. If we get fleas from this field trip, your grandmother will have a fit."

Josie shooed her daughter to the basement laundry room, then brought Amelia her robe and carried her own long robe. She separated the clothes into lights and darks, dropped a load into the washer, and added soap powder. If only she could wash away this evening as easily.

"Do you think we brought some bugs home?" Amelia asked.

"I hope not, but if you start itching or see any little bites, let me know and I'll buy you a flea collar."

"Mom, tell me you're joking," Amelia said.

"Why?" Josie asked. "That would spoil the fun."

"What can we do to save those little dogs?" Amelia said.

"I'll do some research online and find out," Josie said.

"We have to do something," Amelia said. "Those pups were real sick. Their mothers could hardly move. They were cold. All they have are those weird kids to take care of them."

"Don't talk about Bart and Billy that way," Josie said. "Their father neglects them. It's not their fault they don't have warm clothes and decent haircuts."

"Isn't there a child abuse hotline we could call?" Amelia asked.

Josie faced a parent's dilemma: How much did she want to involve her daughter in the dark side of the adult world? Josie knew Jonah Deerford was cruel. His frightened sons and neglected animals proved that. If Josie complained to the authorities, she ran the risk that Jonah could track her down. Jerry might have already told him, if he was part of the miller operation. She hoped not.

Jerry looked as trusting as his puppy. He'd blab Josie's address to Jonah, and the mean man with the black beard could turn up on her doorstep and threaten her and Amelia. Or Jonah could take out his anger on his boys. Once again, Josie wondered how Allegra could have abandoned her children.

Josie knew those poor boys and starving animals needed care. She would have to figure out a way to help them but keep her daughter out of it. If she made a complaint, it would have to be anonymous. Maybe she could turn Mrs. Mueller loose on Jonah.

"Why are you laughing, Mom?" Amelia said.

"I was being silly. I thought we could unleash Mrs. Mueller on Jonah."

"He deserves her," Amelia said. "But what if he married her?"

"Don't go there," Josie said.

"Why does Jerry defend that butthead, Jonah?"

"Amelia Marcus, watch your mouth."

"A blind man can see he's mistreating those dogs, Mom."

"Jerry is a loyal friend. It's possible for friends to overlook the faults of people they like."

"The way Grandma defends Mrs. Mueller?"

"Something like that," Josie said.

Their clothes were tumbling in the basement dryer when Amelia said, "Harry's still hiding under the bathtub, Mom. All I saw was his tail sticking out. As soon as I walked in the bathroom, he pulled it in after him."

"He'll come out eventually, Amelia," Josie said. "He's gone through a lot of change in a few days. Is he eating his food?"

"The whole bowl. I gave him more. He drank all his water. He used his litter box, too."

"That's good," Josie said. "If he stops using that, we have problems."

"He hasn't touched his toys."

"He doesn't feel like playing yet, sweetheart. You don't play when you don't feel well. Let him alone a bit longer."

When Amelia went to bed, Josie sat down on her new-old couch. It was more comfortable than the sagging wreck out by the curb. She dozed off and woke up about eleven o'clock. She went down the hall toward her bedroom. She checked

Amelia's bathroom, but there was no sign of Harry, not even his tail.

Her daughter was asleep. Josie pulled the covers up over Amelia, and thought again of those shivering boys and starving animals.

Josie was a woman with a mission. She was going to close down Jonah's puppy mill and rescue his sons, and not necessarily in that order.

# Chapter 13

"Do you want to identify yourself?" asked the woman who answered the Child Abuse and Neglect Hotline on Sunday morning.

Josie's heart was pounding. She felt as if her future depended on her answer. Yes? No? Yes would be courageous, but could a single mom afford that kind of courage?

"Do I have to give my name?" she asked in a small voice.

"You are not required to give your name unless you are a 'mandated reporter.' In Missouri, that's a teacher, a social worker, a medical professional, someone who works around children."

"No, no, I'm nothing like that," Josie said.

"But giving us your name would help with our investigation," she said.

The woman sounded mature and trustworthy. Josie imagined her looking like a favorite teacher. She would be in her fifties with a plump, comfortable figure and clothes that were neat but not stylish. Her hair would be short and permed.

"But you could still do your report without my name?" Josie asked.

"Yes."

"Then I'd rather not give it," Josie said. I'd rather not do this, period. I'd rather be sitting on my couch at the curb having tea with Mrs. Mueller.

"If you do find a problem, when will you take action?" Josie asked her.

"Probably between twenty-four and forty-eight hours. Emergency situations would be faster."

When Josie hung up the phone, she was still wondering whether she'd done the right thing. The questioning by the Child Abuse and Neglect Hotline seemed to take forever— nearly an hour. Josie was asked questions she could answer, such as the names of the children and their father. And some she couldn't, including what school the boys went to and their ages.

As Josie gave her answers, she wondered whether she sounded like an interfering busybody. She tried to convince herself that there was nothing really wrong with Bart and Billy. But she remembered the bruise on the boy's wrist. The livid red and purple mark seemed to grow larger in her mind. Those poor boys were pale as ghosts and way too thin. Their little red hands sticking out of those too-short sleeves looked pitiful. Someone had to do something.

"Might as well be me," Josie said, then realized she was talking to herself. Was that a bad sign? Only if I start answering myself, she decided, but didn't say it out loud.

Josie didn't think she could take another telephone interrogation. She reported the animal abuse to the Humane Society of Missouri through its Web site. She wasn't required to leave her name. Instead she told them Jonah's name and gave detailed directions to the Deerford Kennels. She described the horrific conditions, including animals without food, water, medical care, or proper sanitation. She mentioned the dead Daisy.

Josie had no idea how many dogs were involved. Possibly a hundred or more. She couldn't count all those poor, shivering puppies. As for breeds, she'd seen Chihuahuas, dachshunds, toy poodles, and maybe some bichons. She could only guess at the others. She wished she hadn't seen any of it, but she could not erase what had happened from her mind.

Josie finished filling out the online report, then sent it off. She hoped it would stop Jonah's ugly little operation and end the animals' suffering. But what if she failed? What if Jonah found out she'd turned him in—and he went free?

She'd worry about that if and when it happened. Something had to be done about abused boys and helpless puppies. She just hoped her mother didn't find out she'd filed those reports. Jane would go ballistic if she knew Josie had ratted out a man like Jonah. Mrs. Mueller, her own personal Neighborhood Watch program, might be some protection, but so far the old woman's snooping had never done anything useful for Josie or Jane.

She did have Stan nearby. He was certainly strong. And loyal. And brave. What if I convinced my sweet musclehead that Jonah is a bad carb? Josie wondered. She hadn't talked with Stan since the day he and Howie had moved the couch to the curb. Maybe she should look up the calorie count for making love. But that probably wouldn't work. Stan would be toning a different muscle group.

What the heck is the matter with you? she asked herself. I'm not begging a grown man to put down his barbells and love me. And Jerry will not be lighting up my life. His defense of Jonah took care of any spark I might have had. We have totally different views of child rearing, and that's fatal to any relationship. I already know that.

She thought of her lost loves, the two men she could have married, but didn't. Her romance with Mike had hit the rocks because of his awful daughter, Heather. Nate, her first love, turned out to be a drug dealer.

If you fall for a man, Josie Marcus, you can almost guarantee there's something wrong with the dude. Your mother picked a man who abandoned her, and you've followed in her footsteps.

Josie shook her head and declared the pity party over.

I have a wonderful life, she told herself. I have a daughter who gets good grades in school. She's healthy. My mom is a bit cranky, but she's there when I need her. I am blessed with good friends like Alyce. As for romance, I had a man I loved with all my heart. How many women get those gifts?

"Mom!" Amelia said in a whisper. A shrieking whisper, if that was possible.

Josie, lost in her own thoughts, jumped. "What's wrong, honey?"

"You gotta see Harry."

"What's he doing? Is he hurt?" Josie lowered her voice to a whisper, too.

"He's out from under the bathtub and playing with his yarn ball. He's so cute, Mom. Come look."

They tiptoed down the hall and peeked into the bathroom. The small, striped cat was batting the red yarn ball with one brown paw, then pouncing on it. Once he captured the ball, Harry paraded around the room with his trophy in his mouth, like a baby tiger showing off his antelope.

Amelia giggled. Harry dropped the yarn ball and ran under the tub again.

"He'll be out again soon, honey," Josie said. "The stitches in his paws are starting to dissolve. He's feeling better."

"I feel better, too," Amelia said. "He's going to be a real cat."

"He always was a real cat," Josie said. "But he's going to be a real member of the family."

Josie decided to quit brooding. She had work to do tomorrow. She didn't usually phone Alyce when her husband was home, but her friend would understand. She called Alyce and said, "Want to go clothes shopping with me on Monday?"

"Oh, no," Alyce said. "I feel bad enough. You're what—a size two? And I'm a twenty-two."

"I'm an eight, which is fat in fashionable circles. And

you're definitely not a twenty-two. I have to mystery-shop dog clothes and both of us are too big for Chihuahua sweaters."

"There are no live dogs involved, are there?" Alyce said.

"Strictly canine couture," Josie said. "We're mystery-shopping the Upper Pup boutiques. The one near you opens at ten o'clock. Should I pick you up?"

"Of course. We need to dish. How's your love life?"

"A dish served cold," Josie said. "Be prepared to be bored silly. I'd better go. There's a knock at my door."

Josie checked the porch cautiously. Amelia was right behind her.

"It's Chloe and Jerry!" Amelia said. "Can I go pet her?" She opened the door without permission and ran outside. Jerry stalked inside, not bothering to say hello.

"Josie Marcus, how could you?" Jerry said. His anger was a living thing.

"How could I what?" Josie said, puzzled.

"How could you have reported Jonah?"

"I don't understand."

"Turn on the television," he commanded. "The story has been running nonstop since he was arrested."

"Arrested!" Josie searched for the TV clicker and found it on the coffee table under a magazine.

Jerry grabbed it out of her hand, turned on the television, and said, "Look what you've done!"

The news showed a video of grim-faced people carrying cages of puppies out of a ramshackle farmhouse. Others had larger dogs wrapped in blankets. At the bottom, a red trailer announced WILDFERN PUPPY MILL RAID.

"More than two hundred dogs were rescued from Deerford Kennels," the announcer said. "Also, two boys, ages six and seven, were turned over to a child protection agency. Authorities say Jonah Deerford was running a puppy mill and breeding dogs in inhumane conditions. Mr. Deerford was arrested and charged with multiple counts of cruelty to animals and also child endangerment. Authorities say the raid on Deerford Kennels was the result of months of investigation."

"Jerry, it couldn't have been me," Josie said. "The announcer said the investigation took months. I just met the man."

Now the story had turned to a man talking into a microphone at a press conference. "This was a cooperative effort by local, state, and Humane Society of Missouri investigators," he said. "We have been building a case against Deerford Kennels for more than six months."

"Six months ago I'd never heard of Jonah." Josie hoped Jerry couldn't hear the relief in her voice. She'd done her duty, but played no active part in bringing down Jonah Deerford.

"There has to be some mistake," Jerry said, his voice rising to a whine. "I've known Jonah all my life. He'd never hurt anyone. He took care of those boys when his wife, Allegra, ran off."

Josie bit back her comments on the quality of Jonah's care. They sat in silence and watched more videos and interviews with rescue workers. Some of them were openly weeping about the sick and dying dogs.

"I know who did that to Jonah," Jerry said. "It was one of those radical animal vigilantes. Those types care more about animals than humans."

I can't take any more of this, Josie thought. He'll feel differently once he's faced the facts about Jonah.

"Jerry," she said, "I'm sorry you are upset about Jonah. But neither one of us has enough information to discuss this right now. Let's wait until we know more about the case. I have to help Amelia with her schoolwork. Good-bye."

Jerry stared at her, then got up and left without a word.

Now I really am manless, Josie thought. It felt good. Tonight, she would lounge about and enjoy her freedom. She spent a luxurious half hour taking a scented bubble bath. She was toweling herself dry when the phone rang.

She heard a whirring in the background and recognized it as a treadmill. Stan was working out—again. "Josie, I've been neglecting you," he said. "It's time for a fun night. Can I pick you up in say half an hour, at seven o'clock?"

"Where are we going?" Josie asked.

"It's a surprise. But dress for a special night. We're going to get away from St. Louis."

Josie felt a rush of excitement. Finally, Stan had gotten the SOS on their love life. She called her mother. Jane was happy to watch Amelia, especially if it might help Josie snag Stan.

"Where are you two going?" Jane asked.

"It's a surprise," Josie said. "But he wants me to dress for a special night."

"Oh, Josie. Maybe he'll give you a ring at last. If you need to stay all night, call me. Amelia can sleep in my guest room and I'll get her to school tomorrow morning."

Jane had never made that offer before. Josie didn't know whether she'd accept Stan's proposal, but it would be nice to be asked.

Josie shooed Amelia upstairs, then pulled out her best short black skirt, off-the-shoulder black top, and high heels. She hummed "Girls Just Wanna Have Fun" as she changed. She was just spritzing on perfume when Stan rang her doorbell.

Josie's face fell when Stan showed up in a baggy gray parka from his premakeover days.

"Wow!" he said. "You look nice. I hope those shoes won't hurt your feet."

"Are we going dancing?" Josie asked.

"Oh, you'll dance down the aisle when you see this," Stan said. She could almost feel the excitement crackling through his hunky body.

The unseasonably warm winter night was lit by the soft

glow of the stars. They crossed the Mississippi River, driving away from the sparkling St. Louis cityscape. The highway signs said they were bound for Chicago.

Josie loved Chicago. We could drive there in four hours, she thought, spend the night in a Gold Coast boutique hotel, have a sumptuous room-service breakfast, walk down Michigan Avenue.

Josie had mentally mapped out the exciting getaway by the time the car was at the exit for Reddingville, an Illinois farm town about thirty miles outside of St. Louis. Stan turned off the highway and drove down a two-lane road lined with car dealerships and franchises, then parked in a vast, crowded lot near a sign featuring a neon farmer in overalls. FARMER FRANK'S DISCOUNT BARN, the sign said. ALL OUR MARKDOWNS MARKED DOWN—70% OR MORE OFF EVERYTHING IN OUR STORE.

"This is where we're going?" Josie said.

"It's an unbelievable sale," Stan said. "You can get a fifty-ounce bottle of Tide with Bleach Alternative for two dollars. That's one-quarter what it would cost you in St. Louis. And paper towels are—"

"Get me out of here," Josie said. "Get me out of here or I'll scream and you'll spend the night in the Reddingville jail."

"What's the matter, Josie?" Stan asked.

He looked clueless, she thought. He was clueless. "Stan, I shop for a living," Josie said. "I get paid to go down those aisles. Shopping for free is not my idea of fun. I'm all dressed up tonight. I'd like to do something spontaneous and relaxing. Take me home. Now."

"You don't even want to buy some Tide?" Stan said.

Josie was screaming as Stan roared out of the parking lot. They rode home in silence.

# Chapter 14

The Upper Pup boutique was somewhere between cozy and claustrophobic. Shelves were crammed with hand-painted ceramic dog bowls, hand-knit sweaters, and what signs called "canine couture." There were tutus for Chihuahuas. A motorcycle jacket proclaimed it was BAD TO THE BONE. Rainbows of collars and leashes hung on the walls. Squeaky toys swung on racks. A low-slung dachshund grabbed a toy frog and scuttled under a display table.

"Rosie! Bad dog," her owner said. "Bring that back."

Rosie whimpered and hunkered down, while her owner dragged her out by the collar. "I'm so embarrassed," Rosie's owner said. "I'd better buy it, but won't that be rewarding her?"

"My name is Patti," a tiny woman said. "I'm the top dog here." Her light brown hair and slightly popped eyes made her look rather like a Chihuahua. Josie was startled by Patti's deep voice. She expected someone so small to make shrill yapping sounds.

"You could put the toy away until Christmas, when she'll have forgotten it," Patti said. "But I can't sell it with teeth marks in it."

Alyce was examining fake-fur dog beds shaped like sports cars. "Look at this one. It even has a Mercedes logo on the hood. It's a 'Furcedes.' Did you ever wonder why cars aren't named after dogs? There are cat cars like Cougars and Jaguars, but no dog cars. I might like to drive a Golden Retriever or a big friendly Labrador."

"Who wants to drive a Pit Bull?" Josie said. "And buying a Doberman is asking for trouble, especially if I had an accident. I could see a lawyer telling a jury, 'That woman's 2009 Doberman ran a red light and attacked my client's innocent 2007 Golden Retriever.' I'd be the bitch behind the wheel."

"Josie!" Alyce said, struggling not to laugh. "We're going to get thrown out along with Rosie the shoplifting dachshund."

"We have to be serious," Josie said. "I have to buy a dress for a Chihuahua. If I start laughing now, I'll lose it."

The manager said, "May I help you, ladies?"

"I was looking for a dress called Strawberry Delight," Josie said. "I saw it on your Web site."

"That's in our little-dog clothes section. It's on sale with the matching hat."

She led them to a round rack with doll-sized dresses on plastic hangers. "What kind of dog do you have?" Patti asked as she pawed through the clothes.

"A Chihuahua," Josie lied.

"What size is she?"

"Small," Josie said. Weren't they all small? she wondered.

"We have small and extra-small sizes for our little dogs," Patti said. "How much does your dog weigh?"

"About five pounds," Josie said.

"And what's her length?"

Josie held out her hands about six inches. "But that doesn't count the ears."

"Do you know her neck size?"

"No," Josie said.

"She's probably an extra small," Patti said. "But if the dress doesn't fit, you can return it in thirty days, no questions asked. 'Any time, any store' is the Upper Pup policy. Just save the receipt. Ah, here it is."

Patti pulled out a red and white dress dotted with strawberry appliqués. A big gingham bow was planted on the back. Josie wished she'd had a dress like that for Amelia when she was a baby.

"You get the dress and hat for only $21.99," Patti said. "Don't you love Chihuahuas? You can buy such cute clothes for them."

"And they come with their own fur coats," Josie said.

Alyce cleared her throat to remind Josie she was supposed to be a mystery shopper, not a canine critic. "Josie, look at this little dog bathrobe with the rubber duckie on it," she said.

"I'll stick with the strawberry dress," Josie said.

"May I show you our specials on winter boots and Christmas costumes?" Patti said. "We have a complete line of Santa sweaters, plus warm raincoats and winter boots."

"No, thank you."

"Look at this harness with angel wings." Patti pulled out a dog harness with floppy white cloth wings.

"Amazing," Josie said.

"We have an excellent selection of sportswear," Patti said.

"Thanks, but she's not athletic," Josie said.

"What is your little girl's name?" Patti asked.

"Amelia," Josie said.

"Lovely name," Patti said. She took Josie's credit card and slipped the dog dress into a bag decorated with paw prints.

"We'd better get home to your *fur child*," Alyce said, nearly dragging Josie out of the store. "She'll be wanting her lunch."

They made it to Josie's car before they collapsed into their seats, laughing. "Good thing you gave your daughter's name as your little girl," Alyce said.

"I don't think Harry the cat would look good in gingham checks," Josie said. "They'd clash with his stripes. I can't believe I paid twenty-two bucks for a dog dress." She pulled out her clipboard. "Let me go through my mystery-shopping checklist quickly."

Josie ticked off the questions on the form. "Patti identified and introduced herself. She greeted me and offered to help. She found the item I wanted. She told me about the holiday specials. A perfect score for Patti at the Chesterfield store."

"Give the woman a bone," Alyce said.

"Give me something to settle my stomach," Josie said. "These cutesy-poo clothes make me sick."

"That's a little harsh, Josie."

Josie looked at her friend's sincere blue eyes. Alyce's light blond hair stuck up slightly from static electricity, giving her an exotic golden crest.

"No, it's not harsh," Josie said. "Little kids are going hungry this winter and shivering in the cold. Buying dog dresses is obscene."

"It's harmless," Alyce said.

"Dogs should be dogs, not child substitutes. It's useless and cruel."

"Josie, why are you so judgmental?" Alyce asked.

"I'm not sure what you mean."

"Many people think declawing a cat is cruel."

"But we gave Harry a good home," Josie said.

"And cut off his toe joints to save your couch. You didn't even try a scratching post first. Not that I'm in a position to criticize. I'm addicted to kitchen toys. The money I spend on high-priced slicers and dicers could be used to feed the poor."

"But you're not a saint," Josie said.

"Neither are you," Alyce said. "We're just trying to live our lives. So are the dog lovers. Cut them some slack."

"I guess so," Josie said.

"How was your weekend?" Alyce asked.

Josie told her about her "special date" with Stan.

"I think it's time for my catch and release program," Josie said. "I'm in the wrong romance. I'd better let him go."

"You're going to have to be cruel to be kind," Alyce said.

Josie asked, "Do you want to go to another Upper Pup with me? I promise not to be righteous."

"Deal," Alyce said.

"We don't have to buy anything at this store," Josie said. "I'm supposed to return the dress and see if this Upper Pup lives up to its 'no questions asked' policy."

This was one of Josie's least favorite parts of mystery shopping. She felt like an idiot returning something she'd purchased an hour before. But it was a good test of customer service.

Josie wrinkled her nose when she walked into the second Upper Pup in the rich suburb of Clayton. The shop smelled like a wet dog. Tufts of dog hair dotted the floor. The door glass was covered with dog nose prints.

A round woman with straight gray hair was talking to a grumpy-looking bichon. The woman wore a bone-shaped name tag that read SALLY—MANAGER.

"Sit up, Amber. Sit!" Sally said in the high voice used for children and pets.

The surly dog refused to move. The manager waved a treat under her nose. The dog snapped it up, nearly biting the woman's fingers.

"Now, Amber, that's not very nice," Sally said.

Josie and Alyce examined dog accessories while the manager cooed at her dog.

"Would you forgive me if I said that puppy bassinet with the lace trim creeps me out?" Josie asked Alyce. "I had one almost like it for Amelia."

"Sh," Alyce said. "You don't want Sally to hear you. I agree the bassinet is too weird."

"She won't hear me. She's too busy training her dog on company time," Josie said.

"Excuse me, ma'am," Josie said, raising her voice. "I'd like to return this." She held up the dress bag.

Sally examined the receipt and said, "But you bought the dress this morning."

"That's right," Josie said, "but it doesn't fit my dog."

"You should have taken it back to the store where you bought it," the manager said.

"Your return policy says 'any time, any store,'" Josie said.

"But it counts against my inventory," Sally said. "Well, I'll take it back."

She refunded Josie's purchase on her credit card, then said, "Come back again when you can buy something."

Josie thought Sally was nearly as surly as her dog.

"Sit up, Amber," Sally was saying as they left. "Come on, eat your num-nums. That's my big girl."

"And likely to get bigger, if Sally doesn't quit stuffing her with treats," Josie said as they headed for the car.

"I'm guessing that manager will not get high marks," Alyce said.

"No," Josie said. "And I won't feel the least bit guilty saying so in my report. The store was not clean. She wasn't helpful. She questioned my return. Sally is going to have lots of time to play with Amber when I turn in this report."

"What now?" Alyce said.

"That's it for today. I can mystery-shop the third Upper Pup later in the week."

"Will you do me a favor?" Alyce asked. "Would you come to lunch at my house Wednesday?"

"Are you kidding?" Josie asked. "I love your cooking."

"There's a price," Alyce said. "You have to meet my new neighbor, Traci."

"Is that a good idea?" Josie asked. "We don't run in the same circles."

"That's why I'm inviting you. Traci is from Miami and she doesn't quite fit in with the other women in the subdivision. She thinks they're snobs. They think she's rude. I think she's a hoot. I'll make lunch and the three of us can talk. Traci wants a new puppy. I'm trying to convince her to get a shelter animal."

"Doing good while eating well. My favorite kind of charity. Count me in," Josie said.

"See you at noon Wednesday," Alyce said.

Later that same afternoon, Amelia came running out of school with a big smile. Josie was delighted by the change. For too many afternoons after her father's death, Amelia had dragged herself to the car and answered questions in mono-syllables. "I can't wait to see Harry," she said. "How's he doing, Mom?"

"He was fine last time I checked," Josie said. "He'd emp-tied his food bowl and filled his litter box, and you know what that means, young lady."

"I'll clean it when I get home," Amelia said, her smile slightly dimmer.

At home, Amelia hauled out the litter jug and trudged down the hall to her bathroom. Soon Josie heard shouts of "Mom, Mom! Look!"

Josie darted out of the kitchen as a small brown blur raced down the hall, made a U-turn at Josie's shoes, then zipped into Amelia's bathroom.

"It's Harry, chasing a yarn ball!" Amelia said. "He's out!"

By that time, he was back under the claw-foot tub. Not even his tail showed. But the yarn ball was in the hall, proof of the cat's first major venture into the house.

"Isn't he wonderful?" Amelia said.

"He is indeed," Josie said. "We should celebrate with mac-aroni and cheese."

"Okay, but I'll make it."

"You won't get any argument from me," Josie said. "Be sure to wash your hands."

An hour and a half later, they were finishing up in the kitchen when Josie heard a knock on the door. She peeked out and saw Jerry. He held a prancing Chloe on a leash in one hand and a big bouquet in the other.

"May I come in?" Jerry said. "I want to apologize."

"Sure," Josie said. "Amelia, you can leave the dishes and play with Chloe on the porch if you want. Put on your coat first."

Amelia had her coat on and was outside in record time.

Jerry stood on the mat inside the door, looking awkward. "I'm sorry," he said. "I accused you of turning in Jonah. When I had time to think about it, I realized it couldn't be you. The news said the investigation had been going on for months. These flowers are for you. I'm sorry."

Jerry handed Josie an enormous bunch of pink and yellow Gerbera daisies, roses, stargazer lilies, and sunflowers.

"They're beautiful, Jerry. Come into the kitchen while I put them in water. Would you like some beer or wine?"

"Coffee would be nice," he said.

"Have you seen Jonah since the arrest?" Josie asked as she trimmed the stems on the flowers, then hunted for a big vase.

"No. He's out on bail. They say he hurt his puppies and didn't take care of his boys. The state has custody of Bart and Billy."

"But if he wasn't properly caring for them . . . ," Josie began.

"They had a few bruises, sure, but that's just boy stuff," Jerry said. "Jonah is a farmer and he comes across as a little rough. Everyone has to be useful on a farm, even kids. There's supposed to be someone else who complained about him, too."

"There is?" Josie said.

"But I know you'd never do anything like that," he said, and smiled at her.

"Would you like a brownie?" Josie asked.

"No, thanks," he said. "I'd better finish taking Chloe for her walk. It's warming up and she's feeling frisky."

"Thank you for the flowers," Josie said. He didn't ask her to walk with him.

"Good-bye," Jerry said. He gave her a quick, coffee-flavored kiss, and left her standing in the kitchen, feeling confused.

Once her daughter was in bed, Josie sat on the couch, waiting for the ten o'clock news. She wanted to see if there was more news about Jonah and the puppy mill. She fell asleep during a Christmas feature about a neighborhood Santa and woke up when she heard, "So enjoy the unseasonably warm December weather."

The final credits were rolling. Josie had missed the puppy mill story. Josie slipped down the hall in sock feet to check on her daughter. Amelia was asleep. Harry was curled up on the bed with his tail wrapped around her daughter's arm.

Josie tiptoed into her bedroom for her camera and sneaked back. Harry put his head up and stared at Josie with big green eyes, but remained possessively next to his new friend. Perfect.

She snapped their picture to show Amelia in the morning.

# Chapter 15

Josie didn't have to wake up Amelia on Tuesday morning. She was awake and at her computer. Harry was sitting on a pile of paper next to it, his brown paws neatly folded in front of him.

"Nice striped paperweight," Josie said. "Did you know Harry slept with his tail curled around your arm last night?"

Josie handed her daughter the photo of the sleeping Amelia with her cat. Amelia's eyes lit up when she saw the picture. "Harry's so cute! I'm taking this to school to show everyone."

"Better get moving," Josie said. "We have to leave soon."

Josie carried a cup of coffee into her bedroom and turned on the television while she dressed. She winced when she saw the story on the screen.

"Funeral services for Edna Prilosen, who was killed at the Pets 4 Luv store in Rock Road Village, will be tomorrow at St. Philomena's Catholic Church," the television newscaster said. He looked professionally sad.

"Police have no leads on the victim's hit-and-run murder in the store parking lot. The fifty-six-year-old saleswoman is survived by her widowed mother."

The announcer's voice slowed and he grew more serious. "We are about to show you the parking lot surveillance video of the hit-and-run incident. We warn you the scene may be upsetting, but it is important that the killer be found."

Josie couldn't stand to see the gray, grainy video. The horrible scene still replayed in her mind every night. She turned down the sound and ransacked her closet for a clean shirt. When she looked back, the announcer was reading the news again. Josie turned up the volume.

"The driver's face is not visible in the video," he continued, "but authorities say the killer is probably a tall man with broad shoulders. The truck is an older Ford F-150 pickup, one of the most popular models on the road. The color is dark, possibly charcoal, black, or deep blue. The license plates were covered by what may be mud."

Josie was relieved that she was not mentioned as a witness.

"Police believe the truck has a broken headlight on the passenger side and several dents on the body. If you have any information or have recently seen or worked on a Ford F-150 truck with a broken passenger-side headlight, please let us know. Pets 4 Luv is offering a twenty-thousand-dollar reward for information leading to the arrest and conviction of the killer."

A phone number flashed on the screen.

Didn't Jerry drive a dark, dented Ford pickup? And Paul? They were neighbors of Jonah Deerford. Were they in business together? Did they help him by killing Edna?

Jerry was still defending the man, though Josie couldn't understand why. Any reasonable person could see Jonah had neglected his boys and those puppies. Both Jerry and Paul were tall men with broad shoulders. Josie didn't know enough about Paul to suspect him. All she knew for a fact was that Edna was dead. Jonah was out on bail. Millions of dollars, and Jonah's family farm, were at risk. The man was cruel and vindictive—and suspicious of Josie. He'd asked Jerry about her. Did Jerry really tell him Josie was a harmless mystery shopper?

Josie felt too sick to drink more coffee. Was Detective Gray right—did her amateur meddling kill an innocent woman?

I can't take all the blame, Josie decided. The store should have hired a professional investigator. Harry shouldn't have stuck me with that stupid purse cam. Edna shouldn't have talked to Nedra and the other investigators. But if Edna hadn't talked, the cruelty would have continued. Now she was dead. And Josie was carrying a load of guilt.

Jonah killed her, Josie thought. Fear gripped her so tightly, she could hardly breathe. What if he comes after me next? What if he hurts my daughter?

Maybe Jonah didn't kill Edna. The store manager also had a good reason to want her dead. Edna's testimony would ruin Dave's career. He was on the run now. He'd seen Josie talking to Edna on the store security camera. Thanks to Dave's visit to Milwaukee, he knew Josie had mystery-shopped his store and discovered his ugly secret. Dave had evaded the police so far. He could come back for her. Josie had no idea what the man looked like. She thought of Edna's mother and her terrible fate: The poor woman outlived her daughter.

I have to protect Amelia, Josie thought. My daughter will be safe at school. Barrington has security on the premises and a good system for carpooling parents. The school would not let Amelia outside after class unless a preapproved driver—Josie, Jane, or Alyce—was waiting for her. The school had their approved drivers' photos and license plate numbers. Jonah wouldn't have a chance.

But she'd better deliver her daughter to the safety of her school first.

"Time to go, Amelia," Josie said. "Are you ready?"

Amelia tucked the photo of her and Harry into her note-book, then stuffed them into her monogrammed backpack. She was wearing her coolest clothes. Josie thought her daughter looked like a junior model in her skinny coral jeans and long, black tank top under a black-checked smocked top. The weather was just right for her vintage blue wash jacket.

It had taken Josie weeks of shrewd shopping at consignment stores, garage sales, and designer closeouts to assemble that outfit. Josie didn't want Amelia to look like a scholarship student. *I don't want her to be a nerd like her mother was,* Josie thought. *Mom couldn't buy me fashionable school clothes. Money was too tight after Dad left us.*

"I'm ready," Amelia said. "Harry and I have had breakfast, I've showered, and he took a bath. I even cleaned the litter box."

"Let me go outside first," Josie said.

"Why?" Amelia said.

"As your mother, I want to greet the day first."

"You're nutso-crazy," Amelia said.

Josie stepped out on the front porch. The sunny morning was crisp and cold. There were no unknown cars—or pickups—parked nearby. No strangers lurked on the sidewalk. Stan's car was still in his driveway. Mrs. Mueller peeked out her side window.

Josie waved to the old snoop, then said, "Let's hurry."

"I hear a dog barking," Amelia said.

"A cat is probably strolling down the back alley," Josie said.

"The dog is barking really loud," Amelia said. "Do the Petersens have a big dog?"

"We can take a dog census later," Josie said. "You're going to be late for school."

Josie was relieved when Amelia climbed into the car and slammed the door. Except for the barking dog, the street seemed quiet—too quiet, as they said in the old movies.

Amelia was not quiet. All the way to school, she chattered about Harry, praising the perfection of her cat's fur, stripes, eyes—even his ears. "Do you know a cat has thirty-two muscles in each ear, Mom? Humans have only six muscles per ear."

"But more muscles between their ears," Josie said, thinking of her erstwhile boyfriend, Stan.

"Huh?" Amelia said.

"Sorry," Josie said. "Tell me about cats' ears."

"I read some fun facts on the Internet. A cat can rotate its ears one hundred eighty degrees."

"That explains why Harry has ears like satellite dishes," Josie said. She saw Amelia's smile waver. "I wasn't criticizing. His ears are amazing."

Amelia was talking about the flexibility of Harry's spine, when they finally reached school. Josie was relieved. They were running out of feline body parts.

She still felt uneasy. Poor Edna's murder was horrible. She hoped Edna's mother didn't see that ghastly video. What must it be like, to watch your daughter die on television? Josie prayed she'd never know.

To distract herself, she drove to the supermarket for odds and ends. The store was nearly deserted. Josie breezed through the aisles, filling her cart with wholesome, everyday items— bread, milk, soup, and cereal.

It was after nine that morning when she turned into her street. It was no longer quiet. The road was blocked by an ambulance with open doors, two police cars, and an animal control van. A carnival of flashing blue, red, and yellow lights strobed across the houses.

What happened? Josie wondered. Thank God Amelia was safely at school. But that left . . .

"Mom!" she screamed. Josie abandoned her car by Mrs. Mueller's house and ran up the sidewalk to her home.

She was stopped by a uniformed police officer.

"I have to get in," Josie said. "I live here."

"Do you know the woman who lives upstairs?" the officer asked.

"She's my mother," Josie said. "Has there been an accident? Is she hurt?"

Josie heard something bumping on the concrete walkway alongside the house. Paramedics were helping Jane onto a stretcher. Josie's mother looked small and pale as they strapped her onto the gurney. One sleeve on Jane's winter coat was torn. Her bare hand was padded with heavy white bandages. Josie could see blood on the stark white gauze.

"She was attacked," the officer said.

# Chapter 16

Josie's street was a swirl of confusion. Police cars and para-medics were parked every which way. Radios squawked. Neighbors gawked. The uniformed officer barring Josie's way was a blue island of calm in the chaos. He refused to let Josie run up her own sidewalk.

"What is your business here, ma'am?" The officer looked young and fit. His name tag said KIRBY.

"Who attacked my mother?" Josie demanded.

"It wasn't a person, ma'am," Officer Kirby said. "A dog attacked her. A mean one. Your mother said she heard loud barking and went to the garage to investigate. When she opened the side door, the dog sprang at her. Her throat was wrapped in a thick winter scarf. That may have saved her life. She grabbed a broom by the door and managed to fend off the dog. Her arm needs stitches, but there's no damage to her face."

"How did you get here?" Josie's voice wobbled.

"Your neighbor Mrs. Mullet—"

"Mueller," Josie corrected.

"Mrs. Mueller heard your mother's screams and called 911. We were in the area and able to respond quickly." Kirby said it matter-of-factly, but Josie could tell he was proud.

"Mrs. Mueller directed us to the backyard. The dog charged me. I shot the animal. The dog is dead."

"Good," Josie said.

"I think it was a rottweiler." He pointed to a dark, bloody heap in the grass by the garage.

Josie thought of Barney, a rottweiler that belonged to a high school friend. Josie had admired the dog's black and brown coat and patted its big head and soft ears. She couldn't imagine Barney as a crazed killer.

Officer Kirby was still talking. "We can't let anyone touch the body. St. Louis County Animal Control will take the dog and test it for rabies."

"Do you think it was rabid?"

"We don't know, ma'am. Rabid dogs can become aggressive, and this dog was definitely threatening. It had open sores on its coat. If it's rabid, your mother will need rabies shots."

"Oh, no," Josie said. "Whose dog is it?"

"The animal was not wearing a collar or tags," Officer Kirby said. "We think someone may have put the dog in the garage, unless it crawled under the door when your mother drove in, which is unlikely. Your mother says she closed the side door to the garage when she came home yesterday, but it wasn't kept locked. Someone could have opened the back gate, then let the dog inside the garage. Does anyone have a grudge against your mother?"

"Of course not," Josie said. "She's a church lady."

"They have enemies, too," Officer Kirby said.

"Church ladies fight over committees, officer. They don't sic rabid dogs on one another."

"Does anyone else park in that garage?" the officer asked.

"I park on the street," Josie said.

Should she tell Officer Kirby about Jonah and her damning mystery-shopping report? Josie wondered. She'd like to trust the officer, but so far, her report had been the death of Edna. What if Jonah was behind this attack and found out it had failed? He might come back and hurt Jane again—or

Amelia. What if Dave the store manager found them? The officer was brave, but he looked young and inexperienced. Josie couldn't risk her daughter's life.

The paramedics were wheeling the stretcher past them. Josie ran alongside it. "Mom! How are you?"

Jane's voice was so low, Josie could hardly hear her. "A dog attacked me when I opened the garage. Someone locked him in there. I hit him with the broom. He bit my arm. He ruined my new gloves."

"Don't worry about your gloves, Mom," Josie said.

"Mrs. Mueller heard me scream and called the police. That young policeman shot the dog. She saved my life, Josie."

"We need to get her to the hospital, ma'am," a paramedic interrupted.

"Can I ride with my mother in the ambulance?" Josie asked.

"It would be better if you met us at Holy Redeemer. You'll probably need your car to get home from the hospital. You know where Holy Redeemer is?"

"Yes," Josie said. It was the hospital where her lover, Nate, had died. Josie ran for her car, her mind blank with fear. Mrs. Mueller barred her way, arms folded across her massive chest. They did an awkward do-si-do on the sidewalk as Josie tried to avoid her.

"I'm on my way to the emergency room," Josie said. "I'll fill you in when I get home. You won't miss any gossip."

"Don't forget, I saved your mother's life, young lady," Mrs. Mueller said.

"I won't. You won't let me."

Josie jumped in her car and followed the ambulance to the hospital, hoping she didn't have an accident in her distracted state. She found a parking spot near the emergency room entrance and ran inside.

A receptionist with a crisp, no-nonsense voice stopped her. "Jane Marcus is with the doctor. Take a seat in the waiting area."

Josie was too upset to sit. She paced the dreary room, waiting for word about her mother. Worried families huddled in groups on orange plastic chairs. A baby cried. The TV blared, but no one watched it.

Josie was racked with guilt. Why didn't I listen to my daughter this morning? she asked herself. Amelia had heard that dog barking. I could have prevented this attack.

A zillion questions ping-ponged in her mind: Who locked that vicious dog in Mom's garage? Was it Jonah Deerford? How did he know where I live? Did he have a rottweiler? I only saw little purse dogs at his kennels.

After an hour of regret and recriminations, the receptionist called Josie's name. "Your mother is in room two," she said.

The room was a curtained cubicle. Jane wore a hospital gown and a big white mitten of gauze. She looked every one of her sixty-eight years. The chubby, pink-faced ER doctor looked like a self-satisfied pig. Josie nicknamed him Dr. Porker.

"The rabies virus is usually transmitted by the animal's saliva," Dr. Porker said. "I've washed your mother's wound for fifteen minutes with medicated soap and water, standard treatment for possible rabies. It stung a little."

"It hurt like heck!" Jane said.

Josie hid a smile. Mom was going to be okay.

"She needed twelve stitches for the wound, and we gave her a tetanus shot," Dr. Porker said. "She's lucky she was wearing a heavy winter coat and a scarf to protect her face and neck."

"If I'm so lucky, why do I feel so lousy?" Jane asked. "Why are you talking as if I'm deaf? I'm right here."

The chunky doctor faced Jane and said carefully, "Here's

a prescription for pain medication if you need it, Mrs. Marcus. The deceased dog is being tested for rabies. We hope you won't need the shots, but they're not as painful as they used to be. Now you get them in your butt and arms instead of your stomach."

Jane frowned. Women of her generation did not like the word "butt" used about their anatomy. Dr. Porker handed Josie a paper. "Call this number to find out the test results. Remember, you can be symptom-free for twenty days or longer after being exposed and still have rabies. Promise you'll come in for the shots if you need them."

"I'm not an idiot, young man," Jane said. "I've heard of rabies. Now let me go before—before I bite you."

Josie laughed. She couldn't help it. The doctor marched out, looking offended.

Josie helped her mother get dressed. She buttoned Jane's blouse as she fumed. "What's wrong with younger people? Why do they treat retirees as if we're simpleminded?"

"Maybe you taught him a lesson," Josie said.

A lanky, dark-skinned man in purple scrubs arrived with a wheelchair. "I'm from transport," he said.

Josie draped her mother's torn coat around her shoulders, then ran for her car. She met Jane at the hospital door. The young man helped Jane inside the car. After her defiant outburst at the doctor, Jane looked exhausted. Her skin sagged and her face was pale except for dark circles under her eyes. Jane settled in the seat and sighed.

"Are you hungry?" Josie asked. "Would you like to stop for lunch?"

"I'd like to take a nap." Jane plucked at her torn coat sleeve. "I don't think I'll wear this coat again."

"I'll buy you another one," Josie said.

"Don't bother," Jane said. "This is my take-out-the-trash coat. I should have thrown it out last year."

Jane closed her eyes. Soon Josie heard a light snore. Once

home, she checked the street carefully, but everything looked ordinary. Josie was relieved that Mrs. Mueller was not waiting for them. The dog carcass was gone, too.

Jane insisted on going upstairs to "my own bed." Josie followed and helped her into a pink flannel gown. Jane sank gratefully into her bed.

"Would you like tea or coffee? Could I heat up some soup?" Josie asked.

"I'd like to sleep. Go away," Jane said. "Josie?"

"Yes?"

"Thanks, sweetie. I don't say that often enough. I'm too rough on you. You're a good daughter."

Josie kissed her mother's forehead. "You're welcome, Mom." Her eyes teared up as she made her way downstairs. Jane didn't hand out many compliments to her daughter.

Josie wanted to talk to Jerry, but not about another date. She left a message on his phone and hoped he'd call soon. Then she left to pick up Amelia at school, once again checking the yard and the bushes around the porch.

Amelia bounced into the car with the boundless energy Josie wished she still had. She knew her current news would upset her daughter, but there was no easy way to break it.

"Your grandma was hurt today," Josie said. "She was bitten by a dog."

"Not Chloe!" Amelia said.

"No, a big ugly rottweiler, probably the dog you heard barking this morning. She had to go to the emergency room."

Amelia looked ready to burst into tears.

"She's fine," Josie added quickly. "The doctor took good care of her. Grandma got stitches in her hand, but there's no permanent damage."

"Can I see her?" Amelia sounded suspicious.

"Of course, honey, if she's awake. She's been asleep all afternoon. You can even make her soup and toasted cheese sandwiches."

Josie drove home as fast as the traffic and the speed limit

allowed. Amelia sprinted into the house to start her grand-mother's dinner. Josie climbed the stairs to look in on her mother. Jane was sitting up in bed with a teacup in her hand, talking to Mrs. Mueller. Actually, she was listening to Mrs. Mueller. The two women didn't see Josie in the doorway.

"I saw a pickup truck go down the alley around two this morning. It was black or gray. An old beat-up thing like the one Josie's new boyfriend drives. It's hard to keep track of all her men."

Josie was tempted to say something, but let the old bat talk. "The truck was going very slowly. I should have called the police. I might have prevented this."

"You couldn't have known," Jane said.

"When I heard you scream this morning, Jane, I knew that wasn't a normal sound," Mrs. Mueller said. "You were seriously hurt. I just happened to be by a window. . . ."

Right, Josie thought.

"I saw that beast lunge forward and I called the police. My hand was shaking so bad I could hardly dial 911. Thank goodness the police got here immediately."

Josie knocked on the doorway. "Hi, Mom. How are you feeling?"

"Better," Jane said. "Mrs. Mueller baked me a lovely gooey butter coffeecake. Would you like some?"

"Thanks, but I don't want to spoil my dinner."

"I have to leave," Mrs. Mueller said. "Please excuse me." She walked past Josie, pointedly ignoring her.

"Your granddaughter is heating up some soup for you," Josie said, "and making toasted cheese sandwiches. She wants to bring them upstairs. She's very worried."

"She's such a thoughtful girl. Don't let her carry that hot soup," Jane said. "I don't want her getting burned."

When Josie walked downstairs to her kitchen, Amelia was arranging a cup of tomato soup and a toasted cheese sandwich on a tray covered with a blue cloth napkin. The sandwich had been cut into triangles.

"That looks beautiful, sweetheart," Josie said. "I'll carry the soup upstairs. Grandma doesn't want you getting burned."

"But it's okay if you are?" Amelia asked.

"I'm a mom," Josie said. She carried the soup upstairs without spilling any. Amelia followed with the sandwiches on the tray. At the top of the stairs, they reassembled Jane's meal. Jane was still sitting up in bed, but she'd combed her hair and put on lipstick.

"Grandma, how are you?" Amelia asked.

"Better now that I see you, baby," Jane said. "You've fixed dinner. Aren't you sweet?"

Amelia perched on the edge of the bed and watched her grandmother eat. "Harry's come out from under the bathtub now," she said. "He likes to play and run all over the house."

"He didn't get near my dinner, did he?" Jane asked.

"Of course not, Grandma. Cats don't like tomato soup."

"Good," Jane said. "I don't like cats."

"You would if you met Harry," Amelia said. She collected the empty plate and cup. "Would you like more tea?"

"No, thanks," Jane said. "I'd like to get some sleep. I'm tired. I like your coral jeans, but I wish you wouldn't wear those baggy tops. Can't you tuck them in? You have such a nice waist."

"They're supposed to be loose and layered, Grandma," Amelia said. "I have to do my homework now."

"You go ahead," Jane said. "I want to talk to your mother a minute."

Jane waited until Amelia was down the stairs. "Does the dead dog belong to that what's-his-name you're dating—Jerrod, Gerund, Gerbil?" she asked.

"His name is Jerry, Mom, and he has a golden retriever mix, not a black rottweiler."

"Right. It piddles on my front porch."

"I'm sorry, Mom."

"Why should you be sorry?" Jane said, suspiciously. "Did you have anything to do with this?"

"I would never hurt my best babysitter," Josie said. It wasn't a lie. Not really.

"What about Jerry?" Jane said.

"He's never met you, Mom."

"Humph," said her mother. "You don't know anything about him, or who his friends are. He could know some bad people. He's behind that attack somehow, Josie Marcus."

"That's a terrible thing to say, Mom," Josie said.

But she remembered the dark truck running down Edna in the parking lot, and wondered if her mother was right.

# Chapter 17

"Do you like your chicken hot?" Alyce asked.

"Honey, I'm from Miami," Traci said. "I like everything hot: chicken, weather, men—you name it." Traci gave a little hip check.

Alyce's new neighbor was a riot of color, from her flaming hair to her sparkly crystal-trimmed heels. Traci's peppermint sweater looked smashing with her bright hair. Gold bracelets jangled at her wrists and her earrings swung merrily. Her dark eyes had that mischievous "I've got a secret" look.

Josie could see that Traci wouldn't fit in with the subdued suburban moms at Wood Winds. The suburban dads might like her curvy figure and tight clothes.

"I like anything you cook," Josie said. "Hot is fine with me."

"I'm making chicken panini," Alyce said, "and, Josie, that's not the name of an Italian gangster."

"My meager cooking skills are notorious," Josie said to Traci.

"A woman after my heart," Traci said. "If I can't nuke it, I don't cook it."

"What gadget did you buy for this lunch?" Josie asked. "Alyce has a serious Williams-Sonoma addiction," she explained to Traci.

"I finally got my panini press," Alyce said, pointing to what looked like a weird waffle iron with wavy plates. "I wanted to test it at lunch."

"Happy to volunteer," Traci said.

"Wait till I get my new roasting fork," Alyce said. She noticed Josie's puzzled look and said, "It helps lift the Christmas turkey. I nearly lost the Thanksgiving bird."

"My mom dropped the turkey one year," Traci said. "Nobody was in the kitchen, so she wiped it off, cleaned up the floor, and served it. Nobody was any wiser but me, and I kept my mouth shut."

"This year, a timely save kept it from skidding across the floor," Alyce said. "I think a thirteen-inch all-clad stainless steel fork should hold that turkey. The fork is due any day now. They've promised me it will arrive before Christmas."

"This is a cool kitchen," Traci said. "I've never seen one with oak paneling. Where's your fridge?"

"Behind that panel there," Alyce said, pointing to a wall section. "Lunch should be ready soon. The salad is already on the table. Take your wineglasses and start eating, ladies. I'll deliver your chicken sandwiches."

Blue violets bloomed on the table in Alyce's sunny breakfast room. Blue gingham place mats and napkins were neatly set at each place. Traci picked the sunniest chair and sat down.

"This is the warmest I've been since we moved here," she said. "Your salad is too pretty to eat, Alyce."

"I've never had that problem," Josie said. "I eat your food no matter how good it looks. Is this your Roquefort, cranberry, and walnut salad?"

"It is," Alyce said, delivering a plate of perfectly grilled chicken panini. "I know you like it."

Traci took a bite and said, "I've died and gone to heaven. Now I need you angels to help me. I want a dog. I finally have a yard where a pup can run and play. We couldn't keep pets in our condo. I want the best place to buy a little dog,

something girlie, so I can dress it up. I'd like a poodle,
bichon, or a Pomeranian."

"The Humane Society of Missouri has all those breeds
and more," Josie said.

"But most don't come with AKC papers," Traci said.
"I'm a designer kind of girl. You can tell by my clothes."

"Escada doesn't make dogs," Josie said. "Humane Society pups are as good as the ones you'd get from a breeder.
They just don't have that piece of paper. Please don't buy a
puppy mill dog. Didn't you see the news stories about the
raid on that awful Deerford Kennels?"

"Those poor things are really sick and they have behavior problems," Alyce said. "What happens to them is pitiful.
You don't want to encourage puppy mill owners."

"But didn't the Humane Society take those puppy mill
dogs?" Traci said. "How do I know they won't palm one off
on me?"

"The news stories said those dogs went to foster care
families so they could be nursed back to health," Josie said.

"But you only have the society's word for it."

"Traci, please reconsider. You could be buying a whole
lot of trouble," Josie said. "If you want a pedigreed pup, at
least visit the breeder, so you can see how your dog is being
raised."

"I'll think about it," Traci said, and took a sip of wine.
Josie suspected Traci's mind was already made up. "You're
so much nicer, Josie, than that other lady I met."

"Who's that?"

"Renata Uppity Liver-something. Snooty old witch with
white hair."

"Renata Upton Liverspot—I mean Livermore," Josie said.
"She lives in the Victorian mansion on the hill. I think she
posed for the gargoyle over the door."

"We live in the Spanish revival down the hill. Well, it's
more like warmed-over Mizner, but my husband and I like

it. I went over to introduce myself, and Renata treated me as if I'd tracked in something nasty on my shoes."

"Welcome to the club," Josie said. "She treats everyone that way." She carried their empty plates to the sink and asked, "Alyce, can I make coffee?"

"It's perking now." Alyce jumped up quickly. She didn't like Josie meddling in her kitchen. "I'll bring it in with dessert."

She returned with more fragrant plates. "This is crystallized ginger gingerbread with warm pears. It's supposed to be healthy."

Josie took a bite. "Are you sure? It's awfully good."

"Mmm," Traci said. "Can I hire you to cook dinner?"

Alyce laughed. "Little Justin is enough to keep me and a nanny busy," she said. "I love cooking, but right now my family is all I can manage to feed."

When only a few crumbs remained on the plates, Josie said, "I hate to eat and run. But I have to pick up Amelia at school."

She started to carry her dishes to the sink, but Alyce said, "I have everything under control here. You go get your daughter."

Josie drove past the Tudor palaces, Italian villas, and French chateaus of Wood Winds. The guard at the gate gave her a mock salute when she waved.

Josie arrived early enough to sit in the car-pool line in the school drive and trade fake smiles with the other mothers. Many of the women at the Barrington School knew Josie was not one of them, and they were cool toward her.

While she waited for Amelia, Josie called her mother. Jane answered on the second ring.

"How are you feeling?" Josie asked.

"Better," Jane said. "My hand is still sore, but otherwise I don't feel bad. I have some good news. That terrible dog did not have rabies."

"That's wonderful, Mom. Gotta go. Your granddaughter is coming out of school now. She'll be happy to hear that."

"Send her upstairs if she wants to see me," Jane said.

It was a warm winter day, and Amelia ran out wearing the stylish multilayered tops that so puzzled her grandmother. Josie was pleased she'd managed to dress her daughter like the other girls in her class. No point being a professional shopper if you couldn't help your own family.

Those cheerful thoughts vanished when Amelia threw her backpack into the rear seat and flopped down beside Josie. Amelia seemed on the verge of tears.

"What's wrong?" Josie asked.

"Nothing," Amelia said, in a tone that meant "everything."

"Something is wrong and you'd better tell me," Josie said. "I'm not going to have you sulking all evening."

Amelia took a deep breath and said, "It's nothing."

"It is, too," Josie said.

Suddenly, Amelia burst out with, "I showed my picture of Harry to Zoe and she laughed. Zoe says that Harry has big ears because he's a mutt cat and her cat is a purebred with little ears."

"Her cat may have purebred ears, but her owner is pure rude," Josie said. "Besides, she's wrong and I'll show you. I have proof at home." What Josie had was a vague memory of fourth grade history.

"How's Grandma?" Amelia said.

"She says she's feeling better. The dog that attacked her didn't have rabies, so she won't have to go through those awful shots."

"Can I see her?" Amelia's bad mood was melting away as she talked about her grandmother.

"She's waiting for you. I'll look for my proof while you run upstairs to see her."

Amelia ran inside their home long enough to check on Harry. "He's sleeping on my bed, Mom," she said. "He ate all his food. I gave him more. I'm going upstairs to see Grandma."

"Okay," Josie said. "But don't ask her to cook with you tonight. Her hand still hurts."

Josie went to the corner where she had her bedroom office on the garage-sale table. While she waited for an Internet connection, Josie wished she could call down punishment on that troublemaker, Zoe. The girl was the bane of Barrington. Zoe wore slutty outfits. She drank booze and fed the other girls dangerously outdated sex information. She told everyone a girl couldn't get pregnant the first time she had sex.

Making fun of Amelia's cat was petty, but at least it wouldn't do any harm.

On the Internet, Josie found photos of statues of Bast, the Egyptian cat goddess, as well as pedigreed Abyssinian cats. She printed the pictures for Amelia.

Her daughter was downstairs half an hour later with a smile and a white smear on her face.

"What's on your cheek?" Josie asked.

Amelia looked in the living room mirror. "Powdered sugar," she said, brushing it off. "Grandma gave me some of Mrs. Mueller's gooey butter cake. I don't like her, but she makes a good cake."

"Maybe she should swallow some sugar herself," Josie said. "Here's the truth about Harry. Look at these pedigreed Abyssinian cats."

Amelia examined the photos. "They have ears just like Harry."

"Big ears," Josie said. "And a long pedigree. Abys may have been the world's first pedigreed cats. This picture is Bast, the cat goddess. The Egyptians worshiped their domestic cats as gods. Bast's ears are big, too, and she has a slender face. Talk about royalty. Harry's ancestors go way back, and they had royal blood. He has a longer bloodline that Zoe's flat-faced feline, and you can show her."

"Thanks, Mom. I don't need to show her anything. Zoe doesn't know what she's talking about. She's a loser face."

Josie checked her phone messages, but she could hardly hear them because of the racket. She looked out into the hall. Amelia was dragging a pale ribbon along the floor while Harry tried to catch it. The little cat made more noise than a herd of buffalo.

"Amelia, could you and your friend hold it down?" Josie asked. "I have to make a phone call."

"Sorry," Amelia said.

Stan had left no message—again. *Is our romance over?* Josie wondered. She rather hoped it would die a quiet death. Jerry was not the man for her, but her relationship with the hunky Stan was limping along.

There was one message from Jerry. "My mom loved meeting you," he said. "Would you and Amelia like to see me tonight? Maybe we could go out for coffee or take Chloe for a walk."

Josie called him back and left a message. "I'd like to see you tonight, Jerry, and it's very kind of you to include Amelia, but she has to study for a quiz tomorrow. She can't go with us. Come by about seven and we'll go for coffee. Bring Chloe if you want, just so long as she doesn't water Mom's porch."

Amelia didn't really have a quiz. But Josie had some questions for Jerry—and she wanted answers. Tonight.

# Chapter 18

"This is a good cookie," Jerry said. "And I'm only eating one." He tilted his head to one side, which made him look rather like a cocker spaniel. No doubt about it, the man was cute.

Jerry's cookie was eight inches in diameter, one of the specialties of the Cupcakery in St. Louis. Josie had nearly convinced herself that her double-chocolate cupcake wasn't a calorie trap. It wasn't as if she'd ordered a whole slab of cake.

Ah, delusions, she thought. They're the only way to survive dating.

Josie had deliberately chosen the little bakery in the city's Central West End neighborhood because it closed at eight thirty. That guaranteed a short night with Jerry. She suspected this evening was going to end badly. Jerry's mood was cooling faster than their coffee. But she kept asking him questions he didn't want to answer. She kept after him, like a mosquito trapped in a room.

"Does Jonah have a dog? What kind of dog?" Jerry echoed her questions, then bit his cookie as if he were angry at it.

"A big dog, like maybe a rottweiler," Josie said.

"So what if he does? He needs a guard dog out in the country," Jerry said. "It takes a long time for the police to get up that back road. A big dog gives him protection."

"Does he still have the dog?"

"How do I know which dogs the cops took?" Jerry raised his voice a notch. "I haven't talked to Jonah since he got out on bail."

The couple in line at the register glanced at him, took their cupcakes, and left the warm, sugary-smelling shop.

"Where were you the night before last?" Josie asked.

"Excuse me?" Jerry asked. "Did we make a commitment? I thought we were just having fun."

"That's us, no strings," Josie said, forcing a smile. "I'll tell you where I was, though. I was home with my mom. She'd been attacked by a big rottweiler, and a police officer had to shoot it dead. She got twelve stitches in her arm."

"And you think I had something to do with that?"

"No," Josie said. But her voice sounded uncertain. Jerry heard her hesitation.

"Jonah!" Jerry said. "That's why you're asking about his guard dogs. You think Jonah's dog attacked your mother!"

His anger bounced off the sweet little shop's walls. Josie was afraid it would smash the cupcakes. The young woman behind the counter stared at them, cell phone in hand. They were making a scene. Was she going to call 911?

"No, no," Josie said, trying to soothe him. "Of course not. But Jonah was arrested for animal abuse."

"And you're going to kick him while he's down," Jerry said.

Fury flashed in his eyes. For the first time Josie was a little afraid of Jerry. Maybe he wasn't as gentle as he seemed. He certainly defended his friend when the man didn't deserve it.

"Everyone hates Jonah after that news story," he said. "Nobody gives a hardworking man the benefit of the doubt. Nobody wants to hear his side."

His side? Josie had seen the video of those shivering, suffering pups. That said it all.

"I just wondered if you told him where I lived, that's all," Josie said.

"Of course I didn't tell him. Why would he care? Jonah called a day or two after our visit. He said you were a nice girl and you could come by anytime to see his dogs. I said I was lucky you lived near me in Maplewood. My last girl— the one with the tattoos that Mom didn't like—was way down in South County. But that's all I said. That was our big, sinister conversation. Some conspiracy, huh? I never gave Jonah your address."

Jerry wouldn't have to. Josie was listed in the phone book. It wouldn't be difficult for Jonah to pick out the Maplewood address. Josie wondered if Jonah had been out on bail when he'd developed a sudden interest in Jerry's "nice" date. Jerry was too easy for the sly Jonah to manipulate. Or maybe Jerry was Jonah's accomplice.

Suddenly, Josie lost her appetite. Her mother and daughter were home alone. Jonah was still on the loose. Dave, the store manager, was still on the run. She had to be with her family, to protect them, if necessary.

She stood up. "It's getting late. I need to get back home."

"Fine with me," Jerry said. He left half of his giant cookie on the table, next to her partly eaten cupcake. Josie picked up the box of cupcakes she'd bought for her mother and Amelia. She and Jerry walked out together, careful not to touch each other.

The drive home was like a punishment. Jerry did not take the romantic route through Forest Park, with its ancient trees and gentle fountains. He avoided Lindell Boulevard, lined with stained glass and stone mansions. Instead, he drove past the garish pizza parlors, gas stations, and bars until they reached a dreary industrial section of Manchester Road.

"How is Chloe?" Josie asked, trying to break the oppressive silence.

"Fine," Jerry said. He flattened any further attempts at

conversation with that one word. His dark battered pickup jerked and groaned on the city streets.

Josie was relieved when Jerry parked in front of her place. She grabbed her cupcake box, said good night, and hopped out before he could reply.

That's the end of that romance, Josie thought. It's just as well. We don't agree on much except that Jerry's puppy is cute.

The first thing Josie noticed was that the awful couch was finally gone. She glanced at Stan's house next door. Before he became a hunk, Stan used to wait for her on his porch. He'd fix little things in her yard or on her car. Now the lights were off. His garage door was closed. Either Stan was still at the gym or home asleep, worn out by his latest body-building effort. The man was obsessed with perfecting perfection.

Josie knew she had to find the courage to tell Stan good-bye. Last Sunday night had been the end. She needed to stop seeing him while they were still friends.

A light went on in Stan's living room. "Josie?" he called from his front door. Josie could see he was wearing the black T-shirt she'd bought him last Christmas. If anything, he filled it out better than he did a year ago.

"Could I talk to you a minute?" Stan asked.

"Sure," Josie said, and started toward his home. He met her halfway.

They stood awkwardly by the curb where he and Howie had moved the ancient couch. "Josie, there's no easy way to say this." Stan held her hand, which looked small and delicate in his massive paw. His wrist was the size of a healthy sapling. His arm was perfectly sculpted.

Stan took a deep breath and said, "I'll always be your friend, Josie, but I don't think we're working out as a couple."

"What!" Josie said.

"We don't see eye to eye. Sunday night, I took you to my special place, and you hated it."

"But—"

"You're a good person, Josie, but it's better if you find someone who shares your interests. I've found my special someone. Her name is Abby. You'd like her. She teaches third grade and we have so much in common. She's terrific with coupons. We shopped together last Monday, and Abby saved seventeen dollars and eleven cents at the supermarket. She has her coupons in a special file, organized by product, price, and store. I want to make a serious commitment to her, Josie, but I'll always be your friend."

"Sure," Josie said. "This is kind of a surprise."

"It just happened," Stan said. "I didn't mean to fall in love with her. It was love at first sight when we met in the checkout line. It's not fair to keep going out with you."

"You're a good man." Josie kissed him gently on the cheek. "Abby is a lucky girl. Good night."

Stan turned to go back inside, leaving a dazed Josie in the same spot where the couch had been. I've been kicked to the curb by a man I thought was too dull for me, Josie thought. He dumped me before I could dump him. Can a woman die of chagrin?

Josie hadn't wanted Stan, but now that their romance was over, she felt foolish and rejected. Rejected! By a man who thought discount shopping was a special night.

She wearily climbed the stairs to her mother's flat, knocked lightly, and entered. Jane was snoring gently on the couch. Amelia was watching television with the sound turned down. Jane woke up when Josie opened her door.

"I brought you a treat," she said. "Raspberry buttercream cupcakes."

"Yay!" Amelia said, and took a bite.

Jane tried a polite nibble. "Not bad."

"Mine are better," Amelia said.

"They probably are," Josie agreed. "You have your grandmother's cooking skills. When you finish your cupcake, it's bedtime."

"How did your date with Gerbil go?" Jane asked.

"Jerry. It was okay." Josie hoped she sounded noncommittal.

"What's wrong?" Jane asked.

"Nothing. Jerry is nice, but there's no spark. I seem to have that effect on men."

"I still don't see why you don't go out more with that nice Stan," Jane said. "I love this raspberry icing."

"Mom, I know you liked Stan, but we broke up tonight."

"Why?" Jane asked. Josie could see her dreams of a wedding for Josie were smashed. "What's wrong with him?"

"No sizzle in that steak, Grandma," Amelia said.

"Amelia!" Josie said.

"Well, it's true."

"We've heard enough truth," Josie said. "Tell your grandmother good night and let's go downstairs."

Amelia ran in to check on Harry the cat. "He's asleep on my bed, Mom," she said. "He hasn't eaten any dinner."

"You gave him a lot of food when you got home from school," Josie said. "Maybe he's not hungry. And you were chasing him all over the house earlier. He's probably tired. Cats sleep a lot."

"I guess," Amelia said.

Josie took a quick, stinging shower to wash away the bad evening. It didn't work. Stan had dropped her for a third grade coupon clipper. She'd get over it. Eventually. It was Jerry who really bothered her. Was he really so naive he couldn't see through Jonah? Or was he a cog in the multi-million-dollar puppy mill? Postal clerks didn't make that kind of money.

She toweled herself dry, slipped on her robe, and looked in on her daughter. Amelia was in bed asleep with Harry beside her. Her daughter had one small hand on Harry's huge ears. She seemed to have forgotten Zoe's cruel critique of her cat. At least it didn't keep her awake.

Josie wasn't so lucky. Her bed felt as if it were paved with cobblestones. She kept asking hard questions that she couldn't answer:

Who was Jerry? If he was such a nice guy, why did he hang around with Jonah? Couldn't he see the man mistreated puppies and starved his sons? What if Jonah came back and hurt her family? What if Jerry helped him? What had she gotten into, just to make a little extra money?

# Chapter 19

"We lost." Alyce's voice was soft and sad. Josie could tell her friend was upset. Alyce didn't bother to say good morning.

"We lost what?" Josie was still foggy from too little sleep and not enough coffee. She tried to focus on Alyce's phone call.

"The battle for Traci's pup," Alyce said.

"What did she do?" Josie asked. It was nine thirty in the morning. It had been a struggle to get Amelia to school. Josie had overslept, then run out of the house without her coffee. She'd never quite caught up, not even after three cups.

"She went over to the dark side and bought a little bichon at that pet store you mystery-shopped," Alyce said. "Pets 4 Luv. Now Traci wants to come here to show us her new pup. She says she's still unpacking and her house is a mess."

"Great." Josie's voice was as bitter as her warmed-over coffee. "Traci asked for our advice and then didn't take it."

"Please, Josie," Alyce said, "don't be rough on her. I'll fix us a little lunch and we can talk. Could you come here about eleven?"

"Sure," Josie said. "What can I bring? Wine? Dessert?"

"Would you stop at a dog store—a good one, not that puppy mill place—and bring treats for Traci's dog?"

Josie swung by the Three Dog Bakery on Ladue Road near the Inner Belt. The long, narrow store featured a display case of artfully arranged dog treats designed to make any human's mouth water. Josie picked out peanut butter "pupcakes"—dog cupcakes with yogurt icing—and "ruffles"—dog truffles. The ruffles were covered with carob, peanuts, and coconut, like real bonbons.

She arrived at Alyce's home in Wood Winds before Traci. "These are too pretty for a dog," Alyce said. She arranged the treats on a little porcelain plate next to a bowl of water.

Traci's arrival was heralded with a chorus of shrill yaps. Josie and Alyce peeked out the front window and watched her wheel a boxy red stroller up the driveway. The nylon stroller was enclosed with black mesh. Traci unzipped it and gathered a fluffy white dog the size of a powder puff into her arms. The tiny dog wore a zebra-striped sweater, red boots smaller than baby shoes, and a red bow in her hair.

Traci's outfit matched. She teetered on red high-heeled boots, which set off her own zebra-striped sweater and skinny black jeans. A red belt accented her dramatic figure.

"Well, aren't you a pair," Alyce said.

"This is my baby," Traci said, petting the puppy. "Her name is Snowball. Not very original, but it fits. She's purebred with the paperwork to prove it. Snowball is a girlie girl and she likes to dress up. I bought us a bunch of matching outfits."

"Her clothes are cute," Josie said, trying a small dash of honesty.

"That's how I got her—through the dog clothes," Traci said. "I saw they were on sale at Pets 4 Luv and figured it wouldn't hurt to look. I saw this little outfit that matched my new sweater. Then I saw Snowball. From the moment I laid eyes on her, I knew she was my dog. The nice saleslady said, 'Hold her in your arms. You don't have to buy her.'

"Snowball felt so warm. She weighs almost nothing and

she fit in the crook of my arm. She licked my nose and snuggled. I just had to have her. Please don't be mad. It's not my fault I fell in love."

Traci looked as endearing as her dog.

"We're not mad," Alyce said. "We just want you to be happy."

"Oh, we are," Traci said. "Snowball is a good dog, even if she acts a little strange."

"How so?" Josie asked.

"Well, she's jumpy. She gets scared when the phone rings and she tries to hide."

"Me, too," Josie said. Alyce frowned at her and she shut up.

"Last night, I had her with me in the great room," Traci said. "The voices on the TV nearly drove the poor thing out of her mind. It was like she'd never heard a TV before. She kept looking around for the people. And she walks funny."

"Is she crippled?" Alyce asked.

"No, watch."

Traci put the pup on the kitchen floor. Snowball looked puzzled, tottered a few steps in her little red boots, and sat down.

"Maybe it's the boots," Josie said.

"No, she doesn't like to walk even without them," Traci said. "She has a whole yard to run and play in, but she won't go outside unless I carry her. I set her down and she sits there. Do you think she's retarded or something? Can you say that about dogs, or is that wrong?"

"The houses here have big yards," Alyce said. "Your little dog probably doesn't feel safe yet in strange surroundings."

"You've barely had her a day," Josie said. "Maybe Snowball needs to get used to her new life. We just got a cat, Harry. It took a while for him to settle in. He lived under the bathtub until he felt it was safe to come out. Harry is fine now. He and my daughter, Amelia, run wild all over the house. They made such a racket yesterday that I couldn't talk on the phone."

"Come sit down in the breakfast room, Traci," Alyce said. "Bring Snowball with you so she feels secure. Josie brought her some special treats."

Alyce unfolded a plush throw rug on the Mexican tile floor near Traci's chair and placed the bowl of water and dish of treats at one end. "These are pupcakes from Three Dog Bakery. And ruffles—doggie truffles."

"They look so elegant," Traci said. "And they're the right size for a little dog."

Snowball sniffed the treats and began chewing on a pupcake.

"She eats fine," Traci said. "So I don't think anything is too wrong, do you?"

"Eating is a good sign," Alyce said. "At least, that's what I've heard. We should eat, too. I have lunch and wine for us."

"Again?" Traci said. "You didn't have to do that."

"I didn't have time to make anything special," Alyce said. "I threw together a warm salad. It's Brussels sprouts with roasted chicken."

"Your 'nothing special' is anyone else's feast," Josie said.

Traci picked at her salad and kept watching her puppy.

Josie ate every bite. "I thought I didn't like Brussels sprouts, but these are wonderful," she said. "Too bad Mom didn't make sprouts like this."

"The secret is walnut oil," Alyce said.

Snowball had finished her food. The puppy was walking in small tight circles no bigger than an old-fashioned LP record.

"That's something else she does," Traci said. "I think it means she's nervous."

"Maybe she needs to see a vet," Josie said.

"I don't know any doctors around here," Traci said.

"I don't have pets," Alyce said. "But I'll be happy to call around the subdivision for you and find out where the neighbors take their dogs."

"I have the name of a vet who makes house calls," Josie said. "He's supposed to be good, but I haven't used him yet. It might be less scary for Snowball if the vet came to your house. I still have his cards." She dug in her purse for one of the cards Nedra had given her that day at the Humane Society.

"I don't know what he charges," Josie said.

"I don't care," Traci said. "If I have money for dog clothes, I have money to get my baby well."

"The vet's fans call him Dr. Ted," Josie said. "Maybe if Snowball doesn't perk up soon, you could call him in a day or two."

"I'm calling him now," Traci said. "If something is wrong, it's better to know right away, so we can fix it. If Snowball is okay, I'll quit worrying. I've never had a puppy before, so I don't know how they're supposed to act. At least my puppy came with a guarantee."

"What kind?" Josie said. "Is it a certificate of health? Will the store pay her vet bills if she gets sick?"

"Let me see," Traci said. "I didn't really read it through. I was so excited, I just dropped it in my purse. It's still in there. Heck, Jimmy Hoffa is probably buried in that purse."

Traci opened a fashionable bag the size of a laundry bag. She pulled out an envelope covered with hearts and paw prints. "That's what Pets 4 Luv gave me. These are Snowball's AKC papers, plus a coupon for dog food. Ah, here's the guarantee. It says—oh, no."

The blood drained from Traci's face, until she was whiter than Snowball. All Josie saw were those bright red lips, as if Traci were bleeding. She read the guarantee slowly, like someone in pain: " 'If your pedigreed puppy dies within thirty days of purchase, Pets 4 Luv will replace it with another dog, free of charge.'"

Two tears trickled from Traci's eyes, leaving a black mascara trail. She picked up her little dog and hugged Snowball until she yelped. "I don't want another puppy," Traci said. "I want this one. And I want her to be well."

# Chapter 20

"Something is wrong with Harry," Amelia told her mo
"He won't play. He just kind of lies there."

Amelia tugged on her dark hair, the way she did v
she was worried, until it stuck out.

Josie smoothed it back into place. "He's a cat, h
They don't do much, period. You've only been home
school a few minutes. Give him time."

"But he likes to jump around and chase ribbons. Ye
day we ran down the hall. Now he won't move. He'
eating. I gave him breakfast and he hasn't touched any c
food all day. And he's not using his litter box."

Uh-oh. Josie knew this could be bad news. What if H
really was sick? More heartbreak for Amelia.

"Where is Harry?" Josie asked.

"Sitting on my bed."

Harry was curled up on the flowered spread. He d
jump off when Josie came into the room. He sat there
stared at her. Was the cat getting used to her, or was h
sick to move? The little brown and black striped an
looked like a bundle of tree roots and shadows on the
ered spread. Josie marveled at the artistry of his desig
permitted her to scratch his soft fur in a circular mo
Josie talked to Harry, telling him how handsome he wa

she examined his skin for wounds or rashes. His coat looked healthy. His green eyes were clear.

But his huge ears, which normally moved at every sound, drooped and were still. Harry looked okay, but felt listless.

"He seems all right," Josie said. "But if he isn't better in a day or so, I'll call the vet."

"Okay." Amelia dragged out her answer to let her mother know she wasn't happy with that decision. "I'll go e-mail Grandpa the picture of Harry and me."

"He'll like that," Josie said. "Grandpa knows about cats. Ask him if Harry needs a vet."

Amelia went to her computer. Josie poured herself more coffee and sat on her new couch. It must be my day for ailing animals, Josie thought, as she sipped another cup. She and Alyce had spent half an hour with the weeping Traci. Finally, Alyce's colorful new neighbor had packed her little dog into its stroller and rolled her home. Traci said she would call the vet, Dr. Ted. She'd left more than three hours ago, and there was no word from her yet.

What if Harry was really sick? Josie wondered. Where am I going to get the money to save Amelia's cat? Vet bills can be almost as expensive as human medical bills. And I owe her school a thousand dollars. Well, I don't care. Harry is worth it. He brought Amelia back to life after her father's murder. I'll do what it takes to get him well, even if I have to sell my new couch.

Josie gave her beige couch a loving pat on its fat bolster. This was the only decent couch she'd ever had. It looked new. She liked its soft, simple style. That should make it easy to resell. Mrs. Mueller might buy it to prevent the shame of a yard sale on her street. I can ask Stan to haul the sofa outside once more, for old time's sake. Too bad that old wreck of a couch is gone. I could have slipcovered it.

Josie felt better once she'd decided to make the ultimate sacrifice for her daughter. That's when Amelia came into the living room carefully balancing a pile of crumpled bills and change in her hands. A nickel slid off and rolled onto the rug.

"What's that?" Josie asked.

"It's all my money," Amelia said, putting it on the coffee table. "We don't have cat health insurance. I saved three hundred eleven dollars and twenty-two cents. You can have it to make Harry well. I know you worry about money a lot."

"Oh, honey, you don't have to spend your own money." Josie blinked back tears. Amelia guarded her stash of birthday and Christmas money the way a miser clung to his gold. She had more in her savings than Josie did.

"If Harry needs a vet, I'll get him one," Josie said. "The money will come from somewhere."

"We can't get it from Grandma. She hates cats," Amelia said.

Josie was too proud to borrow it from Alyce, though her rich friend would lend it without question. She felt sad and guilty that her daughter had to fret about the family finances.

"I want you to enjoy your childhood without worrying about money," Josie said.

"Everybody worries about money," Amelia said. "Even the rich kids at school are having problems. Mason isn't going to Aspen for Christmas. Her family can't afford a ski trip. Jessica got her allowance cut. She used to get twenty dollars a week and now she acts like she's broke on five dollars."

"She is, by her standards," Josie said. "Did she save any of her allowance?"

"She spent it on clothes and junk," Amelia said. "Donna's father lost his job and her mother fired the maid. Donna has to clean her room and change her sheets. You'd think she was a slave or something. I've been doing chores all my life."

Only if I nag you, Josie wanted to say.

"So we all worry about money," Amelia said. "Harry's part of our family and I want to keep him well."

THE FASHION HOUND MURDERS 147

"Me, too," Josie said. "I'm proud that you are so responsible. Put your money away. Taking care of Harry is my job."

Josie was relieved when two phones—her cell and their home line—rang at once, ending that conversation. Amelia checked the home phone display on the living room extension. "It's Grandpa! I'll talk to him."

Josie answered her cell. At first, she didn't recognize the caller's girlish voice.

"It's me, Traci. Alyce's neighbor with the little dog. You told me to call. Is it okay? Are you fixing supper or something? Your vet, Dr. Ted, just left. What a sweetie."

"How is Snowball?" Josie asked.

Now the girlish voice turned sad. "Dr. Ted says you were right. Snowball is a puppy mill dog. He suspected she was raised by that breeder who just got arrested, what's his name?"

"Jonah Deerford. He's out on bail now," Josie said.

"That man better not come around me," Traci said. "He'll be safer in jail. I swear I'll kill him. What he did to my poor little dog was brutal. Do you know why Snowball walks funny? She was cooped up in a wire cage. It didn't have a regular floor. She wasn't let out to run and play. She spent her little puppy life balancing on those wires. When she got tired, her leg fell through the holes in the cage floor. How scary is that?" Josie heard Traci's tears for her dog's pain.

"That's cruel," Josie said.

Traci was wound up now, eager to deliver her news. "You know why Snowball is afraid of the television? Dr. Ted says it's because she never heard a TV before. Can you believe that? She doesn't know what a phone is, either. She's not housebroken because puppy mill puppies just go in their cages. Sometimes they sleep in it."

"I'm so sorry," Josie said.

"Dr. Ted says she's a bright little animal and she likes people, despite what they did to her. Well, one person, anyway. He says if I am patient and loving, I can help her live a normal life. There's nothing physically wrong with her, except she's too skinny, and she has fleas and an ear infection. He gave her medicine for that. He says she's lucky. Some puppy mill dogs are born with deformities or they have rotten teeth. I have to give her a special diet so she can build strong bones and put on weight."

"That's good, I guess," Josie said.

"I know I should have listened to you and Alyce and not bought Snowball. But now I have her and I'm going to make her better. So I guess her story has a happy ending, doesn't it?

"We just have to stop those puppy mills. Dr. Ted hates them. He says puppy mill owners should go to jail. I think prison is too good for them. What if a judge lets them off with a slap on the wrist? It happens, you know. I read it on the Internet. People like Jonah Deerford should die, slowly and painfully."

"Uh," Josie said

Traci was still talking nonstop. "Dr. Ted is working to change the laws. He says people are animals, too, and he doesn't believe in killing them. He wants to make it more difficult to run puppy mills and for the bad puppy breeders to keep the profits. He thinks their money should go to the shelters that rehabilitate the puppy mill dogs and cats. Hit them in the wallet, he says. That's where they really hurt.

"Dr. Ted wants me to write a letter to my state representative saying we need a stricter puppy mill code and the money to enforce it. We have to have more inspections of breeding facilities. I gave Dr. Ted two hundred dollars for his rescue group."

"That's nice," Josie said.

"It's the least I can do," Traci said, with the fervor of a new convert. "That's how much I spent on dog clothes. Dr. Ted works with rescued animals. He also volunteers his time to do low-cost spaying and neutering. He'll even lower his bills if you're in financial need, which I'm not. Isn't he nice?"

"Yes," Josie said.

It's all she could manage before Traci said, "Oops. Look at the time. My husband will be home soon and I haven't started dinner. I have to feed him and my puppy. I just wanted to thank you for suggesting Dr. Ted. I feel so much better about Snowball. If you need a good vet, I recommend Dr. Ted."

"As a matter of fact, I do," Josie said. "I'm glad you called. Thanks for telling me about Snowball." But Traci had already hung up.

Josie was about to call Dr. Ted when Amelia came running into the room.

"Grandpa says Harry could be really sick and we should call the vet. He says he'll pick up the bills. That can be my Christmas present."

"That's not much of a present," Josie said.

"A healthy Harry is the only present I want," Amelia said.

# Chapter 21

"Hunk alert!" Amelia said, peering between the miniblinds out the front window. "Major hottie on the porch."

Josie was horrified to see her daughter had mastered Mrs. Mueller's spying technique. Amelia was lifting a blind by one finger for a better covert view.

"Amelia, what are you talking about?" Josie kept her voice low.

"I think Harry's new vet is about to knock on the door," Amelia whispered. "This dude is sizzlin'."

"Amelia Marcus!" Josie gave her daughter a glare that should have lasered the freckles off her nose. "If you start any of your stupid matchmaking talk, I won't answer the door. If Harry dies, it will be your fault."

A chastened Amelia retreated to her room. Josie opened the door and her eyes widened. Her daughter was right.

Dr. Ted was a hunk. He was a strapping six feet tall. A red plaid lumberjack shirt emphasized his broad chest. His jaw could have been designed with a T-square. He had on jeans and well-worn Timberland boots. Dr. Ted wasn't outrageously ripped like Stan. He was a normal, average hunk with melting brown eyes. And Josie was melting like ice cream in August.

Easy, girl, Josie told herself. Wipe off the drool and reboot your brain. If you fall for this vet, there is definitely something wrong with the man.

"Hi, I'm Dr. Ted. Thank you for the new client."

"Come in," Josie said, pleased she could manage those two words. "I heard from Traci how you helped Snowball."

"I didn't do anything but examine her dog. She's going to have to do most of the work. But I think she has the patience and motivation to work with Snowball."

Modesty. A good quality in a man, Josie thought.

"How can I help you?" Dr. Ted said.

"I'm worried about my daughter's cat." She described Harry's symptoms.

"Could be serious, could be minor," Dr. Ted said. "Won't know until I see the little guy. Do you have a pet caddy?"

"Yes."

"Would you put it outside the door of his room? I don't want to spook him, but I may have to take him to the van for an X-ray."

Josie led Dr. Ted down the hall to Amelia's room. Her daughter was on her bed, petting her lethargic cat. Harry's eyes widened and his ears pricked up, but he stayed there.

Ted deftly turned Harry to expose his belly and expertly probed it with his fingers. "I think the little guy is constipated. He's probably in pain. But I'd like to take an X-ray first."

"Did he break a bone?" Amelia was white with fright.

"No, but pets sometimes swallow strange things. I worked on a dog that ate a needle and a cat that swallowed a plastic bag. Sometimes there's a mass blocking the intestines. I don't think your cat has those problems, but I have to check."

While he talked, Josie handed him the pet caddy. Dr. Ted efficiently packed Harry into it. Harry gave one faint meow and they were out the door. Dr. Ted loped to an oversized blue van. On the side was ST. LOUIS MOBO-PET and a cartoon trio—a dog, a cat, and a bird sitting on the cat's head. Giant letters announced TAKE THE STRESS OUT OF VET VISITS—WE

COME TO YOU. The phone number was the size of a spaniel.
The van was large enough that Dr. Ted could enter without
ducking his head.

"Do you think Harry will be okay, Mom?" Amelia paced
the living room like a worried parent.

"I'm sure Dr. Ted will do his best," Josie said, wishing
she could say something more reassuring.

Dr. Ted was back in ten minutes, carrying a blue gym bag
and Harry's caddy. He was smiling. "Well, that wasn't too
bad," the vet said.

Harry's annoyed meows said otherwise.

"What has your cat been eating?" he asked.

"Cat food," Josie said. "The dry kind. We had a coupon
for a bag of it."

"Any soft food—canned food?"

"No," Josie said. "But the dry food is a good brand."

"I'm sure it is," Dr. Ted said. "Your cat is definitely stopped
up. I brought the materials for an enema. Do you have a bathroom we can use—and a tub?"

"Amelia's bathroom will be fine," Josie said, and showed
him the room. He began unpacking the blue bag.

Amelia opened her mouth to protest, then quickly shut it.

Josie said under her breath, "Your cat, your bathroom."

"Great first date," Amelia whispered. "What are you going to do next time, shoot rats at the dump?"

"It's not a date," Josie hissed. "He's here for your cat."

"Right. That's why he keeps staring at you."

"For that remark, you can also clean up the bathroom,"
Josie whispered.

Josie found a stack of old towels, folded up Amelia's
purple rug, then put down an old one. Amelia talked to Harry,
who was still imprisoned in the caddy. Dr. Ted opened a
prepackaged enema and brought out the cat.

"Is that a Fleet Enema?" Josie asked.

"You can't use the human product for cats. It's too high
in phosphorus. This one is specially designed for felines."

Ted wrapped Harry in an old towel, with only his rear end sticking out. Harry meowed in protest and wiggled around until his head was peeking out and his rear was safely hidden.

After soothing words and a brief struggle, the vet administered the solution, then gave Harry a pat and set him on the floor.

Harry ran for the litter box.

"Let's give him some privacy," Dr. Ted said. They filed out of the room and stood in Josie's living room.

"He should be okay, but if his functions don't resume normally, bring him into my office or give me a call," Dr. Ted said. "You're feeding him good food, but some cats require soft food as well as dry. Give him a few spoonfuls of canned food every day and we may be able to prevent this situation from happening again."

"Thank you," Josie said. "How much do I owe you?"

"Two hundred dollars."

Josie gulped. She hoped she had enough in the bank to write him a check.

"Or you can donate twenty-five dollars to the Humane Society of Missouri and then go out with me for coffee." Amelia pumped her fist in a "yes!" motion.

"I don't want favors," Josie said.

"You're doing me the favor," he said. "Let's go check on Harry."

Amelia ran ahead and peeked into her bathroom. "He's using the litter box."

"Good," Dr. Ted said. "Let's leave him alone. He'll be pretty grumpy for a bit and he may not want you near him, but he'll forgive you when he feels better."

Josie wrote him a check and asked, "Would you like to have that coffee here, Dr. Ted? I have fresh brownies." She didn't add that her daughter had made them.

"Might as well," he said. "I can be here if Harry needs me." He saw the alarm in Amelia's face and said, "Not that

I'm expecting a problem. Now I'd like to wash up, if I could."

"The cat-free bathroom is down the hall on the right, Dr. Ted," Josie said, and prayed she hadn't left any bras hanging in there.

"My name is Ted," he said as he went down the hall.

Josie turned to Amelia. "Go upstairs and visit your grandmother. She'll want to know all about Harry. I'll call you when Ted leaves."

Amelia went upstairs without a word. Josie nuked the brownies and made coffee for Ted. He stood with her in the kitchen and talked. When she started to take the food to the living room, Ted said, "I like the kitchen better."

"I'm not much of a cook," Josie confessed.

"I am," he said. "I like to cook. The kitchen is the heart of the house."

A man who liked to cook. He was perfection. Josie liked that he felt comfortable talking in a kitchen. To her that meant he was good with people. At some of the best parties, the men and women gravitated to the kitchen, where they swapped stories and drank. The stuffed shirts stayed in the living room.

As she set sugar and milk on the table, Josie checked Ted's left hand for a wedding ring or that other deadly giveaway, the white line that signaled a married man on the prowl. She didn't see either, so he was genuinely single, or a good liar.

While Josie poured their coffee, they exchanged the obligatory personal histories. Ted said he was single, with no children, no ex-wives or committed girlfriend—or, in the case of Josie's last serious lover—an ex-girlfriend who should be committed.

"Do you have an aspirin?" Ted asked.

"Are you okay?" she asked. She thought he looked a little pale.

"I'm fine. I think I might be coming down with the flu. I'll probably go home after my shift."

"Do you live nearby?" Josie asked.

"My veterinary clinic is on Manchester Road, about three miles from here," he said. "I live a block behind it with a black Lab and a cat. I take them both to work."

"What kind of cat?"

"Striped. Like your Harry, only orange. Her name is Marmalade. Her owner couldn't afford to pay for her treatment and wanted the cat put down, but I couldn't do it. I liked the cat better than the owner. I offered to forgive the debt, but he wouldn't take her home. Said she ate too much."

"That's so nice of you," Josie said.

"A lot of vets do that," he said. "Besides, Marmalade earns her keep. She's a blood donor. She's saved two cats hit by cars."

"I didn't know you could do that," Josie said.

"My black Lab, Festus, is another donor. He doesn't mind needle sticks, and he gets extra treats for each donation. Festus loves food. My partner, Chris, says I'm making him lazy. That's pretty hard to do. Some Labs are bone lazy and Festus is one of them."

"Your partner, Chris?" Josie was suddenly alert. Was her hunk gay?

"My business partner," he said. "Christine. She's married and has three children, a cockatoo, and a standard poodle."

Josie heard a barking sound. Ted grabbed for the phone in his pocket.

"Sorry," he said to Josie. "That's my cell ring tone. Chris's son programmed it. I have to take this call. I handle mobile emergencies till midnight."

Ted went into the room. Josie could hear him say, "Uh-huh. Uh-huh. What does it look like? Okay, keep Snowball out of the garage. And you stay inside, too. Don't go out and don't turn over that bucket. I'll be there as soon as I can. It could be poisonous. I won't be sure until I see it. I'll have to check if there are any more. I'll be there as soon as I can. No, you don't have to pay me. Consider it an extension of today's visit."

"Sorry, I have to leave," he said. "Traci found a snake in her garage and trapped it under a bucket. It might be poisonous."

"Are you going to kill it?" Josie asked.

"No," he said. "I'll remove it for her. I don't want her—or the snake—getting hurt. Thanks for the brownie. Could I fix dinner next time? I'll call you."

# Chapter 22

"I'll call you."

Those were the three little words Josie wanted to hear from Ted. The only thing that sounded better was his statement, "I'd like to fix you dinner."

A man who cooked. Who was kind to animals. A dude who was "sizzlin'," in Amelia's words. What more could a woman want? All because the cat needed to be unplugged. Thank you, Harry, Josie thought. You've rescued my love life.

Josie was sure she'd never be interested in a man again after she'd refused to marry Mike. Her fling with Stan the Man Next Door was more to please her mother. Stan looked as though he'd stepped off the cover of a romance novel, but he didn't make her heart beat faster. She'd spent more exciting nights with a phone book. She'd been briefly interested in Jerry, but that was another romantic dead end.

But Ted was definitely interesting.

Josie wondered whether Ted really would call her again—and if so, how soon.

Let's be realistic, she told herself. You, Josie Marcus, are not much of a bargain in the marriage market. You're a thirty-one-year-old single mom. You have no money, a lot of debt, and a ten-year-old daughter with a smart mouth. You cannot compete with an unattached twentysomething. You are not exactly Angelina Jolie. Men's jaws don't drop when you enter a room. In fact, your career is shopping at malls without being noticed. And you are very good at that.

So why should Ted look at you twice? Even the brownies you gave him were made by your daughter.

But he did, and he wants to see me again, she thought. Josie wandered happily around her flat like a dazed teen after her first kiss. What would it be like to date a man like Dr. Ted? She'd watched the way he'd handled Harry. Was he as masterful with women as he was with constipated cats?

Cats! Amelia! I promised my daughter I'd call her after the vet left. She was still upstairs with Jane.

Josie dialed her mother's phone. "How are you feeling, Mom?" she asked.

"Better," Jane said. "My arm hurts, but the doctor says it's healing nicely. There's no sign of infection. I felt well enough to give Amelia a cooking lesson. We're making pot roast with carrots and potatoes."

"A perfect winter meal," Josie said.

"I hope so," Jane said. "The weather has been so unseasonably warm lately."

"Mom, I'd eat your pot roast in August."

"Only because you can't cook anything else," Jane said. "Is that man finally gone?"

"Dr. Ted left, if that's who you're talking about," Josie said. "I promised to call Amelia when he did. You can send the kid back down, if you want."

"As soon as dinner is ready. She'll bring you pot roast, potatoes, and carrots. Are you dating that man?" Jane sounded vaguely angry.

"Not yet," Josie said. "Besides, his name is Ted and he's a doctor."

"An *animal* doctor," Jane said. "You don't know what he's been with."

"You make it sound like Ted has fleas," Josie said. "Do you know what he gets for a house call for a cat?"

"It would only upset me to know how much you've spent on that creature. Amelia told me that cat needed an enema. She said you paid good money for it. You could have given it one at home for free."

"Cats don't drink prune juice, Mom," Josie said.

"I meant the old-fashioned way, with an enema bag and soapy water."

"Trust me, Mom, there's no way I could get near Harry with that. It would take four strong men to hold him down."

"I don't know why you insisted on bringing that wild animal into your home in the first place."

Josie didn't usually get angry at her mother. Jane was her free, always-on-call babysitter. Jane picked up Amelia at school whenever Josie needed her. But now something exploded, and Josie lashed out at Jane.

"Because your granddaughter loves that cat. Because she cried herself to sleep for months after her father's funeral. Now she falls asleep with her arm around Harry and wakes up smiling. She talks about all the cute things Harry does. They chase each other around the flat. He's the first creature she's cared about since Nate died. If you love her, you should try to understand that." Josie realized she was yelling at her mother. She didn't bother to apologize.

To Josie's surprise, Jane sounded contrite. "I'm sorry, Josie. You're right. Amelia has been a little cheerier since she got that cat. I don't like cats, but this isn't about me."

Josie thought there must be something wrong with her phone. Jane was actually apologizing. *I should have spoken up sooner,* Josie thought. *I've allowed myself to be a doormat for too long. I know Mom was angry when I came home pregnant with Amelia, but I'm not doing penance for the rest of my life. Amelia is the best thing that ever happened to me.*

"Thanks for understanding, Mom," Josie said. "Send Amelia down with dinner when she's ready. If you need me to help carry the food, give me a ring."

Josie hung up while she was still ahead. And just in time. Her cell rang. This time, Josie recognized the little-girl voice.

"Snowball saved my life," Traci announced dramatically.

Josie couldn't imagine the tiny bichon saving anyone, but she listened to Traci's story.

"After Dr. Ted left, I dressed Snowball in another cute outfit. This one had red polka dots. I went to get her stroller to take her for a walk. I keep it in the garage.

"When I got outside, my little doggie was acting weird. I mean, weird in a different way. She was barking like crazy at the wood we keep stacked in the garage. Alyce said we should keep our firewood outside, but it's too cold to run out there when we want to throw on another log.

"Anyway, Snowball was yapping her head off—even more than usual. I kept telling her to be quiet, but she wouldn't shut up. She stood her ground on the garage floor and barked and barked. I went over to pick her up. That's when I saw a snake's head sticking out behind two split logs. I nearly screamed. We have snakes in South Florida, and I killed one with a shovel once when I lived with Mom in Arizona. But I didn't know anything about Missouri snakes."

Traci paused to take a breath.

"I picked up my little dog and threw her in the house. I was afraid she'd attack that snake. She's very brave, you know. I was going to kill the snake, but I thought I'd better call Dr. Ted."

Josie felt a flash of proprietary jealousy. "I thought you were married," she said.

"I am. But this didn't look like a Florida snake. I was afraid there was a nest of them in that wood pile. What if they thawed out when they got warm and came out of hibernation or something and were all over my garage? I thought I'd better consult Dr. Ted."

"It doesn't hurt that he's cute," Josie added. The words just slithered out.

"Sure doesn't," Traci said cheerfully. "He didn't want me killing the snake. I'd trapped it under a bucket and put a cement block on top. I could hear the snake thrashing around. It was horrible. I ran inside and bolted the door."

"You did?" Josie asked.

"I know, it was stupid. Like the snake could slide under the door. But it was a shock. I wasn't expecting to see a snake in my own garage. We live in a nice neighborhood."

"They have snakes, too," Josie said.

"Well, yes. And rats. Dr. Ted said he was at your house taking care of your cat. Is your cat okay?"

"Harry is fine," Josie said. "It was Dr. Ted I was worried about. He didn't look good. He asked me for an aspirin."

"He drank nearly a bottle of my Pepto-Bismol," Traci said. "He wasn't feeling well, but he helped anyway. Dr. Ted came straight over, just like he promised. He drank some Pepto, then caught the snake with a noose thingy that looked like it would strangle the snake but didn't. Then he put the snake in a special box with airholes. He said the snake was poisonous."

"A copperhead?" Josie asked.

"I'm not sure. I don't know snakes—except the two-legged ones. We had a bunch on our condo board. Dr. Ted drank more Pepto, then took the snake away. I can't tell you how happy I was when he pulled out of our driveway. That snake gave me the creeps.

"Just think. If my little dog hadn't started barking, that deadly snake could have bitten me. I could have died without my Snowball."

Josie heard the tears in Traci's voice. Was the redhead weeping for her dog, for her imagined near death, or simply reveling in the drama?

"You have a hero dog," Josie said. "It's only fair that Snowball saved you. You rescued her from a terrible life."

"Now we're even," Traci said. "Except I'm going to see that nothing bad ever happens to Snowball again. I'll do everything I can to stop people like that awful Deerford man."

"I think the law will take care of him," Josie said.

"That's what Dr. Ted said. I wish I believed him."

"Mom!" Amelia called. "I'm at the back door with two plates. Open up."

"Gotta go," Josie said. "My dinner has arrived."

"Aren't you lucky?" Traci said.

"Yes, I am," Josie said. She helped Amelia set the food on the table. The pot roast was fork-tender. Josie praised her daughter extravagantly.

"I don't like vegetables," Amelia said. "And you don't, either. So why do we like these roasted carrots?"

"Because they don't taste like vegetables," Josie said. "They've been braised in meat juice."

Mother and daughter ate the last of the brownies. While Amelia checked on Harry, Josie cleared away the dishes. She figured it was only fair, since Amelia had cooked supper.

She was tired when she hung the dish towel on the rack and mildly disappointed. It was almost nine o'clock. Josie figured Dr. Ted wasn't going to call tonight. She'd hoped he'd call, but she knew he was busy. She went down the hall to look in on Amelia and Harry.

Her daughter was in bed asleep with Harry in her arms. The cat opened one green eye, then closed it.

Josie smiled. All was well in her small corner of the world.

# Chapter 23

"Mom, look. Harry is having breakfast with me," Amelia said.

The striped cat was balanced on the edge of the kitchen table, his long tail draped over the side. He watched with intense interest as Amelia carefully spread grape jelly on her last bit of toast.

"Amelia, get that cat off the table," Josie said.

"I thought you'd be happy he wasn't scared anymore," Amelia said.

The fearless Harry delicately dipped one paw into Amelia's glass, then licked the milk off the pads on his foot.

"Isn't he cute?" Amelia said.

"Adorable," Josie said. "He's had that foot digging around in his litter box and now he's sticking it in your milk. Maybe I should just pour your milk in the toilet and you can both drink it."

"Mom, that's gross," Amelia whined.

"Not as gross as having a dirty cat foot in your food. By the way, young lady, Harry's litter box is overflowing after his adventures yesterday. You still have time to clean it before you go to school."

"Fine. I'm not hungry anyway," Amelia said. She slammed her milk glass in the sink, picked up Harry, and slung him over her shoulder. "Come on, Harry. Let's go clean your litter box." She stomped out of the kitchen. Harry stared accusingly at Josie as he rode Amelia's shoulder to their shared bathroom.

So much for a sunny winter morning, Josie thought. It's about to turn cloudy and cold. She drove her sulky daughter to school, then spent the day doing dull but necessary chores. She wanted Ted to call her. She jumped every time the phone rang. She stared at it, hoping she could make it ring. But he didn't call that day or the next. Their encounter had seemed so promising. The weekend dragged along without a word from the brown-eyed vet. Harry stayed healthy, so she didn't even have an excuse to call Ted.

But she watched her neighbor Stan and his new love, Abby. The little blonde he'd dumped Josie for drove a powder blue VW. It spent the whole weekend in Stan's drive. Abby was round, shy, and pretty. Stan had said he'd met her in the supermarket checkout line. By the look of her, there must have been a sale on bakery goods. Josie was so embarrassed by that snide thought, she didn't look at Stan's house all Sunday afternoon. She was afraid she was turning into Mrs. Mueller.

By Monday morning, Josie had given up hope of ever seeing Ted again. She sighed, poured herself a second cup of coffee, and turned on the TV news in her bedroom. She nearly dropped her cup when she saw the story on the screen. There was Dr. Ted on television, standing next to his St. Louis Mobo-Pet van. He looked ruggedly handsome in a dark blue flannel shirt.

Uh-oh. The man sticking a black microphone in Dr. Ted's face was a reporter famous for his ambush interviews—Big Ike Ikeman. The station's "I Like Ike" campaign featured a steady procession of flat-voiced folks with bad hair saying, "I like Big Ike because he stands up for the little guy." Most of those "little guys" were somewhere in the neighborhood of three hundred pounds.

Big Ike shared the same shape as his admirers. His hair

was unreal, in all senses of the word. His toupee looked like a squirrel had skittered onto his scalp and died. The fake hair managed to be flat and bushy at the same time. Ike's eyes were small and porky, hidden in pink nests of fat. His smile was mean, especially when he was going in for the kill. He was smiling that way now.

Josie panicked. Poor Ted had walked into a trap, and he was too clueless to know. Maybe she could interrupt the interview with a warning phone call. Josie quickly punched in Ted's number, but her call went straight into voice mail.

Too late, she thought. He'd turned off his cell. Now there was no way to save Ted. She could only watch the disaster unfold. The interview was live, just the way Big Ike liked it.

Ike's smile was as genuine as pleather. "So tell me, Dr. Scottsmeyer, what do you think about the people who run puppy mills?" Ike asked.

"As you know, I've been working to change the law so that puppy mill owners cannot profit from abusing animals." Ted's brown eyes were wide and sincere. "I'd like our legislators to change the Missouri statutes so that millers—people who operate puppy mills—are literally forced to pay for their crimes. Their money should be used to rehabilitate the animals they have mistreated. People should not grow rich hurting innocent puppies and kittens."

So far, so good, Josie thought. But this reporter usually tossed his victims a softball question or two before he played hardball. She tried to send the unwary Ted warning thoughts. Please, please, be careful, she prayed. Ike will torment you the way a bored cat toys with a mouse. Then he'll pounce and destroy you.

"Do you know an Edna Prilosen?" Ike asked.

"No, I don't think so." Dr. Ted looked so innocent, so clueless.

"Yet you were taped at her funeral only a short time ago."

While Ted fumbled for an answer, a video showed mourners filing out of a church behind a dark wood casket. An arrow pointed to Ted escorting an older woman wearing a black hat and coat.

"Do you often go to the funerals of women you don't know?" Ike asked.

"Oh! Edna," Ted drew out the name.

"How many Ednas do you know?" Big Ike asked.

"Only one. Edna was my mom's bridge partner. I took Mom to the funeral because she was too upset to drive herself."

"Do you forget murder victims' names so easily?" Ike asked.

Now the grainy, gray video of Edna's horrific hit-and-run was on the screen, this time without any warning about the content. Poor Edna was pursued by the pickup truck, knocked down, and dragged along the parking lot. Josie winced at the brutal video and hoped Edna's bereaved mother wasn't watching.

"I didn't forget Edna," Dr. Ted said. "I just didn't remember her."

"Isn't that the same thing?" Ike asked.

"Look, I mean no disrespect to the poor lady," Ted said. "Edna was a good friend of my mom's, but I barely knew her." Ted sounded angry and defensive. He was scrambling for an answer. Even to Josie, his excuse sounded lame.

"Did you know her well enough to avenge her death?"

"Her death! I don't believe in killing anybody—or anything."

Ted looked tired and unwell. Had he been sick with the flu for the last three days? Josie wondered. Was he too groggy to defend himself against Ike's attacks?

Big Ike gave his famously insincere smile and abruptly switched topics, another trick to lure his victims into feeling safe. "We have a recent case where a Wildfern man was arrested for running a puppy mill. If convicted, he faces jail time for cruelty to animals. Do you think we should fill our already-overcrowded prisons with people who raise puppies?"

Another softball. Josie held her breath.

"As I understand it, Jonah Deerford didn't raise puppies," Ted said. "He bred them under cruel conditions. Society will be dealing with the damage this man has done for years."

"How so?" Ike asked.

"Homes will have to be found for the rescued puppies. More than a hundred puppies will have to be fed and sheltered. Many of the dogs will need special foster and medical care. That man did a lot of damage. If you ask me, jail is too good for him."

"How about the death penalty?" Ike said.

The camera moved in on Ted's face. "I'm not sure what you mean." He looked puzzled.

Josie dug her nails into her palms. This was it. Ike was going for the kill.

Big Ike smiled again. "I mean the man was bitten by a deadly snake and died. The late Jonah Deerford was the number-one police suspect in the death of Edna Prilosen. Police believe that is his truck in the video tape. They found the killer mobile on his property. And by the way, I wasn't the first to mention Jonah Deerford's name in this interview."

Ike pointed dramatically at Ted as his squirrel rug slipped over one eye. "You were. You knew his name."

"Huh?" Ted looked surprised and completely lost.

"Where were you yesterday?"

"I was sick. I had the flu. I've been out of commission the last three days."

"And before that?"

"I was on call for my clinic. I helped a woman with a sick cat and another lady who had a little dog."

"And did you do something else at the home of the woman with the dog named Snowball?" Ike asked. "The Wood Winds dog owner?"

"My patients' medical histories are confidential," Dr. Ted said.

"Not in the state of Missouri. That's one law you haven't managed to change. Did you rescue a snake and take it away from the home of Snowball's owner? A poisonous snake?"

"I—"

"It can't be too confidential, doctor. Your patient's owner told half the subdivision. One public-spirited neighbor called me. Come, doctor. Haven't you said before that snakes are our friends?" Ike asked.

"Yes," Ted said, relieved to return to a subject he understood. "I've often said that snakes have a useful place in the ecosystem. I believe we must treat them with respect. The public is starting to understand the importance of snakes, thanks to increased education. I tell people if they find a strange snake in their yard, say a copperhead or a rattlesnake, don't kill it. Call me and I'll take it away and put it in a safe environment."

"So you took a poisonous snake out of a subdivision and what? Turned it loose on Jonah Deerford?"

"That's not true. I let it loose in the wild, away from hiking trails and bicycle paths, where it can live in its natural habitat. Snakes kill mice, rats, and other vermin so we don't have to resort to harmful, destructive pesticides. But I never advocated that snakes be used for murder."

Ike's white teeth shone like bathroom tiles. "Interesting, doctor. I never said Jonah Deerford was murdered. But the police believe he was. Did one of your slimy 'friends' kill him?"

"No!" Ted said. "That's absolutely wrong. Snakes aren't slimy."

Josie groaned. Ted would call her, all right. From the county jail.

# Chapter 24

Big Ike's vicious attack on Dr. Ted was followed by a "special report" on the death of Jonah Deerford. First a skillful stabbing, Josie thought. Then murder.

"Accused animal abuser Jonah Deerford was found dead yesterday at the Wildfern farm where he had his kennels," the blond news anchor intoned.

Josie turned up the sound on her television. The news anchor said, "A UPS driver saw Jonah Deerford sitting in his pickup outside his trailer home. The driver tapped on the window to get Mr. Deerford's signature. When the victim did not respond, the driver called the police."

A B-roll festival followed. Josie watched sick puppies being carried out by solemn rescue workers. Then two small, shivering boys wrapped in blankets that hid their faces were helped into officials' cars. It ended with the inevitable body-bag shot. The paramedics had trouble wheeling the stretcher along Jonah's rutted yard to the ambulance.

The video switched to a slow pan of a dark gray pickup. A woman in a crime-scene jumpsuit was kneeling by the truck's right-front bumper, dusting it with a small brush. DEATH TRUCK was the caption on the screen.

"Animal control officers were called to the scene when police spotted a brightly colored snake in the pickup with the deceased," the news anchor said. "The snake was alive. Fortunately, the police did not open the truck to investigate. Animal control officers captured the rare reptile, and it was taken to the St. Louis Zoo. No one else at the scene was injured."

A photo of a snake with red, yellow, and black bands flashed on the screen. Josie thought the exotic creature was pretty, for a snake.

"A herpetologist says the reptile is believed to be a deadly coral snake. The coral snake is not native to Missouri. The expert says the coral snake is not aggressive and does not attack unless stepped on or otherwise handled. Police found bite marks on Mr. Deerford's neck and wrist. There is usually little or no swelling or pain associated with the bite, and symptoms can be delayed for up to twelve hours. The victim may not have been aware of the attack. The bite feels 'faint as a pinprick and people may not know they've been bitten,' the herpetologist said.

"The last reported coral snake death occurred in the United States in 2008 in Bonita Springs, Florida. An autopsy will be . . ."

Jonah Deerford was dead. The man who starved his sons and profited from mistreating puppies had been murdered. He couldn't come after Josie or her family now. Josie thought she would feel relieved at the news, but she didn't know if there were more members of the puppy mill ring out there. What about Jerry? Or Paul? And how did poor Dr. Ted get pulled into this mess?

Josie's cell rang. She heard a little-girl voice wailing, "It's all my fault. I ruined Dr. Ted."

"Hello? Who is this? What happened?" Josie asked.

"It's me, Traci. Alyce's neighbor with the little dog." Josie heard sniffling, followed by a small, shrill bark. "I destroyed that sweet man after he helped me. I didn't know. I didn't know." The voice dissolved into incoherent crying blended with a chorus of yaps.

"Mom!" Amelia stood in the bedroom door, with Harry

at her side. "I'm going to be late for school. We have to leave now."

Josie had lost track of the time. "Traci, I'm so sorry, but I can't talk to you," Josie said. "I have to get my daughter to school. Don't sit home alone. Go straight to Alyce's house. I'll join you as soon as I can. Yes, it's okay if you see Alyce this early in the morning. Her little boy, Justin, wakes up around six. Don't cry. Whatever you've done, I'm sure it can be fixed."

"You promise?" Traci asked, sounding even more girlish. Another tear storm threatened.

"Absolutely. Put on your prettiest outfit, pack up Snowball, and I'll be there as soon as I drop off Amelia. If she's late to school, we're both in trouble. Bye."

Amelia handed Josie her coat and purse. "Come on, Mom."

They ran for the car together. Once inside, Josie gave her daughter the cell phone. "Call your aunt Alyce and keep her on the line until I get to a red light." In Josie's world, good friends were transformed into honorary aunts and uncles. It was old-fashioned, but it worked. Mrs. Mueller was not and never would be an honorary aunt.

Alyce must have answered the phone immediately. "Aunt Alyce," Amelia said, "Mom says I should keep talking to you until she gets to a red light. Harry is fine. He's so cute. Do you know that a cat's ears . . ."

Amelia happily detailed the wonders of her cat as Josie rolled through three green lights. Damn, she thought. There was never a red light when you needed one. She was halfway to the Barrington School before she finally came to a red light. Amelia handed her the phone. "Alyce, Traci's on her way over to your house," Josie said. "She should be there any minute. Something's wrong, but she was too upset to tell me. All I know is Jonah Deerford, the puppy abuser, is dead, and that idiot Big Ike ambushed Dr. Ted on TV this morning. Traci thinks it's her fault. No, I don't know why. The light is turning green. Gotta go. I'll be there as soon as I can."

She handed the phone to Amelia and concentrated on the drive to school. They made it with minutes to spare.

"Out you go." Josie kissed her daughter on the forehead. It was only 7:58 a.m. and she was exhausted already.

She turned on the radio and heard more news about Jonah's death. A man identified as a "police official" said, "We are investigating Mr. Deerford's death as suspicious. Coral snakes are not native to Missouri. We believe someone deliberately put the deadly reptile in Mr. Deerford's pickup truck where it would attack him."

Good, Josie thought.

A news commentator added, "Ironically, the murder suspect was found dead in the very weapon the police believe he used to kill Edna Prilosen."

What? Josie was glad she was sitting at a red light when she heard that news.

"Mr. Deerford's pickup has been identified as the one in the Pets 4 Luv security video hit-and-run. DNA tests are expected to confirm that the truck was used to kill the victim, who worked at the pet store."

Poor Edna died for reporting Deerford's cruelty and greed. It wasn't fair.

The trip to Alyce's house took longer than Josie expected. Now that she didn't need one, she hit every red light on the road. Jane called while she was stopped at one.

"Josie, did you see the news about that puppy mill man?" her mother asked.

"Sure did. Jonah Deerford was murdered, Mom. Couldn't happen to a nicer guy."

"Mrs. Mueller called me. She's sure that's the dark truck she saw prowling the alley the night before that dog attacked me. She wanted the phone number of that nice young policeman who shot the dog. I kept his card. She talked with him and he said she was probably right."

"That's good, Mom. I hope you feel safer now," Josie said. "The light's turning green. I have to go."

Forty minutes later, Josie was waved through Wood Winds' security gate. She parked in Alyce's drive, stepped around Traci's red dog stroller, and knocked on the side door.

"Come in, Josie," Alyce called. Snowball yapped.

Alyce's kitchen smelled of hot coffee and warm cinnamon. She handed Josie a plate with a slab of coffee cake on it. Josie followed her friend to the sunny breakfast room. Snowball and Traci were dressed in matching pink turtleneck sweaters. She held her little dog on her lap and stroked her white fur for comfort. Traci's red hair was a raging fire.

"Amy the Slut's been at it again," Alyce said. She held her cake fork like a dagger. "I swear I'll kill her myself one day."

"You'll do the world a service," Josie said. "But you'll need something sharper. Maybe that fancy roasting fork."

"It's due any day," Alyce said. "Amy better not be around when it arrives."

"Traci, what happened?" Josie asked.

Traci mopped her tear-streaked face with a wad of tissues. "It's all my fault," she said. Snowball gave another sharp bark.

Alyce interrupted. "Now, we've already been through that. You know it's not true. Start again from the beginning, and don't cry. You'll only upset Snowball."

Traci took a deep breath, gulped, and said, "After Dr. Ted left in his van with that awful, poisonous snake, I took Snowball for a walk in her stroller. I needed to get out of the house and away from the garage. That snake gave me the creeps."

"What color was it? Did it have red, yellow, and black stripes, or was it more brown and black?" Josie asked.

"I don't know. I only saw the head sticking out and the light wasn't good. It looked snaky. I was too busy keeping

Snowball from attacking it. Anyway, I was coming down the street when I was stopped by a blond lady. She was wearing a tight black catsuit and really high heels. I guess I should talk—these are pretty high, too." She indicated her black spikes. "But I don't know how she could walk in them. She looked like a South Beach dominatrix."

"That's Amy," Alyce said. "Dresses like a pro but gives it away." She was no fan of Amy's.

"Well, she seemed very sweet," Traci said. "She told me that Snowball was cute and admired my dog's little red boots. She invited me to her house for a drink. I went because nobody in this subdivision talks to me, except Alyce. We drank martinis. They were strong."

Alyce snorted.

"After I finished one, Amy asked who the hottie in the blue van was and how I got him to my house twice in one day. She acted like I'd been hitting on Dr. Ted. I said I was married."

"That's never stopped Amy," Alyce said.

"I told her Dr. Ted was there on business and he was a veterinarian. The first visit he took care of my dog. Then he took away a poisonous snake. I told her all about the snake. I didn't know it would hurt him. I grew up in a tough section of Miami, and she didn't seem like any of the troublemakers I knew there. I thought people were nicer in the Midwest."

"Traci is suffering from the delusion that Midwesterners are kinder and gentler than people on the East Coast," Alyce said.

"Well, you've been kind to me!" Traci burst out. "Both of you. And Dr. Ted, too. How was I to know?"

Tears were threatening again, and she squeezed her little pup tightly. Snowball gave a yip, and Traci patted a furry white ear. "Sorry, baby, I didn't mean to upset you.

"I feel like I should cover Snowball's ears for this next part," Traci said. "But I'm pretty sure she doesn't understand what I'm saying. Amy said, 'Hmm. A hottie who makes house calls. Well, well. I have a pussy he should check out.' I thought she had a cat. I really did."

"She didn't say that!" Josie said. "Even for her, that's gross. If it were any woman but Amy the Slut, I wouldn't believe it."

"Everyone in this subdivision knows her—many in the biblical sense," Alyce said. "She said she had sex with my husband."

Amy claimed to have bedded every man in Wood Winds. She had the kind of body that made a faithful wife doubt her husband's virtue. A man Josie trusted once said Amy wasn't quite the femme fatale she led people to believe. He said as many men turned her down as accepted her favors. But for Amy, half the fun was stirring up trouble.

"Let me guess," Josie said. "Amy called Dr. Ted, he arrived in his van, and she made a pass at him. Ted turned her down and she got even by calling Big Ike."

"I don't know for sure," Traci said. "But I do know he was out of her place awfully fast. Too fast to look at any animal."

"Oh, he saw that bitch, all right," Alyce said.

"Alyce!" Josie said.

# Chapter 25

On the way home from Alyce's house, Josie stopped at a supermarket to buy Harry's soft canned food. The choices seemed overwhelming, from free-range turkey to ocean fish.

Was ocean fish better than just plain seafood? she wondered. Some brands were all natural. What were the others? Unnatural? Was organic better than all natural? Was cat food in a pouch softer than the canned variety?

Was one healthier than the other? What if the cat didn't like what Josie bought? Her financial life depended on her choice. She wouldn't accept more charity from Ted if Harry got stopped up again.

She stared at the selections, as if the answer were sitting on the shelf. Instead, it was in her purse.

What is this? she lectured herself. Are you a 1950s high school girl? Quit waiting for Ted to call. Give him a ring.

Ted's cell phone was busy. It stayed that way three more times. On the fourth try, she reached him.

"Josie!" He sounded happy to hear her voice. "I'm glad you called after . . ." His voice skidded to a stop.

"After what?" she asked.

"After I made a complete fool of myself on television this morning."

"Why do you think that?"

"I sounded like a murderer."

"Don't be ridiculous. Everyone knows Ike Ikeman is a bully. Nobody believes a word he says."

"Three people did," Ted said. "They told me to keep my snake-loving self away from their dogs."

"Ted! That's so wrong."

"The practice will survive without them," Ted said. "But it still hurts. How's Harry?"

"He seems fine," Josie said. "You said to get soft food. I can't figure out what kind to buy. Do cats like turkey, chicken, or fish flavor?"

"Depends on the cat," Ted said. "Why don't I drop by some sample cans tonight? That is, if you still want to see me."

"I'd definitely like to see you," Josie said.

"Good. May I cook dinner for you and Amelia? That way, I can feed the whole family."

"You've had a bad enough day without cooking."

"Josie, I like to cook. It helps me relax."

Josie had heard people say that before. She gave them the same credibility as the health nuts who claimed "a brisk morning workout gives me energy for the rest of the day." But Ted seemed sincere.

"If cooking helps you relax," Josie said, "you are welcome to chill out and cook dinner at my house."

"How do you feel about mushroom chicken marinara?" Ted said.

"Love it. But remember, I have a very basic kitchen."

"I'll bring the fixings over about five. We can sit in your kitchen and talk while the sauce simmers."

"Do you drink wine or beer?" Josie asked.

"Beer. Any kind. As long as it's cold."

Josie stopped by the Schlafly Bottleworks, Maplewood's brew pub. She decided Ted would need something hearty after his illness and on-camera ordeal, and bought six bottles of oatmeal stout. Then she added a six-pack of Scotch ale, and since the holidays were heading their way, one of Christmas stout. She stopped abruptly. A fridge full of beer, even locally brewed, might make a man wonder about her.

Once home, Josie buzzed around her flat, dusting and vacuuming. She picked her laundry out of the bathroom. She polished the kitchen. She dug out her meager supply of pots and pans and her pathetic collection of kitchen tools, and wished she had some of the culinary wonders from Alyce's kitchen. A nice mandoline, maybe, to slice the mushrooms. Or a citrus trumpet to juice the lemons.

When Josie was growing up, her mother had encouraged her to go to baseball games "so you will have something to talk about with your date."

I should have stayed in the kitchen with Mom, she thought. Then Ted and I could talk about food. Well, we can still talk about food, and I can certainly eat it, but we can't have a serious culinary conversation.

Josie's cleaning burst was interrupted by a phone call from Jerry. She'd almost forgotten about the hangdog owner of Chloe the Humane Society pup.

"Josie, did you see the news about poor Jonah?" he asked.

Poor Jonah? That man was a murderer and puppy abuser. Josie bit back her angry words. It would take Jerry a long time to understand his friend's crimes. There was no point adding to his pain.

"I'm terribly sorry for your loss," she said. That was true. Jerry had lost his friend twice—the imaginary Jonah and the real one. It would be doubly hard for him when he finally understood who Jonah was—if Jerry was innocent. She wasn't sure anymore. She wasn't sure about anything. But she didn't want to get involved with Jerry until she knew more about the man.

"Uh, I was wondering if you'd like to go for a walk with

Chloe and me tonight when I get home from work. It's a nice warm day."

"I'm sorry, Jerry," Josie said. "I'll have to take a rain check. I'm busy."

Permanently busy, she thought as she hung up. She hoped Jerry and Chloe would keep walking out of her life.

She checked the kitchen clock. Another half hour before she picked up Amelia. Josie set the table with a bright yellow tablecloth and napkins, then for a centerpiece used a cheerful pot of purple hyacinth from the supermarket. She started to get out her candleholders, then nixed that idea. Candles might send the wrong signal.

The house shone by the time she left for the Barrington School that afternoon. Amelia was having one of her almost-adult days. "You look nice," she said. "What's happening?"

"Ted is fixing dinner for us and bringing by food for Harry," Josie said.

"So do you want me to disappear upstairs to Grandma's?" Amelia asked.

"No, Ted wants to make dinner for both of us. Stick around."

"You need a chaperone," Amelia said.

The kid was way too smart, Josie thought. "No, I don't need a chaperone. But I don't want it to look too romantic too soon."

"Yeah, that litter box last time would get any man hot," Amelia said.

"That's enough." Josie bit her lip to keep from laughing.

Ted was on the front porch at 5:01 with a small cooler balanced on a big cardboard box. He held the cooler steady with his chin.

"I see you've taken my warning about my hopeless kitchen seriously," Josie said.

"I brought a few pots and prep tools," Ted said. "I hope you don't feel insulted."

"You can't insult my cooking," Josie said, removing the small cooler.

"Let me put this down on the kitchen counter and we'll check on Harry," Ted said.

The cat was lounging on Amelia's spread. When he saw Dr. Ted in the doorway, Harry's eyes grew wide and he made a dash to disappear under the bed.

"Oh, no you don't, big fellow." Ted captured the squirming Harry. The cat's back claws came out and slashed Ted's wrist.

"Oh! You're bleeding," Josie said.

"It's just a scratch, ma'am," Ted said, imitating an aw-shucks cowboy. "That's quite a set of steak knives your cat has. Now, Mr. Harry, let's resume our exam."

The vet carefully probed Harry's midsection. "Belly feels nice and soft. I'd say his system is working again."

"Definitely. I had to clean out his litter box," Amelia said.

Ted gently set Harry down on Amelia's spread. The cat slid down the side and slunk under her bed, his body low to the floor.

"Harry," Amelia called, "come on out. It's okay."

"He'll appear when he feels safer," Ted said. "Right now, I'm the scary dude who stuck him in the rear end. Let's leave him alone and go out to the kitchen to look at food."

Ted unpacked three cans of Hill's Science Diet—turkey, chicken, and fish.

"Any of these should work," Ted said. "Just give him one spoonful in the morning and another at dinner."

"What about milk?" Amelia asked.

"Cats need protein, even more so than dogs. Adult cats should not have a lot of milk, or you'll be doing more litter box duty."

"What if he won't eat the soft food?" Josie said. "Cats can be stubborn."

"Don't negotiate with him," Ted said. "Take away his dry food. Put down a spoonful of this wet stuff and don't feed him anything else until he eats it. No dry-food dessert until he finishes his fish."

"Isn't that cruel?" Josie asked.

"Is it cruel to make your daughter do what's good for her?"

"She thinks so, but I don't."

"Cats are too practical to starve." Ted tore back the top on the minced seafood entrée. A smell redolent of Dumpsters in August rolled out of the can.

"Ew," Amelia said. "That's stinky. What is it?"

"Fish lips," Ted said. "I don't know exactly. But to a feline nose, it's as delicious as a burger and fries to you."

Amelia spooned some into a bowl and carried it to the corner of the kitchen floor where Harry's food and water were kept now.

"Let me wash up," Ted said, "and we'll switch to the more pleasant pastime of cooking our dinner." Josie found a tube of Neosporin for the cat scratch on his wrist. It didn't look bad once Ted had washed off the blood.

For the next hour, Ted worked on dinner while Amelia watched.

"What can I do to help?" Josie asked.

"Talk to me," he said.

He sautéed mushrooms and chopped fresh basil for the pasta sauce. He added canned tomatoes and strips of chicken breast. While he cooked, Ted sipped oatmeal stout and poured a dollop into the tomato sauce. "Improves the flavor," he said. He took another drink. "Improves the cook."

Ted unpacked a chocolate cake with a cherry on top. "Here is dessert. This is an old family recipe."

"'Schnucks Bakery,'" Amelia said, reading the box's label.

"Gee, is that right?" he said. "I guess Mom always took

it out of the box first when she brought it home from the supermarket."

Amelia giggled. She enjoyed having a good-looking man in the house. So did Josie.

Josie was mortified when Ted pulled a saucepan out of the box to boil the angel hair pasta.

"Even I have one of those," Josie said.

"Ah, but this is a very special saucepan," Ted said. "Imported from Manchester. Manchester Road, that is."

He drained the pasta, returned it to the pot, and added half the sauce. Then he checked the garlic bread in the oven.

"Madam," he said to Josie, "if you will remove the garlic bread, dinner will be served." Josie transferred the bread to a napkin-lined basket.

Ted tossed the pasta and sauce, poured it onto three plates, and added the remainder of the sauce.

"Voilà!" he said, and waved his wooden spoon with a flourish.

"Yum," Amelia said.

"Sit down and tell me if it's any good."

Josie took a forkful. "This is delicious. I don't want to ruin your dinner, but what's been the fallout from today's show?"

"Chris, my partner, called me an idiot and said I should have known any interview with Big Ike would be an ambush. But I never watch Ike. How would I know? Besides, I didn't do anything wrong, so I thought I had nothing to fear. Guess Chris was right. I am an idiot. She wouldn't let me drive the van. She says I've made Mobo-Pet notorious by defending snakes. She wants me to get rid of Jack."

"Who's Jack?" Josie asked.

"My scarlet king snake. Jim, a herpetologist friend, found him on a camping trip in Florida and gave him to me. Jack is less than two feet long, but he's pretty. His body is striped with bands of red, black, and yellow. He looks almost like the deadly coral snake. Fortunately, Jim knew the difference."

"Is that the kind of snake that killed Jonah Deerford?" Josie asked.

"Close. There's a rhyme that goes: 'If red touches yellow, it can kill a fellow. If red touches black, it is a friend of Jack.' The coral snake has the red, yellow, and black pattern. The harmless scarlet king snake is red, black, and yellow. That's why I named my king snake Jack."

"I don't think I could remember that rhyme if a snake was staring me in the face," Josie said.

"Me, either," Ted said. "But the scarlet king snake has a good disguise. Most creatures run when they see it. Jack is useful in the wild. He pays his way by eating rodents and small lizards. I bring him along on my lectures. Now my partner, Chris, wants him out of the waiting room, even though Jack can't hurt anyone. She says he's too notorious."

"Are you going to take him home?"

"I'll have to," Ted said. "But Marmalade will have a fit. That cat hisses at poor Jack every time she passes him at the clinic."

Josie saw a blur out of the corner of her eye. Harry was braving the kitchen, even with his enemy present. He scooted across the floor, keeping his body so low he looked like a fur snake. Harry sniffed the new food in his bowl, then ate it heartily. He finished quickly and sat back on his haunches to take a bath, carefully licking his paws, and then his enormous ears.

"Look, he's starting to feel relaxed," Amelia said. "He came into the room even though you were here, Ted. He ate all his food. Good boy, Harry."

Josie tried to distract the cat by making dog noises. She whined and woofed softly. Harry put his ears back but refused to run off.

"You make a good dog," Ted said. "I mean that in a nice way." Barking sounds came from his pocket, and Ted took out his cell.

"Sorry," he said. "That's my partner, Chris. I'd better take this."

He wandered into the living room. First Josie heard only the low, singsong tones of greeting. Then Ted's voice got higher and louder.

"What! They killed Jack! Why? What do you mean he was shot while trying to escape? I'll be right there."

# Chapter 26

Ted sprinted out the door, leaving behind his dishes, his dinner, and two dazed females.

"Is he gone?" Amelia asked. "He roared out of here like Iron Man."

"He sure is," Josie said. "I know it wasn't the food. He did the cooking."

Josie found her coat and began buttoning it. "Have you seen my purse?"

"Where are you going, Mom?" Amelia asked.

"To Ted's office." Josie located her purse in her bedroom.

"What can you do for him?"

"Get Ted a lawyer if he needs one. I can ask Alyce's husband to recommend one, if it comes to that."

"Why would he need a lawyer?" Amelia asked.

"I heard the words 'killed' and 'shot while trying to escape.'"

"Do you think we had dinner with a murderer?" Amelia's eyes were bright with interest.

"We most certainly did not," Josie said. "But it's smart to take precautions if the police are involved." What am I teaching my daughter? Josie wondered. I've had way too many unhappy encounters with the law.

"Is Jack a person or a snake?" Amelia asked.

"I don't know. Either way, it sounded like trouble."

Josie hauled out the phone book and looked up Ted's office address. Terrific. It was in Rock Road Village. She hoped Rock Road Detective Gray wasn't at the scene of Jack's killing.

"I'm calling your grandmother to come down now and watch you," Josie said.

"I can take care of myself," Amelia said. "I'll go to bed." She started down the hall to her room, making a comic pantomime of walking. "See?"

"I saw you do that the last time I trusted you home alone for a few minutes. Then you sneaked out of the house."

"Mom, I was only nine then. I'm ten now."

"Big whoop," Josie said.

"You sound like Miley Cyrus. She's stupid."

"Well, we agree on something. You know why you can't be here by yourself, Amelia Marcus? Remember that little problem with the wine coolers when you took your midnight stroll? You've forfeited my trust, young lady. The answer is no."

Amelia flopped down on the new couch and stuck out her lower lip.

Josie dialed her mother's number. "Would you mind keeping an eye on Amelia for an hour or so? It's an emergency, or I wouldn't ask. No, no, nobody's sick. I just have to leave for a little while. No, this won't turn out to be all night like last time. I'll explain why later. I'll send your granddaughter upstairs in a few minutes. You'll come down? Oh, Mom, you're an angel. I agree, it's better for Amelia to sleep in her own bed."

There was a brief silence while Josie listened. "Okay, I'll make sure she locks the cat in her room, but he wouldn't hurt a fly. Or a fish. Yes, Mom, I know what happened to Siegfried and Roy, but we're talking about a tiny cat, not a tiger. Yes, yes, they had the same ancestors. Harry does have tiger stripes, but he's the abridged version of a ferocious feline. And he's declawed. Mom, I promise Harry will be locked up. Your ankles are safe."

Josie softened her voice. Her mother really was doing her a favor. Jane just hated cats, that's all. She couldn't help it. "And thanks."

Josie hung up. "You heard that, Amelia. Grandma will come down here and watch television. Please keep your door shut and keep the cat in your room."

"Oh, Mom," Amelia said, stretching the title into several syllables. "Harry's harmless."

"I know he is," Josie said. "Now you have to convince your grandmother. Meanwhile, close your door, please, and make sure he doesn't escape."

Josie watched her daughter flounce off to her room, then heard Amelia's door slam. Josie was annoyed, but let the gesture go. She put on her gloves and waited until she heard her mother walking down the back steps.

"Bye!" she called. "Love you!"

Josie was out the door and off to Rock Road, the scene of some of her life's biggest disasters. Nate had died here. Poor Edna had been murdered at that awful store. This time, things would go well. There was no such thing as a jinxed town.

She had no trouble finding the St. Louis Mobo-Pet office. A carnival of flashing blue, red, and white lights bounced off the one-story building's pale walls.

In the parking lot, Josie spotted two Wildfern police cars, several aggressively anonymous cars that practically shouted "unmarked police vehicles," and a horde of uniform and plain-clothes cops.

She also saw her Rock Road nemesis, Detective Gray, lurking among the blue uniforms. In the middle of the chaos stood Ted, guarded by a thin, angular woman with straight dark hair pulled into a ponytail. She wore green scrubs and had her arms folded across her flat chest. Josie suspected this was his veterinary partner, Christine.

Josie parked her car down the street and walked to the edge of the scene, careful to avoid the moiling cops.

Ted was talking way too loud. He sounded upset. "But you didn't have to kill him," he said in a sorrowful voice.

"We were acting on an informed tip that you had a dangerous reptile in your office, as well as other material connected with the murder of Jonah Deerford," a young uniformed officer answered. The bright, whirling lights illuminated his baby-fine blond hair and the peach fuzz on his cheeks. "A walk-in visit confirmed that a suspect reptile was sitting in an aquarium in the waiting room where anyone could access it."

A suspect reptile? Josie hid her head in her hands so the baby cop couldn't hear her snorting laugh.

"Why didn't you just take the aquarium?" Ted asked. "The snake couldn't get you through the glass."

"We tried, but a black Labrador retriever galloped straight at us."

"Festus can be territorial," Ted interrupted. "He didn't bite you, I hope?"

"No, he hit me with a glancing blow, causing me to drop the aquarium," the young officer said. "It broke. The snake got loose. At that point we heard a threatening hiss."

"That was my cat," Ted said. "Marmalade always hisses at the snake."

"We didn't see a cat," the officer said. "We heard a threatening hiss, and the snake charged us."

"Charged!" Ted said. "Snakes don't charge."

"This one moved very fast, sir, and it was headed straight toward me. I dispatched it with a single shot to the head."

"And now Jack's dead," Ted mourned. His partner, Chris, tugged Ted's sleeve, possibly trying to shut him up.

"I'm sorry, sir." The officer sounded sorry, but Josie suspected it was because he was about to become a department joke. She could see the older officers trying to hide their grins while he told his tale. The young officer would probably have to endure rubber reptiles in his locker, and hear meows, hisses, and yells of "Charge!" when he walked down the station's halls. If he was lucky, he might avoid a nickname like "Snake Eyes." Cops loved to play pranks on their own.

"But it was only a snake," the officer protested. His face and the tips of his downy ears were as red as the suspect serpent.

"No, you don't understand," Ted said. He was in full martyr mode, dying to make the world believe that snakes were our friends. "Jack was a good snake, a useful snake. He never hurt anything in his life, except rats. If you were a rat, officer, Jack would have been a problem. Otherwise, you were quite safe."

Josie swore she heard more suppressed snorts from his brother officers. Oops, she thought. After that speech, rubber rats would be added to the young officer's torments.

Josie couldn't take any more. She had to save the innocent Ted from himself. She pushed past the crowd of smirking cops and called, "Ted! Are you okay?"

"Josie!" he said. "You followed me here."

"Why, Miss Marcus, what a surprise to see you here." Detective Gray, dreary and dangerous, stepped between them. His voice was full of mock courtliness. "My colleague Detective Winston Dixie wants to meet you. He's on the Wildfern force."

Detective Dixie gave her a small nod, which was about all he could manage with all those chins.

"Winston Dixie?" Josie said.

"Go ahead," Winston said. "Get the jokes out of the way. My nickname is Win Dixie and my mama didn't know she was naming me after a supermarket chain. She was a St. Louis lady who lived here all her life. Her daddy admired Winston Churchill, and that's where I got my name. I'm just glad Grandpa wasn't a fan of General Dwight Eisenhower. But we're here to talk about you.

"Miss Marcus," he said, "you seem to know everybody. You talked to the hit-and-run victim, Edna Prilosen. You visited the late puppy abuser, Mr. Jonah Deerford. And now you're with the snake charmer, Dr. Ted."

"What!" Josie said.

"You're what we call a common link," Detective Dixie said.

"No! St. Louis is a small town," Josie said.

"Very small," Detective Dixie said. "Every time I turn, I run into you. Step into my new office, Miss Marcus, at the clinic here."

"But—," Josie protested.

"Unless you'd rather go to my office way out in Wildfern."

# Chapter 27

"We can drive all the way out to Wildfern," Detective Winston Dixie said. He stretched out the "all" so it sounded like they were going to California. "Or we can just talk here in the doctor's office. He has plenty of exam rooms." He glanced at his watch. "It's eight forty-two. If we go to Wildfern, I'm thinking you'll get back around midnight. If we have our conversation here, it won't take long."

"Am I under suspicion?" Josie asked.

"No, you're not," he said. "I'm asking you for your help as a concerned citizen. You don't have to talk to me in Rock Road Village. But . . ."

He paused long enough to let her consider it.

Now that sentence was ambiguous, Josie thought. Alyce, who'd taken some law classes in college, had taught Josie to look for weasel words. "As a concerned citizen" could mean he saw Josie as a concerned citizen. Or it could mean for some legal reason he couldn't question her in Rock Road. In that case, she could tell him no, citizen to citizen. She knew what Alyce would say: "Never, ever, talk to the police without a lawyer present."

Dixie started up again. "But I could call my good friend Ike Ikeman. Big Ike would try to get another television interview with Dr. Ted. I'm guessing this time Ted would run, while Ike turned the camera on that big blue Mobo-Pet van.

And Dr. Ted would look guilty as hell. Which I happen to believe he is."

It was blackmail and Josie knew it. More bad publicity would hurt Ted. She should just walk away. She could. Except Ted hadn't walked away from Harry. When the cat had needed expensive care, Ted had helped Harry for almost nothing. And Harry was, in Amelia's mind, some link with her dead father. The striped cat looked like Nate's long-vanished tabby, Cookie. To Josie, he was every striped cat she'd ever seen. But Harry the cat was a major part of Amelia's world. Josie had to help the man who helped her.

She knew Detective Dixie couldn't arrest her for failing to help him or obstructing an investigation. But the police knew how to make trouble. In Josie's experience, they stuck together and did favors for one another.

If Josie refused, she would suddenly have a lot of little problems. She'd be stopped for a burned-out taillight on her car. Or because she rolled through a stop. Or dropped a gum wrapper and broke a littering law. When cops wanted to get you, they did. And she didn't have the kind of career criminal mind that enjoyed fighting the police.

Josie mentally hushed her fears. She hadn't done anything wrong, and neither had Ted. She'd get the interview over with and go home. Besides, if the interview got rough, she could walk out.

Detective Dixie interrupted her thoughts. "Do you want to talk at the clinic or go into Wildfern?" he asked. "In the time you've sat there, we could have been halfway to Wildfern."

Josie gave in. "I'll talk with you. But I need to call my mother. She's watching my daughter."

"Fine." Detective Dixie shrugged.

Josie dreaded this call more than the interview with Detective Win Dixie. She speed-dialed Jane. Her mother sounded groggy. She must have fallen asleep on the couch. Good.

Josie hoped to have this conversation over before Jane woke up fully.

"Hi, Mom. Sorry to wake you. I'm going to be a bit later. No, no. Everything is fine. She's asleep? Good. Thanks." She hung up quickly.

"Let's go inside the clinic here," Detective Dixie said. Josie was relieved to get away from the flashing lights and noise. Officers were carrying out cardboard boxes. Dixie opened room two, a small exam room with a blue counter. On the counter were a plastic dog skeleton, a computer monitor, and a rack of pamphlets. The room smelled of dog hair and disinfectant.

Dixie stood behind the counter and nearly filled the room. He was wearing a shirt that could have slipcovered a recliner. The maroon shirt made his skin seem pinker. His goatee looked freshly trimmed. Josie sat in the only chair. She felt tired and bedraggled. She had a spot of pasta sauce on her shirt.

"What is the nature of your relationship with Dr. Ted, the veterinarian?" Detective Dixie asked.

"What relationship?" Josie said. "He gave my sick cat an enema. Tonight he cooked me dinner. My daughter was present the whole time. That's not exactly a relationship."

Josie immediately regretted those last sentences. They sounded defensive.

"So, based on dinner and an enema, you came running to his rescue tonight?"

"It sounds so unattractive when you put it that way," Josie said.

Dixie slammed his huge hand on the counter and spoke each word slowly and distinctly. "I. Am. Not. Joking, Miss Marcus. Tell me the truth or I'll hold you as a material witness and you can spend the night in jail. Remember, you have a daughter to consider."

And a mother, Josie thought. A murder case would be a

picnic in the park compared to an angry Jane. She wanted this detective out of her life.

Josie slapped on a smile and said, "Can we start again, please? Officer, I don't have any kind of romantic relationship with Ted. I got his name from another woman when I was at the Humane Society to adopt my cat. A friend named Traci had a puppy mill dog. She needed a vet, and I gave her one of Dr. Ted's cards.

"He went to her house in Wood Winds subdivision and looked at her little dog. He confirmed it was a traumatized puppy mill dog. After he left her house, my cat seemed sick. My daughter was worried about Harry—"

"Harry is the cat?" Detective Dixie asked.

"Yes. My daughter loves that cat. She picked him out at the Humane Society because he looked like her late father's cat. I called Dr. Ted. He came to our home and found out the cat was constipated."

Dixie's eyebrows went up.

"It's true," she said. "We're new cat owners and we'd been feeding him too much dry food. Dr. Ted unplugged the cat and suggested a diet change. While he was at our house, he got a call from Traci that her dog had found a snake in her garage. She wanted to kill it with a shovel, but he ran out there to save it."

"You're telling me he drove out to West County to save a snake?" Dixie said.

"He's kind of a snake rights person," Josie said. "He believes snakes are our friends and have a useful place in the ecosystem."

"I know, I know. You can spare me the lecture. I've already heard it. Do you know what kind of snake he rescued at this Traci's house?"

"She said it was poisonous, but she didn't know what kind or what color it was. All she could see was the head and she said it looked 'snaky,' which I guess it would."

"But Traci didn't know if it was a cotton mouth, a rattle-snake, or a coral snake?"

"No. She's from Miami. She said it didn't look like any snakes she'd seen there. That was the first time I met Ted."

"And when did you see Ted again?"

"I called him earlier today to ask about the right brand of food for the cat. He offered to bring over some sample cans and cook dinner for my daughter and me. We were eating when he got a call from his partner, Chris, that the police were at the clinic and had shot Jack. Ted ran out the door without finishing his meal."

"Did Ted talk to you about snakes, Miss Marcus?"

"Oh, yes. He said that snakes were misunderstood. They were helpful."

"Did he ever mention coral snakes?"

"Just that they looked a lot like harmless scarlet king snakes. They have bands of red, black, and yellow, except their colors are sort of reversed. How did that rhyme go? 'If red touches yellow, it can kill a fellow. If red touches black, it is a friend of—'"

Dixie interrupted. "Yeah, yeah, 'a friend of Jack.' I'll make sure they teach that at the police academy, so the uniforms don't go shooting the wrong snakes. Can you answer one more question for me, Miss Marcus?"

"Sure," Josie said, hoping the endless evening was coming to an end.

"Can you explain why a real coral snake skin was found in your vet's office?"

"A dead snake skin?" Josie was tired and confused.

"A *shed* snake skin," Dixie said. "But it came off a live snake. Snakes outgrow their skins and shed them. They look sort of like pork rinds."

Josie's exhausted mind flashed on a picture of her horrible boss crunching crispy snake skins. Her stomach turned.

"This particular skin we found belonged to a coral snake,"

he said. "Now, being a careful kind of guy, when we served the warrant, I brought a real herpetologist with me. That's a snake expert. He examined that skin and agreed it came off a coral snake. A full-grown one, maybe two feet long. He also said the snake that got shot was a harmless scarlet king snake. But that coral snake is not harmless. So what is your innocent vet doing with a coral snake skin in his office?"

"I don't know," Josie said. "Maybe he used it at one of his snake lectures."

"I don't think so, Miss Marcus. That snake skin was behind his office couch. A very dangerous place to keep a coral snake. If a cleaner had moved the couch, she could get bit, you know?

"You look kind of sick there, Miss Marcus. Maybe Dr. Ted should be more careful about the friends he hangs around with, huh? Maybe you should be more careful about your friends. Some snakes have two legs."

# Chapter 28

Ted's partner was pacing the clinic's empty waiting room with short, angry strides. Long spiky strands of dark hair had escaped Dr. Chris's ponytail, and Josie felt an urge to smooth them. Even in the shadowy room, the veterinarian's face looked taut and angry.

Dr. Chris glared at Detective Winston Dixie when he walked out of the exam room. "Are you finished now? I'd like to lock up and go home to my family."

Someone had cleaned up the waiting room. The shattered aquarium was gone. So was the slaughtered snake, except for a stain and a bullet hole in the light blue carpet. The side table where the snake used to live seemed bare. Dr. Chris had tried to fill in the spot with a stack of old magazines and a heartworm display.

"Where's Ted?" Josie asked.

"The idiots took him in for questioning," Dr. Chris said. "I think he's going to be arrested."

"But he's innocent," Josie said.

"So was the snake, and he's dead," she snapped. "At least they didn't shoot poor Ted."

That bit of invective set off Detective Dixie. "Our department doesn't believe your partner is innocent," he said. "What was he doing with a coral snake skin hidden in his office?"

"It's not illegal to keep a snake skin," Dr. Chris said. "Besides, I tried to tell you that Ted never had a coral snake at the clinic. We have kids and pets running around this clinic. His cat camps out in his office. His dog sleeps beside the receptionist's chair. A poisonous snake is too dangerous here."

"So a coral snake, which doesn't live in Missouri, just happened to crawl inside your clinic and shed its skin under the couch?" Detective Dixie said. "Or was that a coral snake your partner found in Traci's garage?"

"I told you before. Ted said he found a timber rattle-snake. They're native to Missouri. Timber rattlesnakes go into 'torpor'—it's sort of like hibernation—in winter, but they may come out of it if the weather gets warm. We've had several warm, sunny winter days."

"And what did your good friend Dr. Ted do with the rat-tlesnake after he found it?" the detective asked.

"He let it loose in the woods, where it belonged."

"Where it could kill someone," Detective Dixie said.

"Deaths from rattlesnake bites are rare, detective," Dr. Chris said. "Your chance of dying from a bite is less than one percent if you get proper treatment. Rattlesnakes are rather shy."

"Ted *told* you he let a rattlesnake loose in the woods," Dixie said. "But nobody saw the snake. Not even that Traci lady who thinks he's such a hero. If Ted's a hero, he should have killed the snake to save a human."

"Hikers wear boots to protect themselves from snakes, detective. They're the intruders. Let me repeat: Ted doesn't kill snakes."

"But he does kill people," Dixie said. "He made hostile statements concerning the victim, Jonah Deerford."

"Jonah Deerford was what we call a miller—he ran a puppy mill," Dr. Chris said. "It was cruel. No one who cares about animals likes millers. But Ted was smart enough to know if we eliminated Jonah Deerford's puppy mill, another would pop up in its place. That's why he was trying to change the law, to make puppy mills unprofitable. But I doubt someone like you would understand."

Detective Dixie gave a sarcastic smile. "Good night, ladies. I've enjoyed talking to you, but I'd like to go home to *my* family."

He slammed the clinic door. They heard his car engine start in the loud silence.

"You must have really yanked his chain," Josie said. "He isn't the type to debate issues with civilians."

"Good. Maybe my arguments actually penetrated his thick skull. But I doubt he heard a word I said."

"I didn't introduce myself. My name is Josie Marcus." She extended her hand. "I gather you're Dr. Chris. Ted came over to my house tonight and fixed dinner."

"You can call me Chris. I'm not a doctor unless you have fur or feathers. Ted told me all about you, Josie. I'm glad he's going out with you."

"I don't think we've reached the dating stage yet," Josie said. "He just looked at my cat the other day and made my daughter and me pasta for dinner tonight."

"When Ted cooks for a woman, that means he really likes her," Chris said. Her smile made her seem younger. "I hope you do start dating him. Ted's last girlfriend was one step away from a stalker. He had to give her the 'Let's be friends' speech. She was seriously pissed at him. It's hard to let go of a man as charming as Ted—and one who can cook, too.

"After they split, Ted's car windshield was broken and we found animal feces smeared on the clinic door. I wanted Ted to get a restraining order against her, but he refused. He said we didn't know for sure that she had done it. He told me, 'It's not her fault. She liked me better than I liked her. I hurt her. I feel bad about it, but things just weren't clicking. It would have been dishonest to lead her on.'"

"I definitely understand," Josie said. "Does Ted need a lawyer?"

"I called one. I hope Ted will follow his attorney's instructions to shut up and avoid his 'Snakes are our friends' speech. Especially when one of his 'friends' killed a man. Jonah Deerford was lower than a snake's belly, but his death was still murder."

"Can anyone give Ted an alibi for the time before Jonah died?" Josie asked.

"Yeah, the same woman he dumped."

"Oh," Josie said.

"She could save him, but I don't think she'll want to. Ted had some kind of stomach virus and was dragging around. His car was sick, too. He drives an old 'sixty-eight Mustang. The battery died. She took him home with her, fed him chicken soup and toast, then bought a new battery for his car. He stayed with her three days until he was well enough to drive."

"If she has the battery receipt, she might help him," Josie said. "It would prove he couldn't drive out to Wildfern."

"She says she threw it out. She paid cash for the battery and installed it herself."

"So she nursed Ted back to health, fixed his car, and then he dumped her. I can see why she's angry at him."

"Me, too. Even Ted says she had good reason. She might be too angry to testify on his behalf. Worse, she might lie and hurt him."

"What's her name?" Josie asked.

"I can't remember," Chris said. "I'm not good with names. With all the pet and people names at the clinic, I can't keep them straight. I only met her once. What was her name? It was something New Agey: Arizona? Nevada? Azure? Ursula? Ireland? It wasn't your everyday Cathy or Chris. I named my kids Morgan and Ashley so they'd be different, but their names are just as common as mine used to be."

Josie glanced at the clock next to the clinic's register. "Is it really eleven thirty? I've got to get home. Mom is babysitting and I promised her I wouldn't be late. I have a daughter of my own, but I'm never too old to get in trouble with my mother."

"Oh, I've heard that lecture often enough," Chris said. "Nice to meet you, Josie. And hang on to Ted if you can. He's a keeper."

"Can I call you to check on him?"

"Anytime," Chris said.

It was pitch-black when Josie left the clinic, and cold enough that she could see her breath. There won't be any snakes out tonight, she thought as she started her car. Ted's vintage tangerine Mustang was parked forlornly in a corner. On the short trip home, she tried to think of an excuse to mollify her mother. *Sorry, Mom, but the cat's vet fixed us dinner and then the police had a warrant to search his clinic. . . .*

"Police" and "warrant" were not a good combination, Josie decided. When Jane finds out Ted is a murder suspect, she'll go ballistic. There's no point in pretending I'm not romantically interested in him. Maybe if I . . .

Maybe if I grew a backbone, I could tell my mother I'm dating Ted and if she doesn't like that, tough toenails. The sudden, defiant surge of anger felt good.

Josie parked the car in front of her home and slammed the door hard. If her mother was asleep, Jane would be awake now. The lights were on in the living room. Josie marched up the front walk, prepared to do battle.

Jane met her at the door and used a tone Josie hadn't heard since she was sixteen. "Josie Marcus, it's almost midnight. Your few minutes turned into nearly four hours. What are you doing going out with a man who's mixed up in a murder?"

"How did you know about the murder?" Josie asked.

"It's all over the news. He's been arrested by the Wildfern police. Your daughter was crying. I don't know why you can't go out with a nice man like Stan."

"Because he's dull, Mom. Stan is so dull he makes my

teeth ache. If you like him so much, you date him. Mentally, you're both the same age—sixty-eight."

Jane looked like she'd been slapped. Josie instantly felt guilty. Her mother seemed wrinkled and tired. Her hair was mashed flat on one side, probably from napping on the couch.

"I'm sorry, Mom." Josie tried a more conciliatory tone. "I know you think Stan is good son-in-law material, but I can't force love if it isn't there. Stan's a good man—for some other woman. And he's found her. He loves Abby, not me. GBH. Please?"

Josie held out her arms. Jane refused to move. Her jaw was locked in that stubborn bulldog position.

"Come on, Mom, it's a family rule. If I ask for a Great Big Hug, you have to give me one." She wrapped her arms around Jane. Her mother was rigid and unyielding, but she let Josie hug her.

"I'm only trying to do what's best for you," Jane said between sniffles.

"I know you are, Mom. But Ted is the best man for me right now. Stan has already found the woman he deserves."

"But he's so handsome." Jane sniffed back a tear.

"He is nice looking," Josie said. "If I had any sense, I'd have fallen for him. But I didn't."

"Okay," Jane said. "But I still think you're making a mistake."

"I made a mistake with Nate, but we gave you a beautiful granddaughter, didn't we?"

"Yes, you did, Josie. And I hope you're not calling my granddaughter a mistake."

"No, Mom, the mistake was all mine."

"Well, you've done a good job of bringing her up. Amelia did all the dishes by herself tonight. She likes Ted. I hope that's a good sign. Harry means a lot to her. I finally met the cat."

"How did you and the beast get along?"

"He's quite nice—for a cat." That was a huge admission from Jane.

"Thanks, Mom," Josie said. "I really appreciate your watching Amelia. But I'd better get some sleep if I'm going to drive her to school on time." She gave her mother one last kiss on top of her head and gently guided her to the back steps.

It was midnight. Josie had had enough crises for one day.

# Chapter 29

Harry prowled the kitchen like a tiny tiger while Amelia ate her breakfast.

"Look, Mom. Isn't he cute?" she said, between bites of toast.

"The cutest," Josie said. Two-word sentences were all she could manage this morning. She was seriously sleep deprived and coffee starved. So far, she'd given her daughter dual-word commands: "Get up." "Get dressed." "Eat breakfast." But not all six words at once. That would have been too difficult.

Josie took her first sip of hot coffee and felt the neurons start firing. One more jolt, and she'd be almost up to speed.

She watched the small striped cat pace. By the third sip, she started making dog noises—a series of soft woofs and whines. Josie thought she sounded realistic. So did Harry. His mobile ears rotated, and he began looking under the kitchen table and behind the fridge.

"Mom! Stop that. You're confusing him," Amelia said.

"Since I can't torment the cat, let's head for school," Josie said. A whole ten words at once. She was ready to face the day.

All the way to Barrington, Josie listened to her daughter praise Harry. She was in love with her cat and found something new to admire each day. "Harry looks like a plain dark brown cat with black stripes, Mom, but he's got lots of colors. His stomach fur is yellow-brown with stripes, his vest is white, the insides of his ears are pale beige, his eyes are green, and his nose is red."

"Like a little rubber eraser," Josie said.

She could tell by Amelia's silence this was not proper appreciation. "I mean that in a cute way," Josie added, and wished for more coffee.

Harry's praises ended only in the Barrington School driveway. Before Josie could leave, her cell rang, and she pulled over. It was Harry the human. Well, semihuman.

"Josie," her awful boss said. *Crunch. Slurp.* "Did you mystery-shop that third dog boutique?"

"The Upper Pup?" Josie asked, stalling for time.

"Yeah." *Crunch. Chomp.* "I need your report today."

"I'm shopping it this morning. It opens at ten," Josie said. She'd forgotten all about the store. She'd had too much crammed into the last few days.

"I need the report by three o'clock," Harry said. There was a massive crunch, like tree limbs breaking in an ice storm.

"Harry, what are you eating? It sounds interesting."

"Chicken-fried bacon," he said. "Very big in Texas. The new chef at the diner down the street makes it. He serves it with cream gravy, but that's too fattening."

"Right. Much healthier without it."

Harry crunched good-bye and hung up.

Chicken-fried bacon. Bet that delicacy was endorsed by the heart association, Josie thought. Maybe if Harry kept eating lard-loaded food, his arteries would blow like a birthday balloon, and she'd get a new boss. Anyone would be better than Harry.

Josie wondered if Alyce could go mystery-shopping with her today. She speed-dialed her friend.

"I'd love to go," Alyce said. "Justin can torment the nanny at home." She lowered her voice. "Would you mind if Traci and Snowball went with us?"

"Is she there again?" Josie knew she had no business asking.

"Yes. She's upset about the news of Dr. Ted's arrest. She came over this morning. We're talking about our babies."

"Oh? Did she have a difficult labor?" Josie asked.

"Is something wrong?" Alyce asked.

Yes, Josie wanted to say. Comparing a puppy to a toddler makes me feel queasy. But she knew she'd sound jealous.

"No, just tired," Josie said. "Traci and her dog will be good cover for mystery shopping. You can all meet me in the parking lot at the Clayton Road store at ten o'clock."

Traci was unfolding the doggy stroller from Alyce's SUV when Josie arrived at the Upper Pup boutique. Alyce wore a dark blue winter coat that made her pale skin glow.

Traci and Snowball wore matching Black Watch plaid coats. Traci had a plaid tam and Snowball had a plaid bow. Snowball yapped a greeting. So did Traci. "I can't believe you're letting me mystery-shop with you. I feel like James Bond."

"Sh," Josie warned. "Our mission is a secret."

"Can I buy something for Snowball?" she asked.

"As much as you want. It will make us look like regular shoppers," Josie said.

Shopping with Traci was sort of like going to a store with Amelia, except Josie's daughter would have been more subdued.

When Traci rolled Snowball into the store, Kate, the saleswoman, said, "Oh, you look so cute with your baby."

Kate listened to the dog's rescue saga. "You're so brave to adopt her," she cooed.

"Oh, it's no trouble at all," Traci said. "She's so sweet. But we girls are looking for new clothes."

"I can help you with that," Kate said. "Let me show you the clothes racks, then see to these ladies." She turned to Josie. "I'll be with you in a minute."

The saleswoman was soon back at Josie's side. "Sorry for the wait. How may I help you?"

"I'd like to look at your accessories," Josie said.

"Anything in particular? We have a whole jewelry case of dog charms, barrettes, and collar pendants." Kate had passed two mystery-shopper tests—she'd greeted the customers and offered to show the accessories.

In the background, Josie could hear Traci yelping, "Isn't this cute? . . . Oh, I love this! . . . Snowball, this Santa suit is adorable!"

Josie was losing patience with a grown woman who squealed. You're jealous, she told herself. Alyce has always been your best friend. Now you're acting like a spoiled high schooler. Traci is good-hearted and she's trying to help a pup who had a bad start. Josie mentally repeated Alyce's injunction not to be judgmental. She'd declawed Harry, after all. For a couch.

"I'd like a pearl tiara for my Chihuahua," Josie said. She couldn't believe those words came out of her mouth. At least she was paid to say them.

"We have a Parisian tiara for your little princess." Kate opened the jewelry showcase and removed a bauble suitable for Marie Antoinette. "Look how that pearl hangs in the center rhinestone arch."

"Precious," Josie said.

Alyce raised one eyebrow. Josie wondered if she was overdoing her fake enthusiasm.

"And it's only seven ninety-nine," Kate said.

"I'll take it," Josie said.

Kate wrapped the tiara while Josie and Alyce watched Traci pile her selections on the counter: four doggy dresses, a rhinestone sweater, a Santa suit, three scarves, two sets of boots, four hair bows, and a crystal collar charm. Josie mentally added up the prices. Traci's shopping spree cost more than Amelia's school wardrobe.

"Well, I can see you and Snowball have done well without me," Kate said. "May I show you a collar and leash set?"

"I guess so," Traci said. "Poor Snowball spent her little puppy life crammed in a cage and she's not used to walking on floors. But my vet says I should try to leash train her."

Soon Traci added four leashes, including an "evening" leash trimmed in pearls and rhinestones. She put Snowball on the counter next to the pile. "Look at that! The stack of clothes is taller than Snowball." The fluffy white dog yapped and wagged her tail.

Josie gave an insincere smile and tried not to sulk.

Kate rang up the purchases and put them in a paw-print shopping bag. As Traci rolled the dog stroller out to the lot, she asked Josie, "How'd I do?"

"Nice job, Mrs. Bond," Josie said.

"Would you like to stop for lunch?" Alyce asked. "My neighbor Joanie Protzel has a deli nearby. They make their own corned beef."

"I've been dying for a good deli since I left Miami," Traci said.

Joanie Protzel, a small, brown-haired woman, met them at the door. "I'm sorry," she said. "No puppies are allowed in the store."

So much for your baby, Josie thought meanly. The board of health doesn't let in fur kids with fleas.

"Then we'll go somewhere else," Alyce said.

"No, no," Joanie said. "I'll babysit the puppy while you eat lunch. I'll feed her myself. I have some beautiful turkey. You can sit inside by the window and watch me. It's a sunny day. Your baby won't get cold."

Alyce said, "What do you think, Traci?"

Joanie added, "It's all white meat, and I'll throw in a bit of beef, too. Pups love my food. One has his own account here."

"Well, Snowball is supposed to get used to strangers,"

Traci said. "Dr. Ted says it's part of the socialization process. And I'll be right where I can see her while Joanie babysits her."

Inside, the three women were served homemade corned beef stacked high on light rye, crunchy pickles, and Dr. Brown's cream sodas. Traci watched Joanie feed Snowball turkey scraps. The little dog barked when Joanie stopped.

"Look," Traci said. "She's asking for more."

Joanie asked the waitress to bring a bowl of water for Snowball, but never left the dog's side.

Traci picked at her food as she watched her pup. Josie and Alyce went through their sandwiches as if corned beef would become illegal by sundown.

They stopped for serious conversation when their brownies and coffee arrived.

"I can't believe Dr. Ted was arrested for killing that awful Deerford man," Traci said. "He didn't murder him. I know he didn't."

"Of course he didn't," Josie said.

"So who did?" Alyce asked.

"I guess the real question is who had a coral snake," Josie said. "Those snakes aren't found in Missouri."

"They live in Florida, don't they?" Traci asked. "That's what the TV said."

"Do you think one crawled into your packing boxes and you brought it with you?" Josie asked.

"Ew, no," Traci said. "We didn't live in the Everglades. We lived in a condo in Miami."

"I meant maybe it got into the moving van by accident," Josie said. "I saw this news story where a neighbor's cat stowed away in a chest of drawers in a moving van, and it wasn't discovered for a thousand miles."

Traci's eye widened. "So you're saying a rare poisonous coral snake just happened to crawl into my moving van in the middle of a busy city and wound up in my garage?"

"It's possible," Josie said.

"Then what?" Traci asked. "Dr. Ted rescued it and said, 'Oh, look. A poisonous snake. Think I'll kill Jonah.'"

"Well, that part doesn't fit," Josie said. "Maybe there was more than one snake and . . ."

Alyce glared at her. "And what, Josie?"

And little Miss Sunshine here kept it and killed Jonah Deerford, Josie thought. Traci said she wasn't scared of snakes. And she hated Jonah.

"Nothing," Josie said.

"Nothing is right," Alyce said tartly. "Missouri has laws about owning exotic reptiles. From everything I've heard, Dr. Ted would be too careful to keep an animal that dangerous. He certainly wouldn't use a snake to kill someone, no matter how much he disliked puppy millers."

"You're right," Josie said. "I'm not making sense. I'm upset about Ted's arrest. I know he hated millers, but he was trying to find legal ways to stop them."

Traci patted Josie's hand. "You're right to be upset. I am, too. I still think that Deerford man deserved to die. But I believe Dr. Ted is innocent."

"Exactly what I was thinking," Josie said. Alyce caught Josie's double meaning and frowned.

"Well, how can we stop the millers?" Traci blushed bright red. "I mean besides not buying a puppy mill dog like I did."

"You bought one, but you saved her," Alyce said.

"Ted is trying to get the legislature to change those miller laws," Josie said. "He also wants to get funding so federal officials can inspect more breeders. He wants people to write letters to their lawmakers and to the newspapers."

"I already wrote the letters," Traci said. "I gave money, too. Dr. Ted said it was important to support the organizations that fight puppy mills."

"You can also buy clothes and toys at the Humane Society of Missouri's gift shop," Josie said. "The proceeds support their work."

"Shop and save. I like that," Traci said. "I'll donate the amount of money I just spent today, too. But there must be some other way to make people know. I didn't until it was too late."

They chewed thoughtfully on their brownies. Traci let out a squeal that made everyone in the deli look at them. "I know! I'll put up a video on YouTube about Snowball! I'll tell her story! And other people can talk about their rescued puppies. My little Snowball can model the clothes I'll buy her at the Humane Society gift shop."

"A terrific idea," Alyce said.

"I've got the name, too," Traci said. "I'll call it 'Snowball in Hell.'"

"Isn't that the name of a song by They Might Be Giants?" Josie asked.

"They're an alternative rock group," Traci said. "Nobody's heard of them."

"They won a Grammy," Josie said.

"My puppy will be more famous. 'Snowball in Hell' fits her because that's where she was and that's how much chance she had of surviving. But she did. We'll show the world!" She raised her coffee cup and said, "To Snowball."

Alyce and Traci toasted the new project with coffee. Josie reluctantly lifted her cup.

"I can't wait to get the puppycam running," Traci said. "Josie, would you like to come with us?"

"Wish I could," Josie said. "But I have to file my report today. I'd better get going. But I'd like to buy your lunch."

She dropped two twenties on the table and fled, but she knew she couldn't escape her own pettiness.

# Chapter 30

What's wrong with me? Josie asked herself as she drove home.

Traci is harmless. Dressing up a dog doesn't hurt anyone, not even the dog. And Alyce is generous enough to share her friendship with more than one person.

The problem is me, Josie decided. I don't like Traci, her squeally voice or her cutesy outfits. I hate that she spends so much on dog clothes. And yes, I'm jealous. I wish I had that money for my daughter.

She finished her Upper Pup mystery-shopping report, giving Kate high marks for her customer service, and faxed it to Harry at two o'clock.

She felt something furry rub against her ankle and nearly shrieked. Then she saw Harry's skinny, striped body. He bumped her leg with his forehead. Josie had read that was a cat greeting.

"Hi, guy," she said. "Are you losing your shyness?"

She bent to pet him and Harry scuttled under the couch. Josie tried some dog woofs and growls, and Harry poked his head out to look around. Josie snapped his picture.

"Gotcha!" Josie said. "Wait till Amelia sees this."

Josie couldn't wait to tell Amelia that her cat had greeted her. She printed out Harry's picture and brought it with her to the Barrington School that afternoon.

"Oh, Mom, look at those eyes!" Amelia said. "He looks smart and curious."

All the way home Josie listened to Amelia pile on the Harry praise, but she was delighted to see her daughter chatting and laughing again. Too many of these school runs had been made in dispirited silence, until Josie had wondered if Amelia would ever be happy again.

"I have a cooking lesson at Grandma's tonight," Amelia said. "We're making chicken and dumplings."

"My favorite," Josie said.

"We may need some extra time. This recipe can take two or three hours," Amelia said. "Do you like fluffy dumplings or the flat ones?"

"Fluffy," Josie said. "And take all the time you want. I have things to do."

As soon as Amelia ran up the steps to her grandmother's flat, Josie started making phone calls. The doggy tiara was sitting in a bag on the coffee table, and Josie wondered what she was going to do with it. Maybe she could give it to Traci, along with an apology. She called Alyce.

"I wanted to apologize," Josie said.

"Oh, you've come out of your snit?" Her friend's voice was frosty with disapproval. "You all but accused that poor woman of murder, Josie. She has enough problems with the subdivision snobs."

"I'm sorry," Josie said. "I could say I was tired, or worried about Ted, but the truth is I was a jerk and I'm jealous."

"I forgive you." Alyce's voice was a shade warmer. "Admitting it is the first step to recovery. That was a joke," she added quickly.

"I can give Traci that tiara if she'd like it."

"I'm sure she'd love it. We spent two hours taping Snowball. That pair are naturals in front of a camera. Traci's husband will help her load the video on YouTube tonight. I think she and Snowball are going to be stars."

"I can't wait to see it," Josie said without a sneer.

She hung up before her new halo slipped. Harry was sitting next to her on the couch posed like a library lion. She didn't want to scare away the skittish cat, so Josie ignored him. She called the clinic to see if Dr. Chris had any news about Ted.

The receptionist put Josie on hold for so long that she heard two commercials about dog dental care. The dangers of plaque were being pointed out the second time when Dr. Chris came on the line. Josie heard outraged meows in the background.

"Chris, it's Josie. I just wanted to check on Ted."

"Well, he's been arraigned. The whole city knows that. There's no bail because it's a murder charge."

"But it's his first time," Josie said.

"You don't get a first time with murder," Chris said. "The prosecutor said Ted was unmarried and painted him as a flight risk with no ties to the community. His lawyer mentioned the clinic, but that was discounted. So Ted is stuck in jail and I'm running the clinic without a partner. I just went three rounds with a fifteen-pound cat. I stuck a thermometer in her butt and she wrecked the exam room. Even knocked the computer monitor on the floor and broke it."

"Sounds like you're having a bad day. Is it okay if I visit Ted?"

"Yes, you can track him down through the St. Louis County Justice Center Jail Information Service. They're surprisingly nice to the friends of future felons."

They were, too. A woman told Josie the earliest she could see Ted was at seven o'clock that night. "And for forty minutes only," the woman told her. "Be here on time." Josie listened for signs of disapproval in her voice, but couldn't detect any.

When Josie hung up, she saw she was scratching Harry's ears. Better yet, he'd sat still for it. In fact, he was purring loudly. Why do I feel honored for doing Harry a favor? she wondered. Cats could teach us a lot.

Josie called her mother and said, "I have to run an errand at six thirty. What's the ETA on the chicken and dumplings?"

"They'll be ready in fifteen minutes, if you don't mind coming up here," Jane said.

"Are you kidding? I'd walk to Chicago for chicken and dumplings."

"Upstairs is as far as you have to go," Jane said.

Jane was still wearing long sleeves to cover the wounds from her dog attack, but otherwise she seemed to have recovered. The kitchen was warm and fragrant with comfort food. The chicken was just the way Josie liked it.

"These dumplings are light as clouds," she told her daughter. "How did you do it?"

"Unlike her mother, Amelia listens to me," Jane said. "She dropped the dumpling dough onto the chicken and kept the cover on for fifteen minutes without peeking. You always had to look, and that ruined them."

"I was curious," Josie said. Amelia snickered.

Josie and Amelia did the dishes in Jane's kitchen and Amelia agreed to stay with her grandmother for another two hours. "Can I run downstairs and feed Harry?" she said. "I have to put out his stinky fish."

"By all means," Josie said. "I'll talk to your grandma until you return."

"Thanks, Mom," Josie said. "The lessons seem to be going well."

"She's a natural cook," Jane said. "She's a lot easier to teach than you were. I bought a fat stewing hen at the store. We're going to make chicken soup for tomorrow. The weather is supposed to drop another thirty degrees tonight. Put on your warm coat."

"You're still a mom," Josie said, and kissed Jane goodbye. She passed Amelia on the stairs.

Josie could feel the change in the temperature as she left the house and was glad she'd followed Jane's advice about the coat. The sky was heavy with gray winter clouds. A single star showed through, like the coming promise of spring.

Josie arrived at the jail early. It wasn't the first time she'd visited someone there, but it was just as depressing. Josie stood in a long line of people who looked like they'd just left work: Men and women in hospital scrubs, women in business suits, men in work boots. All seemed tired. The air was heavy with sadness and loud with the cries of children who should have been at home eating dinner.

No one ever comes here because they want to, Josie thought. Imagine building something that people dreaded entering.

Ted looked startlingly handsome seated behind the Plexiglas barrier, though his skin was slightly yellowed by the glaring lights. They spoke on telephones like in the movies. Even their dialogue sounded like a script.

"I didn't do it, Josie," he said. "You have to believe me."

"I do, Ted," Josie said. "I just hope the jury does."

"I didn't have any luck convincing the police," he said. "I tried to tell them I never saw the skin from that coral snake in my life, but they didn't believe me. How do you prove a negative?"

Josie didn't answer that. She couldn't. She changed the subject instead. "What kind of snake did you find in Traci's garage?"

"A timber rattlesnake. And I let it loose in the woods where it belonged. It's a Missouri snake. But I can't prove that, either. And it's getting cold again, so the snakes won't be out sunning themselves."

"Your partner, Chris, says you have an alibi for the days before Deerford's death," Josie said.

"Right now, my alibi is mad enough to see me fry in the electric chair. She liked me better than I liked her, and I had to tell her I didn't want to see her again. I hurt her, Josie. I didn't mean to, but I couldn't love her as intensely as she loved me."

"I've been through that, Ted. I understand all too well. Maybe if you gave me her name, I could talk to her."

"No!" Ted said. "You'd make it worse."

"I know I'm not tactful," Josie began.

"That's not what I meant. You'd make it worse because you're so much nicer and better looking than she is. And cute. One look at you, and she'd want to ruin me for sure. I can't give you her name, Josie. It would rub salt into her wound if she saw you."

Josie was touched. "That's sweet, Ted. If the police think you're guilty, then we have to come up with someone else who might have a coral snake. Do you know any exotic snake collectors?"

"Drug dealers prefer exotic pets, Josie. I don't know any of those people, and they don't usually get much veterinary care for their animals. We have one man who has a boa constrictor he calls Main Squeeze, but he's just a regular guy who likes snakes."

"Would he know any snake collectors? Do they stick together?"

"He's a harmless pothead, Josie, but he's not a dealer. He collects comic books and *Star Wars* memorabilia and sells them on the Internet. I don't think he could help you."

"We have to find someone who could have a coral snake here in Missouri," Josie said. "The police aren't going to look. I'll try an Internet search tonight."

"Anything you can do, Josie, I'd appreciate. I'm going to get out of here. I know I am. Then I'll make it up to you."

They were back to the movie clichés again.

"I hope so, Ted," she said. "I really do. I have to go."

The wind was cold reality. She fought it as she walked to her car. Josie knew Ted was innocent. She also knew she was a lousy judge of men. So far, she'd dated two drug dealers and a man with a homicidal ex.

She'd liked Ted from the moment she met him. He was kind, helpful, charming.

*So was another Ted—Ted Bundy*, whispered a small voice. He was a helpful, charming serial killer who murdered thirty women.

But her Ted loved animals.

*So did Hitler*, said the same treacherous voice.

But Ted is innocent, she practically screamed.

*That's what all the wives and lovers of guilty men say.* Now the voice seemed to be laughing.

The only way to silence it was to prove Ted didn't kill Jonah Deerford. Josie knew Ted had been framed. Framed? That phrase sounded so corny. Still, she knew innocent men were railroaded for murder. If Josie didn't help Ted, who would? The police were convinced he was guilty.

"I have to find out more about the real killer—coral snakes," Josie said out loud.

Oops. Now she was talking to herself. The jail visit must have upset her more than she thought. That was her third meeting with Ted. Their first encounter was a cat enema. The second was an unfinished dinner while the police searched his business during a murder investigation. The third time, Josie and Ted had met in the county lockup, with a Plexiglas chaperone.

We haven't even had a date yet, she thought. I'm fighting for a future we may never have.

# Chapter 31

Josie was greeted by the warm, welcoming smell of chicken soup that cold winter night. She followed the scent upstairs and leaned in the doorway, listening to her mother and daughter discuss ingredients.

"The soup needs more dill," Jane said. "Taste it and see."

Josie heard a light slurp as Amelia sampled a spoonful. "I agree about the dill. But do we have to add carrots?"

"They'll give it body," Jane said. "And they don't taste like carrots."

"They do to me," Amelia said.

"Me, too," Josie said. "Not that I'm qualified to chime in on any cooking discussion. Your soup smells good."

"Grandma says there should be enough meat on the stewing hen to make chicken salad, too."

"Another homemade dinner," Josie said. "I hate to break up the class, but you have school tomorrow and you need to check on Harry."

"I'd better see if he ate his stinky fish." Amelia ran downstairs to their flat. Josie stayed behind to talk to her mother.

"Thanks again, Mom," Josie said.

"I enjoy teaching her."

Amelia yelled upstairs, "He ate it! He ate it!"

"Thank goodness!" Josie yelled back.

"What's the big deal?" Jane asked.

"If Harry doesn't eat his canned food, he gets plugged up. The next enema will cost me two hundred dollars."

"That's outrageous!" Jane said.

"Well, so far he likes the canned fish. But this taught Amelia an important lesson."

"What's that?" Jane asked.

"No matter what you do, there's always an asshole in charge," Josie said.

"Josie Marcus, wash your mouth out with soap," Jane said as Josie fled down the stairs laughing.

"What's so funny, Mom?" Amelia was in the kitchen, refilling Harry's water bowl.

"I was explaining to your grandmother why we were glad Harry ate his fish," Josie said. "It's bedtime for you."

Amelia set the bowl on the floor with a clunk, usually the signal for Harry to appear. He didn't.

"Where's Harry?" Amelia asked.

Josie made her dog noises again, walking up and down the hall. Finally, the little cat came out of Amelia's closet, stretched, and looked around.

"You'd think if I sounded like a real dog he'd stay hidden," Josie said.

"Harry knows he's safe here," Amelia said.

Amelia sent off a final flurry of text messages to her friends while Josie searched the Net for information about coral snakes. One Web site said eastern coral snakes were "extremely reclusive and generally bite humans only when handled or stepped on."

Did the late Jonah Deerford step on his snake attacker— or sit on it? It didn't matter. The coral snake bit him and he died.

"There is little or no pain or swelling at the site of the bite," the Web site said, "and other symptoms can be delayed for twelve hours."

Jonah could have been bitten the night before or early in the morning, and then died half a day later. By the time the venom kicked in, Deerford would have experienced "slurred speech, double vision, and muscular paralysis." Josie wondered if he was trying to drive somewhere for help when he died.

Not a pleasant way to go, but Jonah had hurt too many innocent animals for Josie to feel sympathy for him. He'd treated his own sons worse than dogs. Or at least as badly as the poor pups in his kennel. And Edna's death was too horrible to think about. Jonah did not deserve pity.

According to another Web site, the eastern coral snake was found in parts of North Carolina, Louisiana, and all of Florida. Josie knew plenty of St. Louisans vacationed in Florida. And one recent addition to St. Louis used to live in snake central: cute little Traci.

Wasn't there someone else local who spent a lot of time in Florida? Someone who liked snakes? A name niggled in her brain, but she couldn't remember who it was.

Josie's search turned up two more types of coral snakes in the United States—a Texas coral snake and the western coral snake. The western snake slithered through parts of Arizona and New Mexico, then down into old Mexico. But none came as far north as Missouri. Not naturally, anyway.

Josie knew Interstate 44 ran from St. Louis through Oklahoma and ended somewhere in Texas. The highway was a major drug corridor, or so the news reports said. The highway patrol was always busting someone with a car full of coke. Ted said drug dealers liked to keep exotic animals. Maybe one of them liked the deadly beauty of a coral snake.

That certainly broadened the potential coral snake population, Josie thought. But their owners were likely to be even more dangerous than their pets. Didn't Traci mention something about living in Arizona? What was that all about? She'd have to find a way to ask, without sounding jealous.

Josie yawned. She could hardly keep her eyes open. Enough research. She peeked into her daughter's room for a final check. Amelia had fallen asleep with her bedside light on. Josie tiptoed in and turned it off. Harry was curled at the foot of the bed, guarding Amelia. He raised his head.

"Woof!" Josie said softly. Harry began searching the room for the imaginary dog.

"Good night," Josie whispered to him. "There's no dog. You're safe here."

Strange things slithered on the edge of Josie's dreams, but they didn't wake her. When her alarm went off at seven the next morning, Josie felt better after more than ten hours of solid sleep.

Morning brought the real horrors. It started harmlessly enough, with a wake-up call from Alyce. She was breathless with excitement.

"Josie, turn on your television, now," Alyce said. "There's a news story coming up you don't want to miss."

THE KENNEL OF DEATH headline filled Josie's screen.

"How melodramatic is that?" Josie said.

"It's Deerford Kennels," Alyce said. "And the story is melodramatic. They've found another body there. A woman."

The blond anchor intoned, "Police made another grim discovery yesterday at the Deerford Kennels in Wildfern. Authorities were continuing the investigation into the death of Jonah Deerford when they discovered the body of his wife in an abandoned refrigerator on the property."

"I wondered how any woman could abandon those boys," Josie said.

"Shut up and listen," Alyce said. "It's important."

"Dental records confirmed that the dead woman was Allegra Coleson Deerford, mother of the two boys child welfare officials removed from the farm," the news anchor said. "Mrs. Deerford appeared to have been shot, a police spokesperson said. An autopsy is being performed.

"Mr. Deerford had told authorities that his wife had abandoned their sons. Two years ago, he went to court to bar his wife's parents from visiting the boys. In legal documents, Mr. Deerford claimed the boys' grandparents were 'unstable hippies' and 'drug users' living on a commune in California. He was granted the injunction. The boys' grandparents had no known drug charges that would support Mr. Deerford's claim, but said they lacked the money to fight the custody battle."

The video switched to shots of investigators clustered around a beat-up truck. "Mr. Deerford died in his truck from a deadly coral snake bite," the announcer said. "The Wildfern police are treating his death as suspicious. Rock Road Village veterinarian Dr. Ted Scottsmeyer was arrested and charged with Deerford's murder. Police confirmed that the same pickup in which Mr. Deerford was found dead had been used in the hit-and-run murder of Edna Prilosen, a Pets 4 Luv salesclerk."

Mercifully, the station did not run the security video of Edna's murder.

"Police believe she was killed by Mr. Deerford because she was giving animal activists information about sales of his puppy mill dogs to the Pets 4 Luv store in Rock Road Village. The store's former manager is wanted for questioning. A Pets 4 Luv spokesperson denied any knowledge of the puppy mill dogs and said the dogs were bought without corporate authorization."

The announcer said, "But now there may be a happy ending to this tragedy, at least for the children. Recently, the commune where Allegra Coleson Deerford's parents lived was sold to a California developer. The commune dwellers shared the substantial profits. Allegra's parents bought a home in San Diego and hoped to be reunited with their grandsons. They flew to St. Louis when the children were taken into protective custody. The grandparents have begun the process to adopt the two boys. To speed the process, they paid for a home study in California. Missouri authorities are cooperating with the California child welfare officials."

The station broke for a shampoo commercial. Models showed off impossibly silky manes.

"It's early in the morning and I'm confused," Josie said. "Jonah Deerford killed poor Edna because he thought she was going to ruin his puppy mill business."

"Right," Alyce said.

"Then Jonah was found dead in the same truck. He was bitten by a poisonous snake that doesn't belong in Missouri."

"Also right," Alyce said. "And good riddance, too. You don't have to worry about him anymore."

"I guess not, but I don't know if he's acting alone or not," Josie said. "Dr. Ted was arrested, even though he was innocent."

"And you're going to leave that investigation to the police," Alyce said.

"Now it looks like Jonah Deerford killed his wife, the mother of those poor abused boys," Josie said.

"Wait! The commercial's over," Alyce said. "We're getting to the fun part."

"I hope so," Josie said, "because this is a grim way to start the day."

Alyce hung up.

The blond news reader beamed at the camera. "And now we have a special report on the fate of one animal that may have been rescued from the Deerford Kennels puppy mill. Ms. Traci Teeger believes the puppy she bought at Pets 4 Luv is a survivor of Deerford Kennels."

Josie's jaw dropped. There were Traci and Snowball, both wearing matching rhinestone hoodies, like a pair of rock stars.

"This is my baby, Snowball," Traci said, in that annoying, shrill voice.

"Yap!" Snowball said.

"I may barf," Josie said to the television.

"Did you say something, Mom?" Amelia was standing in Josie's doorway, dressed for school.

"Look at that silly woman," Josie said. "She calls a bichon her baby."

"So?" Amelia said. "I think it's cute. Their outfits are awesome."

"Would you dress Harry in rhinestones?"

"No. He doesn't need them. He's not a fluffy dog. Why are you so down on her, Mom? She's a nice lady who helped a sick dog. And look at her puppy. Snowball seems happy. Her tail is wagging."

Tears brimmed in Traci's eyes as she cuddled her pup and looked straight into the camera. "My poor little baby was never allowed to play," she said. "Her tiny feet never touched the ground. When I got her, she was covered with flea bites and she had ear mites. She was underweight. The vet said she was lucky—lucky! Many puppy mill dogs have far worse problems. Puppies like Snowball suffer so I could have a silly piece of paper that said she was pedigreed. I don't need any paper to know she's special."

Traci kissed her dog. A single tear started down her face. "Snowball is learning to walk and play. She's getting medicine. She's gained half a pound. She's getting better every day. If you go to my YouTube site, 'Snowball in Hell,' you'll see her progress on my puppycam. If you want to talk about your own rescue pup, e-mail me at snowballs-mommy@aol.com."

"Gag me," Josie said.

"Mom, stop it!" Amelia said. "You sound like Zoe when she's ragging about Harry."

At the mention of his name, the little cat appeared and bumped his forehead against Josie's leg to greet her.

"Hello to you, too," Josie said. "There's my good boy."

"Excuse me?" Amelia said. "Did you just call a cat your boy? I've always wanted a brother, but I never expected one with four legs."

"It's just a figure of speech," Josie said. Shame seared

her mind. She'd thought she'd gotten over her jealous impulses, but they were definitely alive. Her daughter was right. Josie was acting like a spoiled child.

"Why can Harry be your boy, but Snowball can't be Traci's baby?" Amelia asked.

"Let this be a lesson to you," Josie said.

"Another one?" Amelia rolled her eyes. "What do I need to know now?"

"Just because someone is older doesn't mean they act like an adult."

# Chapter 32

Harry the cat met Josie at the door, his striped tail at a jaunty angle.

"You've come out to say hello," Josie said, falling into the baby talk that people use around pets. "You're my good . . . uh . . . animal companion."

That sounded lame. But she couldn't call Harry her "good boy." Not after what Amelia had said. Josie knew she sounded as silly as Traci. She reached down to scratch Harry's ears and said, "Amelia will be back from school this afternoon. I just dropped her off."

What am I doing talking to a cat? Josie thought. He doesn't understand a word I'm saying. She sent Traci a mental apology. I'm sorry. I'm only a rhinestone away from you.

Josie gratefully answered the ringing phone. Anything to escape her own thoughts.

"So what did you think?" Alyce said.

"About what?" Josie said.

"About Traci and Snowball's television debut," Alyce said.

"They were okay," Josie said, her tone grudging.

"Okay? They rocked!" Alyce said. "The viewers went crazy. Traci's YouTube video has had three thousand hits so far. Her e-mail box is filled with people who want to tell their rescue-puppy stories."

"That's nice," Josie said.

"Is that all you can say?" Alyce asked.

Here goes, Josie thought. This is your last chance to grow up. "I mean I'm delighted. Yes, delighted. Happy for her and Snowball. I'd like to give Traci the tiara. I promise I'll listen to every word she says about Snowball. I'll even buy you both lunch."

"You bought us lunch yesterday," Alyce said, "though you weren't very gracious. Why don't you meet at my place for brunch tomorrow?"

"Deal. And you can kick me if I get surly."

"I was thinking of a muzzle trimmed in rhinestones," Alyce said, and laughed.

Josie hung up the phone and sighed with relief. She'd gotten over that hurdle. She needed a moment to relax and she'd be fine.

She didn't get it. Before Josie could start a fresh pot of coffee, she had a phone call from Jerry. Chloe's owner was talking faster than an auctioneer. "Josie, I'm on my break and I have to ask you something quick. Now that you can't go out with that killer vet, you have time to date me."

"What?" Josie said. She wanted to slam down the phone. Then she wondered if Jerry might have given the police that tip about Ted's snake. Maybe Jerry planted the coral snake skin under Ted's couch. He could have walked in with Chloe. Who'd notice one more dog at a vet's office?

"Mom really likes you," Jerry said. "She wants me to invite you to dinner tonight with her and Paul."

"Who's Paul?" Josie asked.

"You know. He rents the duplex attached to Mom's house. The guy with the snakes."

Bingo! Just the man I want to meet, Josie thought. I wonder if Paul has a coral snake in his collection. And if he was in league with Jonah.

"Hello? Josie? Are you still there?"

"I'd love to have dinner at your mom's," Josie said. "Would we have time to see Paul's snakes?"

"Paul always has time to show off his pets," Jerry said. "I'll pick you up around five thirty. Can Amelia come, too?"

"She has school," Josie said.

Cooking school. It really wasn't a lie. Much.

Josie drank a whole pot of coffee, then spent the day on a caffeine high. She cleaned the kitchen, sewed a button on her coat, did three loads of laundry, vacuumed the rug, and suddenly it was time to pick up her daughter at school.

"Tonight Grandma and I are making chicken salad," Amelia announced as she dropped her backpack in the car.

"That should taste good," Josie said. "I'm supposed to have dinner with Jerry at his mother's house. He invited you, too."

"Ew, all those skanky cats—and the cat hair in the food."

"But you'll get to see Paul feed his snakes," Josie said.

"I'd rather have a front row seat at a Miley Cyrus concert."

"I gather that's a no."

"It's an ew, no," Amelia said. "I like Jerry's dog, but I'm not hanging around snakes or those disgusting cats. One sat in the roll basket and then Jerry's mom served us bread from it. Some of the cats are sick. One had a drippy eye. I might bring a disease home to Harry."

"Good thinking," Josie said. "You help Grandma make chicken salad tonight and enjoy your soup. It's even better the second day."

"Can I bring Harry upstairs while I visit Grandma?"

"You'll have to clear that with your grandmother. It's her home," Josie said.

Amelia spent ten minutes pleading on the phone until she convinced her grandmother that Harry would behave if she brought him upstairs. "I'll keep him in the little bathroom, Grandma, so he can't hurt your furniture. No, he won't wrap himself around your ankles, I promise. Yes, I realize this is a one-time trial. No, we won't make it a habit."

Josie watched with amusement as Amelia carried the

freshly cleaned litter box upstairs to her grandmother's flat. The bowls of cat food and water followed next.

"I'm sure Grandma would let you use her bowls," Josie said.

"She doesn't like cats eating out of her dishes," Amelia said. She picked up Harry and cradled him while Josie waited for Jerry's truck to arrive.

"Why are you going out with that loser face, Mom?" Amelia asked.

"Jerry?" Josie asked. "I'm not going out with him. I'm having dinner at his mother's house."

"And looking at snakes. Wait—are you hanging out with Jerry so you can help Ted?"

"Jerry doesn't have any snakes," Josie said.

"But that weird guy next door does. That's it. That's what you're doing. It won't work, Mom. You'll get hurt."

"Hah! Who's the mom here?" Josie asked.

"Remember what you said yesterday—just because someone is older doesn't mean they act like an adult."

Why didn't I think before I said that? Josie wondered. Talking baby talk to a cat has rotted my brain.

"I'll be having a quiet dinner with his mother, Bernie," Josie said.

"Don't snakes eat rats?" Amelia said. "I wonder if they eat the ears and tail first, the way we eat chocolate Easter bunnies."

Josie's stomach rolled. "There's Jerry's truck out front," she said. "I have to go."

"Be careful," Amelia said. "Watch out for the rats. They come in all sizes."

Jerry's truck looked disturbingly like Jonah's fatal pickup, but Jerry had made a touching effort to shine it up. "I got most of Chloe's hair off the passenger seat," he said, "but I put a blanket over it just in case."

"Where is your dog?"

"I can leave her at home now without her piddling on the floor," he said. "Provided we don't stay too late."

"Fine with me," Josie said, a little too enthusiastically.

"I just hope she doesn't eat something important," Jerry said. "She gnawed my good shoes last week."

"She'll be out of that stage soon," Josie said.

"She'd better be. I'm down to two pairs of shoes."

They rode in a silence that grew heavier by the minute. Finally Jerry said, "I still can't believe all this stuff about Jonah."

"Do you think he killed his wife?" Josie asked.

"I think someone else killed her and hid her body on his property," Jerry said. "There was a lot of junk around the farm. It would have been easy."

Great, Jerry believes Jonah was set up, Josie thought. Just like I think Ted was framed. We make quite a pair.

"But who would want to kill her?" she asked.

"Jonah said Allegra was sneaking around on him. Maybe her lover shot her."

"And then he killed Jonah with a snake?" Josie asked.

"No, no. Your vet did that," Jerry said. "He's one of those radical animal rights types. Did you hear him go on about snakes being our friends with Ike Ikeman on TV? The dude's a nut. He killed Jonah because he sold puppies. He put one of his snake friends in Jonah's pickup."

"How could he?" Josie asked. "Dr. Ted didn't have a key to Jonah's truck."

"Didn't need one," Jerry said. "Jonah didn't lock his truck. A lot of farmers don't."

Jerry's truck was bumping up the rutted road to his mother's house. Josie hung on to the door handle to keep from bouncing across the seat.

"Aw, look," Jerry said softly. "Mom's left the porch light burning."

Bernie was waiting at the front door, surrounded by a

half-dozen multicolored cats. More cats were perched on chairs, the couch, and the television. Cat hair floated through the air like dandelion fluff.

"You look nice, Mom," Jerry said. He kissed his mother's cheek. "Is that a new dress?"

"Nope, just one I haven't worn in a while. Dinner's ready to go on the table. Why don't you and Josie go sit down. You can introduce her to Paul."

Paul stood up when Josie entered the kitchen. He was a tall man about sixty with wide shoulders and a nose like a new potato. "Pleased to meet you," he said, and extended a calloused hand. Paul had had a lifetime of hard work.

Jerry threw a fat gray cat off a chair and said, "Have a seat, Josie. What would you like to drink?"

"Beer," she said. "Any kind is fine."

Bernie hauled a huge platter to the table, avoiding the cruising cats.

"Boy, that looks good," Paul said. "I can't tell you the last time I had homemade fried chicken."

"It's my mama's recipe," Bernie said. "Help yourself to the mashed potatoes and gravy. Josie, would you start passing the string beans?"

Josie passed them without taking any. She'd rather eat cat hair. But the chicken smelled delicious and there had been no cats near the stove.

"Did you ever eat snake?" Paul asked, as he handed the platter to Josie.

"Uh, no," Josie said. "Does it taste like fish?"

"More like chicken," he said. "White meat."

Josie carefully backed her fork out of the chicken breast she'd speared and stuck it into a leg. "Guess you wouldn't find a drumstick on a snake," she said.

"That's a good one!" Paul said. "Snakes don't have legs. Wanna see mine after dinner?"

"Your snakes?" Josie asked.

"Well, my legs aren't as interesting, but you're welcome

to look." Paul laughed at his own joke. "I've got quite a collection next door. And it's dinnertime for one of the big guys."

The last of Josie's appetite disappeared.

"I keep them in the spare room," Paul said.

"If one of your houseguests wiggles his way over here, you're out on the street," Bernie said.

Josie managed to eat her cherry cobbler, then helped Jerry's mom with the dishes. Jerry and Paul retired to watch television. She thought longingly of Ted, who cooked for her and entertained her—and languished in jail.

"You ready to watch me feed my snakes?" Paul asked, popping his head into the kitchen.

"You go next door, honey," Jerry's mom said to Josie. "I'm finished here. I have to feed the kitties."

Paul lived in three small, square rooms tacked onto the side of Bernie's house. "I built special shelves in the back room here," Paul said, as he led them through a living room just big enough for a recliner and a television.

He switched on a light. "Here they are."

The room was lined with what looked like aquariums in different sizes. The snakes were loathsome, Josie thought. And they were moving. Some were barely bigger than belts. Others were six or seven feet long. Their colors ranged from bright spring green to autumnal orange and the brown of dead leaves. None had the colorful coral snake bands.

"Now that one there is a corn snake," Paul said, tapping on one aquarium. "They're pretty common. I've got an orange one, which is sort of unusual. That yellowish one is Herman, a rat snake. Herman's mean. He bites, but his bites aren't poisonous."

Josie backed away from the aquarium and Paul laughed. "Herman ain't coming through the glass, honey. You're safe."

"That's good," Josie said, her voice shaking slightly.

Paul turned to the rat snake. "It's time to feed you, isn't it, boy? You're hungry."

Josie didn't feel quite so bad about talking to Harry the cat if Paul spoke to Herman the snake.

"Now, over here is his dinner," Paul said. He put on thick work gloves, opened a cage of live white rats, and grabbed one behind the head. The fat rat struggled.

"Most collectors feed their snakes frozen mice or rats, but I like the live ones. Makes the snakes work for their dinner. Gives 'em an interest in life, you know?" He dropped the struggling rat into the cage.

Josie felt sick.

"What's the matter, honey? You're as green as a grass snake."

"I didn't know the rats would be so alive," she said.

"You gotta kill to eat. That's the rule of the animal kingdom. Heck, you didn't think that chicken committed suicide for our supper? You'd better never see how they kill chickens."

If I could stand vegetables, I'd become a vegetarian right now, Josie thought.

"Look at that! Look at that! He's got him!" Paul said, as if he were cheering on a football team. Out of the corner of her eye, Josie saw the snake unhinge its jaws and swallow the rat whole. She couldn't bear to watch Paul smile.

"Look!" Paul said. Josie saw the rat's tail disappear into the snake's jaws.

Well, at least I can answer Amelia's question, she thought. Head and ears first, tail last. I never thought I'd feel sorry for a rat.

"Do you have any rattlesnakes?" Josie asked. "Or copperheads?"

"Nope, I don't keep venomous snakes," Paul said. "Too dangerous. Bernie would have my hide. I wanted the boa that turned up on the lawn last year, but then I decided it was a bad idea. Those big snakes can squeeze you to death. Don't keep poisonous ones, either. Don't want any pets killing me."

"Did you say you vacation in Bonita Springs, Florida?" Josie asked.

"Sure do," Paul said. "My brother's got a condo there, and I spend a couple of months with him every year. Winter if I'm lucky, summer if I'm not."

Bonita Springs. "Isn't that where a person was killed by a coral snake a few years ago?"

"Talk of the town when I was there," Paul said. "A couple of illegals were camping out in the woods and a coral snake bit one. Same kind of snake that killed old Jonah. He made a go out of that farm of his. Who'd a thought things would turn out the way they did? I kind of liked the guy, until I got a good look at those kennels of his. Mistreating puppies. He should be ashamed. And the way he raised those poor boys. He starved them and used them as cheap help. That's no way to treat your own flesh and blood. Then he killed that store clerk. I knew Edna. Nice lady. She sold me these rats. She didn't deserve to die like that. I'll tell you—whoever murdered Jonah did the world a favor.

"Well, that's it," Paul said. "Show's over. Herman's going to sleep after a good dinner, and so am I."

"Thank you for a most unusual evening," Josie said. "Jerry, don't we have to get home before your dog eats your shoes?"

# Chapter 33

"What did you think of Paul's snakes?" Jerry asked.

"Incredible," Josie said. That one word summed up the whole evening, no matter how Josie looked at it.

Jerry's pickup rocked and swayed down Bernie's unpaved road toward civilization, while Josie clung to the door handle to keep from sliding around the cab. She hoped this would be her last trip along these ruts. Jerry downshifted as the truck lumbered past the Deerford Kennels' entrance. Ghostly yellow police tape flapped in the cold winter wind. Josie shivered. What a lonely place to live—and die.

"You're very quiet tonight," Jerry said.

"Just tired," Josie said. "I had a long day."

They rode the rest of the way in silence, but it wasn't the easy silence of two people who enjoyed being together. Josie desperately wanted to go home. She had nothing more to say to Jerry. She could feel their friendship dying as he drove along the highway.

An hour later she saw the warm, welcoming lights of her house. Jerry's truck was still rolling when Josie opened the door and jumped out. She was afraid he might try to kiss her good-bye—or want an even closer encounter.

"Good night. Thank you," Josie said. "Pet Chloe for me."

"Wait! I'll walk you to the door."

"Gotta go. It's a school night," Josie said.

"When can I see you?" Jerry said.

"I'll call you!" Josie said, and sprinted up the sidewalk. She was out of breath by the time she ran upstairs to her mother's second-floor flat. She knocked gently and heard Jane whisper, "Come in."

The scene on the other side of the door was Josie's biggest shock that day: Harry was asleep in Jane's lap. Her mother was scratching his huge ears.

"I thought you didn't like cats," Josie whispered.

"I don't," Jane said. "But this cat acts like a dog."

Josie made sounds like a dog whining. Harry sat up and looked around.

"Why did you do that?" Jane asked. "He was perfectly happy."

"I thought he'd want the company of his fellow dogs," Josie said.

"Josie, you don't have the sense God gave a goose. Your daughter is asleep in my bedroom."

"I'll wake her up and walk her downstairs," Josie said. "Thanks for watching her."

"Humph!" Jane said. "She should be babysitting you."

The three made a peculiar procession down the back stairs: A sleepy Amelia carried her cat like a teddy bear. She was followed by Josie bearing the litter box, which was no longer pristine. Jane held Harry's food and water bowls.

Amelia put on her pajamas and fell into her own bed with Harry beside her. By the time Jane had set down the bowls in the kitchen and Josie had planted the litter box, Amelia was asleep with her arm around Harry.

"Aren't they adorable?" Josie whispered to her mother.

"You used to be that cute," Jane said. "Don't forget to wash your hands after carrying that litter box."

A simple hand washing couldn't wipe away the traces of her awful evening. Josie's skin felt itchy from Bernie's floating cat hair and crawly from Paul's snakes. Even a long, hot shower didn't make her feel better. She tried to sleep, but her mind replayed the horrible end of that poor rat. Paul claimed it was only natural for a snake to eat a rat. Josie thought Nature could be one mean mother.

I've wasted a whole evening at Bernie's house, Josie thought, and learned nothing that could help Ted. Paul says he didn't like Jonah, but he didn't keep poisonous snakes—and Bernie wouldn't let him. Maybe he had his treasures out of sight in his bedroom.

Someone must know something that could clear Ted's name, someone familiar with dangerous snakes. She racked her brains. The name seemed tantalizingly close.

When the alarm went off at seven the next morning, Josie remembered the name.

Nedra!

Josie didn't know how Nedra felt about snakes, but the woman was an animal activist. She belonged to People Are Animals, Too, an organization that Ted supported. Surely they protected snakes.

Josie found the PAT card with Ted's name on it in her purse. On the back were printed NEDRA NEOSHO—PEOPLE ARE ANIMALS, TOO and a phone number. The PAT office was on Manchester Road, near Ted's clinic. She'd call later this morning and set up an appointment.

Meanwhile, Josie needed a coffee transfusion and a shot of daily news.

She turned on the television and stared at Traci and Snowball for the second day in a row. Today, they both wore matching St. Louis Cardinals ball caps and warm-up jackets. Traci held her white puppy while she talked to the same blond announcer in a studio setting. With her red outfit and brilliant hair, Traci and her dog made a dramatic pair. The studio lights shone in Snowball's bright eyes.

Seated beside Traci was a slender woman with short blond hair and a simple, blue striped shirt. She held two tiny black dogs. One looked like a fur muff. The other dog was smaller and had a round, domed head. His fur was short and velvety. The short-haired dog tried to snuggle in the crook of the woman's arm. Compared to Snowball, who had more clothes than Paris Hilton, the two black dogs seemed naked.

The announcer looked professionally serious. "Yesterday, Traci shared the story of her puppy mill rescue dog, Snowball. Our viewers wanted more. This morning, we brought Traci back with a special guest, Karen Reibman. Traci, tell us what's been happening."

"Thank you for the hundreds of e-mails you sent," Traci said. "I promise I'll answer them all, but it will take time. Many of you also told your puppy mill rescue stories." Traci seemed born to sit in front of the camera. "On my YouTube page, I have links to informational videos about puppy mills. Some of you said, 'I can't stand to look at those videos. Those poor little pups are too sad.'

"I'll tell you what's sad: what happens to those puppies. Every time we close our eyes, we allow people like Jonah Deerford to hurt more animals. It's time to look at what's going on. I want you to know that those stories can have happy endings. Today, you can meet Karen Reibman. She rescued two dogs several years ago. They're now healthy and happy."

The camera shifted to the blond woman. Now her dogs were leashed and sitting on the floor. One sniffed Karen's shoes.

"Both these dogs are from Missouri puppy mills," Karen said. "Some people think the littlest one is a puppy, but he's really seventeen years old. He's just extra small. His name is Joey and his hair is cut short."

Joey was walking round and round.

"He's walking in small, tight circles," Traci said.

"That's how some puppy mill dogs react when they're nervous," Karen said. "He's pacing the dimensions of his cage like a prisoner. When I adopted Joey, he was filthy and disgusting. He's a Pomeranian, but we had to cut his hair short. He had horrible teeth. Many puppy mill dogs do."

Karen picked up Joey and hugged him. The dog barked.

"It's okay," she said, soothing him. She put Joey down and picked up the fluffy dark dog. "This is my black Pomeranian, Magic. She has a long name and the AKC papers to go with it. Magic is very possessive. Puppy mill dogs are like that. They love their families, but they don't care about the rest of the world.

"When you adopt puppy mill dogs, you may have animals who are five or ten years old, but they're still like puppies. They've been kept in cages and they know nothing about our world. They're not housebroken. They walk into glass doors because they've never seen them. They don't know how to play. If their food bowl is empty, they panic because they don't think they'll ever eat again. That's how their lives used to be.

"It takes months just to calm them down. With lots and lots of love, you can start training them. Both my puppies are housebroken and leash trained. Magic still won't accept my husband, David. He's the kindest, gentlest man, but she's frightened of him. She's frightened of almost all people. It's been a struggle to bring my dogs out of their shells. But Joey and Magic have given me more than I've given them."

Traci was back, holding Snowball. "It takes a special person to adopt a puppy mill dog, but Karen has the patience to do it."

She turned the subject artfully back to herself. "My little baby wants to help less fortunate puppies," Traci said. "We bought her this baseball cap and warm-up jacket through the Humane Society of Missouri gift shop. The proceeds will help save more animals."

"Yap!" Snowball said.

"I want you to go to my Web site and look at the animal rescue organizations," Traci said. "Then make a donation of your time or money. Some organizations need food and medicine. Others could use old towels and newspapers. Everyone has those. Have the courage to help the helpless."

Snowball and the two black dogs barked madly as Traci's e-mail and YouTube addresses went on the screen.

Amelia appeared at Josie's side. "That's sweet, Mom. How come you aren't barfing this morning?"

"Because Traci is sincere," Josie said. "She wants to help. We're meeting her for brunch at your aunt Alyce's this morning."

"Cool. Would you get her picture? All the kids at school were talking about her crusade."

"I'd be glad to," Josie said. "But you'd better get to school first. Today, we're leaving on time."

The sun was shining through a cold, lead gray sky as Josie dropped Amelia off at the Barrington School. She picked up some groceries, then drove to the People Are Animals, Too office. She arrived as Nedra unlocked the storefront. Once again, Josie was struck by the woman's curious, old-fashioned appearance. The long skirt and flat, straight hair were from an antique folk singer's album. Nedra had a pale martyr's face. She seemed to want to suffer for a cause.

The PAT office was plain as a nun's cell. The narrow room held only a lumpy brown futon, a dusty philodendron, and a desk that looked like it had been beaten with chains. The poster over the desk turned Josie's stomach. A platter of human arms deep-fried like chicken wings was captioned, YOU DON'T HAVE TO KILL TO EAT. GO VEGETARIAN.

"I'll be right with you." Nedra settled herself behind the old desk. She checked the message machine, put more pamphlets on a rack, then said, "How may I help you?"

"You probably don't remember me," Josie began.

"I do, Josie," Nedra said. "You were at the Humane Society when I was walking my Chihuahua."

"Bruiser," Josie said.

A smile lit Nedra's pale face. "That's right. You remembered."

"You told me about Dr. Ted, a vet who makes house

calls," Josie said. "When a friend adopted a puppy mill dog, Dr. Ted took care of her."

"That's one of his specialties," Nedra said. "We've referred many people with rescue animals to him."

"Now that Dr. Ted is in jail, I wondered if you could help me rescue him."

"How?" Nedra asked. "As you can see by this office, we're not rich. I could spare maybe five dollars, but I can barely make the payments on my Dogtown home. You probably don't know that Dr. Ted was distancing himself from PAT. He started supporting more conventional organizations. We think that distance is wise, in view of the circumstances."

"But he's accused of murder," Josie said. "The police say he killed Jonah Deerford with a snake. I thought you might put us in touch with someone who knows poisonous snakes. Someone who could help Ted."

"Ew!" Nedra gave a stagy shudder. "I hate snakes. I've pledged my life to saving animals, but I can't make myself like reptiles. That's a prejudice I can't overcome."

"Me, either," Josie said. "Snakes give me the creeps."

"Jonah Deerford deserved his horrible death!" Nedra said. "I'm glad a snake killed him. Sweets for the sweet . . ."

"Snakes for the snakes," Josie finished.

# Chapter 34

"Yap!"

Josie heard Snowball's greeting when she walked into Alyce's garage.

"Is that our star?" Josie asked outside the kitchen door.

"Come in," Alyce said. "The door's unlocked."

Snowball was sitting on Traci's lap at the breakfast room table. They both wore their red Cardinals outfits. Josie sniffed the kitchen air and caught the mouthwatering scent of warm cheese, fresh spices, and cinnamon.

"What's for brunch?" Josie asked.

"Just something simple," Alyce said. "A salad and crepes with goat cheese and plum tomatoes. We have cinnamon rolls for dessert."

"I love your idea of simple," Josie said. "It only takes a Cordon Bleu chef."

"The crepes are simple. Even you—well, even Amelia could make them. Pour yourself some white wine."

"Congratulations on your success," Josie said, raising her glass in a toast to Traci. "I'd like to snap your picture for Amelia. You're a hero at her school."

Traci and her pup posed like pros.

"I have a present for Snowball," Josie said.

Traci opened the tiara bag and said, "It's perfect for my

princess. She's going to need it now that she's being welcomed into Wood Winds society."

"Let me guess," Josie said. "Renata Upton Liverspot, the queen of Wood Winds, has stooped to invite you to Castle Dracula."

"She says I can come for tea. She wants me to bring Snowball."

"Are you going?" Josie said.

"Maybe I can talk her into making a contribution for the puppies."

"She'll throw parties if she can lord it over some volunteers," Josie said. "But any cash will have to be pried out of her cold, dead hands."

"Well, I've lived without her for thirty years," Traci said. "I'm sure I can go on."

"You don't need her acceptance," Alyce said.

Josie did not remind her friend that not too long ago, Alyce had been reduced to tears by Renata's refusal to see her. Josie started to take her empty plate to the kitchen, but Alyce said, "No, stay seated. I'll bring the rolls and hot coffee."

Josie took a bite of a warm cinnamon roll. "These rolls are to die for," Josie said.

"I hope not," Alyce said. "I want you to enjoy my food for a long time. They have healthy ingredients like raisins, pecans, and cinnamon."

"You sure can't tell," Josie said.

"Any luck helping Dr. Ted?" Alyce asked.

"None," Josie said. "I've hit one dead end after the other. If I can't help him, Ted will have to stay in jail until the trial. He can't get bail. That could be at least a year."

"There's nothing you can do?" Traci asked.

"I have a few ideas. I'm going to visit my old boyfriend, Josh, at Has Beans. He may know some drug dealers who have pet snakes."

"Is that wise, Josie?" Alyce asked, her voice serious with concern. "Josh was no fling. You really cared for him. You hurt for a long time after the breakup. Do you want to go back there?"

Traci and Snowball watched this drama. Both had their mouths hanging open.

"It's a risk I'll have to take," Josie said. "I know you said you used to live in Florida, Traci, but didn't you mention Arizona, as well?"

"My mom had cancer and I spent the last four months with her in Arizona. She died in October."

"I'm sorry," Josie said.

"I miss her every day, but I didn't want her to live with that kind of pain."

"What a good daughter you were to move out to Arizona," Alyce said.

"That's where I met my husband," Traci said. "He was visiting his father at the hospital. It was love at first sight. We married while Mom was still alive. She loved Jonathan almost as much as I did. After Mom died, Jonathan got a good job offer in St. Louis. I was tired of the desert dryness and didn't want to return to the Miami craziness. St. Louis seemed like a good place to start a family and have a normal life."

Alyce's doorbell rang. She looked out the front window. "It's the UPS man. I hope it's my roasting fork," she said.

It was. Alyce opened a long box and took out a heavy steel fork more than a foot long. "That should lift a turkey," she said with satisfaction.

"It should lift a buffalo," Josie said. "Do you need a license to carry that?"

"While we're talking about lethal weapons, Josie, please tell me you aren't going to poke around in Jonah Deerford's murder. It's too dangerous."

"I can't let Ted go to jail for a murder he didn't commit. The Wildfern police aren't going to do anything."

"So you're going back to see Josh at Has Beans? You're playing with fire, Josie. Is that your only choice?"

"I can try one other thing," Josie said. "If I can find the woman who can alibi Ted for the time Jonah Deerford was murdered, that would clear him. But Ted won't give me her name. He says she's been hurt enough."

"Such a gentleman," Traci said, and sighed. "You don't find men like him anymore."

"What about that Nedra person?" Alyce asked. "Didn't she used to work with Ted at People Are Animals, Too?"

"Her name is Nedra Neosho. She might know the woman's name, but Nedra says Ted has distanced himself from the PAT group. I saw her this morning."

"Still, to save his life, she might help," Alyce said. "After all, he is a mammal."

"Good thing, because she's antireptile. But she might help. Edna said she was a good person. I'll give her a call. It's worth a try before I see Josh again and open old wounds."

But visions of dangerous Josh danced in her head—exciting visions Josie couldn't ignore. To make them disappear, she dialed the PAT office.

"Good afternoon. People Are Animals, Too. This is Jennifer speaking."

"Hi, I'm Josie Marcus. I was in this morning talking to Nedra Neosho. May I speak with her?"

"She's not here," Jennifer said. "Perhaps I could help you?"

"No, I really need to speak with Nedra. When will she be back?"

"She volunteers one morning a week," Jennifer said. "You'll have to wait another seven days until she comes in again. Sorry." She didn't sound sorry.

Josie hung up, discouraged. "That's that," she said. "No way to talk to Nedra for a week."

"Not quite," Alyce said. "See if her home address is in the directory."

The St. Louis phone book seemed to shrink every year.

But for once, Josie had some good luck. Nedra was in the white pages. "She lives in the perfect place for an animal rights activist," Josie said. "Dogtown."

"You're joking," Traci said.

"No, it's a real neighborhood on the western edge of St. Louis. Dogtown used to be the Irish section. It has some cute older houses. I have enough time to stop by and see her before I pick up Amelia at school—if I leave now."

"Take her a cinnamon roll," Alyce said.

"She won't be able to resist," Traci said.

"Yap!" said Snowball.

Josie left, loaded with leftover cinnamon rolls and good wishes.

Nedra lived in a neat, white vinyl-sided house with crisp green trim. The home had a striped awning over the front door, rambler roses next to the porch, and a fenced back-yard. The front lawn was being dug up and reseeded. About half the yard was yellow-brown clay soil. The rest was strag-gling brown weeds.

Nedra's concrete drive ended in a narrow one-car garage. The garage door was up. Josie saw, parked inside, a brown Subaru plastered with bumper stickers: DON'T EAT THE DEAD—GO VEGETARIAN and I'D RATHER BE CAMPING. Josie hoped the car in the garage meant Nedra was home.

After several minutes of Josie's energetic knocking, Nedra came to the door, wearing the same outfit she'd had on at the PAT office. She had sleep wrinkles in her right cheek.

"I hope I didn't wake you up," Josie said. "May I come in? Ooh, it's your little puppy."

Bruiser was hiding behind Nedra's skirt. Josie bent down to pet the pup's ear. She was in.

"Uh," Nedra said.

Josie stepped into a clean, small room with white cur-tains and mint green walls. Long, brownish things were in shadow box frames on the walls. Leaves? Old lace? The room had a dark couch, a chair, and a long, narrow table against the wall by the door. A bushy green vine trailed down the edge.

Bruiser, Nedra's pound pup, was now gnawing on a flat shoe near the table.

"Hi, cutie," Josie said to the pup, getting down on the floor. Bruiser dropped the shoe and started chewing on a book cover. Josie reached over to rescue the book from Bruiser's puppy teeth and heard a dry rattle, like dead seeds in a gourd.

She was eye level with the cruel face of a tan and black rattlesnake. The reptile coiled and uncoiled in a long, closed tank on the table. Josie backed away and dropped the book with a thud. The pup yelped and ran under the couch. The book was *Venomous Snakes of the World*.

"Looking for your boyfriend's picture in the book?" Nedra said.

"I thought you didn't like snakes," Josie said.

"I lied," Nedra said. "Just like your vet friend lied. Ted said he wasn't serious about anyone. But he was serious about me, until you came along. So I guess I'm nobody." The bitterness in Nedra's voice was like snake venom.

"It was you," Josie said. "You put that coral snake skin in Ted's clinic."

"It was my snake skin," Nedra said. "I went to the clinic when he was out with the mobile pet van and left the snake skin behind his couch."

"But he's being railroaded for murder," Josie said.

"Ted deserves to be in trouble. Just like Jonah deserved to die. The world is better off without both of them. Ted was right—snakes are useful."

She smiled. The snake could have learned a few lessons about scary from Nedra.

Josie looked at the closest brown item on the wall. A snake skin.

"The coral snake skin was a souvenir of our trip to New Mexico," Nedra said. "We visited PAT's headquarters there. At least Ted let me keep that."

"That's where you found the coral snake, isn't it?" Josie asked.

"I found it when Ted and I went camping there. He wanted to leave the coral snake in the wild. He said we were disturbing its home and that wasn't fair. Fair! To a snake! I hid the coral snake in a minnow bucket in my trunk. It survived the trip back to St. Louis."

"And this snake in the tank here is the one Ted found in Traci's garage?" Josie asked.

"Maybe." Nedra smiled a death's-head grin. "Ted wanted to set it free in the woods. He asked me to go with him. He said it had to be released near where it lived. That was the day he met you. All the way to the site, he talked about you— how cute you were, where you lived, your darling daughter, and your stupid, constipated cat! He was too dumb to know it, but I figured it out. Ted was in love with you."

"He was?" Josie was strangely pleased.

"He dumped me three days later. Oh, he was nice about it. Ted said we could be just friends. Hah! They all say that. Ted didn't even know if you liked snakes. I was the only woman he ever dated who did."

"Uh, you have a lot in common," Josie said. "I brought you these. They're vegetarian." She dropped the bag of cinnamon rolls on the couch and started backing toward the door.

"Ted took me to a rock ledge where some fifty timber rattlesnakes were brumating. That's a light hibernation, except this was a sunny day and the snakes were sunning themselves. Those fat suburbanites in Wood Winds would have a fit if they knew a den of rattlesnakes lived so close to their silly gated subdivision."

"I never liked subdivisions," Josie said. She started edging toward the front door, but Nedra and the snake tank still blocked her way. Another five feet and she would be out of there.

"I sacrificed my beloved coral snake to a good cause," Nedra said. "I put it in Jonah's truck. I parked my car at the end of that awful road, hiked up, and left the snake in his truck. It was unlocked. The next day was warm, and the snake did its job. Jonah died."

"Why not kill him with a rattlesnake?" Josie said.

"Because a rattler would have warned Jonah," Nedra said. "If he got to the hospital in time, an adult could survive the bite. But a coral snake is quiet. Dead quiet, you might say. Most people don't know they've been bitten until it's too late. And coral snake antivenin isn't made anymore. But I missed my pet, so I went back to the timber rattlesnake den and brought that beauty home."

"Glad you're not lonely," Josie said. She slid another foot toward the front door.

Quick as a striking snake, Nedra grabbed an odd reaching device off the long table, opened the top of the tank, and stuck it inside the tank. The rubber-lined jaws caught the rattlesnake behind the head. It writhed and undulated. Nedra expertly removed the snake from the tank.

"Well, thanks. Better go," Josie said.

Before she could get out the door, Nedra thrust the snake tongs at her. The snake was close enough that its long tongue nearly touched her shoulder. It hissed and lunged, but Nedra hung on to the snake tongs and kept the snake millimeters from Josie.

"Don't worry," she said. "There's no poison in a snake tongue. But if it sinks those fangs in you, it's bye-bye. Now go outside through the kitchen, or I'll drop the snake on your neck. It will bite a carotid artery and nobody will be able to save you."

The muddy-colored snake bared its fangs and gave a warning rattle.

Josie backed slowly through the kitchen, looking for something to use as a weapon. She started to reach for a kitchen chair.

"Don't even think about it," Nedra said. "And don't bother going for the knife by the sink, either."

They were through the small kitchen now. Josie was backed up against the side door. Only one short step separated her from the garage. Nedra pressed a button on the kitchen wall and the garage door rumbled shut.

Josie opened the shed door slowly, blocking her escape into the backyard.

"Get inside," Nedra hissed. She was starting to sound like a snake.

"I am inside," Josie said.

"I mean in that toolshed. Move or I'll let him sink those fangs in you right now."

Stall for time, Josie told herself. Maybe there's a weapon on the garage wall. Then you can hit her with it and bolt down the drive.

There was barely room for Josie, Nedra, and the rattlesnake in the cramped space between the car bumper and the toolshed. One escape route was blocked by trash cans and recycling bins. Nedra held the snake carefully and threw open the shed door. That blocked the other way out.

"Get in," Nedra said. "The snake is pissed and so am I. Congratulations. You're about to become a statistic—one of the few Missourians killed by a timber rattlesnake."

Josie's terrified brain took in four stacked sacks of mulch and a big bag of grass seed. There was no sign of a shovel, rake, or hoe. They must be out on the lawn.

"I'm running out of patience," Nedra said. "Get in. Now." The snake writhed, hissed, and rattled. "In!" Nedra screamed, and held the snake close enough that Josie could see its mean little eyes in that deadly, triangular face.

Josie slipped into the shed. "It's awfully small," she said.

"It's big enough for you and the snake." Nedra threw the snake inside and slammed the door.

Josie screamed and climbed atop the stack of mulch bags. The snake rattled again and struck at the lowest bag. Josie whimpered and clung to the walls. Wood splinters pierced her hands. The shed was black as the inside of a cave. She felt along the wall and found something silky and sticky in the closest corner. A spiderweb? There were no spiders this time of year, were there?

Josie heard the snap of a padlock.

"Nedra," Josie said, "how are you going to explain the padlock to the police?"

"I'll just say I saw the shed was unlocked when I came home and locked it again. Imagine my surprise when I opened it days later and found you dead."

# Chapter 35

Josie heard that fatal rattle and stayed perfectly still. A thin band of light from the garage filtered under the padlocked shed door. She could see the snake, now that her eyes were adjusting to the dimness.

The rattlesnake was coiled in the opposite corner on the bag of grass seed. There was enough light to read the writing on the bag: *50 pounds grass seed, 49% Kentucky bluegrass, 20% perennial rye, 29% creeping red fescue.*

The snake was one-hundred-percent creepy. The predator's flat, triangular head had terrified humans for centuries. The colors—the yellow-brown of spring mud and the black of decaying leaves—were cruel tricks.

Now Josie could see she wasn't standing on four bags of mulch. These were fifty-pound sacks of corn gluten organic weed control—*Prevents and eliminates weeds. Stops crabgrass, spurge, dandelions, bent grass, and other common weeds. Safe for kids and dogs.*

Trust Nedra to go for the greenest lawn, in all senses of the word.

The coiled snake stretched its jaws and sank its fangs into the bottom sack. An evil stream of venom shot out and trickled down the bag.

Just three feet higher, Josie thought, and I'm dead.

She pounded on the shed walls. "Let me out! Let me go! I have a daughter."

"Shut up, Josie," Nedra said in a bored voice.

How could she sound bored when I'm locked in with a killer reptile? Josie wondered. No wonder the woman likes snakes. She is as cold-blooded as they are.

If Nedra wouldn't listen, a neighbor might hear her shouts. "Help!" Josie screamed. "Somebody help me!"

"Forget it," Nedra said. "The Hendersons next door are both at work and the old lady on the other side is deaf. No one can hear you. Except the snake. Oooh, is that another rattle? Isn't that sweet? Snakes don't drop in on people in the middle of the afternoon. This one announces his visit. You can learn many valuable lessons from our friend the snake." Nedra gave a mocking laugh.

Light! Josie needed more light. She had to escape. The walls felt like they would close in and crush her. Josie ran her hands along the wall for a light switch. Nothing.

She searched blindly with her hands for a ridge, molding, or small shelf along the top of the shed. If she found something, Josie could hang on to it while she pushed the fifty-pound sacks on top of the snake. If two hundred pounds of corn gluten weren't heavy enough to kill the rattler, the sacks might immobilize the snake until help came.

But when was that?

Josie moved her hands carefully above her head. A long splinter sliced her palm. Then another.

"Ouch!" Josie said.

"Ouch?" Nedra taunted. "This will be more than an ouch, Josie. Oh, listen—he's rattling again."

The coiled snake struck the second corn gluten bag. Again, the awful jaws unhinged and the fangs attacked. More venom sprayed the bag. The snake was working his way up to the top of the pile.

Josie felt her feet start to slide off the stack of bags. She grabbed the wall and fell heavily against the corner. She heard a rattle—a metallic rattle, not the dead, hollow sound of the snake's warning. The noise seemed to come from over her head.

Josie reached straight up and prayed she'd find something useful. Her hand touched a smooth wooden pole covered with dust. Her hands followed the pole till it ended in a bent, curved piece of rusted iron. She felt four prongs.

A pitchfork. She had a pitchfork. It must have been stored in the shed's rafters ages ago, possibly before Nedra bought the house.

Josie was so relieved, she nearly fell off the stack of bags. She heard that horrible warning rattle again. The coiled snake unhinged its jaws and struck at the third bag. She didn't see any venom from this strike.

Josie screamed. She could hear Nedra laughing. The woman was as creepy as Paul, who seemed to enjoy watching that snake eat the rat. Except this time I'm the rat, she thought. One bag to go and I'm a dead woman.

Josie grasped the pitchfork handle. I need to move faster than the snake does, and I'm not giving any warning. She would have one chance, and she'd have to aim carefully. The snake was coiled, poised to strike the fourth bag. This time, it would nail her foot with its fangs.

If I fail, my daughter will be an orphan, Josie thought. I can't let that happen.

She rammed the pitchfork tines into the snake as hard as she could, pinning it to the seed bag by its coiled midsection. Blood spurted from the body and ran down the bag. The snake didn't move.

It looked dead, but Josie knew she had to be cautious. She'd seen stories when she did her snake research on the Internet about people being bitten by a "dead" snake. Even a beheaded snake could bite. Those horrific jaws didn't need a body to function.

Thanks to the pitchfork, the snake was no longer a threat. The reptile lay perfectly still.

Josie was shivering uncontrollably. She couldn't stop. She'd left her gloves in the car and her purse in Nedra's living room. There was no way to call for help on her cell phone.

How would she get home to Amelia?

She could see her breath in white puffs. It was getting colder. She might die of exposure, even if she survived the snake. Somehow she had to get Nedra to open the shed door. Then Josie would attack her with the pitchfork. She would have to summon all her strength. She felt as weak as a puppy.

A puppy! Bruiser was her way out of here. Josie stayed balanced on the bags and pounded on the door. "Nedra, your dog is locked inside here."

"Liar!"

"Listen!" Josie made soft whimpering sounds and little, short barks. Her dog noises had fooled Harry. She hoped they'd convince Nedra.

"The snake is going to kill it," Josie said. She whimpered again. She hoped her puppy sounds didn't have a terrified wobble.

"I don't believe you."

"Then where is Bruiser?" Josie asked. "He follows you everywhere. He came to the front door with you. But he isn't with you now, is he? He ran into the shed when you opened the door and hid in the corner behind the grass seed. The snake sees him now."

Stay under the couch, little pup, Josie begged. She hoped the thudding snake book had traumatized the tiny creature into hiding.

"Bruiser!" Nedra called. "Here boy. Here boy."

Josie made frantic whimpering sounds and scratched at the shed walls with her nails, jamming more splinters into her hands.

"The snake is coiled for a strike," Josie said.

Nedra called Bruiser's name and waited. Josie whim-

pered and tried a yelp. There was no sound from the real
Bruiser.

Josie heard the garage door rumble open. Nedra was
leaving. Josie's heart sank. She'd gambled and lost. She was
going to die of hunger and cold in the toolshed. She'd never
get to see her daughter grow into a young woman. They'd
never shop for prom dresses. She wouldn't get to read Amelia's college entrance essay or be with her when she got her
acceptance letter

Wait! Josie heard the screech of tires in the driveway,
followed by a door slam.

"It's going to be too late, Nedra, if you walk away," Josie
called. "Hear that rattle? Nothing a snake likes better than a
fat puppy. This is a dog-eat-dog world. Better Bruiser than
me. You know once that snake eats your tasty puppy, it won't
bother me. It won't eat for days."

"Open that toolshed door," a voice commanded.

That sounded like Alyce. It was Alyce. "I'm in here,"
Josie screamed. "With a live rattlesnake."

"I'm out here with another one," Alyce said. "Nedra! I've
called 911. Now open that door or I'll run you through."

Why did Alyce sound like a discount Johnny Depp? Did
Williams-Sonoma sell pirate cutlasses?

"What is that thing?" Nedra asked.

"It's a meat fork," Alyce said. "And you're dead meat if
you don't open that door and let Josie out. This fork is thirteen inches long. It will go right through you. The police are
on their way. If I run you through, you'll bleed to death before the ambulance arrives."

Josie heard footsteps. Nedra was returning to the shed.
Josie made more whimpering sounds, hoping they sounded
as desperate as she felt. She could hear Nedra unlocking the
toolshed padlock. Yes!

Josie stayed in the corner, perched precariously on her
stack of fifty-pound bags. Slowly, silently, she pulled the
pitchfork out of the snake's body. The reptile stayed inert.

Josie stayed on guard. She made more whimpering sounds, but these came naturally. Her life depended on Nedra's next move.

"Bruiser?" Nedra whispered. "Are you in there, baby?" She opened the shed door an inch.

Josie made happy whimpering sounds and tried a small yap.

The shed door creaked open. When sunlight poured into the shed, the snake suddenly came to life, rattled its tail, whipped its head around, and sank its fangs in Nedra's leg, right through the long skirt.

Nedra screamed as if all the demons of hell had attacked her. The snake let go. Josie hung on to the pitchfork.

"Be careful, Nedra," Josie said. "Stay very still. The snake bite may be near the femoral artery. Don't move or the poison will go straight to your heart and kill you."

"Is that true?" Nedra asked.

"You don't have any choice but to believe me," Josie said. "Let me pass."

"Let me think about it," Nedra said.

"You don't have time!" Josie said. "You're going to die. You're afraid. That makes your heart beat faster. That will spread the poison quicker. Your leg is starting to swell already."

Josie could see Alyce behind her, armed with a thirteen-inch meat fork. Her skin was pale, her eyes were wild, and her ghostly blond hair was standing straight out. She looked like a creature from a slasher movie.

"The cops are on their way," Alyce said. "And it's a good thing. Otherwise, I'd run you through."

A police car slammed into the driveway, followed by an ambulance.

"Do you think I'll lose my leg?" Nedra whimpered.

"I certainly hope so," Josie said. "Snakes don't have legs."

# Chapter 36

Hours after Alyce's daring rescue, Josie was in an emergency room cubicle, wrapped in a thin hospital blanket. Alyce's call to 911 had summoned platoons of police and paramedics to Nedra's home. A uniformed officer, and then a detective, questioned Josie. Josie had signed a statement, but it was difficult. Her hands hurt. That's when Alyce had insisted she be taken to a hospital.

Now a doctor, who looked like he should wear a Boy Scout uniform, was picking splinters out of Josie's hands with long tweezers. He looked lost. Josie half expected him to check her north side for moss.

"How did you know where to find me, Alyce?" Josie asked.

"Your mother called," Alyce said. "She asked if I knew where you were. You didn't pick up Amelia at school. Barrington called her at four o'clock."

Josie sat straight up. "Ohmigod!"

Dr. Scout gently pushed her back down. "Ms. Marcus, you must stay still or this will hurt even more. I still have three more splinters to remove."

"Amelia is safe, Josie. Your mother has her." Alyce sat in the chair next to Josie's stretcher, holding her purse primly on her lap. The strain of her attack on Nedra had turned Alyce's creamy skin the thin blue-white of skimmed milk.

"But I'm in trouble big-time." Josie couldn't stop shivering. The hospital staff kept piling on heated blankets, but they couldn't warm her.

"If I know your mother, she'll give you a good lecture," Alyce said. "But Jane will forgive you. She always does. Lecturing you is her way of blowing off steam. Jane reminds me of a mother cat we had when I was growing up. When one of her kittens irritated Molly, she'd swat it on the head, but Molly loved and defended her babies."

"Ouch!" Josie said.

"Sorry," the doctor said. "That one was in there deep." He laid another splinter on a square of gauze, next to a long row of them. Josie thought this one was the size of a toothpick.

"How did you know where to find me?" Josie asked.

"You'd told me you were going to see Nedra Neosho and ask her for the name of the woman who used to date Dr. Ted," Alyce said. "Then you were going to pick up Amelia. If you'd been delayed, you would have called me or your mother. I found Nedra's phone number and address in the directory. She didn't answer her phone. I knew something was wrong, so I went to her house. There you were, trapped with a deadly snake."

"What if Nedra just wasn't picking up the phone?" Josie said.

"That wasn't a risk I wanted to take. I figured she was the woman Ted had been dating. They had a lot in common— their love of animals."

"You were smarter than I was," Josie said.

Alyce tactfully avoided commenting and continued her story. "I didn't know what I was going to find, so I took my new roasting fork, dropped it in my purse, and drove to Nedra's house."

Josie was touched. She knew what good kitchen utensils meant to a real cook. "You risked your roasting fork for me? That's a thirty-one-dollar fork."

"Always buy the best," Alyce said. "It makes a good first impression."

"You came roaring in like a crazy woman in a slasher movie—and I mean that as a compliment," Josie said.

"Thank you. It's nice to be fearsome, instead of a silly suburban lady. I put the fork back in my purse when the police arrived." Alyce patted her fashionably fat purse. "It would be a forkin' shame if I was caught with a weapon."

"Ouch!" Josie said. "That hurt."

"Sorry," Dr. Scout said. "Almost done."

"You'd better be," Josie said. "My friend here is armed and dangerous."

"You showed up at exactly the right time," Josie told Alyce. "I was trying to persuade Nedra to let me out, but it wasn't working. You made the call, roared into the driveway, and a million cops and paramedics poured in. Everything after that was a blur. Is Nedra going to lose her leg?"

"I doubt it," Alyce said. "The hospital won't release any patient information, but I heard the paramedics talking about a 'dry bite.' I think that means no venom was released when the snake bit her."

"The snake saved all its poison for me," Josie said.

"Nedra is still in plenty of trouble," Alyce said. "There were so many uniformed officers and detectives, they couldn't fit into her ER cubicle. I think she's going to be charged with first-degree murder and attempted murder and maybe importing dangerous reptiles into Missouri."

"Good," Josie said. "That means Ted will go free."

"That's it, Ms. Marcus," Dr. Scout said. "I've put antibiotic ointment on your hands. I'm wrapping them in gauze now. Leave the dressing on overnight. The nurse will be by with your discharge instructions and paperwork." He was gone.

"That was quick," Alyce said. "Maybe our murder talk made him nervous."

"Anything to speed up the process," Josie said. "I'd better call Mom to pick me up."

"I told her I'd take you home. You can delay the inevitable lecture awhile longer."

"What time is it?" Josie asked.

"Six o'clock."

"That late? What about your family?"

"The nanny agreed to stay and take care of Justin. Jake can nuke a chicken cassoulet in the freezer for his dinner."

"I need to get my purse," Josie said. "I left it in Nedra's living room."

"We'll stop for it on your way home."

The fleet of police and emergency vehicles was gone from Nedra's street. A single police car was left with an older uniformed officer. He was fit for his age and had a "seen it all" face. He got out of his car when Alyce pulled into the drive.

Josie went up to him. "I'm Josie Marcus," she began.

"I know," he said. "I remember you were tied to the scene. I'm trying to write my report about this circus. I'd rather do it in longhand like I've always done it, but now everything has to be done on this piece-of-crap mobile data terminal thingy. The detectives said I should watch the place. Those who were more important went to the ER to find out if that snake lady was going to die."

"She was still alive when I left the hospital," Josie said.

"Then I'm waiting to get the okay to lock up here and put the keys in evidence."

"I left my purse in the living room here. It's a black Coach bag. On sale," she said, as if she had to justify an expensive purse.

"It's still there, miss. Follow me in and for God's sake don't touch anything."

The purse was right where Josie said it was. "Can you tell me what's in it?" the old cop asked.

"My cell phone. It's black with a silver band and has a camera. A black wallet with thirteen dollars, two credit cards, and pictures of my daughter, Amelia. A hairbrush, tissues, lipstick . . ."

"Sounds right." He opened her wallet. "Cute kid. Let me check if your face matches your driver's license." He studied the license. "Yep, that's you."

"It's a sad day when I look like my driver's license photo," Josie said. "What happened to the snake?"

"It's dead."

"Good," Josie said. "Did the officer shoot it?"

"Killed it with a shovel."

"What about the puppy?" Josie asked.

"Don't know about any dog," the old cop said.

"Nedra had a Chihuahua puppy. Last I saw, Bruiser was under the couch. Can I look for him?"

"Knock yourself out," the older cop said.

Josie got on the floor gingerly, careful to protect her bandaged hands. She looked under the couch and found the tiny pup cowering in the far corner. Bruiser was curled into a shape as small and tight as a tennis ball—a tennis ball with huge ears. Josie gently pulled him out from under the couch with her bandaged hands.

She held the quivering ball of brown fur in one hand. "It's okay, boy," Josie said. "You're going to be fine. The snake is gone."

"He's adorable," Alyce said, petting one giant ear. "I'd like to take him home permanently."

"You want to adopt a dog?" Josie asked. "What about little Justin?"

"My son is three now," Alyce said. "It's time he learned the difference between a stuffed animal and a real one. Let me ask the nice officer."

The cop mumbled a word that sounded a lot like "shit."

"What's wrong?" Josie asked.

"I get off in twenty minutes, lady. I can't wait and I'm not getting overtime. It will take animal control two, three hours to get here. Let me call the boss on the phone."

After another delay that took up most of the old cop's remaining twenty minutes, he was back. "The boss is with the suspect at the ER. The suspect says she doesn't care about the dog, but she's suing us for killing the snake."

"Can she do that?" Josie said.

"Anybody can sue, if they've got the filing fee. Can she win? There are a lot of reptiles on the bench, but I doubt they'll feel sorry for a dead rattler. Boss says you can take the puppy. Just give me a phone number."

"Then I can keep the dog?" Alyce asked.

"What dog?" the old cop said.

# Epilogue

"What are you doing, Mom?" Amelia asked.

"I want to watch Traci and Snowball's show," Josie said, turning on the television set at seven in the morning. She could hardly use the clicker with her bandaged hands.

"I thought Traci made you barf," Amelia said.

"Shh! The show is starting," Josie said.

"Happy holidays and welcome to *Snowball's Corner*," Traci said. "As you can see, we girls are ready to celebrate."

A red Santa hat perched on Traci's bright curly hair. Snowball wore a Santa suit. Behind them was a Christmas tree decorated with dog and cat ornaments. The camera focused on a "Dogs Make a Home" ornament. The tree was topped with a bichon in white angel robes. A fireplace mantel was decorated with a Howling Hound Menorah—dogs making joyous music. Snowball was crunching a puppy bagel.

"All these holiday gifts and more are available from the Humane Society of Missouri gift shop," Traci said. "Don't forget, when you buy from their gift shop, you help save the animals.

"Thank you all for your e-mails and letters. Many of you said you want to help, but can't buy things right now. Megan, who is eight and lives in Affton, said, 'My daddy is out of work. I want to help the animals, but I don't have any money.'

"That's okay, Megan," Traci said. "You can still grant wishes, even without money. The Humane Society, like most animal protection agencies, has a wish list. Go to their Web site and look at the gifts you can donate that won't cost anything. The society's foster parent program needs gently used towels, washcloths, blankets, and quilts. Everyone has those around the house, don't they? They need newspapers. Shredded copy and computer paper. Fluffy bathroom rugs. Cardboard flats from soda or pet food cases make good temporary litter boxes. You can organize your friends or Scout troop, if you want."

"Yap!" Snowball said, and wagged her tail.

"I also have a letter from William. He says, 'I'm a retiree with more time than money.' Time is a luxury the Humane Society needs, William. You can volunteer. You can be a Pet Pal, and help exercise and socialize the shelter dogs. Or a gift shop volunteer. If you have office skills, they need those. The Humane Society needs your time, William.

"I think everyone can afford a stamp to write a letter to their state and national legislators—or even an e-mail—asking the government to protect our animal friends."

"Yap!" Snowball said.

"Remember our puppy mill fighters' motto, 'The situation is serious, but not hopeless.'

"Don't forget, folks, on Monday, we move to a new time. Snowball and I will still be on this affiliate station, but our show is going national, thanks to all you viewers.

"Bye-bye, and see you Monday," Traci said.

"Yap," said the little dog in the Santa suit.

A commercial for cat food came on the screen.

"Mom, why are you crying?" Amelia asked.

"I don't cry," Josie said. "I'm getting a cold."

As the winter wore on, Traci and Snowball became a regular network feature. Soon the whole nation knew about Traci's heroic pup. She also mentioned the kindly vet, Dr. Ted Scottsmeyer.

As Traci and Snowball's fame grew, Renata Livermore wanted them at her February soiree. Traci, warned of the woman's tightwad habits and smarting from Renata's snubbing, refused unless Renata donated one thousand dollars to the puppy rescue charity of Traci's choice.

Once Traci saw the canceled check, she consented. Renata invited forty members of Wood Winds society and charged them twenty-five dollars each. Alyce was unable to attend, but sent a check. Amy the Slut sent a check, but was not invited.

Nedra Neosho moved to a new home, too, but not by choice. After her arrest, she called a first-rate criminal defense lawyer and refused to speak to the police. But Wildfern detectives found evidence that Nedra had driven to New Mexico for a vacation. A herpetologist found scales from a timber rattlesnake and a coral snake in the minnow bucket she kept in her Subaru.

A search of her home yielded evidence of Dr. Ted's innocence. It included e-mails from Dr. Ted saying he didn't feel well, an e-mail invitation for Dr. Ted to stop by for dinner at Nedra's Dogtown home, a text message on her cell phone inviting the ailing Ted to stay with her until he felt better—all at least three days before Jonah Deerford's death. In a kitchen drawer, police found a cash receipt for a car battery bought during that time. The battery in Nedra's Subaru was determined to be at least two years old, and the clinic van's was even older. The battery in Dr. Ted's orange Mustang was nearly new.

Nedra never asked about her puppy again. But she continued to mourn the loss of her snake. The bite wound in her leg healed and she walked with only a slight limp.

Against the advice of her attorney, Nedra gave an interview to the *St. Louis City Gazette*. She told a reporter that snakes were ecologically useful and downright erotic, then revealed the location of a large winter den of timber rattlers near Wood Winds. A photo of more than fifty rattlesnakes sunning themselves on a rock ledge behind the gated community appeared with the article. Two Wood Winds families with toddlers put their homes on the market after the article appeared. The houses sold for a considerable loss in an already-depressed market.

Mrs. Renata Livermore wrote a letter to the editor complaining that the *Gazette* article had damaged Wood Winds property values. Her attorney threatened to sue the paper for its irresponsible reptile photo. The *Gazette*'s managing editor issued a directive banning any mention of snakes near commercial or residential real estate.

Nedra's top-flight lawyer resigned from her case after her *Gazette* interview. He told her there was no point in hiring him if Nedra wasn't going to follow his advice. Unfortunately for Nedra, she'd sold her house for his retainer. After her attorney fired her as a client, she was given a public defender, who urged her to plead guilty to manslaughter and attempted murder. He told her she was lucky he'd gotten the charge reduced from murder one and the state had agreed to drop the charges for owning an unregistered deadly reptile. The reptile charge was dubious, since the law states reptiles more than eight feet long must be registered. It was difficult to measure the length of the rattlesnake after Josie had stuck it with a pitchfork and the cop chopped it to pieces with a shovel.

The police closed Edna Prilosen's murder and the murder of Jonah Deerford's wife. Evidence said Jonah was the killer. Edna's mother told Ike Ikeman in a tearful television interview that she was trying to find comfort in that. "Jonah got the death penalty, which he deserved," she said. "But it won't bring my Edna back."

Josie figured Jonah had also locked the rottweiler in her mother's garage, based on Mrs. Mueller's account of the dark, battered truck driving slowly down their alley late at night.

The parents of the late Allegra Coleman Deerford sold Jonah's farm and took the two boys, Bart and Billy, to California. They enrolled in public school.

Dr. Ted Scottsmeyer was released two days after the incident at Nedra's home. The exonerated vet refused to let Ike Ikeman interview him. He resumed his practice and continued to help puppy mill dogs, becoming a hero in rescue circles, in part thanks to the praises of Traci and Snowball. The publicity increased St. Louis Mobo-Pets' practice so much that Dr. Ted and Dr. Chris hired two new doctors from the University of Missouri School of Veterinary Medicine.

As soon as he was released, Ted came to Josie's house to thank her. He brought a single rose and a case of Harry's favorite canned food. Harry came out and got an ear scratch from the doctor. Amelia was thrilled to see him. "Mom," she called, "Harry's vet is here."

"Talk to Ted until I'm ready," Josie said.

Josie flew around her bedroom, changing into a cashmere sweater, putting on fresh lipstick, and fluffing her hair, before she strolled out as if she always looked that way.

"Please go to your room," Josie told Amelia, "so Dr. Ted and I can talk. And take your furry friend with you." She waited for her daughter and the cat to leave.

Dr. Ted was thinner after his jail stay, but his eyes were still a melting brown and his manner still gentle. "I owe my freedom to you," he said.

"And I owe the scare of my life to you," Josie said. "None of that would have happened if you hadn't lied to me about Nedra."

"I didn't lie," he said. "I didn't want to reveal her name since you knew her. It was awkward."

"Awkward!" Josie said. "I'll tell you what's awkward—standing on four fifty-pound sacks while a rattlesnake is trying to kill me. Snakes are your friends? Some friends you have."

"I'm sorry, Josie," Ted said. "Please forgive me. But the snake was only trying to protect itself. It died, too."

"I forgive you," Josie said. "I don't forgive the snake. I'm glad it's dead."

"Please, Josie, will you go out to dinner with me?"

"No!" Josie said. "I don't want to go out with you."

"But Josie . . ."

When Josie banned him from her home, Ted looked as woebegone as Nedra's abandoned Bruiser. She escorted the vet to the porch and watched his tangerine Mustang leave.

Amelia waited for her in the living room. "Dumb move, Mom. That one is a keeper."

"Amelia Marcus, you are not to comment on my love life ever again," Josie said. "You've caused enough trouble. Go to your room and stay there."

Amelia and Harry did not come out until dinner, when Amelia fixed a tuna casserole and wisely made no mention of Ted. She was learning more than cooking.

Josie's life settled into a dull winter routine of work and more work. Jerry called her two or three times for a date, and Josie turned him down.

An anonymous tipster reported that Bernie, Jerry's mother, was a "hoarder." According to a television news story, hoarders had a pathological addiction to saving animals but were unable to properly care for them.

The three dogs and all but two of Bernie's cats were confiscated by animal welfare authorities. Bernie cried on television that only she could take care of those cats. The court sentenced her to counseling and a course in pet care. Josie did not report Bernie, but she was glad someone did. After Bernie's sad television appearance, Jerry walked his pup, Chloe, on a new route through the neighborhood.

Josie waved to Stan and his new girlfriend when they went in and out of Stan's house, but that was as close as she got to her one-time lover. On Saturdays, she would see the two of them laughing and carrying in bags of lumpy winter vegetables from the farmers' market. The lights were on in Stan's bedroom until very late on the nights Abby stayed over.

On New Year's Day, Stan rang their doorbell. Josie could see Stan's muscles bulging even under his heavy winter coat. He had his arm protectively around a small, shy blonde. The blonde's face was cherry red from the cold. She held a fruitcake with a big blue bow on it. A modest diamond sparkled on her ring finger.

"Josie," Stan said, "I want you to meet my fiancée, Abby."

"Come in," Josie said. "Happy New Year."

Abby handed Josie the fruitcake. Josie recognized it as a brand on sale at a local discount store.

Stan and Abby sat side by side on the couch he'd moved into Josie's living room. "I wanted you to meet Abby now that she's going to be your neighbor," Stan said.

Abby flashed her diamond solitaire.

"It's lovely," Josie said.

"It was on sale," Abby said. "This style will hold its value longer."

"When's the wedding?" Josie asked. "Will you be a June bride?"

"Oh, no." Abby seemed shocked. "That's a peak time when weddings are more expensive. I think—and Stan agrees—that August would be ideal. We've already reserved a pavilion in Forest Park. We'll have a picnic reception afterward."

"The park is a beautiful place for a wedding," Josie said.

"And cheaper than a church and a hall," Abby said.

"You're invited, of course," Stan said. "And your mother."

"I know Mom won't want to miss it," Josie said. "Where are you going for your honeymoon?"

"We thought we'd stay home and fix up the house," Abby said. "We're going to live in Stan's home. It's paid for. We'll need a nursery. We plan on children eventually. I told

Stan he could keep his awful exercise equipment, but it's going in the basement. I want a real living room."

They sat in awkward silence until Stan said, "Well, that's our news."

"And good news it is," Josie said. "Thank you for stopping by and telling me. You seem perfect for each other."

Stan was the last man to enter Josie's home for months, but she couldn't get Dr. Ted out of her mind. She thought about his kindness, his gentle touch with frightened animals, his brown eyes. But she was resigned to living alone. Josie decided she had no choice.

One Friday night in June, Amelia was upstairs learning to cook lamb. She'd left Harry with Josie. Josie had settled in for another dreary night in front of the television. To cheer herself up, she put on cool shorts, a pretty lace top, and added a touch of lipstick. Harry was curled next to her. She was surprised by a knock on her door at seven o'clock.

She peeked out and saw Ted standing on the porch. He was trying to keep a bottle of red wine, a tray of cheese and crackers, a bouquet of roses, and a DVD from slipping out of his arms.

Josie opened the door and Ted said, "Hi, want to watch a chick movie with me? I rented *Sex and the City*."

"You'd watch a chick movie?" Josie asked.

"For the right chick, I'd make any sacrifice." Ted smiled. Josie didn't.

"Uh, could I come in before I drop all this stuff on your porch? The red wine might stain if the bottle breaks."

Josie opened the door reluctantly. Ted slipped in and said, "I know you're still angry. But would you at least have a glass of wine with me?"

Josie brought in two glasses and a corkscrew. Ted opened the wine and began a speech he'd obviously rehearsed.

"I was wrong about Nedra," he said. "I made a mistake. I thought we both liked animals. We did, but it wasn't enough for a real relationship. She wasn't the right person for me, and I thought it would be better to tell her the truth so she could find the person she deserved. Haven't you ever felt that way about someone?"

Stan, Josie thought. She kept a stony silence.

"Josie, I am sorry. I don't know what else to say."

Harry jumped into Ted's lap and nudged the vet's hand with his striped head. "Look, Harry has forgiven me after we got off to a bad start."

He scratched the cat's ears. Harry closed his eyes and purred loudly. "I'm better with animals than I am with people," Ted said. "But I'm begging you. Forgive me. Please go out with me."

"I forgave you long ago," Josie said. "I'd kiss you, but it would disturb the cat."

"Harry will understand." Ted gently transferred the cat to a couch pillow and kissed Josie.

The kiss was worth the wait.

# Shopping Tips

**Hounded for the Holidays:** Some dogs love to dress up in cute clothes. Others look embarrassed in anything but their own fur coat. If you have a fashion hound, the holidays are an ideal time to trot out the canine couture.

For Halloween, there are "bad to the bone" shirts and jackets, ladybug sweaters, pumpkin and dinosaur outfits. You can find them at many pet boutiques, or by prowling the Internet.

At www.lovelonglong.com, click through to the rhinestone I LOVE SANTA tank tops, bright red Christmas hoodies with fleece trim, Santa suits, red Christmas sweaters with matching socks, doggy boots, and angel-wing harnesses.

Dog boots and pet shoes protect cold paws on icy winter sidewalks. Pardon the pun, but there are houndstooth boots at www.DoggieVogue.com.

Don't forget. For many dog clothes, you'll need a size. The chart may ask for your pet's body length, chest circumference, neck circumference, and leg length.

**Shop and save . . . the animals:** Your local shelter usually has a gift shop featuring clothes, jewelry, and toys for humans and animals, as well as pet beds and carriers. A portion of the proceeds goes to help the animals. Pick up a fashionable dog carrier purse or a sporty stroller and help care for other rescued animals.

The Humane Society of Missouri gift shop sells Christmas and Hanukkah items. Prices may change, but when last we checked, here is what the items cost. The Howling Hound Menorah is $62. The Playful Pups Bagel Tin is $39.50. There are treetop angels of your favorite breed and angelic dog ornaments, too. Cards and gifts for year-round celebrations from Mother's Day to Valentine's Day are at the Humane Society of Missouri. Shop online at www.hsmo.org.

**For a dog's night out:** Your princess will shine in a Parisian pearl tiara ($7.99) or a rhinestone tiara barrette ($9.99). Jeweled leads start at $10.99. Fancy bows, crystal charms, and bling are at www.DoggieVogue.com.

Well-bred gentlemen dogs about town may prefer the black-tie collar for $18 at hsm.petfulfillment.com. Black tie works for best dogs at weddings, too.

**Walk on the wild side:** Even animals wear animal prints, if the items are natural fibers. Funky zebra-print dresses, dog carriers, collars, and sliders are available at www.DoggieVogue.com. Prices range from $3.99 for safari sliders to $24.99 for cotton zebra-print dresses with red bows.

**Puttin' on the dog:** Looking for cute dog clothes, collars, and canine accessories? Save your own paws and shop online for discount and designer duds at the outrageously named Bitch New York (www.bitchnewyork.com). Be sure to look up your dog's weekly horoscope. That's free.

**Where Josie shops for pet treats in Maplewood:** Customers at Airedale Antics, 7316 Manchester Road, are greeted by Harrybear and Sassybear, animal friends of Sheri and Tony Phipps. Sassy and Harry are Airedales, of course. The shop has pet treats, as well as "fine wines" for dogs and cats, including Sniff-N-Tail, Barkundy, and Meowlot from Bark Vineyards.

Tony says the wine is "a gravy with vitamins and minerals and is all natural."

Many pet lovers have a hard time brushing their pet's teeth. Tony suggests ProDen PlaqueOff, a ground seaweed product to put in your pet's food.

Airedale Antics is also a good place to meet animal lovers in various breed rescue groups. For information, go to www.airedaleantics.com or call 314-781-PETS.

**If you aren't lucky enough to live in Maplewood:** Three Dog Bakery has shops around the world, including Canada, Hong Kong, Japan, and across the United States. Three Dog's treats and food include "All Natural Baked Food for Dogs," "Beagle Bagels," and "Gift Boxers."

Felines can enjoy that fat-cat special, lobster. Three Dog sells We Pity the Kitties treats. Three Dog treats are also available at Wal-Mart, Costco, Walgreens, and other outlets. The Three Dog Bakery, 8861 Ladue Road (314-726-1674), is close to Alyce's home. For a store near you, go to www.threedog.com.

**Pet Baskets:** Is your friend thrilled to be adopting a new puppy? Delighted with her new kitten? Worried about her dachshund's back operation? Celebrating her basset's birthday? Commemorate these and other pet milestones with gift baskets from www.mypetgifts.com. Prices range from $30 to $44. There are also gifts for cats and dogs for under $20.

**When the inevitable happens:** Sympathy baskets let your friends and family know you care. Three choices include Mrs. Beasley's Sympathy Basket (www.mrsbeasleys.com), a Harry and David Sympathy Basket, and the Gourmet Basket for Sympathy from 1-800-flowers.com.

Prices range from $63 to $99.

**Looks like our dog might have a little Labrador in him:** or maybe some golden retriever, or oodles of poodle. Many dog owners guess at their pet's background. A Breed DNA Identification Kit can settle the question.

Why bother? Because a dog's DNA can govern its appearance, behavior, and health. The Helen Woodward Animal Center sells the Breed DNA Identification Kit. Swab the inside of your dog's cheek and send the sample to the Bio-Pet Vet Lab in a prepaid envelope. Answer those vital questions for about $60. Check out www.pawsitivelypets.org.

**Sixty-seven percent of Americans sleep with pets on their beds:** If you belong to the thirty-three percent who refuse to let a dog sprawl across your mattress, a pet bed may lure the pooch from his favorite perch. The Canine Couture Dog Spa and Boutique in Somers, New York, has unusual pet beds, including the "Furcedes" car-shaped bed.

For dogs who dream of adventure, there are Benji's Beds. The "Top Dog jet fighter" and the "SS *Seadog* cruise ship" are designed for small- or medium-sized dogs. Your pet can sleep in oval-shaped luxury. Benji's Beds are at select retailers or at www.BenjiVentures.com.

The Chihuahua Shoppe has a plush puppy bassinet with a canopy and eyelet trimming ($19.99 at www.chihuahua-shoppe.com).

Buy your pet a heated bed for those cold winter nights from www.pawsitivelypets.org. Proceeds will benefit the Helen Woodward Animal Center. Heated beds for small, medium, or large dogs range from $32 to $112. There's also a heated cargo bed if your pup likes to ride in your SUV.

Some pets sleep soundly in furry, snuggly beds. But if the covers aren't washable, these beds can become a problem, especially for incontinent animals. Other dogs regard pillowy beds as personal chew toys. For these dogs, Kuranda beds can be custom designed. Kuranda also has a "Donate a Bed" program. Give a Kuranda bed to the shelter of your choice and get up to thirty-five percent off the retail price. For more information, go to www.kuranda.com.

**Charging for the Animals:** *Pittsburgh* magazine said the nonprofit Animal Friends shelter has the city's best pet boutique. Every purchase benefits homeless animals, including the shop's eco-friendly, organic cotton dog toys. If you open an Animal Friends Visa, the organization will receive $50 plus a portion of every purchase. For information, check out www.ThinkingOutsideTheCage.org.

**Bag it:** Dog walking is a good way to meet interesting humans. You've dressed your dog from nose to tail in coat, boots, and bling. But it's hard to look glamorous when you're holding that telltale plastic grocery bag in your manicured paw. The Chihuahua Shoppe has a heart-shaped waste bag holder that comes with a roll of twenty heart-print bags. The holder clips to a belt or a leash, so you'll look as cute as your little dog. Check it out at www.chihuahuashoppe.com.

**I wouldn't send a dog out on a night like this:** That was inventor Nan Siemer's problem. Benji, her bichon frise, refused to go outside in the rain—for four years. Finally, Nan figured out who was top dog in her family. She invented the Poop Tent, an outdoor relief station for pets. The waterproof tent keeps dogs dry in the rain and snow. Sick and injured dogs can use its shelter, as can pups like Benji who doggedly refuse to get wet.

Pop open this puppy porta-potty near your dog's favorite spot, right before bad weather strikes. The Poop Tent retails for $59.95. For details, go to www.PoopTent.com.

**Strut your mutt:** If your dog is a genuine original, there are clothes designed for your pet—Pure Mutt. The original Pure Mutt is Spike, "half retriever, quarter spaniel, a little bulldog, shepherd, shih tzu—even a dash of dachshund."

"Like any good Pure Mutt, Spike remembers to give back," this site says. Part of your purchase goes to a no-kill animal shelter. Prices start at $3.95 for a jaunty Pure Mutt dog bandana. People apparel is about $9.95. Celebrate your dog's unique ancestry by dressing in matching Pure Mutt T-shirts. For more information, go to www.puremuttinc.com.

**For felines and friends:** Harry, Amelia's cat, is much like my own brown and black tabby. My Harry is a rescue cat. While I write, he keeps me company by sleeping near my computer. He has more leg room since I switched to a flat-screen monitor.

Harry refuses to wear cat clothes. He believes his own fur is quite handsome, and it's all natural.

Here's Harry's secret vice. He likes a natural high—catnip toys from www.catshigh.us. The brightly colored cloth toys, about the size of a business card, are stuffed with certified organic catnip. Harry turns backflips for this catnip—literally. Prices range from $2.50 to $25.

**The other hairy:** Cats look so peaceful curled up on a sofa, chair, or window seat. But what they do to the furniture isn't so pretty. Most cats shed, and their claws aren't kind to upholstery. Removing cat hair can be a chore. Rita Scott makes handsome kitty quilts for your cat's favorite furniture. Toss the quilts in the washing machine when it's time to remove that hair. Prices range from $15 to $20. For kitty quilt information, mouse over to www.catshigh.us.

**If your cats insist on a wardrobe, there are cat clothes:** Cat lovers may get a kick out of the Mouse Patrol T-shirt, made of washable cotton jersey, and other selections at www.BaxterBoo.com.

Calm and contemplative felines do fine with soft fabrics and Velcro closures. But Velcro won't hold if a cat really wants to be free. One cat-loving friend bought her cats holiday costumes designed for small dogs. She found that the dog styles didn't fit her cats. As any feline knows, cats are different from dogs.

**When your cat wants out:** Some cats love to roam, but many pet experts say that may not be good for you feline's health or for your neighbor's flower beds. If your cat has a yen for the outdoors, try a safe outdoor enclosure.

The Humane Society of Missouri has deck and patio cat runs, penthouse enclosures, and a wild "Ferris Wheel" enclosure. The feline "Funhouse" and a giant "Town and Country" enclosure work for multiple cats or one fat cat. Prices range from $75 to $259.95 at www.hsmo.org.

**If you want to adopt a puppy mill dog:** Of course, you want to help those poor dogs. Many animal lovers read about puppy mill animals, or see the heartrending videos and rush out to adopt one.

Animal shelters warn against this generous impulse. By all means, adopt a puppy mill pet if you have the time, money, patience—and don't mind replacing your carpeting.

But the Humane Society of Missouri says puppy mill dogs can be difficult. The dogs are not house-trained and may never be. "They will eliminate anywhere and everywhere," HSMO says.

Puppy mill dogs may be fearful, shy, difficult with children, and terrified of visitors. They could have ongoing medical expenses and psychological problems.

If you adopt puppy mill pets, be prepared for years of hard work and disappointment. Even if you believe you can take on a puppy mill animal, your family may not want to live with the stress and mess of a rescue dog.

There are many ways to help besides adopting a rescue pet. Animal shelters need volunteers with a wide range of talents. Some volunteer jobs involve direct contact with animals, such as socializing and exercising shelter dogs. Others require people skills or office abilities.

Check with your local animal shelter volunteer program, or look at their online wish list. Donations of supplies are welcome and may be tax deductible. The Humane Society of Missouri has a wish list as well as a gift-in-kind donation form at www.hsmo.org.

You can also make a donation in your pet's name to the animal shelter of your choice to help less fortunate animals.

**One more thing:** The ASPCA, the American Society for the Prevention of Cruelty to Animals, is one of many organizations working to prevent cruelty and pass tougher laws. If you want to help, campaign for federal and state laws that protect animals and punish their abusers. Go to www.aspca.org to find out how. Then let your legislators know you are part of the animal protection lobby. Get laws with teeth in them.

**Read on for a sneak peek at the
next novel in Elaine Viets's national bestselling
Dead-End Job Mystery series,
*HALF-PRICE HOMICIDE***


**Praise for the Dead-End Job Mysteries
Winner of the Anthony Award and the Agatha Award**

"A stubborn and intelligent heroine . . . a wonderful South
Florida setting."
  —Charlaine Harris, #1 *New York Times* bestselling author
of the Sookie Stackhouse novels

"Clever." —*The New York Times Book Review*

"Wickedly funny." —*The Miami Herald*

"Viets keeps the action popping until the cliff-hanging ending." —*Publishers Weekly*

"Hilarious." —*Kirkus Reviews*

"A fast-paced story and nonstop wisecracks. . . . Elaine Viets
knows how to turn minimum wage into maximum hilarity."
  —Nancy Martin, author of *Murder Melts in Your Mouth*

"Fans of Janet Evanovich and Parnell Hall will appreciate
Viets's humor." —*South Florida Sun-Sentinel*

"A quick summer read for fans of humorous mysteries with
clever premises." —*Library Journal*

"Laugh-out-loud comedy with enough twists and turns to
make it to the top of the mystery bestseller charts."
  —*Florida Today*

"A heroine with a sense of humor and a gift for snappy dialogue." —Jane Heller, author of *Some Nerve*

"I need to see Vera right away," the pocket-sized blonde said. Her voice was a sweet whisper.

Helen Hawthorne could barely see the woman's curly head over the counter. She reminded Helen of a cream pie with her high-piled sugar white hair and lush curves. A size two, Helen estimated, based on her years in retail.

Cutie-pie was no tourist vacationing in Fort Lauderdale. She belonged on fashionable Las Olas Boulevard. But Helen figured Cutie-pie would pay full price for her skimpy white dress, not hunt bargains at Snapdragon's Second Thoughts.

Cutie-pie dropped a stack of soiled men's shirts on the counter. They landed with a thud that told Helen extra starch wasn't what weighed them down. She hoped the dark red stain on the white shirt was ketchup.

"Do you have any dry cleaning for pickup?" Helen asked.

Cutie-pie looked around as though checking for spies, then said, "Tell Vera it's Angelina Jolie. It's urgent."

"She's in the back room," Helen said. "I'll get her."

"Hurry," the blonde said. "He can't know I'm here."

Helen didn't run through the cluttered store. But her long, loping stride covered several feet at a time. She cut through bins of dirty laundry, dodged a display of designer purses, tiptoed past the Waterford, and powered through the consignment-clothes racks. Versace, Gucci, True Religion, and other designer names flashed by.

Helen parted the print curtains leading to Vera Salinda's office. The owner of Snapdragon's Second Thoughts nested in a welter of bills, invoices, and boxes. Vera's sleek dark hair was like an ax blade. Her plump red lips looked like fresh blood. Her pearl white skin had an otherwordly glow in the underlit room. She was frowning at her computer.

"What?" Vera asked Helen.

"Chrissy Marlet is here," Helen said. "She wants to see you. She says it's urgent."

"Hell's bells," Vera said. "Not her. The only thing worse would be Kate Winslet."

Vera hurried toward the front, adjusting her bloodred mouth into a scary smile. Tight black Versace jeans and a pink tank top showed off her gym-toned body.

Helen picked up the Windex and starting cleaning the costume jewelry case so she could listen. She didn't want to miss this.

"Chrissy Marlet, how are you?" Vera asked. She swung her cutting-edge hairstyle and leaned on the counter. Muscles rippled under her hot pink top.

"In a hurry," Chrissy said. Her sweet, breathy voice was a breeze through a bakery. "I have something to show you."

She moved the soiled shirts to reveal a brown leopard print purse with a Prada logo. "It's a pony-hair purse. Still has the original tags and the certificate of authenticity."

Pony hair, Helen thought. A purse made from a baby horse? She decided the material wasn't any creepier than calf.

Vera ran her fingers over the gold Prada logo, prodded the hairy purse with her long, bone white fingers, and unzipped it. Helen saw the signature brown lining.

"It's the real deal," Vera said. "I can sell it for four ninety five."

Chrissy went even whiter. "What? That means I'll only get half. Two hundred fifty dollars."

"Two forty-seven fifty," Vera corrected. "And that's if I sell it."

"I can't do anything with that kind of money," Chrissy said. Her sweet whisper changed to a thin vinegar whine. "That purse was three thousand dollars."

"It's like a car, Chrissy. Once you drive it off the lot, it loses its value. Leopard print is so last year." Vera's voice was harder than her fake nails.

"What about Tansey? Call her. She'll take it." Chrissy couldn't hide her desperation.

"Tansey hasn't been buying," Vera said. "Her ad agency is laying off staff."

"Couldn't you give me a little more money? I have the tags *and* the receipts. Unlike some of your sources, I don't steal."

"Nobody cares about your receipts," Vera said.

"The police would," Chrissy said, then returned to sweet-talking. "Please, Vera. You know me. My code name is—"

"I know your real identity," Vera said, quickly cutting her off. "Hush. You never know who could walk in."

With a screech of brakes, a black BMW with a grille like a hungry mouth slid into the loading zone in front of the shop. The driver's door slammed. A man filled the shop door, blocking out the harsh August sun.

Chrissy looked frightened. "It's Danny," she whispered, and hastily dropped the soiled shirts back on top of the pony-hair purse.

Big didn't begin to describe Danny Marlet. He was as dark and threatening as a thunderstorm. His black eyebrows were like low-hanging clouds. His eyes flashed with barely controlled anger. He wore a navy suit, but didn't sweat in the sweltering August heat.

"Chrissy, pumpkin, you're up early," he said. "It's not even noon." His smile showed sharp teeth that made Helen shudder.

"I'm taking your shirts in for laundering." Chrissy's voice trembled slightly. "Vera is the best dry cleaner in town. I want only the best for my hardworking man."

"Be sure and show her that ketchup stain on my white shirt," Danny said. He grabbed the Hugo Boss shirt, exposing the pony-hair purse.

"What's that?" he said.

"It's a purse," Chrissy said.

"I can see it's a purse. I also see that Gucci bag on your shoulder. Since when do you carry two purses? Are you trying to spend twice as much of my money?"

Helen heard him accent "my."

"No. I must have picked it up by accident."

"Unless you were trying to sell it. This is a designer consignment shop. Was she bringing in that purse to sell, Vera?"

"I told her leopard print is so last season," Vera said.

"You didn't answer my question, Vera," Danny said. "You sell designer clothes on consignment and my wife is addicted to logos."

"So what if I am?" Chrissy exploded. "You want me to look better than all the other wives, but you won't give me any money."

"I don't trust you around cash, sweetie," Danny said. "It disappears at the touch of your little white fingers. But I let you shop as much as you want. You have unlimited credit at Neiman Marcus, Gucci, Prada, and every other major shop from here to Miami."

"Did it ever occur to you I might want my own money?" Little Chrissy looked like a Chihuahua yapping at a Doberman.

"Then get off your lazy ass and make some," Danny said.

"I can't! I gave up my acting career when I married you."

"I hardly think a mattress commercial and a straight-to-DVD movie counts as an acting career," Danny said.

"I didn't have a chance to develop my art," Chrissy said.

Danny snorted. "The only acting you do is in the sack." He meanly mimicked a woman in the throes of pretended passion: "'Oh, Danny, more. More. More.' More sex or more shopping, dear heart?"

Helen kept her head down and scrubbed at the already clean display case. This was way too much information.

Danny's diatribe was interrupted by the clip-clop of high heels. A jingle of bells signaled Snapdragon's door was opening. Vera slipped between the warring couple and said, "Continue your conversation elsewhere, please."

Danny dragged his wife by the arm to the back of the store. There was a tiny tinkling sound in their wake. Helen found a woman's gold wrist watch on the floor. Was it Chrissy's?

She heard a dressing room door slam. She waited, then knocked on the door. Chrissy and Danny were facing each other in the cramped space. Chrissy's face was bright red.

"Sorry to interrupt," Helen said. "Is this your watch, Chrissy?"

"Yes, thank you. The clasp is loose. That's my next errand." She absently fastened it on her wrist as her husband shut the door in Helen's face. She caught snatches of their argument over the store's background music.

"What do you mean, am I cheating on you?" Danny said.

"I saw the way you stared at her last night!" Chrissy said.

"I wasn't looking at her designer dress, that's for sure."

"No, you were looking at her fake tits," Chrissy said. "Mine are real. So are my designer dresses. She wore a knock-off and everyone knew it."

"And none of the men cared," her husband taunted.

Back at the front of the store, Helen picked up her Windex bottle again. She heard Vera loudly welcome her new customer. "Loretta Stranahan. How nice to see the best-dressed woman on the Broward County board of commissioners."

Helen nearly dropped the spray bottle. Loretta could have been Chrissy's twin sister. Her blond hair was a shade or two yellower, but she was as small, creamy, and curvy as Danny's wife. And as well-dressed, in a black Moschino dress and polka-dot heels. She looked about thirty and dangerous. No one would ever call her "little Loretta."

"There are a lot of women commissioners," Loretta said. "But I like competition. I came by to see if you got in more suits from Glenn Close."

"Sorry," Loretta said. "Glenn hasn't made a delivery lately."

"Is she hanging onto her suits longer now?" Loretta asked.

"Even the rich have money problems," Vera said. "Men who never noticed the price of laundry now want their shirts on hangers instead of in boxes. You know why? Shirts are seventy-five cents cheaper on hangers. Seventy-five cents! These same men used to leave their change on the counter because it made holes in their pants pockets. Now they count pennies."

"Please, let's not go there," Loretta said. "I've had endless meetings about the budget cuts. With the picketers, postcard campaigns, and petitions, I'm about to snap."

"Let me show you my new arrivals in the back," Vera said. "I'll give Helen some instructions first."

"Watch the store, Helen," Vera whispered. "I have to make sure Loretta doesn't run into Danny."

Loretta trailed Vera through the store. Helen could hear Vera saying, "I have a Chanel suit in your size."

"Too expensive looking," Loretta said. "My constituents will think I'm on the take."

"A black Ferragamo then?" Vera said. "That's rich looking but not rich."

"Vera, honey, I have a hundred black suits. They all look alike."

"I'll find you a new blouse. A touch of color would freshen them."

"Well, I could look. That wouldn't cost anything." Loretta was weakening.

Helen heard a small surprised shriek. "Why, Danny," Loretta said. "You're the last person I expected to see here."

"I'm shopping with my wife," Danny said.

Helen checked the overhead security mirror to see the drama unfold. Chrissy and Loretta had squared off. Chrissy's back was arched like an angry cat. Danny loomed above the blondes like a dark mountain.

"That's right," Chrissy said. "He has a wife. I'm Mrs. Danny Marlet." She wrapped her arm protectively around Danny's.

"Trust me, honey, I'm not interested in your husband," Loretta said.

"Then why do you call him a hundred times a day?"

"It's business," Loretta said.

"Until midnight?" Chrissy asked.

"Important business. A little cream puff like you wouldn't understand."

"I'm not stupid!" Chrissy said. "I know about those three thousand new jobs Danny's project will bring to the city. And the house with the seven toilets. It's not exactly the house of the seven gables, is it?"

"Shut up!" Danny said, his voice dangerously low.

"Danny can't afford to get rid of me, can you?" Chrissy said. "He tells me everything."

"If he told you everything, he'd tell you why he spends so much time with me," Loretta said. "I can't see why you shop here, Chrissy. With all Danny's money, he could buy this store."

"Hey!" Danny said, stepping toward her. "I'll barely break even on the Orchid House project."

"Right," Loretta said. "That's why you're fighting so hard for that height variance. For nothing."

Vera broke up the discussion. She took Danny's arm and dragged him to a rack of men's shoes. "I have some wonderful Bruno Maglis," she said.

"I don't wear used shoes," Danny said. "They're disgusting."

"They're new. These are four hundred dollars, Danny, and I'm selling them for less than a hundred. I think they'd fit you." She slid shoes the size of sleds into Danny's hands, then steered Chrissy toward the dresses.

"Try on this pretty cotton dress. It's cool, but simple."

"Perfect for a simple person," Loretta said.

"Ladies!" Vera sounded like a disapproving schoolteacher. "Chrissy, you are the wife of a major developer caught in a controversy. You can't be seen fighting." She handed her the dress and pushed her toward the back dressing room next to her office.

Vera took Loretta's hand. "And you, dear, are an elected official who must behave as well as she dresses. Come see my new blouses. I haven't put them out yet. Perhaps I can find you a little extra tact."

Loretta docilely followed Vera into her office.

At the front counter, Helen did the paperwork for Danny's shirts. She'd just dropped them into the laundry bin when the door's bells jingled. A woman with light brown hair wanted to see some Escada. Helen showed her the rack when she heard the bells again.

Helen recognized this new customer. Jordan lived in Helen's apartment complex. She practically haunted Snapdragon. Jordan had straight dark hair, slanted green eyes, and a long nose that made her look rather like an anteater. A stylish anteater. She shimmied in wearing a summer dress that was as tight as a tourniquet.

"Helen!" she said. "Any new cocktail dresses from Paris Hilton?"

"Going someplace special?" Helen asked.

Jordan dropped her voice and said, "I've found a man—a special man. He wants to take me clubbing in South Beach. Paris's clothes would be perfect."

"But what about—?" Helen said, then stopped. Jordan was living with Mark. But that was Mark's problem, not hers.

"What?" Jordan asked.

"The price," Helen finished. "Paris left two dresses, but they're three hundred each."

"Don't worry, I can get the money from Mark. A girl has to move up in the world, doesn't she? Let me see the dresses. Are they slutty?"

"Slightly," Helen said.

"Good. I want raw sex. My new man has to pop the question. I'm not getting any younger." Jordan's green eyes were as hard as bottle glass.

"Then try them on. But I'd better warn you, you could walk into a domestic argument back there."

"Oooh, free entertainment." Jordan gave extra swish to her hips as she followed Helen to the back. Danny was walking between the racks and Jordan walked straight into him. Helen watched Jordan's face light up and her gem-hard eyes soften. "Why, Danny," she said.

Danny surveyed her as if she were a virus under a microscope. "Do I know you?"

Jordan stepped back as if she'd been slapped. "Danny, how can you say that? After—"

She never finished. Danny dropped the monster Maglis on the floor with a clatter. "You!" He pointed to Helen. "Tell Vera I'm not interested in castoffs." He stormed out.

Jordan stood there as if she'd turned to stone. Maybe the skintight dress had cut off her circulation.

"Prick!" Jordan wiped away tears, smearing her mascara.

"He's not worth crying over," Helen whispered. "And his wife is in the back dressing room. Look at these dresses." She steered Jordan to the cocktail dress rack. "The pink and the red dresses were Paris's."

"What about that yellow one?" Jordan asked.

"That's a handpainted silk scarf." Helen picked it off a hanger. "Feel it."

"Not interested in covering anything up," Jordan said. "It's showtime."

Helen settled Jordan and the two dresses inside the other fitting room, then picked up the shoes Danny had dropped on the floor and put them back on the shelf.

Vera came out of her office, took a deep breath, and said, "Anyone still here?"

Helen looked around. The Escada lady had slipped out during the drama. Loretta, the best-dressed county commissioner, had also disappeared.

"I have Jordan in the fitting room," Helen said. "She's trying on dresses."

"I need a break," Vera said. She settled wearily behind the front counter. "Is it really only eleven fifteen?" She took a long drink of bottled water and popped two aspirin.

"Is it always this crazy here?" Helen asked.

"You ain't seen nothing yet," Vera said. "This is an emotional business. Everyone wants to look richer than they are. Loretta didn't want the blouses, but she's the easiest type to deal with—a professional who has to look good. Your neighbor Jordan is hunting for a man. She's convinced if she finds the right dress, she'll get a rich guy and be happy."

"It didn't help Chrissy," Helen said.

"Poor Chrissy. Her husband is a control freak."

"I couldn't imagine my fiancé, Phil, caring how many purses I have," Helen said.

Vera took another long drink and said, "Phil doesn't need to control you. I doubt he could. Danny is a developer. Until his Orchid House hotel complex is approved, he's in the spotlight. He doesn't like it."

"Then why do it?"

"Despite the way Danny was poor-mouthing, he stands to make millions. Developers are like riverboat gamblers: One year they're rich, the next they're busted. He can't help that. The only thing Danny can control is his wife. He won't give her a dime. Chrissy outfoxed him. She buys superexpensive merchandise, keeps it until she can't return it to the store, then brings it to me for consignment. I sell it and we split the money. She's hauled off about two thousand dollars so far this year. Danny never tumbled onto her scheme until today. He's usually too smart to blow up in public, but right now, he's playing a dangerous game."

"How?" Helen asked.

"He needs the approval of the county commission to tear down the old Orchid House and build a new project. That's why he's cozying up to Loretta. He's after her vote, not her ass. She's one of two holdouts."

"Danny doesn't play around?" Helen asked.

"Of course he does. Chrissy is his third wife. He has at least one sweetie on the side. I've seen him drinking with pretty ladies around town. I don't think he was asking them for loans."

"Too bad for Chrissy," Helen said.

"She's no angel," Vera said. "She's a customer of the Exceptional Pool Service."

Helen looked at her blankly. "What's that mean? Our pool is cleaned by my landlady with a long-handled net."

"Exceptional Pool Service lives up to its name. Their ads promise, 'We get into places you never consider.' The joke is they're exceptionally good at getting in bed with unhappy wives. Check out their ads online. Their employees look like Chippendales and their service uniform is tight white shorts and a tan. Almost makes me wish I had a pool.

"I'd better check on Chrissy," Vera said. "Where is that pony-hair purse? I'll ask what she wants to do with it." Vera spotted the purse, picked it up, and headed toward the back dressing room.

"I'll see about Jordan," Helen said.

She was almost at the dressing room when she heard the first scream.